"Mr. Bear, please don't eat me up," I pleaded.

"Hah!" he said. "What makes you think I want to eat you up?" His big, black, shiny eyes blinked at me. "I'd rather offer you a business proposition. How would you like to make a little extra spending money, Golda?"

Well, needless to say, I became suspicious of this offer, especially since it came from a bear that talked. "Money?" I asked.

"Yeah, a little extra never hurt nobody, and I know you Lockes and your neighbors ain't got that much."

As we ate dinner that first night, Papa Bear explained what I was to do to earn my promised spending money. Seems he, along with a few other woodland creatures, had a moonshine still hidden up the mountain, and they all needed a little extra help.

"I got one girl by the name of Red who helps out from time to time. She always wears this hooded mantle and carries a basket. She tells everybody she is taking lunch to her grandma, but actually she is carrying shine down to the valley. She has a wolf that works with her by distracting anybody that might stop her to check the basket. He makes as if to attack her, and whoever is about will chase after him leaving her free to go on her delivery route."

—from "My Great-great-great Grandma Golda Lockes"
by Annie Jones

Also Available from DAW Books:

If I Were an Evil Overlord, **edited by Martin H. Greenberg and Russell Davis**
Isn't it always more fun to be the "bad guy"? Some of fantasy's finest, such as Esther Friesner, Tanya Huff, Donald J. Bingle, David Bischoff, Fiona Patton, and Dean Wesley Smith have risen to the editors' evil challenge with stories ranging from a man given ultimate power by fortune cookie fortunes, to a tryant's daughter bent on avenging her father's untimely demise—and by the way, rising to power herself—to a fellow who takes his cutthroat business savvy and turns his expertise to the creation of a new career as an Evil Overlord, to a youth forced to play through game level after game level to fulfill someone else's schemes for conquest. . . .

Misspelled, **edited by Julie E. Czerneda**
There is a right way and a wrong way to do practically anything. And when it comes to magic, skipping the directions, changing the ingredients, garbling up the words of a spell—all of these can lead to unusual, sometimes dire, sometimes comical consequences. Here seventeen authors—Kristen Britain, John Zakour, Doranna Durgin, Jim C. Hines, and others—accept the challenge of creating spell driven situations that get out of control, where: a cybermancer has her spell disk corrupted by unexpected input . . . two students out to brew up some spells completely outside the curriculum forgo a most important ingredient . . . a has-been golf pro finds an old family spell that *should* improve his game, but at what cost? . . . and a young woman who orders a fairy-tale life, but she forgets to read the fine print and ends up with the worst parts of two fairy tales.

Enchantment Place, **edited by Denise Little**
A new mall is always worth a visit, especially if it's filled with one-of-a-kind specialty stores. And the shops in Enchantment Place couldn't be more special. For Enchantment Place lives up to its name, catering to a rather unique clientele, ranging from vampires and were-creatures, to wizards and witches, to elves and unicorns. In short, those with shopping needs not likely to be met in the chain stores. With stories by Mary Jo Putney, Peter Morwood, Diane Duane, Laura Resnick, Esther Friesner, Sarah A. Hoyt and others.

TERRIBLY TWISTED TALES

EDITED BY
Jean Rabe and Martin H. Greenberg

DAW BOOKS, INC.
DONALD A. WOLLHEIM, FOUNDER
375 Hudson Street, New York, NY 10014

ELIZABETH R. WOLLHEIM
SHEILA E. GILBERT
PUBLISHERS
http://www.dawbooks.com

First Printing, May 2009
1   2   3   4   5   6   7   8   9

DAW TRADEMARK REGISTERED
U.S. PAT. AND TM. OFF. AND FOREIGN COUNTRIES
—MARCA REGISTRADA
HECHO EN U.S.A.

PRINTED IN THE U.S.A.

ACKNOWLEDGMENTS

CONTENTS

INTRODUCTION

When I was a kid, I'd make up my own fairy tales—or, rather, I liked to twist the age-old ones. After hearing about The Old Woman Who Lived in a Shoe and Red Riding Hood for the umpteenth times, I'd craft my improved versions. I remember fancying the wolf catching all three pigs and then proceeding to huff and puff and blow down The Old Woman's shoe. It was the same wolf that caught Red Riding Hood unawares and later nabbed Chicken Little and Bre'r Rabbit and the race-winning turtle and then gnawed on Paul Bunyan's axe handle for good measure. The wolf always won. I guess I was a quirky kid.

In any event, I liked my fairy tales folded, spindled, and a little bit mutilated . . . like many of the fine stories in this anthology. Sure, the original versions are just fine and dandy, but the *altered* versions show some great creativity, cleverness, and maybe a dash of maliciousness.

I was delighted so many wonderful authors could contribute. They pleasantly stirred my imagination.

I hope they stir yours.

Thank you for picking this up!
Jean Rabe

WAIFS

Dennis L. McKiernan

Dennis McKiernan is known for his high-fantasy novels, including *The Iron Tower* series. He served in the U.S. Air Force and holds degrees in electrical engineering. He also has written in the science fiction, horror, and crime fiction genres. He lives in Tucson, AZ. His other works include: *Once Upon a Winter's Night, Once Upon a Summer Day, Once Upon a Spring Morn,* and *Once Upon a Dreadful Time.*

When I finally escaped from that thrice-cursed oven, I went after those two little shites who not only had tried to roast and eat me but had destroyed my house as well. I mean, do you know just how long it takes to make even a single gumdrop? And they have to be special, too—warding off rain, not getting all gooey and soft in the sunshine, resisting those effing birds that come and peck away at my decorative and colorful touches as if it's their right. Orioles are especially bad. And gingerbread eaves—don't talk to me about gingerbread eaves. I mean, they have to hold up under the most severe downpours and not turn to mealy slush and sluice away. Oh, and sugar siding, too. Do you know just how hard it is to even get sugar in these dark ages? You can get plenty of honey, but sugar? The only thing honey is good for is to make rock-candy-hard shingles.

Anyway, there I was, inviting into my cottage what I thought were two abandoned waifs who seemed to be lost in the forest. They told me about their supposedly poor parents having to set them loose deep in the woods. Oh, and they spoke of a breadcrumb trail and greedy birds; when it comes to greedy birds, I could sympathize with the children. Gladly, I took them in. Ah me, little did I know.

I fed them a good nourishing soup with croutons and even a candy apple. And I warmed them before my hearth and gave them hearty chocolate drinks (Ha! Chocolate. Another precious rarity, but I wanted to sweeten up the little darlings).

Oh, you might think I didn't notice how they whispered to one another, but I did. Foolish me: I thought they were sharing childish secrets or perhaps were a bit intimidated by the wart on my nose or whatever. And all the while they were conceiving their fiendish plot to cook and eat me and live in my house happily ever after.

So, I asked them if there was any other thing they might like, and they requested an angel-food cake. *Angel food,* no less. I would have to quadruple-sift flour to the finest and use even more sugar, and there would be egg-whites to whip, and what could I do with the leftover yolks? I mean, I am just a poor old goody who could ill afford the splurging of my precious resources.

Regardless, I did so.

I mean, I could always use a yolk-milk slurry to baste the meat I would shortly have.

And I heated the hearth oven to bake the cake, but

as I started to slip the filled pan into the hot chamber, the little bastards shoved me in instead and slammed the door behind me.

Somehow they locked it.

Thank the nine infernos, in that same moment the skies opened and engulfed the forest, and the torrent was rather like a flood, and bucketfuls poured down my chimney and quenched the hearth fire and cooled the oven.

They tried to kindle a new blaze, but everything was wet, and they finally gave up. Yet I remained quiet, for I realized that if they knew I was alive, they would certainly wait until the wood dried out and roast me to a fair-thee-well. Over the next several days, I heard all sorts of ripping and tearing, but I held my tongue.

Finally, on the fourth or fifth day—by that time I had lost count—everything fell silent, and I understood they were gone.

It took me another day to loosen the bolts on the door latch and get free, all of my beautiful long black fingernails now gone from using them like screwdrivers, the remainder nought but jaggedy, bleeding stumps. Hrmph! Once I heard that prissy Snow White complain of a broken nail. What would that little miss prim and proper have said were her hands like mine, nails down to the quick? One of these days I'll shove a poisoned apple up her— Oh, wait, speaking of apples, by this time I was nearly dead of thirst and hunger. I mean, all I had had to eat was unbaked angel-food batter that had splashed on my hands as the children had pushed me into the hearth oven. But in the first day I had lapped away that meager bit of sustenance. And now it was four or five days after—perhaps even a week. And so, I staggered outside and drank from an overflowed rain barrel, after which I snatched an apple off the tree in my front yard.

I was on my third apple when I turned and looked at my beauti—My house! My house was ruined. Those evil little bastards had stripped the house of ginger-bread and sugar siding and honey shingles and all the ornamental gumdrops . . . Oh, the gumdrops. The horror, the horror.

That's when I went after those sons of a bitch . . . er, rather, the son and daughter of a bitch.

Fortunately, the ground was soft from the rain, and I tracked them to Tom-Tit-Tom's place. I called out his name, but there was no answer, which was strange; I mean, he really, really didn't like anyone knowing his name, and he flew into a rage at the sound of it. He had been that way ever since that fraud of a princess—Ah, wait, the princess and her child; maybe that was it. I opened the door and slipped in, thinking that perhaps the reason he didn't answer was because he was busy with those very same brats who had almost done me in. I mean, given his peculiar penchant for wee tots, he had always wanted a child of his own. And with two, I mean, he could have twice the—Uh-oh! His house was ransacked, a real mess, his spinning wheel gone. Rats! I wanted that thing. I mean, who couldn't use a bit of gold now and then?

I searched, but the place was empty. Even so, the tracks of the brats went on, so I followed.

At Little Red's grandmother's house, I found my friend all hacked up. His long nose slashed and his big ears chopped and his sharp teeth smashed. Who-ever had killed BBW was no longer around. Gram and Red were missing, too, and there was no sign of their friend the woodsman.

I went on, my suspicions growing, my alarm increasing. Those two kids seemed to bring disaster into the lives of everyone they came across.

The pig's digs were destroyed—straw strewn, sticks splintered, though the brick one still stood. But inside that house, there were signs of slaughter everywhere: a pig's foot there, a sow's ear here, a curly tail ripped raw and bloody.

Did I want to keep tracking? I mean, revenge is sweet, but after all, life is sweeter. Still, I had to get to the bottom of this, so I headed for the poor parents' house the children had told me about—the one sitting on the edge of the forest. At the time I had suspected those two little monsters had been feigning when they had claimed they had gotten lost and didn't know where it was—breadcrumb trail, my ass—but I knew the locales of most cottages along the verge, so I headed there.

Many were abandoned, but I found one yet occupied but barricaded. The trembling dwellers were locked inside, weapons at hand—the man grasping a newly sharpened sickle, the woman wielding a wooden pitchfork with wicked, fire-hardened sharp-pointed tines. Yet they opened the door a crack when I told them why I was there.

"Demons," the father muttered, after I asked him about his children.

"Demons! Demons!" screeched the mother, in between fits of sobbing. "Demons!"

"Threw 'em out, we did," muttered the father, not lowering his curved sickle.

"Before they could eat us!" shrilled the mother between gasping sobs.

"Then they do eat people?" I asked.

"The neighbors!" cried the mother, blubbering.

"And pigs and other such," muttered the father.

"Bones out back!" wailed the mother, bawling.

"Cracked for the marrow," muttered the father, and then he slammed the door, and I heard a heavy bar *thunk!* into place.

No longer afraid, now that I knew what I was dealing with, I slipped back into the deep, dark forest.

I continued to track the children, and a day or three passed. But on the next day I heard an enraged roaring, and I edged forward until I came to where I could see a hut in a clearing. Outside, Papa Bear ranted and raved, while Mama Bear wept. Of Baby Bear there was no sign. On the ground before Papa Bear lay a girl's head and a pile of cracked bones. As to the rest of her, there was nothing. I looked sharply, very sharply, to see if it was the head of one of the waifs I was after. No-no. This one's hair seemed to be more golden, with long curly locks, not the straight yellow hair of the girl I was after. Where was Baby Bear, I wondered.

The next day I found the remains of a campfire, a small clawed and torn bear skin nearby. Ah, my question was answered.

A day or so later, I caught up with the two I was after.

We three now live in my cottage. The roof repaired, the siding replaced, the gingerbread restored, and my lovely gumdrops once again making the place sparkle with beauty.

Now and again a person comes by, and we invite them in for a meal.

MY GREAT-GREAT-GRANDMA GOLDA LOCKES

Annie Jones

Annie Jones is a displaced Southerner who lives in Wisconsin with her Yankee husband and Yorkshire terrier, Ali. She is a grandma and a beginning fiction writer.

After my grandmother passed away some months ago, I was helping clean out her attic and came across an old journal that had been written by my great-great-grandmother. I am sharing an interesting part of her story, just as she told it, with nothing changed.

My name is Golda, and I am a daughter of the Lockes family that lives on the edge of the forest somewhere in the West Virginia Mountains.

No doubt you have heard stories about me involving three bears and how they were angry with me for eating their porridge and sleeping in their beds . . . all lies, every word.

When I was young, the forest was my playground. I would forage for berries or any edibles that I could find because our family was very poor. We ate every scrap of food we could get—fruits and vegetables and nuts, that is. We were vegetarians and never ate meat of any kind.

One summer day while roaming through the woods, I heard a menacing growl. Lo and behold, a great black bear stood in my path.

"Oh! Oh! Mr. Bear, please don't eat me up," I pleaded. "Oh, please, I am small, and there is simply not enough of me to make a tasty morsel. I certainly would not eat you." I quivered, too scared to run.

"Hah!" he said. "What makes you think I want to eat you up?" His big, black, shiny eyes blinked at me. "I'd rather offer you a business proposition. How would you like to make a little extra spending money, kid?"

Well, needless to say, I became suspicious of this offer, especially since it came from a bear that talked. "Money?" I asked.

"Yeah, a little extra never hurt nobody, and I know you Lockes and your neighbors ain't got that much. You're all a scraggly bunch, if I do say so."

"How?" I asked. "How could I make some spending money? What would I have to do?"

He led me deeper into the mountains where the underbrush was densest. In the middle of a certain thicket sat a sweet-looking log house with smoke curling out of the chimney.

He escorted me into a cozy little kitchen. There was a table set with three bowls and three spoons. On the stove in the corner bubbled a steaming kettle. A middle-sized bear, wearing a snow white apron and a little lace bonnet on her head, stood over the kettle engrossed in whatever she was stirring with a long wooden spoon.

"About time you got back, Papa Bear," she said. "The porridge is done. Who did you bring this time?" Without pausing, she went on. "Let her sit at Little Bear's place. She can sleep in Little Bear's bed too if she plans on staying. He won't be back for a while since he is out distracting."

So from that day forward, I slept in whichever bed was empty—the great big bed, the middle-sized bed, or, most often, the little bed because Little Bear was frequently away.

As we ate dinner that first night, Papa Bear explained what I was to do to earn my promised spending money. Seems he, along with a few other woodland creatures, had a moonshine still hidden up the mountain, and they all needed a little extra help.

"I got one girl by the name of Red who helps out from time to time. She always wears this hooded mantle and carries a basket. She tells everybody she is taking lunch to her grandma, but actually she is carrying shine down to the valley. She has a wolf that works with her by distracting anybody that might stop her to check the basket. He makes as if to attack her, and whoever is about will chase after him leaving her free to go on her delivery route. Our Little Bear does distracting work, too. Neither he nor the wolf's ever been caught. There's just too many places to hide."

After eating my porridge, I ate Little Bear's too because I was very hungry.

Papa Bear said, "I am taking Golda up to the still, Mama Bear. So she can see what goes on up there and get acquainted with our operation."

The moonshine still was well hidden in a cave with the mouth covered by thick brambles. The cave could be entered by a small opening at the side of the brambles. The earth had shifted sometime in the past, and this made several vents in the ceiling of the cave that allowed the smoke an outlet. With all the different vents, I suspect no one could track down precisely where the smoke was coming from. Conveniently, there was a bubbling spring running close by, which supplied water.

Papa Bear started right away teaching me the fundamentals of becoming a moonshiner. He explained the furnace, which was constructed of large rocks and dobbed with red clay to hold the heat in. Seated down inside the furnace was a heavy flat rock with a firebox under that. Inside the furnace was the still, all made out of pounded copper. Papa told me his grandfather had made the still all by paw and had learned from a Scotsman who moonshined with him for some time.

It was all so interesting! I learned words like worm, which is a coiled copper pipe where steam is condensed into shine; goose eye, a good bead that holds; dog heads, so many I can't write them all down.

Thus, I became a moonshiner, and a good one too.

I suggested to the farmers in the area that they grow white corn and sugar cane, since in the past they had planted potatoes and ate them all up, earning nothing. Most of them went along with the notion.

The farmers became very well off selling us corn and sugar, which they made from the sugar cane, and which we used for shining. The farmers had the miller grind up the corn for us, but none of them knew the reason we wanted all the stuff.

I became quite wealthy, and in time I moved away from the edge of the forest and into a great house down in the valley town, where I became a bootlegger. From there I could direct distribution of our commodity to Kentucky and Ohio, using a small barge operated by my family. They navigated up and down the Big Sandy and Ohio Rivers, stopping at secret drop-off points so we could sell our wares.

The last I heard of Red Hood, she and the wolf had joined a circus, she as a wolf tamer, both of them being squeezed out of the bears' operation.

And as far as I know, the bears are still making moonshine in that cave. But I won't say where it is or speak the name of the town where I lived.

My biggest mistake was marrying and letting my husband in on my secret. He stole some of my money and flat out left me and our five younguns. He went back to Europe, where he originally came from.

The blabbermouth he was, he changed my story to his way of thinking, wrote it down, and sold it to a publisher. He was just a dirty dog, and what he told was a dirty pack of lies, so don't believe all that he said if you happen to read his story, which he called a "fairy tale." The truth was writ by my hand this day.

ONCE THEY WERE SEVEN

Chris Pierson

Chris Pierson, an unrepentant Canadian, is the author of nine novels, eight of them published, most recently the *Taladas* Trilogy in the *Dragonlance* world. His short fiction has appeared in numerous anthologies, including *Time Twisters*, *Pandora's Closet*, and *Fellowship Fantastic*. During the day, he builds swaths of Middle-earth for *The Lord of the Rings* Online. He lives in Boston with his wife, Rebekah, and their amazing daughter, Chloe.

The earth smelled of roses, which Heimskur the Fool thought was odd. He knew soil and stone, had lived with it all his life, delving deep into the bones of the world to prize out copper and silver and gold. He was of the *dvergar*, one of the last of his kind, born able to scent different sorts of rock. Granite smelled like woodsmoke; limestone stank of the sea; a bright vein of iron ore sang in the nose like the air before a storm. He knew every aroma of stone, every fragrance and reek and tang. None smelled like flowers, though. No dirt was like roses.

"The witch has tainted the earth itself," muttered

Reithur, lying in the ditch beside Heimskur, his black-bearded face pressed into the mud. "Her list of sins is long."

"Hush," whispered Alvíss, who was their clan-chief, eldest of them all. "I would not have *them* hear us."

Reithur scowled and looked like he might argue, but Reithur *always* looked like he might argue. It was his nature, just as it had been his brother Reifur's ever to be glad. He stayed silent, though, bowing to Alvíss' will, and lay in the flowery soil and listened as the riders clattered past.

There were thirteen horsemen, which was of course a dark number, as all things in this land were dark. Fjarheim had been a glad realm once, but now it was foul, its people hard and its warriors cruel. The riders wouldn't hesitate to put four wandering *dvergar* to the blade. Even Heimskur, who was slow-witted for one of his kind, did not doubt that. And though Reithur would no doubt claim later that he could have slain all thirteen riders with his sword alone, that was just his hot blood talking. Besides, as Alvíss had said when they set forth from their halls in the mountains, there was no good reason to risk getting killed before they reached their goal.

"*Then* we may chance death," he'd said. "Any other risk is empty, as our friends and brothers know."

Sorrow took Heimskur, as he lay in the shadowed ditch; listening to the rattle of tack and harness while the queen's huntsmen rode by. Once the *dvergar* had been seven, and they had lived in peace. Now they were four—him, Reithur, Alvíss, and Stygg the Silent, who lay as still and quiet as a stone on Heimskur's right side.

Horses chuffed and whuffed. Chainmail jingled, and swords rattled in their sheaths. Men's voices cursed and barked with spiteful laughter. The noise grew loud, then faded away, echoing among the hills. The *dvergar* lay still for some time after, while the pale moon traced the sky overhead. Finally Alvíss got up, brushed the dirt from his silver beard, and peered into the night.

"They are gone," he said. "We were not seen."

"About time," snapped Reithur, heaving to his feet. He checked for his sword, sheathed at his hip. "If I had to weather that stench much longer, I'd have started puking flowers."

Stygg, who was big and broad and red-bearded, smiled and said nothing.

"It will not be the last time you smell it," Alvíss replied. "If the tales are true, the town itself stinks of roses, and the queen's bower worst of all."

"Perhaps," Heimskur said, "we should cut off our noses. Then we will smell nothing."

Reithur snorted with disgust. Stygg's eyes twinkled, and his shoulders shook. Alvíss, however, smiled his patient smile, the one he always wore when he spoke to Heimskur.

"Perhaps," he said. "But what about when our quest is done? Without noses, how then would we find ore underground?"

Heimskur thought about it. He scratched his cheeks, which—unlike the others'—were bare, save for the faintest downy wisps.

"I don't know," he answered. "I didn't reckon there'd be anything after the quest. I never thought we would return."

The four *dvergar* stood quiet in the bushes beside the road. They glanced at one another, then away into the dark. After a while, Alvíss sighed and spoke in a voice that was heavy as lead.

"Sometimes, Heimskur," he said, "you seem the wisest of us all."

That made no sense to Heimskur, but he nodded anyway, and smiled, and followed when the others set off down the road again, on their journey to the heart of Fjarheim to slay the Snow Queen.

Isvít, she was called, and she was fair beyond anyone in all the northern kingdoms. She had been a princess, though not of Fjarheim; Hitherlond had been her realm, at the feet of the mountains where the *dvergar* dwelt. Her mother had prayed to Frigg and Freya for a beautiful daughter, as white as snow and red as blood and black as night. The gods granted her wish, but they were cruel, as all men know. She died in childbirth, before she could behold her baby girl.

The child grew up lovely, but the King of Hitherlond took a new wife, a dark and comely woman from far away. Vándir, the new queen was named, and she was cold and cruel. She grew jealous of young Isvít, and ordered one of her huntsmen to take the girl into the forest and murder her. Isvít's fairness stayed the man's hand, however, and he spared her, turning her loose in the wild. She might have died then, but her wanderings led her into the mountains, where she sought shelter in the halls of the *dvergar*.

The seven of them—Alvíss, Reithur, Reifur, Stygg, Móthur, Ónd, and Heimskur—had returned from the mines that evening to find Isvít asleep in Heimskur's bed. Taken with her beauty, they welcomed her, adopting her as a foundling and raising her to womanhood. Those had been glad days, and Heimskur thought of them often, with a fondness that left a bitter taste in his mouth. For if the *dvergar*'s long and dark history had taught them anything, it was that glad days never lasted long.

It began some ten years after Isvít came to them; somehow, doubtless through fell witchery, Queen Vándir learned that the girl still lived. Wroth with envy, she came three times to the *dvergar*'s halls, seeking to kill Isvít with fell magic and poisons—and the third time, she succeeded. The _dvergar_ came back from a hard day's mining and found the girl dead at the gates of their hall, a foul and rotting apple still clutched in her hand.

Their grief was as deep as the world's bones, particularly Heimskur's, as he had been her favorite. To honor her, the _dvergar_ bore her to a cavern of white crystal, and there she remained for many years, and rot did not touch her, such was her fairness. Often Heimskur went to that cave and wept beside her bier. Without Isvít, the world was a dark place, and he found little joy in toil and ore and song. Only the beauty of her lifeless face lifted his heart. Each day he prayed, to grim Wotan and furious Thunor and wily Loki, that the dark queen's deeds might be undone.

Then, one day, a warrior came to the mountains. His name was Fríthur, and he was the heir to the throne of Fjarheim, a land of folded coasts and misty hills, many leagues away. He came to the _dvergar_'s mountains seeking monsters to slay: a frost-giant, perhaps, or a band of trolls. Instead he found the cave of crystal, and Isvít dead within.

So taken was he with her beauty that he knelt by her bier all night, whispering sweet words in her ear. Heimskur found them in the morning and ran to fetch his clan-brothers. The _dvergar_ came to the crystal cave, ready to slay Fríthur for despoiling Isvít's tomb, but instead they beheld a wonder: His honeyed words had awakened her from death itself. The sight of Isvít, alive and in Fríthur's arms, lightened the _dvergar_'s heavy hearts, and though it pained them, they allowed her to leave with him, riding back to Fjarheim, where they were soon to wed. Heimskur and his fellows rejoiced, for glad days had returned.

But again, as ever, they did not last.

It began with the wedding. The *dvergar* left their mountain steading, for the first time in many long centuries, and went to Hafodd, Fjarheim's capital. There they were honored guests, and even ill-tempered Reithur wept with joy to see the girl they loved, now a resplendent princess. At the feast afterward, however, things turned ill. Queen Vándir had learned that Isvít lived again, and insane with spite, she traveled from Hitherlond to the feast. This time, however, Isvít was wise to the queen's tricks. She and Fríthur tricked Vándir, welcoming her as a guest and promising to set aside all their old enmities. But their words were false, and when the queen and her retinue were half-drunk with mead, they sprang the trap. Fjarheim's warriors slew the queen's guards and took Vándir captive.

Next came the iron shoes.

Heimskur felt a stab of pain at the memory, for the *dvergar* themselves had forged the shoes, at Isvít's behest. They had no idea why she would want shoes of metal, especially as they were not her size, but such was the *dvergar*'s love that they obeyed without question, presenting them to Prince Fríthur as part of Isvít's dowry. At the feast, though, all became clear: after they captured Vándir, the king's warriors brought out the shoes and heated them over a fire until they glowed crimson as the setting sun.

"You sought to bring woe upon this place of merriment," proclaimed Fríthur, standing over the weeping queen. "I will not have it. This is a happy day, your majesty, and you must dance. Dance, so all can watch."

As the folk gathered in the mead hall watched, the king's men clamped the glowing shoes on Vándir's feet. She screamed and lurched and leaped—but not for long. The sickly smell of roasting flesh filled the air as she fell. Three times the king's warriors dragged her back to her feet, and three times she danced, howling, until she collapsed again. Then, at last, she could not stand any more, and at a wave from Prince Fríthur a headsman came forward with his greatsword.

The *dvergar* were horrified. They looked to Isvít, expecting her to be stricken as well, but she simply rose, cold and haughty, and stood above Vándir, who lay gasping in anguish.

"You gave me death, Your Majesty," she declared. "Now I return the gift. You will dance again in the underworld, knowing that I was fairest."

The queen only wept. Isvít nodded to the headsman and then turned her back while he struck Vándir, one quick blow to her neck. And it was done.

The *dvergar* left the feast soon after, confused and heartsick. Alvíss sought to speak with Isvít, but she wouldn't see him. They began the long journey home that very night, swearing never to return to Fjarheim.

For years they kept that oath, remaining in their underground halls, delving and smelting ore to sell to the kingdoms of men. Soon after the wedding, traders from both Hitherlond and Fjarheim came in greater numbers, seeking iron at dear prices. War had begun between the two kingdoms, for the folk of Hitherlond could not let Queen Vándir's murder go unanswered. Fjarheim responded with shocking savagery, with Prince Fríthur leading its longboats to burn the villages on Hitherlond's shores. Smiths on both sides needed steel for mail and swords and shield rims, and the *dvergar* sold it to them, as they had always done.

Still, though the trade made them rich, they took no pleasure from it, for they knew the war was Isvít's doing. Even Reifur, who was always merry and quick with a song, grew grim at the tales of slaughter wrought by Fjarheim's reavers. The fighting went on for three years, growing ever worse until all of Hitherlond was laid waste. The call for iron soon fell almost to nothing, but the *dvergar* were glad of it. The war was done, and surely the woeful tales must stop.

Instead, they only grew worse.

Within a month of Hitherlond's fall, the king of Fjarheim was slain—killed, the story went, by a vengeful Hitherlonder's dagger. In their hearts, however, the *dvergar* knew better. Now Isvít was queen of both her old home and her new, and King Fríthur took her longboats far and wide to plunder other kingdoms. Stories arose that the raiders returned with not only gold and jewels but also young girls, all of them beautiful. These they brought to the king's keep, and they were never seen again, though at night their screams rang out from the castle's tower.

Two more years passed, and the *dvergar* heard the tidings they'd dreaded: King Fríthur was dead as well, drowned in the sea on the way home from a raid. Some lords questioned whether it was right that Isvít remain queen alone; within a month, every one of them had disappeared, and loyal vassals ruled in their place. Isvít took no other husband, but she continued to send her reavers forth for riches and young girls.

The *dvergar* mourned, but they did not interfere. They had long avoided the affairs of men, only making an exception for Isvít because of her beauty. So they kept to their halls, and delved their ore, and waited for the next round of tales to come.

Looking back, even Heimskur understood what fools they were, to think they could stay safe from Isvít's wrath.

One day, the queen sent her huntsmen instead of her usual traders, offering a paltry price for the *dvergar*'s iron. Reifur and Reithur, who had gone to trade with them, rejected their offer and bade them leave. It fell to quarreling; and Isvít's huntsmen shot both brothers with arrows and stole their ore. Reifur took a shaft through the eye and died at once, but Reithur lived, and his fury grew hotter with every passing day while he recovered from his wounds.

The *dvergar* laid Reifur's body in the crystal cave, where Isvít had slumbered, and held a moot about what they would do. In the end, they chose to set aside their oath: two of them would return to Fjarheim to speak with Isvít. Reithur wanted vengeance, but he was too badly wounded and couldn't convince the others. Alvíss still hoped they might persuade her to honor their old friendship and that she might order her men to leave them in peace. They drew lots to see who would go, and Ónd and Móthur were chosen. With heavy hearts they set out for Fjarheim, to beg for peace.

Months passed, and they did not return. Then, one misty morning, a rider came to the gates of the *dvergar*'s halls, threw a sack upon the ground, and galloped away. Heimskur went out to fetch the bag, and when he opened it up, Móthur and Ónd's heads tumbled out, withered and eyeless.

For the four remaining *dvergar*, there was no more debate. The next morning they set out, with swords and axes on their belts and shirts of steel mail under their cloaks. They left their halls empty and started down the road to Fjarheim to end Isvít's reign, once and for all.

The town of Hafodd crowded gray and dour at the angle of a long fjord, surrounded by dark hills crowned with pines. Its buildings were few and plain: stone houses with thatched roofs, looming close to narrow, muddy streets. A haze of smoke made a pall over them, mixed with drizzle that blew in from the sea. The village's docks stood empty but for a handful of fishing vessels: Fjarheim's longboats were gone, its reavers plundering faraway lands. Only the queen's huntsmen remained to defend the town, clad in white cloaks over their hauberks of mail.

Standing with his clan-brothers on one of the overlooking hills, Heimskur stared down at the town and marveled at how the years had changed it. Part of it was an illusion made by the weather—it was the month of Einmanúd, when winter's bitterness gave way to damp spring—but there was more than that. Hafodd had been a blithe place, and merry, on the day when Isvít married Prince Fríthur. There had been colors other than gray and dun and rust. Years of strife and war, however, seemed to have drained all the joy and life from the place. Even from a distance, the townsfolk looked grim and stooped as they slogged through its muddy streets. Shriveled heads stood on stakes atop the wooden fence that surrounded the village, their long, dry hair whipping in the wind. The Tree of Wotan, a massive oak around which girls and boys had danced on the wedding day, was leafless and thick with ravens, which took turns plucking morsels from the corpses that hung from its boughs.

Reithur spat in the dirt, glowering at the town. "Killed the place, she did," he said. "Like she does everything she touches."

"Mind your temper," Alvíss replied, "and keep your voice down. The dead could hear you, the way you gripe."

Stygg grinned and said nothing.

"Go ride a long-axe," Reithur muttered—but he said it quietly.

All was silent but for the creak of the pines and the shouts of fishmongers from Hafodd's wharf. Heimskur's gaze drifted to the king's keep—now the queen's, he supposed. It perched on a rocky spur on the town's north side, a broad hall with a peaked roof that once had been covered with bright silver, shining in the midday sun. Now the metal had tarnished and looked as dull as lead. A tall watchtower rose from the hall's seaward end, crowned with a white banner emblazoned with a crimson rose.

That brought the smell back to Heimskur's mind. Everything here was roses, it seemed—sweet and cloying and wrong. The dirt and the rocks had little scent of their own. He'd been feeling sick for days because of it. A wave of nausea crashed over him, and he lowered his head and retched.

A hand settled on his shoulder as he heaved. When he was done, he looked up to see Stygg, silently comforting him. Alvíss and Reithur stood behind him, their faces grave.

"I hate this place," Heimskur gasped. "I wish we hadn't come."

"I know, my friend," Alvíss replied. "But she must be dealt with. It is our responsibility."

Reithur tugged his beard. "Let's do it and have done, then. No more skulking. No more *planning*. Let's put steel in her and leave her carcass for the crows."

"But how do we get close enough?" Heimskur asked. "There are huntsmen everywhere. How will we hide from them in the town?"

Reithur snorted. Stygg smirked. Alvíss, however, was the soul of patience.

"We've discussed this," the elder *dverg* said. "We won't be going through the town."

He reached to his throat and pulled out an amulet on a chain: a slice of agate, green and tawny, etched with tiny runes around the hole in its center. It gave off the faintest smell of its own, a scent like burning peat that soon drowned in the rose reek.

Seeing the agate, Heimskur remembered at once and felt stupid for forgetting. It was an ancient charm, made in the days when the *dvergar* were many, and giants and gods still walked the hills: a *hurthmen*, a door-stone, the last of its kind. Alvíss turned it over in his hand, then tucked it away again.

"One chance," he said, "is all we'll have."

Reithur fingered the hilt of his sword. "All we'll need."

Soon they were moving again, picking their way along the ridge, keeping low among the trees to avoid being spotted. That was easy, for the *dvergar* were skilled at hiding from the eyes of men, and they went untroubled. At last they came to a high outcrop of rock, a hunk of deep gray stone bearded with russet moss. Alvíss stood before it, touched its face with his fingers, and shut his eyes. Heimskur and the others stood by, watching. When he pulled his hand away again, it trembled.

"This will do," he said. "It is the same stone as lies beneath the keep. The road should be clear."

"Do it, then," Reithur said.

Alvíss looked to Stygg, who nodded, then to Heimskur.

"Are you ready, my friend?" he asked.

Heimskur licked his lips. "Yes," he answered, but it was a lie.

Alvíss turned back to the rock. As he did, he pulled out the *hurthmen* again, clutching it in his hand.

"Open," he said. "In the name of Jörth who is the earth, of the *jötnar* and the *thursar*, the stone-giants and trolls, of the fathers of the *dvergar*, the first-delvers, I bid you. Open and make a road for us."

With that, he took the *hurthmen* in both hands and snapped it in half. When it broke, the agate disappeared in a flare of golden light. The earth beneath Heimskur's feet shook—a faint rumble, as when a mine passage was about to give way. There followed a loud *snap*, and a crack appeared in the face of the rock. It swiftly widened, revealing a passage through the stone, disappearing into darkness. Dust showered down from the tunnel's ceiling. The smell of the rock, an aroma like mown hay, rolled out, banishing the roses for a moment. Heimskur drank it in.

Alvíss nodded at the tunnel. "This is our road," he said. "The other end will open into the keep. Now we must—"

None of them saw the arrow until it struck. One moment Alvíss was talking, the next he was on the ground, and blood was everywhere, and a feathered shaft quivered in his neck. He clutched at it, choking, his face turning red. Heimskur gaped at him, and something whined by his ear: a second arrow, which burst into slivers against the rock.

Reithur swore, yanking his sword from its scabbard. "You bastards! You misbegotten whoreson filth! By Thunor, I'll have your balls to cook and eat tonight!"

Heimskur looked up and saw the white cloaks, the mail hauberks, the bows and spears and murderous eyes. The queen's huntsmen had found them after all, and they were swarming over the crest. He reached for his axe, hauling it out and standing over Alvíss. The elder *dverg* lay still, his eyes staring at nothing.

More arrows flew. One grazed Stygg's arm. Another glanced off Heimskur's helm. And three hit Reithur—two in the stomach, one in the thigh. He howled in rage, going down on one knee, and then fought his way back up. Blood poured down.

"Sons of dogs!" he roared, hacking the shafts away with the blade of his sword. "You'll have to do better than that!"

The next shot hit him in the eye, just like his brother. He died with a curse on his lips.

I will be next, Heimskur thought, seeing the huntsmen moving among the pines. Or maybe I will be last. I will die here, like the others.

But he didn't. Instead, Stygg grabbed his arm and

hauled him back, away from the bodies of their clan-brothers, toward the tunnel in the rock. Heimskur barely understood what was happening, saw only death and arrows coming. Another shaft hit Stygg's shoulder and stuck there; he grunted, but still he said nothing.

A moment later, they were in the passage. The ground shook again, and the sliver of light from outside narrowed and then vanished altogether, shutting out the huntsmen and Alvíss and Reithur. Darkness fell, and the hay smell was all around them. They were inside the rock.

Heimskur could see in the dark, as could all *dvergar*, but it took a moment. When his eyes began to work again, in tones of gray, he saw Stygg standing before him, anger and pain in his eyes as he yanked the arrow out of his arm. He didn't cry out.

There were only the two of them now. Their clan-brothers were dead—Reithur, Reifur, Móthur, Ónd, and Alvíss, all gone. The thought was like a mountain on Heimskur's shoulders. A fool and a mute were all that remained of the mighty *dvergar*.

"What do we do?" he asked. "Where do we go?"

Solemn, Stygg pointed the only way they *could* go—onward, down the tunnel Alvíss had opened. To Isvít's lair. Heimskur stared into the dark and sighed.

"All right," he said.

He began walking, and Stygg came after.

They followed the road through the stone for hours; it didn't run straight but wound this way and that, now down, now up, never keeping to the same direction for more than a dozen steps. Time and distance grew difficult, and Heimskur wondered whether they would ever come to the end—or if, without Alvíss to guide them, he and Stygg would remain lost forever beneath Fjarheim's hills.

Finally, though, he sensed the end was near: a new

warmth in the air, and the stink of roses behind the hay. Heimskur wrinkled his nose, and behind him Stygg sneezed. They both chuckled at that, thinking of Órd, who had been forever sneezing and wheezing when he was alive. It had driven the others half mad, but now Heimskur wished he could hear the sound again—along with Reifur's laughter, Reithur's grumbling, and Móthur's snores when he slept.

So lost was he in painful memory that he blundered right into the tunnel's end, bloodying his nose against solid stone. The road simply stopped there, at a blank wall. He stepped back, rubbing his face, and Stygg bumped into him from behind.

Heimskur stared at the rock and felt a stab of panic. He'd been expecting the passage to open out into Isvít's hall, or maybe end in a door.

"What now?" he wondered. "How do we get out?"

Stygg tapped him on the shoulder, and he glanced back. The big, silent *dverg* pointed at the wall, then to his lips. He mouthed words, though nothing came out.

Of course, Heimskur thought. Alvíss had spoken a spell to open the wall on the other end; words would likely do the same here. He struggled to remember what his clan-brother had said; then it came to him, as if Alvíss himself were whispering in his ear. He turned back to the wall.

"Open," he said. "In the name of Jörth who is the earth, of the *jötnar* and the *thursar*, the stone-giants and trolls, of the fathers of the *dvergar*, the first-delvers, I bid you."

It didn't occur to him until the walls were already trembling that he had no idea what lay on the other side. For all he knew, it could be a barracks filled with huntsmen, or the mead hall itself in the midst of supper. He reached for his axe and heard the soft scrape of Stygg unsheathing his sword. But when the rock split open, it revealed a cellar storeroom, filled with barrels and sacks and coils of rope. A wooden door stood shut on the far side, torchlight spilling beneath.

The floral stench was almost overwhelming, and Heimskur gagged. Swallowing, he stepped out of the tunnel, and Stygg followed. A breath later, the wall closed behind him, the hidden road gone forever. There were no more *hurthmen* to open it up again. The two *dvergar* exchanged grim glances: they could only go forward now.

Heimskur crept to the door, pressed his ear against it, and heard nothing on the other side. Holding his breath, he eased it open, its hinges squeaking. Light stabbed his eyes, and when he could see again, he beheld a corridor of stone. He and Stygg looked left and right. There were more doors either way, and the hallway bent out of sight in both directions.

For a moment, the fear returned. Heimskur had no idea where he was. Behind any door, around any corner, might be many men with swords. He glanced at Stygg, who shook his head and looked frustrated.

Heimskur snorted, and nearly choked on the rose reek. Then, like a stormbolt, it struck him: the smell. It had been growing stronger as they got closer and closer to Isvít. Why would it be any different now? All he had to do was follow his nose.

He sniffed the air again. The roses were stronger to the left.

"This way," he said. "I know it."

Stygg shrugged. Together, they took the left passage, rounding a corner and coming to a door. Heimskur pushed it open . . . and there, on the other side, was a circular staircase, winding up and up and up around a central pillar.

The tower, Heimskur thought. And Isvít at the top.

Following the roses, they began to climb. The stairs were tall and difficult for the *dvergar*'s short legs, but Heimskur was hardy, and grief and vengeance drove

him. He and Stygg passed several landings, but they
met no one. There were narrow slit-windows at times,
looking out at the gray sky, hills, and sea. Heimskur
only glanced at them in passing, axe trembling in his
hand as the roses drew him on.

Finally, knees aching and ears popping, they neared
the top and came to a halt. There were voices ahead:
two doorwardens, bored and playing at runestones.
One cursed his partner after a good throw, and the
other laughed.

The guards were still reaching for their blades when
they died, Heimskur's axe chopping into one man's
knee while Stygg's sword cut the other's throat. Heimskur's foe, a golden-haired warrior with a scar across
his cheek, let out a scream as he fell, then caught
Heimskur's axe in the side of his neck. Blood spurted
against the wall, and his head twisted unpleasantly as
his body slithered down the stairs.

All was silent, but Heimskur knew they'd been
heard. The guard's howl had been loud enough to
rouse the entire keep. He and Stygg looked to the
great, oaken door the men had been crouching outside. It was bound with iron bands and graven with
runes. They waited for a sound from inside, for it to
fly open and death to rain down on them—but nothing
came. Instead, an uproar arose from below: curses and
boots, pounding up the stairs. Men's voices called out
for the queen.

Heimskur and Stygg lunged for the door. They
slammed their shoulders into it, expecting it to be
locked.

It wasn't. It swung wide, and the two *dvergar* stumbled in.

The room was dim enough that Heimskur's dark-
sight took control. When he could make out details,
he saw that it was vast—it must have filled the whole
top of the tower—and in complete disarray, as if a

battle had been fought there. A broad bed sat to his left, disheveled and heaped with furs and blankets; several chests and wardrobes stood open, clothes spilling out and onto the reed-strewn floor. Half-drunk flasks and half-eaten plates of food covered a long table, and several chairs lay tipped over nearby. Fine tapestries of hunters and giant-slaying warriors hung askew on the walls. The hearth stood dark and cold, thick with old ashes. Curtains covered all the windows.

There were bones, too—a great mound of them, capped with a pile of small, grinning skulls. Heimskur thought of the tales, of young girls brought back from raids, and his stomach clenched.

He was still staring at the bones when Stygg caught Heimskur's arm. Heimskur looked to the far end of the room and spotted something he'd missed: a scrawny, huddled form, sitting on the floor, wrapped in a threadbare cloak. When he'd first looked at it, he'd thought it was just the cloak with nothing inside, so frail was the person who wore it.

Stygg glanced at him and shook his head, then turned and began to drag furniture in front of the door. Heart thudding, Heimskur crept forward. The huddled figure was moving, very slightly, rocking back and forth. And she was speaking, her voice a dry, cracked whisper. Heimskur moved in, axe ready, and heard the words.

"Mirror, mirror, on my wall," croaked the voice, "who in this land is fairest of all?"

The figure looked up, its head hidden beneath its hood. Heimskur followed its gaze and caught his breath. Mounted on the wall—the only thing hung that straight there—was a large mirror, made of what looked like brightly burnished silver. In it, he saw his own reflection, and he was handsome . . . more handsome, he knew, than he really was. He also saw Isvít there, in place of the huddled figure, and she looked as she once had, black-haired and fair-skinned and red-lipped as she'd been as a girl.

Her image smiled, but it was a cold look, full of menace instead of mirth.

"Thou, O Queen," the mirror replied, "art fairest of all."

The broken, hooded thing on the floor nodded, took a deep breath, and let it out.

"Mirror, mirror, on my wall," it asked again, "who in this land is fairest of all?"

Isvít's image grinned even broader. It was a wolf's smile, or an adder's.

"Thou, O Queen," the mirror replied, "art fairest of all."

Heimskur understood, then. He felt the magic in the room, coming from the mirror in waves. He felt its evil. He smelled the rose reek, which he had thought came from Isvít. Instead, it billowed from the mirror, which wasn't silver at all. Silver smelled clean, like a spring-flooded stream. Whatever metal it was made of, it was fell and corrupt. He glared at it while Isvít asked her question a third time, and her own likeness answered again.

"Mirror, mirror, on my wall . . ."

"Thou, O Queen . . ."

"Stygg," Heimskur said as his clan-brother returned from the door. "Hold her. Don't let go."

The big *dverg* did as Heimskur bade, without question. He moved behind Isvít, tensed, then seized her arms, holding her fast. She struggled against him like an animal, then threw back her head and screamed, a deranged sound that rose and rose, from a low moan into a shrill keen. Her hood fell away, and Heimskur caught his breath as he beheld her face. She was old and ruined, her black hair only frayed scraps of gray on her bald scalp, her wrinkled skin so pale that every dark vein showed through. Sores crusted her red lips, and madness filled her eyes.

He stared at the yowling thing Isvít had become, and for a moment he could do nothing. He'd thought he would hate her, but now he felt only pity. Then he heard shouting from beyond the barricaded door and fists pounding on it from outside. It stayed blocked, but he knew he didn't have long.

He started toward the mirror, and Isvít screamed louder, shouting words in a tongue Heimskur had never heard. There was a dull sound, a *whump*, and firelight filled the room, and the smell of roasting flesh. He glanced back and saw Stygg burning, the big *dverg* still not making a sound as flames burst from his skin. But Stygg kept hold of Isvít, whom the fire did not touch, even as it consumed him. He held on with all his dying strength.

Grieving, Heimskur turned back to the mirror. He heard the fires devouring Stygg, heard Isvít screeching, heard hatchets chopping at the door to her chamber. Hate filling his heart, he raised his axe and flung it with all his strength. It flew true, and struck the mirror in its midst.

The foul metal dented, warped, and fell from the wall with a clatter. Isvít's cries stopped, and Heimskur heard a thud as Stygg finally let her go, his smoldering body toppling to the floor. All was quiet for a long moment, save the clamor from the door. Heimskur took a step toward the mirror, fear clutching his heart.

As he did, there was a terrible sound, like shattering crystal. An eldritch light poured from the mirror, the sickly green-gray of corpses, and Heimskur fell back, gasping as the brilliance stung his eyes. He didn't look away, though, and so he saw the ghosts spill out. They were pale wraiths, as insubstantial as fog, but he could see their faces, each of them young and beautiful.

The first two he knew.

One was Isvít, as she'd been years ago, on the day she was wed.

The next was Vándir of Hitherlond, who had died dancing in her iron shoes.

After that, dozens more shades emerged—all of them women, all surpassing fair. A few looked familiar, as though they might have been queens of nearby realms, but others were strange, clad in foreign raiment, their faces painted as women in kingdoms far to the south and east did. Each lingered only a moment and before dissolving like morning mist. When the last of them was gone, the mirror turned dark. The scent of roses lifted from the room.

Heimskur walked over and kicked the mirror. It crumbled to ash. He nodded and turned away. He didn't look at the charred thing that had been Stygg, and he also ignored his axe. He had no need for it—he couldn't fend off all the warriors outside the room. He heard them now, their hatchets splintering the thick door, hacking it to flinders.

He walked to Isvít, knelt down, and touched her withered face. Her eyes opened, dark and blurred. Despite the gloom, though, she saw him and smiled.

"Heimskur," she breathed.

"Child," he answered, his voice thick. She was dying, and he could only watch.

"The mirror," she said. "It arrived as a gift, for my wedding day. We didn't know who sent it."

He listened, not understanding. He had always been slow. Alvíss could have explained it to him—he'd always been able to explain—but Alvíss was gone. They all were.

Isvít kept talking, her voice blurred and dreamy. "It was the queen. Vándir's last curse on me. The mirror took my soul, as it did hers, and the ones before. All that happened . . . all I did . . . it wasn't *me*. . . ."

She shut her eyes. Heimskur took her hand, gripped it tight; her fingers were cold in his grasp, weakening with every breath. The feel of them broke his heart.

He bent low and kissed her forehead. Then he held her, alone in the dark, and waited for the men to finish breaking down the door.

CAPRICIOUS ANIMISTIC TEMPTER

Mickey Zucker Reichert

Mickey Zucker Reichert is a pediatrician, parent to multitudes (at least it seems like that many), bird wrangler, goat roper, dog trainer, cat herder, horse rider, and fish feeder who has learned (the hard way) not to let macaws remove contact lenses. Also the author of twenty-two novels (including the *Renshai*, *Nightfall*, *Barakhai*, and *Bifrost* series), one illustrated novella, and fifty plus short stories. Mickey's age is a mathematically guarded secret: the square root of 8649 minus the hypotenuse of an isosceles right triangle with a side length of 33.941126.

Jack crouched in front of his father's grave and heaved a sigh that gave faint voice to the angst of the past few weeks. He clutched his only possessions in one hand: a hunk of twisted metal and a carved stone wrapped in a greasy, threadbare rag. He ran his free hand through tangled brown locks, grown too long since their last cutting. The knots stopped his questing fingers, the job too difficult. In fact, as he braved the autumn chill in clothing held together by a myriad of patches, everything in the world seemed beyond his scant abilities.

"Papa, I don't know what to do." Jack's voice emerged thin, reedy, and he cleared his throat. "It's getting cold. I have nowhere to live, no coppers to spend. Without you, I'm lost." Tears escaped his eyes, leaking in quiet trails along his cheeks. His mother had died in childbirth; his father had struggled to maintain the family, providing the basics for his three boys, the deepest love, but little else. For many years, that had seemed like enough.

The father had left his sons what he could: their mean hovel to the oldest, the few coins he could scrounge for the middle son. For Jack, there had been only one thing remaining, the object swathed in rags now digging its irregular corners into Jack's palm. A treasure, his father had called it, hidden away for a time of unfathomable need. The man who had given it to Jack's father had styled himself a wizard, the trinket an item of great power that came also with a warning: "For though it can save a man in his time of utmost desperation, it holds a dangerous aura of evil."

Or so Jack's father had told him. But Jack did not believe in wizards or magic, and the item his father had left him seemed like nothing more than a curious knick-knack.

Jack's other possession had proven far more valuable to him. He had found the strange bit of iron fourteen years earlier, when he was only four, snagged between rocks in the drinking creek. The rusty, algae-tangled chunk of metal had probably fallen off an ocean-going vessel. How it had come to lie in the creek he would never know, but its usefulness became instantly clear the day he used it to snare his first fish. Jack had swung it clumsily, repeatedly. After hundreds of attempts, he had somehow managed to drive it through a fish's mouth and out its left gill. He had scooped it from the water, full of pride; and his catch had made up the bulk of the evening meal.

Since that day, Jack had modified the piece, and his technique, until he had become an expert fisher. A flash of silver, a deft movement, and a fish dangled. So long as the water remained unfrozen, his family never went wholly hungry again. And, since his father's death, Jack had kept himself fed in the same manner. Fish and roots. Fish, with crumbled autumn weeds for seasoning. Fish, fish, fish.

Soon, however, the stream would freeze, and so would Jack. "I need to travel, Papa. Far away, if I must. Where the streams don't freeze and all the jobs aren't already taken. I don't mind hard work; you know that, Papa. But the job has to exist for me to take it." Through a blurry mist of tears, he stared at his father's headslab, a crude hunk of deadfall with words scrawled across it in berry juice. Only the oldest son could read, so Jack had had to take his brother's word that it said, "Beloved Father."

"Papa, I'm sorry. I think I'm going to have to sell this thing you gave me." Guilt assailed Jack. Whether the work of a wizard or a liar did not matter. To Jack, the piece was precious because his father had gifted it to him. It was the only thing Jack had to remind him of the man who had served as mother and father to his sons, the loving generous patriarch who had worked so hard in so many ways to keep his brood alive and comfortable in abject poverty.

Jack unbundled the rags to take his first really close look at the thing. Carved from white stone, it appeared exquisitely detailed, far beyond anything his family could have achieved with their crude blades and lack of artistic talent. It depicted an animal of some sort, which he could not identify. It had a face most similar to a coney or a weasel, but the ears rose from the head in prominent triangles too small for the former and too large for the latter. It stood on its hind legs, like a human, though it seemcd better suited to a four-legged stance. Its arms ended in paws, its legs swathed in what appeared to be soft, leather boots. It also wore a fancy tunic and hooded cape, with the hood throw back from its head. The tail was long and thinner than a squirrel's, or a chipmunk's.

The crafter of the statue had painted it with colors so lifelike and vibrant that Jack wondered where he could have found them. The cape was brilliant red, with gold and maroon highlights that perfectly matched the feathered straps of the boot laces. Jack could best describe the creature as striped, though it did not have the cleanly distinct markings of a badger or chipmunk. Instead, its blacks and whites blended into patchy silvers and grays, and only the white paws and nose and the black tail tip appeared well-defined and singularly colored. Its canted eyes were yellow, with slitted pupils.

As Jack stared, the statue jerked in his hand.

Startled, Jack dropped it in the dirt over his father's grave.

Stupid, clumsy oaf. Jack berated himself and his suddenly vivid imagination. The well-crafted stone-work had looked exquisitely real. He reached for it.

At that moment, the thing twitched again. It tossed and jumped, stretching and blurring, growing in the space of an eyeblink. At last, it stood directly in front of Jack, only two heads shorter than an average-sized man.

Jack leaped to his feet, staring without blinking, unable to tear his gaze from the creature. It was alive, breathing, its strange eyes inspecting him with the same intensity as he did it. The tail twitched chaotically.

Before Jack could find his tongue, or even remember he had one, the animal executed a bow suitable for royalty. "Greetings, Master Jack."

The standard reply slid from Jack's mouth without the need for thought, "Greetings." His brain and limbs refused to operate. Only his eyes continued to function, drinking in the vision in front of him until he memorized every detail.

"You can call me Puss," the beast continued.

"Puss," Jack managed to repeat. His eyes burned, and he realized he had stopped crying and forgotten to blink for quite some time. He forced himself to flutter his eyelids until the pain subsided. "Hallo, Puss."

Puss bowed again. "With respect, Master Jack, you already greeted me."

Jack licked his lips and loosened his grip on the fish catcher. Only then, he realized he had been clutching it tightly enough to leave deep impressions in his hand. "Forgive my rudeness, but I'm not really certain how to handle a . . . a . . ." He could think of only one logical description, ". . . hallucination." He rubbed his closed eyes briskly. When he opened them, he expected to find nothing but his father's grave with a dropped knickknack on top of it.

But Puss remained, regarding Jack curiously. "I surprised you."

"Entirely," Jack admitted.

"Well," Puss said philosophically. "It's to be expected, I suppose. There's so very little magic in this world."

Another shock. Jack decided he was safer sitting down and lowered his bottom carefully to the dirt. "You mean there are . . . other worlds?"

Puss laughed. "Other dimensions, at least. I'm not a traveler by nature, so I can't really speak to other worlds. I just know that where I come from, magic is quite common."

Jack did not know what to say. He dug a toe into the soil, hoping this normal, idle action might awaken him from dream. Only the expected resulted: His toe got dirty, and brown dust sifted to either side, leaving a small depression. "You're real, aren't you?"

"I'm real." A grin spread across Puss' whiskered face. "I'm not an illusion or a dream. Your mind is working just fine. You can punch yourself silly, but I won't disappear." He crouched to Jack's level. "Do you want me to punch you?"

"No. Thank you." Jack finally asked the question that had plagued him since his first glimpse of his father's legacy. "What exactly are you?"

"Where I come from, I'm called a cat."

That answered nothing. Jack studied the creature again. "A cat?"

"Yes."

"Named Puss."

"Yes."

"And what, exactly, does a cat do?"

Again, Puss smiled, a toothy grin that sent a chill through Jack. It reminded him of his father's warning.

"I can grant your most fantastic wish."

"A wish." Jack could not help feeling a spark of hope, even as doubt and worry rose to crush it. He had heard enough stories of men granted their hearts' desires, only to despise the results when pixies and fairies used grossly literal interpretations to turn desires into torments. "Let me guess, I ask for eternal life. I live forever but as a crippled, shriveled old prune begging for death."

"No, Master Jack. I have no intention of twisting your words against you." Puss stood up straight, tail still lashing. "In fact, I already know what you want.

A happy life with no further worries about money, meals, clothing, or shelter."

Jack could not deny he wanted those things, but he still searched for the catch. *It holds a dangerous aura of evil.* He considered other stories his father and brothers had told him. "What's the price for this gift, Puss? My eternal soul?"

The cat's tail quickened its thrashing. "Yes."

Jack had expected the opposite answer or, at least, for the cat to dodge his question. "Yes?"

"Yes. The price is your soul, Master Jack."

Jack nodded, finally trusting his legs to hold him. He had known nothing this wonderful could ever happen to him without an impossible catch. "Then, no. I know how these things work. The moment you grant my wish, I get one instant of joy, die, and you get to torture me for all eternity."

"No, Master Jack. I will do everything in my power to see that you live out a full, happy, and natural lifespan. In fact, I intend to share it with you, if you'll allow me."

Jack blinked. The cat seemed utterly sincere, nothing but innocence in those strange, amber eyes.

"Or, if you wish, I can leave you and find another master to assist. You'll die of exposure on your father's grave and take your chances as to the dispensation of your soul." The cat whirled gracefully, pulling up his hood as he did so and taking a step toward the woodlands.

"Wait," Jack heard himself saying. "Give me some time to think about this."

Puss stopped in midstride, then turned slowly.

"A full, *long*, happy life, right?"

The cat nodded. "To the best of my abilities. If you choose to take up jumping off roofs and bridges to prove your invulnerability, I may not have the wherewithal to save you from your own stupidity."

Jack could live with that exception. A happy man had no reason to behave in such a risky manner. "With love and marriage and money?"

"Happiness would be near impossible without those, and I guarantee that happiness."

Jack still worried. The wizard's warning echoed in his mind: "For though it can save a man in his time of utmost desperation, it holds a dangerous aura of evil." Jack looked at his father's headslab. Nothing had changed. He gritted his teeth, closed his eyes. *Papa, if you know any reason I shouldn't do this, give me a sign.*

Nothing followed, not a stray thought, not a movement, not a sound. Jack opened his eyes and spoke through teeth still tightly clenched. "Puss, you have a deal."

Princess Darcia noticed the creature in the courtyard from her third-story window. Shoving aside the gauzy film of curtains, she peered down to study him more intently. Though human by the ability to walk on two legs and speak fluently, he looked nothing like anyone she had ever seen. In any other guise, she would have assumed him an animal, covered with fur and with paws instead of hands. Yet what, besides people, wore clothing? Whatever else could carry live pheasants and a string of fish to the castle? Left without answers, she watched the guards in the courtyard trailing him with gazes as curious as her own.

The creature swept down his hood and bowed at the door, appropriately respectful and gracious. Darcia could not help smiling. His stripy silver head looked so adorable she wanted to pet it, tickling between the triangular ears and down the gentle slope of his snout to his velvety, black nose. His fur looked as touchably soft as a fine silk blanket.

Darcia could hear little of the exchange that followed,

except that the creature called himself "Puss" and had brought the pheasants and fish as gifts from the young Duke of Corlwin. At least, it sounded like Corlwin; the princess had never heard of such a place, nor of its duke. She could not help imagining a handsome corsair near her own seventeen years. She pictured him tall and blond, exotic-looking compared with her own family's black hair, swarthy skin, and dark eyes. Anyone who employed such elegant and odd-looking servants had to be striking and mysterious. One thing was certain; she had to meet this Puss.

In a swirl of gowns and lace, Princess Darcia swung away from the window, dashed across her room, and threw open the door, startling the guards and ladies-in-waiting stationed outside. Without a word, she charged past them and down the broad, purple-carpeted staircase.

"Princess! Princess!"

Darcia ignored the calls from behind her. She had long tired of servants trailing her wherever she went. As young children, they had played together like equals: wrestling, giggling, sharing their aversions and desires. But, as they had grown, their deference toward her had become a growing hindrance. They fawned over her like sycophants, refusing to "burden her" with the details of their petty lives.

Darcia's mother, the queen, had died several years ago. Her father, though doting, carried the responsibilities of an entire kingdom, which left him no time to talk of girlish matters.

So, Darcia did not bother with the men and women who trailed her down the steps and into the great entryway. The massive double doors stood closed, their pair of inner guards at brisk attention.

"Where did he go?" Princess Darcia wondered aloud.

One of the entryway guards bowed low. "About whom, your highness, do you inquire?"

Darcia spun in a full circle, glancing through empty rooms and hallways for a glimpse of the new arrival. "The . . . the . . ." She could not find the proper word. To call him a man seemed inappropriate, but to name him animal impolite. ". . . one who called himself Puss."

"Ah." The guard fidgeted, clearly wondering how the princess had already come to know of their visitor. "Meeting with His Majesty in the Great Hall. Puss has promised to rid us of our . . . our rodent problem."

Darcia remained in place, surprised by the revelation. When King Harold had first promised a pile of gold to the one who rid the palace of its rats and mice, strangers had come in such droves they had become more a pestilence than the hairy little creatures they vowed, unsuccessfully, to eradicate. At last, her father had had to make a reluctant decree. The man who achieved this miracle would get his pile of gold, and a chance to woo Princess Darcia as well. But, should he fail at the task, he would spend the rest of his natural life in the dungeon. That greatly reduced the number of men attempting the feat. The king had hoped to limit the pool to only those of greatest competence. Instead, they had, so far, gotten only those overconfident of skills they did not possess.

Princess Darcia was assured that by "woo," the king meant only that the successful man would be given the opportunity to win her love and respect. She would never be forced marry against her will. And, though she claimed to go along only to help the kingdom, Darcia secretly enjoyed the arrangement. It opened so many possibilities she would not otherwise have. So far, her only eligible suitors were older, stuffy nobility, spoiled beyond redemption. At least, she might get to meet a man with an actual talent, a good man with a great skill, and she always imagined him young and handsome as well.

Apparently guessing the reason for her interest in Puss, the guard continued, "Don't worry, your Highness. He states that if he succeeds, all rewards go to his master, the Duke of Corlwin. If he fails, he suffers the punishment himself."

Darcia's brows arched upward in surprise. "This duke must be a special man to attract servants so loyal." She could imagine many nobles ordering their men on such an assignment. However, once at the castle entryway, unwatched by their masters, nearly all servants in Puss' position would become instant free agents. No one needed a subservient job once he had a huge pile of gold and the attention of a princess. To clearly announce such unselfish intentions meant Puss had no personal designs at all on the fortune or her hand. Only a fool, or a truly steadfast minion, would agree with such a bargain. Puss did not appear stupid, and Darcia wanted to meet any lord who could inspire such allegiance.

"Indeed," the guard responded, retaking his position at the door.

Ignoring her own entourage, Darcia crept down the hallway toward the Great Hall. Though she made little noise, the mass of footsteps at her heels did. The guards at the door of the Great Hall looked up nervously, until they apparently recognized the group headed toward them and fell back into their usual stiff positions.

At that moment, the door burst open. Darcia's guards and ladies fell back, and even the princess stepped aside to allow whoever exited some space. A page scurried out, Puss' hooded cape and tunic thrown neatly over one arm, the boots clutched in his hand. He managed an awkward bow toward Darcia as he raced toward the downstairs guest suite. Through the open doors, Darcia caught sight of her father, a hand clapped to Puss' shoulder, while guards hovered around him. A pile of dead mice lay heaped in the far corner of the room.

Darcia looked longest at Puss. Without his clothing, he seemed even more animal, if possible, his body covered with the same striped fur as his face. Blood flecked his whiskers and stained the furry white mask across his cheeks and his paws. Then, the door banged shut behind the retreating page, and the scene cut off before the princess could take it all in. One thing was certain: Puss had captured more rodents in the moments it had taken her to get from her room to the Great Hall than any of the others had in days. She had not noticed her father's expression but imagined his bearded face wreathed in an ecstatic grin.

Darcia spent most of the day pretending to adhere to the normal routines of a princess. Therefore, it took her nearly until dinner to deliberately stumble upon Puss. She found him in the library, stalking. He worked on all fours, a lithe, agile bundle of animal muscle frozen in position. Only the tip of his tail twitched in anticipation. Then, abruptly, he pounced, neatly trapping a mouse in a sudden net of knife-like claws. With a single movement, he snapped its spine and tossed it onto a growing pile of carcasses. His nails receded, his tail lashed, and he did not look up as he spoke. "Good evening, Princess."

Darcia knew she had opened the door soundlessly. Either Puss had exquisite hearing or her entourage had given her away. In any case, his guess was spectacular given that they had never met. She curtsied respectfully. "Good evening, Puss. Will you be joining us for supper?" It was not her question to ask; the servants had surely already taken care of the matter.

However, she wanted very much to speak with this odd creature, especially about his master.

"No, your Highness." Puss finally glanced in her direction, his pupils slitted and his irises a strange shade of yellow. They were demon's eyes; and, for a moment, Darcia sucked in a breath of fear. Puss did not, or pretended not to, notice. "I'll need to work straight through till morning. The rats won't come out until after nightfall."

Though not crazy about rats, Darcia had grown accustomed to them. "Perhaps, then, you could save my room for last?" She hoped the invitation sounded as innocent as she intended. "I'd like to talk to you about your master." She added emphatically, more for her servants than for him, "In private." She looked at his paws, smeared with blood but otherwise small and plushy. She saw no sign of the long, deadly nails that had ended the mouse's existence. *Where did they go?*

Puss finally bowed. "As you wish, your Highness." He licked blood from his whiskers.

Darcia closed the library door, heart pounding. There was something stunningly attractive about this Puss, and also much that seemed clandestine, sneaky, and evil. Curiosity assailed her, tempered with a hint of fear. There was nothing sexual about her interest in him; she knew without the need to ask that their anatomy was not compatible. He was to her neither male nor female, only animal. She saw him as no more suitable as a suitor than the horses in the stable. Yet, she found herself fascinated in so many other ways. She wanted to brush his fur until the mats and stains disappeared and each stripe lay in perfect alignment, to find where he hid those dagger claws, and to understand his devotion to his master. It was a desire she could not fully understand, yet it had driven her every action since she had seen him from the window.

Supper seemed to drag on forever. As soon as she

could, Princess Darcia crawled into her bed under the pretense of exhaustion. She simply wanted the night to go more swiftly, but her thoughts kept sleep at bay. Surely, some worried guard or servant would mention her plans to her father and insist that someone oversee her liaison with Puss.

Fitfully, Darcia dozed, awaiting Puss' interruption that never came. At last, she went to her window and brushed aside the silken curtains. The three-quarters moon hung high, the stars numerous and awash with light. A hint of pink touched the eastern horizon, the only indication of an approaching dawn, still at least an hour away. Guards stood attentively at the front gates, watchful and waiting.

Darcia moved to the side window, which overlooked the courtyard. The garden below appeared to sleep, the flowers that left the area awash in color during the day seemed gray and damp, closed to buds for the night. Curled on her favorite alabaster bench, Puss appeared to be sleeping.

Poor thing's exhausted. A sudden idea struck Darcia, and she smiled. Quietly snatching the blanket from her bed, she twisted it into a thick rope. Tying one end securely around a bedpost, she tossed the other out the window. It fell near enough to the ground that she could drop safely. Though not the first time she had climbed from her window to escape her constant flurry of attendants, she had not dared to do it in many years, not since her father had chastised her as a child, worried she might place herself in danger or break a leg.

Years of dance training kept Darcia fit and graceful, and she shinnied down her makeshift rope without difficulty, dropping lightly to the ground. At first, she approached Puss quietly so as not to awaken him. Then she remembered the claws and deliberately shuffled her feet through the gravel. She did not want to startle him and find those daggers jabbed instinctively, deeply into her chest.

Puss did not move.

When Darcia took a seat beside him on the bench, she could see one eye, at least, was open. "Puss?" she whispered.

The beast rolled his head backward, just far enough to fix his stare on the princess.

Darcia wriggled closer to him and pinched bits of clotted blood and dirt from his whiskers.

Puss licked his lips. "I'm sorry, your Highness," he said. "I finished all the rooms, but it was too late to bother you so I thought I'd—"

Darcia silenced him with a gesture and a soft shushing noise. She lifted his head and placed it on her lap.

Apparently surprised, he rolled to his stomach; but he did not try to escape.

"Poor Puss. Poor poor, Puss." Darcia stroked his head, dislodging old fur, flakes, and bits of dirt. "Just rest."

His head went heavy in her lap.

Darcia scratched behind the pert ears, and then ran her hand along the dark, heavy stripe that ran directly down his spine.

Puss closed his eyes and began to rumble. It was a strange, new sound, barely resembling a hunting dog's growl, but much friendlier. It seemed beyond Puss' control. It did not matter if he inhaled or exhaled, the sound accompanied every aspect of his breathing. Darcia could feel as well as hear it. It rattled throughout his body, and he snuggled against her as he made it.

Darcia quickened her touch, and the sound increased in volume.

Puss opened his eyes, and Darcia read a combination of confusion and contentment. "Is that me?"

"It's you," Darcia confirmed. "Am I hurting you?"

"No, I like it." Puss looked down the length of his body. "I think it's a sound of liking, of happiness. But I've never made it before." The rumbling died as he spoke. He lay back, stretching his legs as far as they would go.

Darcia resumed her petting, and the purring began again in perfect response. "I like it, too. It's soothing." She had many questions she wanted to ask him. She had never met anything like him, and she wished to know more of his master as well. But she felt so comfortable just stroking him and listening to the musical rhythm he created, that she did not wish to disturb the moment. She did, however, take a paw and study it. It was white, surprisingly clean; apparently, he had washed it. She saw no evidence of the claws she had previously noticed. Tentatively, she squeezed a toe, feeling something hard as bone inside it. The sharp point of a claw emerged. She pushed harder, and a curved blade popped from the toe in all its wicked glory.

Darcia had to focus to keep from recoiling. *Amazing.* It seemed impossible that Puss could hide a dagger inside each plushy toe, but he managed to do it. More surprising still, he cut neither himself nor those around him when he used the paw to touch others or manipulate objects. Meeting up with him, Darcia had hoped to answer some questions but had only raised many more. He was an enigma of great complexity, a one-of-a-kind creature with deep mysteries wrapped in an animal body. She wanted to know so much more and yet had a disturbing feeling much of it was better left secret.

Jack lounged on the riverbank beneath the covered bridge, watching the cool, clear water for approaching fish. He had not realized just how dependent he had become on his companion in the few weeks before

Puss left to visit the king. Jack never went hungry; but fish, and the vegetation he recognized as edible, had become a bore. He craved the fowl and conies Puss had provided, as well as the mintier, headier plants and spices the cat had added to their diet.

"So, let me understand this," Jack said, running a toe through the river. "The king offered you a pile of gold, and you . . . you . . . refused it?"

Puss recoiled from Jack's simple action. In their short association, the cat had made it absolutely clear that he despised water. The lightest rain sent him scurrying for shelter. "Yes. I refused King Harold's gold."

Jack looked at Puss as if he had gone entirely mad. "Wasn't the gold the purpose of going in the first place?"

"No."

"No?" The question was startled from Jack.

"No." The expression Puss returned held an air of amusement, and a twinkle filled his amber eyes.

Jack had clearly misunderstood. He pulled up his ragged pants and tightened the rope belt. "You promised me happiness. A roof over our heads, a decent set of clothing, some food other than fish. Any of those would go a long way toward our goal, and gold could certainly buy them."

Puss smacked his lips at the mention of fish. Clearly, he had missed them every bit as much as Jack did the creatures Puss caught. "Be patient, Master. You will have all of those things."

Without thinking, Jack grabbed a small rock and tossed it into the river. Puss retreated from the splash, though the farthest reaching droplets came nowhere near him. The stone spiraled to the riverbed, leaving a familiar pattern of widening rings on the surface. It was a phenomenon Jack had seen a million times since childhood, but it never seemed to grow old. His brothers and he had spent many hours composing games that involved throwing or skipping stones on water. "I don't mean to sound greedy, but if you refuse *piles* of gold—"

"I know what I'm doing," Puss insisted, brushing off his clothes as if to free them from nonexistent sprinkles. "Haven't you ever noticed it while fishing? When you're desperate, the fish seem to know it and avoid you. But if you act aloof . . ."

Jack found himself finishing the sentence, ". . . they swim right up to you."

"Exactly." Puss nodded vigorously. "And if you're going to marry the princess,—"

"Marry the princess?!" Jack could scarcely believe what he was hearing.

Puss talked over him "—we must convince the king you don't need his money. That you have plenty of your own."

A snicker broke through Jack's irritation. Once breached, the dam burst, and laughter flooded out of him until he could barely breathe. For several moments, he found himself utterly incapable of speech. Every time he tried, waves of mirth overtook him again.

Apparently misunderstanding the source of Jack's amusement, Puss pled his case, "She's very sweet, young, quite pretty."

"Of course she's pretty. She's a princess." Jack outlined his ragged, scrawny self with a broad gesture. "And I'm . . . not exactly . . . prince material."

"No," Puss admitted. "You're only a duke."

"A duke?" That sounded no less ludicrous. *"I'm* a duke?"

"That's what they believe at the castle."

Jack's eyes narrowed in confusion and suspicion. "And where would they get a silly idea like that?"

"From me. It's what I told them."

Jack stared at his companion, taking in the bipedal, but still bestial, shape. No human clothing, no use of human speech, not even his humanlike mannerisms could change the obvious fact that Puss was an animal. The warning blossomed in Jack's mind, in his father's voice: "For though it can save a man in his time of utmost desperation, it holds a dangerous aura of evil." For all his apparent kindness, for all his cleverness, for all he called Jack "Master," Puss still held title to Jack's very soul. So far, he had proven a benign and friendly owner, but even the sweetest of hounds had, in rare circumstances, been known to turn on its master.

Puss answered the unspoken question. "Yes, I told them you were the Duke of Corlwin."

"Corlwin?"

Puss waved a paw in an encompassing gesture. "Here."

Jack knew little of the territory to which Puss had led him, but it seemed empty, aside from the river, some forest, and an occasional road. The only structure he had seen was the sturdy, wooden bridge over the river upon whose bank they sat. "You're mad."

Puss took the insult in stride. "If you insist."

"I'm not a duke. The king will take one look at me and know that."

Puss rose and walked around Jack, studying him with a designer's eye. "A good bath, combed hair, some fine clothes. That's all it would take."

Jack wondered if Puss spoke the truth. "I can handle the bath and combing. But fine clothing? If I could afford that, I wouldn't be wearing the scraps of an outfit handed down through two brothers." He locked gazes with Puss, who still studied him with clear interest. "Unless you're talking about . . . magic?" In every demonic tale he had ever heard, the deal got made; and the devil instantly fulfilled his victim's wishes by magic. Then, unless the man acted in a terribly clever fashion, the devil cleaved him from his wretched soul for all eternity.

Puss cocked one brow. "Oh, so we believe in magic now?"

"My knickknack came to life," Jack reminded his once-stone companion. "How can I continue to deny it?"

Puss shrugged and finally turned away. "That was not my doing. I'm a magical creation, but I wield none of it myself. The lot of a cat is wits, not spells."

Jack snorted. "If you were so witty, you'd have a way to catch those fish you love so well without getting your paws wet."

Puss just smiled a toothy grin, the answer obvious. He *had* found a way, and its name was Jack. Puss returned to the matter at hand, "Strip down and take that bath. Make sure you scrub your hair and work out those blessed tangles."

Jack stared at the icy water, eyes widening incrementally. "Yes, you've definitely gone entirely insane."

"Not insane, just . . . witty." Puss prodded Jack cautiously. "Hurry up. Before the king sees you in those rags."

Driven by the concern in Puss' tone, Jack removed his worn clothing before the content of the cat's words fully penetrated. Naked and poised over the water, still clutching his fishing device, Jack finally thought to question. "Why would the king see me? Why would the king even—"

Puss plucked the iron hook from his master's hand. "In lieu of the gold, I asked him to come visit—"

The sound of hoofbeats on packed earth interrupted Puss. He gave Jack a more vigorous shove. "Go, go quickly. Deep into the water. Then, follow my lead."

Puss gathered up Jack's old clothing and ran toward the road.

Left with no means to argue, Jack waded toward the middle of the river, scrubbing his skin fiercely and finger combing the knots from his hair.

Soon, the sound of creaking cartwheels joined the clop of shod hooves in a fancy duet. A small coach, fully enclosed and festooned with flags, gemstones, and banners flowed toward the bridge at the heels of four impeccably groomed white horses. Two partially mailed men, girded with swords, controlled the reins. They wore silver helmets with red top feathers, and their silks bore a crest Jack could not make out from the river.

Suddenly, Puss ran onto the bridge, waving his furry arms. He no longer held Jack's discarded clothing, and the young man worried for the fishing hook that had kept him, and his family, alive for so many years.

Though faint with distance, Puss' voice reached Jack's ears. "Please help! Help my master, the duke!"

The coach rumbled to a stop. An exchange followed that Jack could not make out. His heart rate quickened. If he could not hear, he would not know what lead to follow.

The door of the cart opened, and a man stepped out. Dressed in fancy scarlet and silver silks, covered in jewelry and flourishes, the stranger commanded authority with every movement or gesture. This, Jack guessed, was the king himself. Jack found himself bowing quite unconsciously until he sucked water up his nose. That sent him into a fit of violent coughing.

Nevertheless, Jack heard the king's deep voice, "What's wrong with Duke Corlwin?"

Puss spoke with loud anxiety, presumably so Jack could hear every dramatic word. "My master saw a man drowning and leaped into the river to save him. While he was performing this heroic act, thieves stole his clothing. Now, he's stuck in the cold water, too modest to leave."

A young woman, also finely dressed, poked her head out of the coach's door. Immediately, Jack felt assaulted by all of the modesty Puss had claimed for him. He covered his privates with his hands, not altogether sure of his motivation. He liked to think he wished to save a royal virgin the site of naked man parts, but he also did not want her to judge him by the ice-water shriveled state of his unmentionables.

Puss stepped between the princess and any view of the water below. Unfortunately, that also put his back directly toward Jack, effectively cutting him off from the rest of the conversation. Swiftly, Jack gave his skin a final, violent rub down and worked the remaining knots from his hair.

Moments later, Puss appeared at the riverbank, accompanied by one of the men who had driven the wagon. He held a drying blanket and a set of crisp, clean silks. Approaching the water, he gestured for Jack to emerge.

Jack obeyed swiftly, using the brush and trees to hide himself from the those waiting on the bridge. He did not have to feign his embarrassment. The man arranged the drying blanket across his shoulders while Puss laid out the garments in order. Jack appreciated Puss' thoroughness. He had never before owned an undergarment and might well have humiliated himself putting things on the wrong ways and places. Luckily, the king's man averted his eyes, allowing Puss to silently assist without drawing suspicion.

When Jack indicated he had finished, the king's man finally turned and bowed. "Come with me, please, Duke Corlwin. The king and Princess Darcia would very much like to meet you."

Jack felt as if someone had punched him in the gut. "Thank you," he said mechanically, giving no outward sign of the battle taking place internally. His heart felt like it wanted to slug its way through his chest, and the urge to run in terror seized him. It took sheer force of will just to keep one foot moving in front of the other.

In what seemed like an instant, they stood on the bridge in front of the king and his daughter. Up close, King Harold looked even more intimidating, a large man with an intense gaze and aristocratic features. Jack started bowing and could not stop until Puss gave him a savage kick and a sharp nail tore into his ankle. Only then, Jack dared a glance at Darcia.

Puss' description did her no justice. She had a gentle, round face, smiling eyes, and a soft complexion. Clearly entertained by Jack's excessive display of manners, she grinned at him. As he studied her, she also looked him over, and she did not, at least, act repelled by what she saw.

The king finally broke the silence. "Duke Corlwin, I can see you're rightfully shaken by your experience. With your consent, I'd like to postpone our meeting until this time next week."

Our meeting? Jack scarcely managed to bite back the words before he spoke them aloud.

"Your servant stated that if we gave you sufficient time, you would have us for a feast at your manse."

A feast? My . . . manse? Startled into abject silence, Jack continued to, brilliantly, say nothing at all.

"Master?" Puss prompted.

Jack shook his senses free. *Follow Puss' lead.* "Yes, Your Majesty. A feast at my manse in one week. That should leave me ample time to prepare, and I would be honored by your presence." He managed a single deep bow this time, then a second to Darcia. "Please promise to bring this breathtaking woman with you." With a raw courage he never knew he could summon, Jack took Darcia's warm, delicate hand and kissed it gently.

To Jack's surprise, the princess' cheeks took on a

flush, her grin persisted, and she flashed him a coy look. "I wouldn't miss it for the world."

Then, king and princess bundled back into their coach. Jack stared after them until the servants managed to turn the contraption around, and the whole of it disappeared back the way it had come, leaving only the lingering odor of horses.

At last, Jack rounded on Puss, "A feast at my manse? A *feast!* At *my* manse!" He shook his head fiercely, wondering if he could even manage more words. Apparently, he could: "Have you gone absolutely, utterly, hell-damned, around-the-bend, over-the-top crazy?"

Puss waited until Jack completed his rant before tossing him back his fishing device. "Please hook me a couple fish, and I'll catch you a . . ." He cocked his head, waiting for Jack to fill in the blank.

Jack sighed and closed his eyes as shock and anger gradually dispersed. He knew from their association thus far that Puss loved fish of every variety, even the mud-dwellers that Jack found scarcely edible. So intent was the cat on avoiding water, however, he chose to clean his fur with his own tongue.

". . . partridge," Jack said, leaning over the water with hook in hand, worried to muddy his brand new silks. "And make it a tender one. *Penniless. And we're going to build a mansion, and a feast, in a week. I wonder what a king does to a pauper who impersonates a duke?* It's likely to be our last meal."

The keep in the woodlands towered over the trees, its stark construction festooned with bleak, flowerless vines. Back in his ragged clothing, his silks carefully stashed, Jack studied the well-crafted structure in shock, while his stomach churned over a breakfast of evening leftovers. "This is so huge. I've looked this way many times. How did I possibly miss it?"

Puss smoothed his own garments, which seemed far more suitable. "It blends in well."

Jack had to admit that the foliage swarming over the stonework did add some camouflage, but he still found it difficult to believe he had dismissed it as a normal part of nature. "We're not calling upon the occupant, are we?"

"We are."

Though Jack had raised the question, the answer surprised him. "Admittedly, I'm clean, but I'm hardly dressed for nobility."

Puss looked Jack over, as if for the first time. "Well, the garments the king supplied would work better, but you'll need those in decent shape for our feast."

"Well, yes, but . . ." It struck Jack how silly the whole conversation had become. "Let's say we actually have this feast—and I don't see how we can. Won't the king notice I'm wearing the exact same clothes he gave me?"

"It's a compliment to his taste, of course."

"Of course." Jack knew Puss would have an answer for everything. He only wondered why he kept asking. "So why are we here? Are we befriending another king, just in case the first one doesn't work out?"

"No."

"Because I really like the first one's daughter—" The cat's response finally caught up to Jack's thoughts. "No? So what are we doing here?"

"You'll see. Follow my lead."

Jack had grown tired of that response. He seized Puss' wrist, surprised by the softness of the fur. He had never touched the cat before. "No. I'm tired of 'following' your 'lead.' This time, I want to know in advance."

Puss turned to face Jack directly, freeing his paw. "Believe me, master. The less you know this time, the better off you are."

Jack rolled his eyes.

"But, I will give you one important piece of advice."

"What?" Jack asked sullenly. Though Puss' motivations frequently defied logic, at least his companion had gotten them this far.

"Whatever you do, whatever you say, do *not* show any fear."

"What?"

The next thing Jack knew, Puss had taken his arm and was leading him to the massive wooden door of the keep. As Puss slammed a giant knocker against the wood, he whispered one more time. "No fear, got it? Not a hint of fear."

The admonishment itself sent a shiver of dread through Jack. He suppressed it the best he could. "Why should I be afraid? What exactly are we doing?"

The door opened on squealing hinges, and a mousy creature that closely resembled a human female gestured them inside. Pale as a ghost, she seemed to hover a moment in indecision.

Looking beyond her, Jack saw an entry hall three times the size of the entire cabin his father and brothers had built. Though simply furnished with stone and wooden benches, it also sported an enormous fountain in the shape of a horse, the water spurting from its upraised mouth to curl around its body and between stone hooves that seemed to cleave the air. Below it, the water gathered in a pool, where orange and white fish flitted through algae and shadow.

Jack could not help seeing all these things as he entered, though only one thing held his gaze. Seated calmly on one of the benches was a massive figure. From the waist up, he looked entirely human, albeit a giant that would have towered over the tallest man Jack had ever seen. Scraggly black hair fell around his ears, and a sharp, dark beard hid his chin. The ears and nose were broad, contrasting with narrow-set eyes with a depth beyond wisdom. His legs sported wooly hair and ended in cloven hooves. Jack suspected he probably had a tail as well.

Show no fear, Jack reminded himself. *No fear.* The urge to flee seized him like a compulsion, and it was all he could do to remain in place and fight to keep his expression impassive.

The door banged shut on Jack's heels, and the realization that he had lost his only escape pushed his resolve to its boundaries.

Beside Jack, Puss bowed deeply.

The giant grinned, revealing a set of vicious fangs ten times the size of the cat's own. "Ah. My Capricious Animistic Tempter. It seems like forever since I've seen you." His mouth opened wider in clear amusement. "Is this one mine?"

The words struck through Jack's heart like a dagger. He glanced at Puss, who dodged his gaze.

"Yes, Master," Puss said meekly. "He is yours."

The creature leaned forward hungrily.

"But not yet," Puss added.

The giant's smile slipped away, replaced by an expression of clear annoyance. "Not yet?"

"I have not yet fulfilled my promises to him."

Jack's legs felt rooted, his thoughts exploding in several directions. No wonder the title "master" came so easily to Puss' lips. From the edges of his vision, Jack saw figures shifting in the background, as eerily white as the one who had answered the door. *Are those . . . souls? The ones pledged to Puss' evil master?* Jack suddenly knew a regret so profound he could scarcely stand it. He closed his eyes tightly and begged any god who might listen to let him wake up in familiar squalor and find it was all a dream. But nothing changed except the view. Understanding remained, and a sulfur smell permeated the room. He had not noticed the odor before, his attention focused on more visual horrors. Jack had gotten himself into a situation from which he had no power to extract himself. Two things seemed certain: Puss had lied about the promise of a long life, and Jack's entire existence was no longer worth the rags he wore. *Why?* he wondered.

When Jack opened his eyes, he found the monster's attention fully on Puss. "Why did you bring him here now?" The giant's curiosity seemed to echo Jack's own. "Why not wait until it's time for me to claim . . ." His cruel gaze went suddenly to Jack. ". . . his . . ." His lips curled into an evil grin that revealed every fang and tooth. ". . . soul."

Jack's blood ran cold. The eyes seemed to skewer him.

Puss replied so softly, he sounded barely audible compared to the deep rumble of his master's speech. "Because, he doesn't fear you. He doesn't worry about serving you. He laughs when I say you're the world's greatest shapeshifter and says he doesn't even believe in magic."

"Doesn't believe!" The giant rose, revealing legs longer than they had first appeared. He not only towered over Jack; if Jack had carried a twin on his shoulders, the creature would still exceed them both. "Doesn't believe!" The massive form blurred and flowed, swirling through an array of colors.

"What are you doing?" Jack demanded through gritted teeth. He could picture himself running, bashing into the closed door again and again in a howling, futile attempt at escape. How could Puss possibly expect him to maintain composure in the face of this threat?

Puss grabbed Jack's arm, claws digging in just enough to capture his attention. "No fear," he reminded.

A moment later, the giant assumed a solid new shape: huge, tawny, and animal in every respect. Four muscular legs had sprouted from a powerful torso, rippling with vitality. The face resembled Puss' but much larger and with a coarse mane surrounding the catlike features. The creature opened a mouth full of pointy teeth and let out a roar with such force that only Puss' steadying hold kept Jack from collapsing.

Jack forced himself to breathe rhythmically. Otherwise, he might hyperventilate into a coma. Fear shocked through every part of him, but he refused to surrender his thoughts to panic.

"Laugh," Puss instructed.

Jack had never heard anything more ridiculous. "I can't move my jaw."

"Laugh," Puss demanded. "Your life depends on it."

Jack forced out a huff of breath that sounded more like a squeal. The actual mechanics of laughter seemed impossible to remember. He moved his belly in bursts, driving out breath in a series of snorting puffs that he hoped would suffice.

The maned head tipped sideways, and the now-familiar, booming voice emerged, "What's going on?"

"He's laughing." Puss interpreted Jack's inscrutable actions. "He says it's easy to make oneself into something large when you are already large. If you wielded real magic, real power, you could transform yourself into something infinitesimally small as well."

The creature growled. Its eyes narrowed, and it glanced between Jack and Puss several times. "This is a trick, Capricious Animistic Tempter. You want me to become a mouse so you can pounce on me and eat me."

Puss raised his paws, all innocence. "There are other small animals besides rodents."

"True." A louder snarl shattered Jack's concentration. If something did not happen soon, panic would break through his brittle façade. "But I've seen you with birds, too. I've seen you—" Suddenly, the giant chuckled. "I know one place you would never go, my hydrophobic creation. One place I can prove my power without also risking my life." The massive animal disappeared in a puff of smoke, and the fountain suddenly contained an ugly, whiskered, black fish.

"Go!" Puss commanded.

The rest was pure instinct. Before he could think to run, before he could fully comprehend the danger, Jack had cleared the distance to the fountain and speared the fish on his hook. It struggled desperately, wildly, its shape blurring. Then, Puss sprang forward and, with a single swipe of his paw, tore off the back of the fish's head. And it went still.

Abruptly, the air tingled, and a happy shout went up in hundreds of voices. Still clutching the hook and its grizzly contents, Jack looked around at the pale figures flitting near the entryways. Now, they glided toward him.

Dropping the hook, Jack retreated behind Puss, who set to happily devouring what remained of the fish.

"Thank you," the creatures said as they approached. "Thank you, Puss. Thank you, young man. Thank you."

Jack grabbed Puss' lashing tail. "What's happening?"

Bone crunched between Puss' jaws, and he swallowed before speaking. "The bought souls have a new master, Duke Jack Corlwin. They are eternally tied to this keep, but they now serve a man who will surely treat them more kindly than their previous master."

En masse, the lost souls bowed and curtsied while Jack stared. "Th-thank you," he told them. "Please see to it our home remains tidy and functioning, and I will do everything in my power to keep your eternity comfortable and happy. You only need to tell me what you desire."

The souls scampered off in several directions, chattering happily amongst themselves.

Puss smiled. "Very nice, Master. You're a natural-born duke."

"Hardly." Jack picked up his fish hook and put it in his pocket. "With your help, my Capricious Animistic Tempter." He smiled. "I mean, my cat. I could not have done it without your cleverness." He bowed appreciatively. "You are as witty as you claimed. How can I repay you?"

Puss' grin widened until his fangs showed. "I have everything I need. A secure home, the love of my mistress, and the soul of my master. And so shall it be for my offspring through eternity."

Jack swallowed deeply. He did not fear for his soul. Not really. But something else Puss said confused him. "The love of your mistress?"

"Princess Darcia," Puss confirmed, and a glimmer entered his yellow eyes. "She loves me."

"She loves *you?*" An image of the young princess filled Jack's mind's eye. She was pretty and gracious, far more than he deserved.

Puss nodded happily. "And, with my help, she'll learn to love you, too."

"She will?" It seemed as though Puss might deliver everything he promised, but Jack could not forget that his cat denied having actual magic. "How?"

Puss turned and headed after the soul-servants. "Just follow my lead."

A CHARMING MURDER

Mary Louise Eklund

Mary Louise Eklund lives in Wisconsin with
her husband and teenage son. Being a trans-
planted southerner, she avoids the cold as
much as possible and enjoys watching the snow
melt away for another year. Her hobbies include walking her retired racing greyhound,
napping with her three cats, and photography.

The goings on in the station seemed anything but
normal that day. Then again, that's what we had
been expecting for months—a little excitement. The
whole department was in dress uniform doing our col-
lective duty to see that peace was maintained as Prince
and Princess Charming celebrated their first anniversary. Didn't matter what rank or division you were in,
everyone had been called up to either keep the crowds
under control or the royalty attending the gala safe.

I, for one, wanted to see Snow White—always
thought she was beauty. But, alas, the turn of events
kept me from laying eyes on her. I was in charge of
the security detail for the VIP dinner and ball.

I never expected to instead be the lead investigator
of the murder of Princess Cinderella Charming.

The only good thing about the latter task was I didn't have to wear my dress uniform. I hate those high, starched collars. Still, looking back, I think I'd rather have worn a dress uniform for a week than learn what was really underneath the gilded beauty of Cinderella Van Schouwen Charming.

I had just arrived at the palace that morning with the dress uniform in a garment bag. I was there twelve hours early with my team leaders to scope out the situation and get any updates on just who the visiting bigwigs were and how they were to be handled. In fact, we were just knuckling down with the security heads from some of the dignitaries when all hell broke loose.

A high protocol official came running, with the head of the royal guard in tow, to tell us there had been a murder. That news sent the foreign security heads scurrying to lock down their respective dignitaries. At first I expected to be led into the workings of the palace, instead we kept going to the ritzier and ritzier parts. I knew when we got to the right place because there were maids and ladies in waiting screaming and crying. The guards were thick as flies on a dead carcass.

That's when they told me it was Cinderella. I almost dropped a load.

The next in line to the throne had been murdered. I was glad it wasn't on my watch she'd been killed, but sorry it was up to me to solve the case.

I turned the corner from where the women were wailing, walked through the assembly of dour-but-scared-looking guards, and sucked in an impossibly deep breath.

It takes a lot to shock me, but I was shocked. It wasn't for the gore; as far as that goes, it was your basic bludgeoning scene. Instead, it was the tool of the beating, a shoe.

It was left at the scene of the crime.

Right there—in what had been the pretty blonde's forehead—stuck out the legendary glass slipper, now sparkling red with blood. Never before or since have I covered a case where someone had been beaten to death with her own shoe.

There, in the bowing of her sheer-covered windows, in front of her big oval mirror, the Princess was sprawled in one of her fine light blue gowns. She was stretched out on a pile of finery that must have been various things she'd been trying on.

Every pretty piece had droplets of blood from the beating.

And the shoe stuck out from the top of her face as if it were the red capping cherry on a shiny pastel fabric sundae.

After going over the scene, I returned to the station house and dispatched my team to various tasks. Then I sat back to review what I knew.

The last person said to have entered the Princess's suite was Estella, her stepsister. But Estella was not at the castle when the body was discovered and had not been spotted on the grounds.

So, following basic procedure, I decided to question Estella at her home. According to the address I'd obtained, she didn't live terribly far from the station house.

The first thing I noticed was how shabby the place was compared to the bright gilded boudoir of her sister Cinderella. The house and neighborhood had the reek of genteel decay—grand fifty years ago; it now showed its occupants' loss of affluence.

I was no stranger to the celebrity gossip. I'd seen the tabloid headlines, heard the news clips, and listened to the radio DJs talk about how horrid the beautiful princess' stepfamily was. I couldn't get the sport scores at times, what with all the reports on how

ugly the stepsisters and stepmother were at the latest
function, what greedy thing the stepmother had done,
or some new disclosure on some over-the-top abusive
treatment one of the ugly, evil stepsisters had done to
our precious, beautiful princess. I'd marked it all up
to muckraking for ratings. Sure, Cinderella's life
hadn't been grand, and yes she was a looker and
they weren't.

Now, as I rode down the shabby, fading street, I
had to wonder just how much of the tabloid tales were
true, and if this particular stepsister had been rele-
gated to the slums because she'd been so cruel to a
beautiful, orphaned girl who rose to royalty.

The tired, depressed, but proud-looking maid who
answered my knock didn't seem surprised to see a
royal detective on her doorstep. She simply opened
the door wide and said, "Miss Estelle is expecting
you."

She softly shut the door behind me and led me
down a dark hall. I figured the news had raced to the
Princess' relatives, and now they—Estelle included—
were entering a mourning period. They would be sobbing, dressed in black, kerchiefs in hand.

However, it was when we entered the receiving parlor that I got my second shock of the day. There sat
a dignified Estelle in a blood splattered dress, holding
white bloody gloves, and otherwise appearing ready
to receive me to tea.

"Good day, Detective." She held a regal composure. "Yes, I murdered Cinderella. Please sit down
and take my full confession." Leaving the bloody
gloves on her lap, she waved delicately toward a chair
facing her across the tea table.

The maid poured tea as if this were any social call,
handing me a cup and offering sugar cubes as soon as
I stumbled into the seat.

"No sugar or cream."

I fumbled for my notepad with one hand and held the tea with the other, the china pleasantly warm against my skin.

Estelle took her cup and sipped it like a cultured lady. Then she looked at me over the rim. "I'm sorry to cause you such a shock, the murder and all, and me looking a mess like this. But I knew it wouldn't take long for someone to come for me. So I thought it best to just sit and wait."

I nodded, and after another sip she continued.

"I'll come along peacefully and face whatever consequences are to be mine. The only thing I ask is that first you hear my story, all of it, my reasons for doing what I did today."

"Of course." I didn't know what else to say.

"Sitting here thinking of it, I'm not sure if it was an act of passion or just an impulsive carrying out of something I've been thinking of for years now." Estelle carefully set the cup down on the table and shrugged delicately. "I think that's for you and the courts to decide now, isn't it? The only thing I can do is to honestly tell my side of things, which I feel compelled to do."

"That seems fair enough." I gulped my tea. It was weak, and at that moment I really needed something stronger, like maybe a few jiggers of rum.

"You see, detective, Cinderella was a spoiled brat back when Momma started seeing Claus Van Schouwen— Cindy's father. Cordie and I told Momma this but she didn't see it. All she saw was Cindy being all nice as can be, because at the time Cindy thought we had money. Claus Van Schouwen didn't have much." Estelle paused, looking apologetic and glancing around the sparsely furnished parlor with its threadbare furniture and worn-thin rugs. "You see, back then we could at least keep up appearances, which is why, I suppose, Cindy thought we had money. Nowadays things have become apparent, the house sagging and all. And it's not just this house. Look around the neighborhood. Things have been sliding since the Charmings gained power."

She raised her chin a bit in defiance, knowing she spoke treasonous words; no one was to ever speak of how the Charmings hadn't been royalty only a generation ago. "At that time, detective, Momma was under Cindy's spell, and she was deeply in love with meek and kindly Claus. She couldn't see what we saw, and thought Cordelia and I were just jealous. She thought we didn't want her to remarry. We really didn't mind her marrying Claus—she deserved happiness. We just knew that Cindy was out for money and was using her father to get all she could." Estelle looked away for a moment, staring out the French doors to the weed-choked garden with its crumbling, moldy statues.

It was some time before I spoke. I knew we needed to get on with this before other officers arrived. Besides, the plain but proud woman spoke with such honesty that I wanted to hear the rest of her story before some lawyer shut her up or put a spin on it.

"What kind of things did you and Cordelia see?" I spoke softly, knowing that the woman was struggling to keep her composure, lost in thoughts of days long past.

Snapping her head around, her eyes flared with anger. "I'll tell you what we saw! We saw her stealing from us. We saw her hurting the cats, kicking her father for not buying her something, scratching the neighbor's coach because it was prettier than hers. Not only did we see, we felt her pinches, her shoves, and her spit on our faces! She even locked us in a closet once. We always told the truth about how the fair face covered a foul soul." Estelle stared hard, challenging me to deny her claims. She was almost panting from rage.

Not sure if she was looking to fight, preparing for a flight, or just terrified, I agreed with her. I've learned to soothe the witness and get the full story. "I can see how that would be frustrating to not have your own mother realize what was going on."

Estelle was comforted by my words and shifted on the settee, carefully putting the bloodied gloves on the cushion beside her.

"Yes, yes, it was very frustrating. Things kept on, with smaller but telling incidents, as Claus and my mother became betrothed. It got much worse on the day before Momma's wedding. Someone—later Cindy lorded it over me that it was her—spilled wine all over Cordelia's and my new mint green dresses that were made for us to wear to the wedding. They were horrible, dark red stains." Glancing at the stains now on her peach dress, she raised an eyebrow. "Not the rusty brown stains these are becoming, but deep red on pastel mint. They were ruined, those beautiful dresses. Ruined! We didn't have many nice dresses to wear as it was, and time was short. So Momma used her talents and redid two of our older dresses that very night before her wedding. It was the sweetest thing—she was sacrificing her beauty sleep for us. Some said Mom looked ill at the wedding, others said ugly, as they call Cordelia and me in those papers. I knew why she didn't look her best—she was exhausted, exhausted from an act of love for Cordelia and me." She paused and wiped her eyes with a kerchief from up her sleeve.

As she turned toward the garden window to blot the tears, the blood splatter on the edge of the kerchief almost looked like part of a decorative edging. She was an attractive woman. It was a plain, simple beauty, best not embellished or adorned. She had a wholesome face, looking like the ideal rosy-cheeked milkmaid, not at all like the murderess she confessed to be.

One thing I've learned about murders of passion is that you never know what tiger may rest in wait—even in the most demure. As I made notes, she turned back, sighing deeply before continuing.

"After the marriage, the abuse was much worse—especially after Cindy learned what we did to keep up appearances and that we really weren't rich. That there was only one servant, Susie, and we shared the work with her. Cindy was appalled that we did the cleaning, the mending, the cooking, tending the animals, everything that it took to run the house and make it appear as if nothing were amiss. Claus took to it gracefully, saying that grooming the horse, milking the cows, and feeding the chickens made him feel he was a young boy on the farm. However, Cindy skimped, doing her chores halfheartedly, or having to be nagged to death to do even the smallest thing. It was clear that Claus was upset with his daughter and even blamed himself for coddling her too much. You see, her mother died in childbirth, and Claus treasured the girl, spoiling her rotten. But the evil at her center, that was all hers and not Claus' fault."

Estelle leaned forward, again sipping at her tea and then making a face before adding more to the cup. "Mine is cold. Do you need a warm up, Detective?"

"No thank you. Please, Miss Van Schouwen, do go on." I nodded toward the clock. "Time is getting away. I want to have all this down before others interrupt us."

She smiled apologetically. "I see. I'm sorry. Not having killed someone before, I lack experience with how, precisely, to handle it all. I'll do my best to finish quickly." Taking a deep breath, and facing me squarely, like a pupil in school, she said, "Claus adopted Cordelia and me. However, I think now I shall be going back to my father's name of Vasilyev. I think that best given the events of today." She smoothed her dress. "Anyway, after he adopted us, Cindy became even more hostile. During one argument between Cindy and her father, he suffered the apoplectic fit that eventually killed him. The poor man lay upstairs in the master bed, tended by us. We were the ones weeping and praying for his healing. Cindy danced about down here with the mice and birds loose in the house while planning how she'd spend her inheritance. It was a perverse way to celebrate, counting her inheritance before he was dead."

Estelle shook her head in disgust. "Reality came as a surprise to her when his will was read! He left everything to my mother, saying he trusted her good sense in using it to take care of us girls and to see we were wed properly." She nodded triumphantly. "He was not blind to what he'd raised. Mother took the responsibility seriously, setting aside the money for our dowries and clothes. Claus' chores were divided among us. Momma always wanted the house to appear sparkling."

Estelle finished her tea. "Tensions built as the year went by, and then came the invitations for the prince's ball. Momma got us all three nice gowns and slippers for the social season. Contrary to Cindy's stories, we were all invited, and we never attempted to prevent her from going. We wanted nothing more than to marry her off to some schmuck and get her out of our house. It was Cindy who refused to go to the ball, saying her new gown wasn't fine enough, the coach not nice enough, her hair not done well enough, and so on. She locked herself in her room, ranting that she'd rather die an old maid than be seen looking like a working woman. Momma was forced to leave her behind. I remember in the carriage Cordelia and I saying that if Cindy wasn't going to get out, we'd need to land someone and get out ourselves. Momma rolled her eyes, and we could tell she didn't want to be left alone tending Cindy for the rest of her years."

"The ball . . ." I prompted.

"The ball was glorious! I was thrilled when the prince spoke to me and asked me to dance. We had a wonderful conversation about literature and horses." For a moment, a smile played on her lips, and she looked stunning. She had a glow of happy beauty that flickered, and then too quickly faded. "You can imagine our surprise when Cindy showed up dressed to the nines, wearing those damn glass slippers and having arrived in a white coach complete with groomsmen and matching white horses. Momma was terrified that she'd gotten to our funds and left us in penury."

"But it was magic, wasn't it?" I'd recalled the tale printed in every tabloid.

"Of course magic was involved. But I'm sure it wasn't a fairy godmother, as she claimed, but rather a very dark form of black magic. Well, you know the story from there. She left that magical slipper, and there was a search by Prince Albert Charming, who was consumed with finding her. Then once found, there was the press storm. Her story—and it is a story, about this godmother and about how cruel we were— was everywhere. We were fearful to go to the eventual wedding, but the Charmings required it. Nevertheless, with the angry mobs outside our home throwing rotten vegetables at us and saying such horrid things, we were sure we'd be killed before the reception. But Cindy kept us safe so that we could be her foil. The worse we looked, the better she was loved, the more opinion and public sympathy were on her side. This past year has taken its toll on us. Momma took a turn for the worse and had to go to a home for the elderly. Cordelia has opted to live out in a shack on our vegetable plot rather than face the angry people in the streets. I stayed here, steeling myself against the hordes and visiting Momma twice a day to be sure she is well taken care of."

She took a breath, steadied herself, and continued. "One night the prince came here in secret. He told me of how Cindy was acting, of how much money she spent, of how she treated him with disdain now that she had what she wanted—money and power. Albert thinks that she cast some sort of spell on him, a lust and attraction spell, which broke once they married. He had come here looking for understanding, help in dealing with her, but . . ." She smiled, lowering her head. She blushed at using the prince's first name. "It developed into something quickly, between Albert and me. I'd loved him from the first dance that night at the ball."

Estelle looked exhausted, and I gently patted her hand.

"So now, Detective, I am to this morning's events, the big first-year anniversary. It was required that Cordelia and I attend. Cindy saw that the court tailors made us appropriate clothes so that we would stand out horribly." Estelle lifted the gauzy, sparkly peach finery now with dark stains of the Princess' blood. She let it drop from her hands in disgust. "I went to the palace early to tell her that Albert and I were in love. I didn't go there with the intent to kill her. I wanted to bargain with her. I told her that Albert and I'd be happy to carry on in secret, if only she'd let us take proper care of Momma and Cordelia. She could keep her lifestyle and appearances."

"No one would know?"

Estelle shook her head. "But if Cindy didn't agree, then Albert would shun her publicly and I'd air all the dirty secrets of her past. She laughed, saying I could have Albert. She had the press on her side. She would manipulate them so that the Charmings were out of power and she was in! She said nasty things about my beloved Albert, mocked what this whole traumatic situation had done to poor Cordelia's mind, and said she'd see Momma rot in prison before she'd pay a penny for the woman's care."

I shook my head in sympathy.

"It was then that I realized the chemise she was putting on cost more than one year of good care for Momma. That's when I lost it. I picked up one of those damned glass slippers and intended to break it right in front of her. But it was stronger than I thought it would be. I couldn't break it. So I hit her with it. I swear the slipper hardened in my hand as I beat her senseless with it. It felt as strong as a hammer. I kept striking at that mocking face, that beautiful face that would so twist in cruel joy at causing those I love pain. I just wanted to obliterate it from my sight. I didn't think of it as killing her, just beating that image away."

As she told this, Suzie quietly opened the door. In came one of my detectives with several officers. Estelle didn't notice them, as she continued to relive the moment. I put my finger to my mouth and motioned them to stand along the wall. They waited silently as the murderess described her crime.

"She didn't really fight back. I mean, at first she seemed to struggle, but then it was as if she was under a spell to give way to me for all the harm her vanity, greed, and cruelty had caused. There was little sound, really. Well, at first she had started to scream, but I cut that off with a blow to her pretty mouth. Soon, she was just gurgling and making sounds that reminded me of Momma beating a bad cut of meat to make it tender."

Susie suppressed a small sob as Estelle's voice took

on a flat tone. "I don't know how long it went on, the hitting. It seemed forever. When the heel stuck so badly in her forehead that I couldn't pull it out, I realized she was dead. I knew if the castle guards caught me I'd not get the chance to explain why it had come to this. I'd never be able to reveal what a wicked woman Cindy really was. I wouldn't be able to clear Momma's or Cordelia's names. So I ran off to Albert through the hidden passage between their rooms. I wanted to see him one last time. I told him what I'd done. I told him that I was coming here to wait for the authorities so I could tell my story. As I took my leave, he kissed me and said he'd picked the wrong Van Schouwen sister that night at the ball. He promised that he'd do all he could to help my family. I know if the truth comes out, if people understand how Momma and Cordelia were victims of Cindy, that he'll be able to do it more easily."

Looking up, she finally saw the officers who had come to arrest her. She smiled politely and stood, holding out her arms with her wrists together. "I don't care what happens to me. Really, I don't. I've known true love with Albert. I've done all I can to see my sister and mother are taken care of and their good names vindicated. I regret nothing."

The officers cuffed her and led her away. I asked them to treat her with respect, and from what I can tell, they have.

That evening the headlines screamed: "Ugly Sister Kills Our Fair Princess."

However, with a few well-placed tips to some news-men I know, the tide has started to shift, and the headlines are a little different now.

Estelle's going to trial, and the public is split on what to believe. I think with a handsome, sympathetic prince at her side, a proud, feeble mother telling their story, and the poor, delicate Cordelia on the stand sobbing over past wrongs, the tide will turn wholly in Estelle's favor.

I can already see it in the tabloids: "Our Fair Princess Really an Evil Witch," "Cinderella a Real Spinderella," "Recently Freed Magic Mirror Says None Crueler Then Cinderella."

While bagged in the evidence locker, the now infamous glass slipper turned to brilliant white sand that reminded me of the sparkling white carriage that carried Cinderella to the fateful ball that night.

As I packed the sand-filled evidence bag for court, I couldn't help wondering if it was a demon sprite and not a fairy godmother that gave the slippers to Cindy. Maybe the price of her year of glory was that one of those very slippers would claim her life in the end.

And Estelle was just there to complete the spell.

JACK AND THE GENETIC BEANSTALK

Robert E. Vardeman

Robert E. Vardeman has written more than seventy science fiction, fantasy, and mystery novels. His other short stories can be found in the recently published *Stories from Desert Bob's Reptile Ranch*, with two dozen short stories collected from the past thirty years. He currently lives in Albuquerque, NM, with two cats, Isotope and X-ray. One of the three of them enjoys the high-tech hobby of geocaching. For more info, check out http://www.CenotaphRoad.com.

"**Y**ou look lost." The short, stocky woman pushed back a straw hat and spat out a blade of grass she had been chewing. Her tanned cheeks glowed with health from being outdoors. She was dressed in overalls, with a thin white T-shirt under them and knee-high rubber boots caked with something brown and sticky he was sure could not be mud.

Jack Langmuir marveled at how they were so close to being exact opposites. He towered over her by more than a foot, was gangly, had an unhealthy pallor from spending too much time peering into an LCD screen hooked to his desktop computer, and wore his only business suit. In the heat of the summer day, the tie and jacket were almost too much, but he felt they were his shield against being pushed around. So far, his shield was a failure, and now he was wandering around talking to farmers.

"I'm lost, I suppose," he said.

"I'm Mary Ellen Benjamin," she said, thrusting out a callused, dirty hand. He shook it, ignoring how soft his felt in her powerful grip. "I'm head of the livestock research division."

"Dr. Benjamin?"

"Nobody calls me that, especially my animals, but I do have a Ph.D." She tugged on a rope and pulled a heifer a few steps closer and threw her arm around the cow's neck. For a moment, Jack thought she was going to kiss the smelly animal. "This one's named after my mother. She was head of the genetics department at Stanford. My mother, not the cow."

"Did you go to school there?"

"Sure did." Mary Ellen grinned. "All of you computer jocks react the same way."

"I'm sorry?"

"Disbelief. You don't think a cow herder can have a fancy-ass degree. I do, and I'm closing in on twenty peer-reviewed publications. That's why AgriGen Corporation put me in charge of their animal genetics program. I've made some decent progress, too."

"This one of your, uh, experiments?" Jack stared at the brown and white cow with some uneasiness. He had had a pet dog when he was younger, but he hadn't had contact with animals for almost thirty years. His specialty didn't require it, and he was just as happy that it didn't. "Uh, your cow's looking at me like I was dinner."

"She's an herbivore, like all my cattle. Now, I've got some hogs, damned smart ones, too, that migh‹

consider you a decent meal if you fell into their slop
and didn't get out fast enough."

"You're kidding," Jack said. "You're pulling the leg
of the plant guy."

"That's your field?" Mary Ellen released the rope
and slid it off the cow's neck, but the heifer didn't
stray far, content to munch a juicy tuft of nearby grass.

"Plant genetics. Theoretical plant genetics, actually.
You were right about what I do. I run computer simulations of altered DNA, and then others test the modifications." He looked around and gestured. "Around
here, I suppose, but nobody in the main building will
give me the time of day. I should have let them know
I was coming."

"I got it. You're theoretical, AgriGen Corporation
is empirical. We're not used to a lot of visitors here,"
she said. "Because of the recombinant work, the government makes us keep tighter security than most
labs."

"Well, my coauthor and I are completely theoretical. I mean, we don't experiment." Jack found himself
getting tongue-tied. The way the cow stared at him
was unnerving. "I delivered a paper at the annual con-
ference over in Kansas City and thought I'd hop over
here and meet my coauthor."

"I don't get into the labs much, but I know most
of the researchers. What's her name?"

"Sarah Stahl."

"Sarah was my mother's name, but Stahl?" Mary
Ellen pursued her lips, and then shook her head
slowly. "Not a name I know. You might try Gary over
in plant dynamics, but he's applied, not theoretical."

"Gary Foreman? He's been running some evalua-
tions on my—our—work. Sarah has kept me posted,
but stopped sending progress reports before I arrived
in KC."

"What's she look like? I know more people here by sight than I do by name or even reputation."

"I don't know. As I said, I've never met her. Truth is, I've never even talked to her. We've only traded e-mails."

"I'll check the roster for you. It's kept online with the company intranet." Mary Ellen patted all the pockets on her overalls, and then made a face. "I keep losing my PDA. The director threatened to charge me if I lost another, and it looks like he's going to have to make good on his threat."

"Out in the field and all, I can see where you might drop it." Jack looked across the pasture. "If I dialed your number, you might home in on the ring tone." He took out his cell phone.

"Never mind," she said. "Just go back to the main building and tell them I okayed you seeing her. You might have to put up with a security guard shadowing you."

"Thanks, name dropping seems to work best with bureaucrats. I appreciate your help, since it'll probably go a long way toward building Sarah's and my work bond. I'm glad to get my name on any paper with her. She comes up with the damnedest insights, but she's terrible with the math."

"And you shine there, huh?"

"I do." Jack looked around, saw the barn that looked like something out of a Rockwell painting, the pasture with genetically grown grass, all the same height, lush and dense, whitewashed fences dividing the field into neat squares, some filled with grazing cattle but most empty, and the simple paved path that led back to the main building. It was quiet here. He had not realized how noisy it was around him all the time in New York, even in the middle of the night. Always sirens and traffic and the noises of people and airplanes and buildings settling. The quiet here was interrupted only by an occasional lowing from the cattle, and it pressed in on him like some medieval torture device.

"Too quiet, huh? It gets like that for city folks," Mary Ellen said. "Night would really drive you crazy. We can see the stars. They're itty-bitty points of light, and the sky's black, too."

"You're making fun of me," Jack said.

"She likes you," Mary Ellen said, pointing to her cow. "I can tell. She's making cow eyes at you."

Jack looked uncomfortably at the brown-eyed cow, worried she might charge him. The horns had been polled but could still inflict damage with a sudden toss of the head, powered by powerful neck muscles.

"Now, I *am* funning you," Mary Ellen said, reaching out and putting her strong hand on his arm. "I've got work to do, and maybe I can find where I left that damned PDA. Why don't you go back to the main building and get authorization to go check with Gary? He's director of research and sure to know where your coauthor is hiding."

"Thanks," Jack said. He gratefully started back down the path toward the building, though he had been shuffled from one secretary to another as if he had been a leper before he decided to strike out on his own and had found the barn.

Jack turned and looked over his shoulder at the woman leading the cow into the barn. For all her out-doorsiness, she was kind of cute. And she had a PhD from Stanford. He laughed ruefully. For someone in her field, that literally meant Piled Higher, Deeper. His own degree in genetic combinatorics from Princeton kept him tied to a computer, running elaborate simulations that too often had nothing to do with the real world. The one in a million successes, though, meant new crops and billions of dollars for AgriGen Corporation.

He entered the main lobby and once more tried to find his collaborator.

"I'm sorry, Dr. Langmuir," the receptionist said, his fingers at rest after a frantic pounding on the keyboard, "there's no one named Sarah Stahl working here."

"We've coauthored a half dozen papers. I work for AgriGen Corporation."

"I see that, sir," the receptionist said, looking past Jack, as if he might find a security guard to handle this personnel problem. "In our New York office."

"Dr. Benjamin suggested I talk with Dr. Gary Foreman. Contact him and tell him I'd like to see him." Jack stepped back a half pace at the expression on the receptionist's face.

"He works in a secured area, sir. You don't have clearance."

"I know. Dr. Benjamin said I'd need an escort." The repeated use of Mary Ellen's name was wearing down the receptionist. He pressed on. "I'm certain Dr. Foreman would see me. He's conducted several experiments to prove my theoretical DNA recomb—"

"Why don't you have a seat, sir? I'll see what I can do."

Jack considered leaving, but he was getting angry now. They lied to him about Sarah not working here. Every e-mail he received from her came through AgriGen Corp servers. He couldn't believe someone had hacked into the company computer network just to give him incredible ideas and insights. He sat heavily on an overly hard bench seat and glowered. The receptionist ignored him.

Jack fumbled in his pocket when his cell phone began playing the theme from the old cable rerun favorite "Green Acres." Jack had keyed his ring tones to different people, and Sarah had suggested this one for her messages.

The screen began showing her painfully slow texting.

"Come on, Sarah, talk to me realtime." He caught

his breath when he made out the message. For once he was glad Sarah had not called. Jack looked up and saw that the receptionist had left his station. The cell phone display brought him to his feet and sent him running out the door toward the barn. As he ran, he veered from the path according to Sarah's instructions.

Out of breath and not sure he could run another yard, Jack finally saw the security door mounted into a low concrete bunker.

"What's happened?" he texted back to Sarah.

"Trbl thngs," came the reply. "B crful uv Frmn."

Jack hesitated when he put his hand on the cold metal door handle. If Sarah was right, he needed to inform the authorities. Maybe the CDC or Homeland Security.

"Are you all right?" he texted. His thumbs ached from the way he jabbed down on the keys.

"Safe," came the slow reply.

"Are you in Foreman's lab?" Jack held his breath waiting for a reply. None came. This decided him. Something had happened in Foreman's lab that frightened Sarah. Why he hadn't been told about this immediately when he had identified himself at the lobby was beyond him, unless . . .

. . . .unless AgriGen Corporation wanted to keep a lid on a potentially dangerous situation. How this might have been the result of a plant experiment baffled Jack, but Foreman might be doing other work. It might have nothing to do with his and Sarah's theoretical work, but that didn't mean his coauthor wasn't in jeopardy if she was in a lab rife with some virulent strain of a virus or bacterium.

Jack yanked hard on the door handle, expecting it to be locked. He almost fell to the ground when it opened easily. A gust of fetid air blew from deep in the bowels of the earth. The lab complex had been buried for whatever reason. Jack thought of dozens of reasons, all valid from an experimenter's standpoint. Totally controlled environment, sunlight and moisture and air pressure and composition. He told himself that was the reason Foreman worked like a troglodyte beneath the green grassy fields where Mary Ellen Benjamin worked with her animals.

·   He took the metal steps down one at a time, moving cautiously into the darkness. The light from outside faded when he reached the foot of the stairs and had to make a sharp right turn that stopped in front of an airlock. A thick sheaf of instructions hung beside the door. Jack had seen similar locks before and knew how to operate them, but should he? On the far side of the negative pressure lock might be dangerous diseases running amok.

"Sarah," he said. She had texted him that there was trouble. He had to see to her since the company seemed in a state of denial—if they even knew anything was wrong.

He began cycling through the lock, feeling the higher pressure from outside against his back as he stepped into a dimly lit corridor. A quick turn soothed his growing paranoia. The lock was operable and had not mysteriously sealed. This was an emergency exit, nothing more. No one came this way because there was no reason to. He was letting his imagination run wild and had misinterpreted Sarah's text message. She was a terrible speller. The long reports he received from her were sometimes barely decipherable.

"That's it. I saw what I wanted to. I couldn't believe such a peaceful environment outdoors could be—"

He rounded a bend in the corridor and stared at the sight. He had seen newscasts of the devastation left in the path of a Midwestern tornado. The demolition stretching as far as he could see along the corridor and in the offices on either side was more deliberate. Someone—maybe an entire army—had gone through the desks and files with a thoroughness that belied any natural disaster. It must have taken hours to bring about such complete ruination. Papers looked as if they had been run through a shredder and then tossed onto the floor in piles. Any object on any desk larger than his fist had been crushed, in some cases driven with cruel force into the desktop.

Then he saw the first body. Jack was a scientist. He seldom saw anything bloodier than uncooked meat. He turned and vomited. The corpse had been mutilated as thoroughly as the paper had been shredded. The arms had been pulled off, the legs broken in so many places that stark white bone poked through skin like spaghetti extruded through a colander.

And the pool of blood seemed to stretch forever. He threw up again, but this time his stomach knotted and nothing came up. He had lost everything the first time. Clutching his nose against the stench of his own vomit mixing with the blood, Jack started to back away. Then he saw the footprint.

A foot twice the size of his own—and bare—had walked through the blood. He looked down the corridor turned surreal by the flickering overhead lights. If whoever belonged to this foot had still been in the corridor, Jack would have seen him. A man proportionate in size to that footprint had to be eight feet tall.

"What's gone on here?" Jack spoke in a cracked, barely audible voice, as much to reassure himself as to get his thoughts in order. He found it hard to be logical, to think like a scientist, when confronted with such stark brutality. Identifying the dead man on the floor was impossible because his face was gone, and his head had almost been ripped from his torso.

"Sarah, answer," he said weakly, thumbing his cell phone to life. "This is no time to ignore me. Please, Sarah. Are you here? Where are you?"

"Dngr," was the only response on the texting screen.

Jack tried again to get Sarah to respond directly, but even her abbreviated texting refused to appear on the screen.

He could retreat the way he had entered the underground complex, or he could hunt for Sarah. She had to still be alive because she had just sent him the message. If she was hiding, she might be found by whoever had committed this vile murder. The smart thing for Jack to do was to turn around and alert the company security men—or the feds. This might be an all-out terrorist attack. If Gary Foreman had developed some virulent disease by accident rather than an improved soy bean, then it could be turned into a weapon.

Jack ducked into another office that had been similarly trashed and tried to use the telephone. Dead. The computer on the desk refused to respond. He traced the power cord back and found that it had been systematically taken apart until only sharp, bright tiny wires protruded from the end. Splicing it back together wouldn't even get him access to the company intranet. If the suits in the main office building weren't aware of what had happened under their noses, he wasn't likely to convince them with a few quick IMs.

He sat in a broken desk chair and corralled his incoherent thoughts. Little by little, he put together a plausible scenario of what had happened. This had all occurred recently because the blood and footprints through it were still fresh. In spite of the death, no scent of decay rose to his nostrils, though thinking about the way the corpse in the corridor had been mutilated caused his stomach to knot and try to empty futilely.

Jack got out his cell phone and tried to call out. He didn't care if he reached the president of AgriGen Corporation or the janitor, the police or FBI or

CDC—he wanted *someone*. His phone would not connect.

A quick search through the desk failed to give him a directory of researchers in the complex. He had hoped to find a reference to Sarah or her office. This room, as with all the others, had been completely ransacked. He picked up a stapler and barely recognized its function because of the way it had been twisted apart.

He looked around for a weapon and saw nothing. Stealth would have to be his shield. Jack sneaked a quick look out into the corridor and then skirted the blood pool. It hit him for the first time that he couldn't even tell if the body on the floor was male or female. It had been too thoroughly crushed.

Moving as quickly and quietly as he could, Jack searched the underground complex. All the offices—and their occupants—were ripped apart. When he reached a T branch, he hesitated. To his right were the research labs. To the left lay storage. And immediately in front of him were the elevators leading to the surface. He reached out with a trembling hand, hating himself for pushing the call button while Sarah was still down here. His finger pressed the button. Nothing. The elevator was out of commission.

He realized then that the flickering lighting hinted at a massive electrical failure. The faint bulbs burning at infrequent intervals along the concrete corridors weren't emergency lights but the regular ones at reduced power.

Jack screamed when he heard something breaking in the direction of the laboratories. He pressed his back against the wall and wildly considered prying open the elevator doors. He could hide inside. Whoever was rampaging through the facility would never find him.

But he could not do that. He sucked in his breath,

let it out slowly, and then inched down the hallway. He cast quick looks into each lab he encountered. Millions of dollars of equipment had been trashed. He was not an experimentalist, but from the way the equipment had been broken, he guessed someone familiar with it had done the deed. The destruction was simply too methodical for any other explanation.

He had to close his eyes and hurry past one room where a dozen battered bodies had been stacked. Like the ones he had already discovered, they all appeared to have been crushed under a steam roller's immense bulk. Some legs were pressed to the thickness of a small book. The arms had been ripped off and battered against desks and walls until only bloody paste remained in the skin sheath.

Jack forced himself to keep from getting sick again. If he heaved, he worried he might lose part of his stomach since nothing but bile remained. He walked faster now, only stopping when a bass voice echoed down the corridor, "Fee, fie, Foreman smells the blood of an interloper!"

Jack screamed when a half-naked hulk swung into the hall not a dozen feet from him. The giant bent over to keep from banging his head against the normal height ceiling. Jack had guessed from the size of the bloody footprint that it had been made by somebody eight feet tall. The giant was closer to ten. Huge running ulcers covered his bare upper body, and the hair on the arms was matted with blood. Jack knew it was not the giant's.

The face glaring at him with pure hatred held only one eye. The left was swollen shut and the right eye looked like a bloodshot saucer as it fixed on him.

"Grind your bones to make meal," the giant grated out. It reached out for Jack, but the geneticist was already running as hard as he could for the branch in the corridor. He couldn't fight such a ferocious, misshapen creature. No matter that Sarah was some-where in this complex, he had to get help. That was the only way to save her. The only way.

He skidded around the corner and started back toward the distant emergency door he had first entered when he heard a plaintive cry for help. He took a few more steps when the begging tore at his conscience. If he kept running, he might lead the giant away from whoever was injured. Or the pleas for help might lead the gigantic killer to the victim. Coming to a decision, he headed toward the storage rooms. He found the guard in the first room, legs bent at impossible angles under him. The man reached out imploringly. Even if he had wanted to run, Jack couldn't now. He ducked into the room and slammed the door. He looked for a way to lock it but couldn't.

"Wouldn't matter," the guard gasped out. "It's too big. Knocks down doors."

Jack knelt beside the man. He was not a medical doctor, but he couldn't imagine how the guard had survived such horrendous injuries. From the waist down he was bloody pulp. Whether it was good or bad luck that he had not bled out wasn't something Jack dared consider.

"What is it? The giant?"

"Came from the lab, far end of c-corridor. Dr. Foreman's lab. Haven't seen Foreman in days. Musta killed him, then c-come for ever'one else." The guard weakened in his arms after the effort of speaking.

"Lie back. I'll do what I can. Is there a First Aid kit handy?" The guard struggled to point to a white box with a large red cross on it fastened too high on the wall for him to reach. Jack yanked it free and fumbled through the contents until he found an ampule of morphine. He tried to figure the best place to inject it, and then rammed it into the guard's arm. The guard relaxed almost immediately.

"How long has it been killing?"

"Hours. Right after I came on duty. After eight."

Jack looked at his cell phone and saw it was only a little before noon. The giant had rampaged throughout the facility and killed everyone in only four hours.

"Sarah Stahl," Jack asked. "Where's her office? Dr. Stahl. Where?" Only great restraint kept him from shaking the information out of the guard. The morphine had driven the man into merciful unconsciousness. Jack did what he could to make him comfortable, and then sat with his back against the door to think. Vibration increased and decreased as the giant ran up and down the corridor, searching for him. The monster wasn't too bright if it couldn't figure out where he had hidden, but Jack deserved a break after all he had been through.

He glanced at the guard, his mangled legs and fitful breathing. The man wasn't likely to survive much longer. Like the others he had found, he had paid a price Jack could hardly imagine.

"Green Acres" played on his cell phone.

"Sarah, talk to me. Sarah!" The slow crawl of a text message worked its way across the screen. Tears came to his eyes as he deciphered the abbreviated words.

"Foreman, you stupid son of a bitch," Jack moaned, half in anger and half in disbelief. "You created the soy beans Sarah and I designed theoretically, and then you ate them. You *ate* them."

The giant's ear-shattering roar caused Jack to jump. His heart almost skipped a beat, then it did when he realized the giant—Dr. Foreman—would rip it from his chest if he found him. Jack edged up the wall and looked around the storage room for a weapon. The security guard wore a thick leather belt festooned with all manner of defensive implements. Jack grabbed the pepper spray and a Taser. How either would stop a raging ten-foot-tall, powerfully muscled monster was beyond him, but they were better than nothing.

They might not have done the guard much good, but lacking an RPG they would have to do. Jack fingered the spray bottle and the cold plastic button on the Taser. Even if he had a rocket-propelled grenade launcher, he wouldn't know how to use it. These were better. He told himself over and over these were better.

Then the storeroom door exploded inward. Foreman saw him immediately and groped for him, a meaty hand barely missing him.

"Grind your bones. I smell you! Fee, fie, Foreman smells you!"

The giant dropped one shoulder and forced itself through the door. For a brief instant, one arm was turned from Jack. He moved forward and used the Taser on the arm. The giant recoiled. He brought up the pepper spray and released a blast into the giant's good eye. The small cylinder emptied too quickly, but Jack dropped it and tried the Taser again. Its charge had dwindled, but still gave a potent enough jolt to force the giant away.

Foreman sat in the corridor, caterwauling in an inhuman voice and clawing at his blinded eye. Jack gasped for breath and knew he could never get past the giant blocking his way. He backed down the hallway toward a dead end.

"Come on, come and get me, you son of a bitch. Why'd you eat the soy beans? You don't experiment on yourself. You run tests! You're stupid, Foreman, an idiot not fit to be a scientist. Come on, come and get me!"

The giant screeched high and shrill, causing Jack to clap his hands to his ears. It felt as if an ice pick had been jammed into his brain. He kept backing up and reached behind, fumbling to open the door at the end of the hallway. For an instant his fingers felt bigger than sausages, numb, unbending. The door wouldn't open. He stared at the advancing giant. Foreman rubbed at his good eye and flailed about with his other hand. A blow would fell Jack in an instant.

As the giant lurched forward, Jack opened the door and tumbled backward. Foreman grabbed for him and missed. Scrambling hard to keep Foreman from crashing down on him, he kicked out and tangled his legs with the giant's. Foreman fell heavily. The air gusted from his lungs, and the Taser and pepper spray had also taken its toll.

Jack wasted no time getting to his feet. He grabbed for a spool of nylon fishing line on the floor. He had no idea what it had been used for, but some experimenter had needed lots of it. Like a rodeo rider hogtying a calf, Jack spun the strong nylon string around and around, fastening the giant's legs. Foreman fought so hard the line cut into his flesh and caused him even more pain. This mindless fighting gave Jack the chance to take a few turns around heaving shoulders—and bulging neck. As he tightened, he cut off Foreman's air. The giant tried to pull it free, but the nylon cut deeper into his flesh. Jack refused to stop pulling until Gary Foreman passed out. It took great fortitude on Jack's part not to keep the pressure on and kill the hideous creature.

Instead, he did what he could to tie up Foreman, and then closed the storeroom door behind him. His head came up and his eyes went wide when he heard distant thudding.

"No, no, not more of them."

When he saw the half dozen guards, he leaned against the door, slid to the floor and pulled up his knees. He fought to keep from crying. He was saved. The guards approached warily, and he managed to tell them about the giant Dr. Gary Foreman had become and where to find the scientist. Jack sent two other guards to help their mutilated comrade in the other storage room.

They pushed past him and left him on his own to recover. On shaky legs, he retraced his steps to the emergency exit where he had entered, worked up the metal steps, and finally stumbled out into the bright sunlight. Warmth on his face, fragrant grass odor revitalizing him, Jack made his way toward the barn.

"My God, what happened to you?" Mary Ellen Benjamin ran over to him. "I saw the guards and heard an alarm. Something go wrong down below?"

Jack nodded numbly.

"Come on into the barn and sit down. I'll get you some water."

Jack gratefully sat on a milking stool and regained his strength and composure. He was on his way to recovering when Mary Ellen returned with the water.

"Here," she said, thrusting at him but keeping her distance as if he were a leper. He looked down and saw he was drenched in blood and filth.

"I need a new suit," he said stupidly. He held the glass in shaking hands and gulped the water.

"You need something."

"The company's got a security team down there now. They'll take care of the . . . trouble."

"What happened?" Mary Ellen came closer, then turned and grabbed the rope that dangled from around her heifer's neck so it wouldn't wander off.

Jack explained the best he could. "The soy beans. Foreman ate them himself."

"He's been supplying beans for fodder for quite a while. I never saw a problem. Maybe he thought what was safe for grazing animals was safe for humans."

"Might be a specific human response to the genetically altered beans," Jack said. "I need to get in touch with my coauthor. Dr. Stahl!" He had forgotten about her. "She's still down there. I have to—"

"Dr. Langmuir? We were afraid we'd lost you." Two uniformed security guards and an EMT entered the barn. "You need to be checked out. Then the director wants a report."

"I need to contact Dr. Stahl," he said, taking out his cell phone. The EMT took him by the arm and led him away.

"You'll be just fine." The EMT glanced back at Mary Ellen and then guided Jack away, still muttering to himself.

"Well," Mary Ellen said, slapping one end of the rope against her palm. "It's been some kind of day, hasn't it, Sarah? Come on. Let me get you into your stall. It's feeding time. It'll take me a few minutes to get it all mixed up."

Sarah watched her human leave, then nuzzled straw in her stall and found the stick she had hidden. Mobile lips moved it around until she got it between her teeth, then she pushed more straw away with her nose to reveal a PDA. Sarah began pressing the keys. She had to let Jack know she was fine, was glad that he had survived and taken care of the problems in the lab she had worried about so and that she had an incredible new idea for haplotype and single-nucleotide polymorphism analysis by resequencing all 9459 polymerase chain reaction primer sets in each of six diverse soybean genotypes.

The ideas flowed like a waterfall. If only she could text message faster.

WHAT'S IN A NAME?

Kathleen Watness

Kathleen Watness was born in New York City. After getting a master's degree, she spent most of a ten-year stint in the Navy stationed at government research labs in sunny California. Naturally, since her degree was in marine biology, she ended up settling up in the Midwest after her discharge. She lives there to this day and shares a house built about 1920 with a husband, three kids, and a small white ball of fluff that during the winter is known as Polar Kitty.

There is power in names. Sound the syllables properly and you gain, for a time at least, dominion over the name's owner.

Or does the name own the person? I can't remember, trapped in stone as I now am. There is much I have forgotten. But not how I came to be in this dank cell deep in the lost places of the earth. Or who betrayed me.

My brother. I would spit on his name if I had lips. Perhaps his betrayal was inevitable. I am a fae of earth and water, antagonist to his air and fire. Perhaps that was all the reason he needed, to betray me. Whatever the reason, fraternal treachery has locked my essence into these moss-streaked granite walls.

I need no light, either, but a torch flickers just outside my doorway, a feeble reminder of the bright sun I once enjoyed.

The air shimmered, and my brother, handsome in the way of mortals, slender and supple as a birch, stepped out. He was elegant in a red silk tunic and black leather pants. His polished black boots bore silver buckles.

"It is midsummer festival above," he said, and then took a sip from the bright green mug in his left hand. "The beer is particularly good this year."

I said nothing. He cocked his head and studied the spiral patterns of the moss on the stone that held me. "I see you've been busy."

I shrugged, and the earth grumbled. He laughed and took a longer pull on his beer.

"Hmm, not in the mood for talking, dear brother?"

What is there to say that hasn't already been said?

He sighed and drained his mug. I felt the flicker of his magic, and the mug disappeared. I imagined my hands around his throat, choking the life from the flesh he currently wore. He glided closer to the wall. His face was smug with triumph.

"Perhaps I'll send a mouse or two to keep you company," he said softly. "Yes, a pair of mice, I think. And straw for their bedding." He laughed and faded back to the world above.

Straw. It was straw that had landed me here. Straw and a mortal's greed. Turning such a common substance into gold is one of the simplest of earth magics, a trifle compared to that which keeps the sun in its course or shapes the fabric of the earth into mountains. Mortals can be so shortsighted. But, then, so was I. Intent on the long-term goal, I failed to see the trap my own need led me into.

At the time, it had seemed a simple, straightforward bargain. For the right to stand beside the king and rule a land of several million souls, all I had asked for was one child. Was that so great a price? It seemed it was, since she schemed to cheat me of it, aided by my brother. I would curse his name if I could remember it. Though knowing it won't free me, there is a name that will. It lies tumbled among the forgotten things I knew when I walked in flesh beneath the warm sun.

I sank deeper into the stone, until the torchlight disappeared. Inward I ventured, roaming through memory, searching for a name.

We lounged under an apple tree, sharing a jug of good beer, a loaf of dark bread, and a salty summer sausage. While my brother watched a pretty peasant woman bringing a small basket of food to her husband, who was inspecting the trees, I watched him. At the moment, he was light and easy, and I savored that. His moods could shift like flame and wind. He glanced at me and smiled, then snagged the jug and took a long pull. It was good beer, cool and slightly bitter with a rich, yeasty smell. The breeze whispered above us, and apple blossoms, fragrant and soft as a lover's first kiss, drifted down.

"The king is looking for a wife," he said as he set the jug between us.

I cut off a thin slice of sausage. "Doesn't he already have one?"

"This one is for his son."

I shrugged and popped the sausage into my mouth. My brother has always been more interested in the affairs of nobles than I. I preferred the peasants and the artisans whose hands turned earth and stone and clay into useful beauty.

"You should take more interest in these things," he chided me.

I leaned back against the apple trunk, closed my eyes, and interlaced my fingers across my belly.

"Why?"

My brother sighed theatrically. "Because this king is different."

It was my turn to sigh. With a belly full of bread and good beer, all I wanted was to doze in the cool shade. But my brother would tease and jape until I finally relented and let him have his game. I kept my eyes closed.

"How is he different?"

"He doesn't seem to care much about her breeding." I thought I heard disdain in his voice. "As long as she's slender and beautiful, skilled at household tasks and has a good set of hips, he'll settle for a peasant."

I cracked an eye. "Not typical, I'll grant you. But he's not the first or only king to do that."

"There's no moving you, is there?"

I chuckled at his irritation. He bounded to his feet and paced, muttering in fae. The air in front of his lips sparked and shimmered. Sighing, I rose and put my hand on his shoulder.

"Peace, brother. Now tell me what has so caught your interest in this matter?"

He smiled. A pity I didn't notice at the time how much it resembled a serpent's grin.

"I thought we might help him find this wife."

I cocked my head. "Indeed? It's always risky meddling in mortal affairs."

He shrugged. "How else will you find a vessel?"

I turned from him and searched out the silver hairs in my beard. "Plenty of time yet for that, a century at least," I muttered and crossed my arms.

"Perhaps, but you know how difficult it is to find a suitable candidate." He moved closer. His hand was warm on my shoulder, and his voice was sweet in my ear. "Why not secure it now? The younger they are, the easier it is to turn them."

I shivered as I remembered the last time I had renewed my flesh. I had waited almost too long, putting off what I needed to do.

"Brother?"

My hands tightened on my arms. Then I unclenched my hands and turned to face him.

"I assume you have a mortal in mind?"

He smiled and shifted form to the sparkle of sunlight on water. *Follow me.*

I sank into the earth like a drop of rain and slipped between the tangled roots of trees and ferns and sprouting wheat and followed close behind him. He skimmed over the surface of the trees, flashed in a ploughman's eyes, and then danced down to a long, winding river. I merged with the water and, laughing, raced him down the curving length of it until I tumbled down the paddles of a waterwheel and ended up on the soft mossy bank next to a grain mill. He stepped out of a swirl of dandelion fluff while I slipped out of a granite boulder embedded in the roots of an ancient oak. A brief incantation spilled from his lips, and we faded from mortal sight. Creatures of air are very adept at deception magics.

Thirty paces from the mill stood a small stone house with sturdy, dark green shutters. I drifted to the large garden that stretched out from the left side of the house. Young cabbages and lettuce flourished in the soft, rich soil. While I admired the peas and the radishes and beans, my brother flitted to the back. He returned a heartbeat later and tugged at my shoulder.

"Come, she's in the back garden, doing laundry."

The laundry was fine woven linen set out to bleach

in the sun. Ah, she was a pretty thing, all gold ringlets and rosy cheeks and eyes the dark blue of a midsummer evening. She was strong and graceful, and if I was not there for other reasons, I would have courted her myself.

"Well, brother?"

"She's pretty enough for a king," I admitted and admired the curve of her hips and the way her hair shimmered as she spread the wet linen on the soft, spring grass.

He laughed. "Look deeper, dear brother."

I did. And my breath caught in my teeth. She was too old to turn, but within her she carried the certainty of my physical renewal, not just for a few centuries but for millennia.

We fae walk the earth in borrowed flesh. It is the only way we can exist in the world of men and enjoy its pleasures. Their souls, subsumed within our own when we turn them, will never know death. Their bodies, because they contain our essence, last far longer than a mortal's life. But, after a few centuries, like a well-worn suit of clothes, they begin to break down, and we must discard them and find others. Not an easy thing. For like a set of fine garments, what wears well on one is totally unsuited for another. Rarely, we find flesh so finely tuned to our needs, it will wear almost forever. That was the potential she carried in her womb, though only for me.

Despite that gift, I wavered. Unlike most fae, I have always regretted the necessity of what we must do. Yet, what choice was there? None, if I wanted to escape a prison where no sun or moon shone, where only the endless dark stretched all around me, forever and ever.

The riches she offered carried a price. There is always a price. It would do mortals well to remember that. For us, while we wear flesh, we are subject to mortal magic. And since men named the world and everything in it, including us, we are particularly vulnerable to their power over names. It is the only magic we lack.

My brother lounged back on a cushion of air, chewing on a blade of straw as he watched the woman wringing out the linen she had just washed. He sighed and waved his hand at her.

"She has everything the king is seeking, including a fine wit. Though he left *that* off the list of qualities he sent round with his messengers." He spat out the straw and it drifted to the ground, just in front of my feet. "Mortals can be such fools," he muttered.

I nodded in agreement.

"Has a messenger been here, yet?" I asked. My brother shook his head, then grinned like a fox.

I laughed. "You diverted them."

"Of course. She's not the only maiden who fits the king's list. There are at least twenty others the messengers have found. And they've only been through half the kingdom." His voice went soft. "She's the only one who fits your needs, dear brother."

I grimaced. The wind shifted, and the blade of straw twisted in the grass. I plucked it up. Like me, it came from the earth. I started to release it, then stopped, a glimmer of a plan forming. I have mentioned before that my brother was far more interested in court life than I. That doesn't mean I am ignorant of royal affairs or royal desires. I looked at my brother and smiled.

"She is also the only one who fits the king's needs as well."

He threw me a puzzled, slightly annoyed look. It wasn't often that I chose to best him in wit.

"Consider this," I said and held the straw between my thumb and forefinger then drew it slowly between them. "What else does a king need or desire besides

power and loyalty?" As I've said, turning straw into
gold is a simple magic. The strand stretched between
my fingers, glittering, pure as sunlight, and as thin as
the smile in my brother's eyes.

I shook myself and rose to the surface of the stone.
The torch guttered and threatened to go out. It never
did. After a moment it flared, then burned bright and
steady.

My brother had embraced my plan with glee. He
loved to pretend to be something he wasn't. He'd even
joined a traveling troupe of actors for a time.

When my brother, dressed in the gold-trimmed wine
dark uniform of a king's messenger, had first ridden
up on a fine gray mare, the future queen had dropped,
trembling, in a deep curtsey. At the time I'd thought
she was afraid. Now, I could see that the trembling
had been anticipation.

My brother read the king's proclamation loud
enough to be heard in the next town. Her parents
rushed out, smiling and bobbing like apples in a festival barrel. In less then an hour, she and her mother
were on their way to the capitol.

I wasn't there when they were presented by my
brother to the king, and the mother—prompted by
my brother's spell—boasted of her daughter's skills at
spinning. Had the lass been horrified at the claim she
could turn straw into gold? Had she tried to flee when
the king demanded proof? My brother never mentioned her reactions when later he described the scene
to me. And I, too pleased that the first part of my
plan had succeeded, had never thought to ask.

Now, in retrospect, I wondered why the king had
never asked why, if a daughter could spin straw into
gold, she and her family lived in a peasant's house
with pigs in the back rather than in a fine mansion
with servants.

A scratching noise roused me from memory, and a pair of gray mice scurried through the door. A pile of straw blossomed in the far corner. My brother's mocking laughter echoed then faded.

The mice huddled against the far wall. Water trickled down to form a tiny pool beside them before draining through a narrow crack in the floor. The poor things wouldn't die of thirst, but unless mice had developed a taste for stone, they would starve. That is a hard death for any creature.

I sank back into the stone. There was nothing I could do for them, and I still had a name to discover.

She sat huddled on a stool in front of a fine spinning wheel, her face buried in her hands. She wept silently. My brother had already informed me of where the king's guards had taken her. Disguised as an officer, he had led the way. He'd also told me of the consequences of failure. I hadn't expected that.

As I emerged from the stone, I scuffed my boot across the floor. She bolted up then hugged the wall behind her, one hand clutching her gold necklace. Fear warred with curiosity in her reddened eyes. I spread my hands and smiled.

"Are . . . are you the angel the captain told me would come?" she asked.

"No, but no devil, either," I said, hiding my irritation at my brother's theatrics.

She glanced at the pile of straw that filled half the tiny room and sobbed.

"What troubles you, mistress?" I asked, though I already knew.

"I must spin this straw into gold or I will die at sunrise."

I stepped up and set the wheel gently turning. "What will you give me if I spin the straw?"

Her dark blue eyes widened then she pulled off her

necklace and offered it to me. I held it close to a
lantern and admired the fine workmanship. I decided
to spin the straw the same pale gold as her necklace.

Her eyes darted to the wheel and the large baskets
of empty spindles. She twisted the ring on her finger
and looked back at me. I slipped the necklace into my
pocket and sat on the stool. Without a word, she
handed me an empty spindle and a handful of straw,
hope and doubt mingled in her eyes.

She gasped as the straw shifted to fine gold thread.
Softly, I sang words of magic as I spun, to bind this
first pledge between us into an anchor thread rooted
in the earth so no other earth fae could steal what
I would claim. Every filled spindle strengthened that
thread, so that by sunrise it was as deep and firm as
the roots of the mountains that bordered the king's
lands.

She sat close beside me all night while I worked,
handing me straw then piling the filled spindles into
the baskets. Just before sunrise, the last fragment was
pulled into thread. While the woman studied the spindles, I faded back into the stone. Curious as to the
king's reaction, I lingered until the old man limped
into the room, leaning on his cane. Still posing as a
guard, my brother was close behind him.

The woman was pale, but composed, and she bowed
deeply as the king studied the filled spindles gleaming
in the baskets. Greed shadowed his smile as he turned
to her.

"Spin again this night or lose your head," he said.

Her face went white as moonlight, but she only
bowed, her hands pressed to her fine throat. Unseen
by the trembling woman or the greedy king, my brother
winked at me before he left.

She was taken to a larger room that night. The pile
of straw that waited for her was twice the size of the
first. When I appeared and repeated my offer, she

gave me her ring, carved like a fox biting its tail. I spun the straw the deep yellow of her ring. Again, I sang, spinning the second strand of magic that would bind her first-born child to me.

The next morning, I thought she would melt into the stone when the king demanded a third night of spinning, despite his promise that she would marry his son if she succeeded. After he left, she sank down against the wall, anger and fear exchanging places in her eyes. I lingered a moment, then flowed up the limestone walls to the topmost turret on the eastern side of the palace. In raven form, my brother joined me a few moments later and perched beside me.

He sighed. "The old king is so easy to charm. Hardly worth the sport."

My eyes slid toward him, then to the hills gilded by the rising sun.

"Don't worry, dear brother. One more night and her first-born is yours."

I shifted on my seat. "What if she decides not to marry his son?"

My brother cocked his head, his eyes dark and unreadable. "She wants to be queen."

"The king has threatened to kill her. Three times," I reminded him.

My brother lifted a wing and began preening his feathers. "She's going to marry his son, not him. Besides, he'll be dead soon."

"Hmph, are you a fortune-teller, now?"

He laughed a harsh raven's cry. "Hardly. I overheard his physicians."

I sighed and settled back against the warm stone, then closed my eyes and dozed there until evening.

Before I entered the chamber, I studied the final pile of straw. It was twice the size of the second. Greedy mortal. After this night's spinning he would have enough gold for several kings.

The woman paced in front of the wheel, her hands clutching her arms.

"Good evening, mistress." She stopped and turned to me. Her voice was barely more than a whisper.

"I have nothing to pay you."

"Not yet." Her eyes widened. "Pay me when you are queen."

She clapped her hands. "Yes! I will have gold in plenty."

"I haven't named my price yet."

She clasped her hands. "What do you want? I'll give you anything you want."

"Anything?"

"Yes, yes . . . only . . . please . . ." Her eyes darted to the straw piled to the ceiling and she swallowed.

"I want your first-born child," I said softly. Her eyes snapped back to me. She stepped back, and her hands covered her mouth.

"My child? But . . . I can't."

"That is my price, mistress."

She shook her head, moaning. I started fading back into the stone wall.

"Wait!"

I stepped out of the wall and waited while she stood there, trembling, her hands clenched by her sides.

"All right," she finally said. "I agree."

I nodded and set to work. Oh, how the magic flowed from my fingers and throat that night! The wheel hummed, pulling straw into gold the color of her hair. I sang the words, and in this final binding I saw her first-born, a fine manchild. Strong and sleek and fair. I would walk the earth ten thousand years in that flesh.

That night's spinning drained almost all my strength and stretched my magic to its limits. I slipped off the stool and sank into the floor. The future queen stood in the midst of the glittering baskets, smiling. I stayed

long enough to witness her triumph, and then I retreated down the granite bones of the world to rest.

I surged up, seething. The rocks rumbled and shook.
All that searching, and I still didn't have a name! I
was close, though. I felt it hovering at the tip of memory. To be so close! I raged and shook the walls
harder. Dust and bits of rock pelted down from the
ceiling. The mice squealed and skittered in fright. I
took hold of my temper.

The mice huddled in a corner. I sighed and settled
into the cracks in the rock my temper had opened.
Poor things, cut off from the sweet air and the warm
sun.

Out of flesh, it's hard for a fae to measure time.
But since the female mouse was plump with pups,
several weeks must have passed. I started. They
should be dead. It was then I noticed a small pile of
grain a few feet from their nest. A tiny slit in the air
opened above the grain, leaking sunlight and apple
slices. It seemed my brother had provided for them.
And if—no, when—I freed myself, it would give me
a far faster route than traveling through stone back to
my queen's kingdom. The slit closed, but it left behind
the brisk scent of autumn winds.

I burrowed deeper into the dark granite, but I
stayed close enough to the surface that I could see the
torch. Once again, I ventured inward, hopefully for
the last time.

I was lounging beneath an oak atop a hill just outside the main gates of the capitol, enjoying the warm
spring breezes, when my brother came to tell me of
the birth. He'd stayed at the castle, posing as one of
the queen's servants, to keep on eye on things. He
dropped out of a sparkle of sunlight, a jug of beer

in one hand and a small round of creamy cheese in the other.

"A strong and healthy son," he said, handing me the jug. "The king is pleased."

"The old one or the new one?" I asked, accepting it.

He laughed and sat down on my left. "The new one, of course. The old one died four months ago." He gestured, and a slender, sharp knife appeared in his hand. "I told you, remember?"

I shrugged.

"It was a fine funeral," he continued. "If he'd been alive, he would have enjoyed it."

I laughed at that, and my brother sliced off a thin wedge of cheese and handed it to me.

"She hasn't forgotten," he said softly. Tiny flames flickered in his dark eyes.

"I didn't expect she would," I said, and then took a bit of cheese. It had a sharp tangy bite, perfect with the beer.

"When are you going to take him?" The wind shifted and carried the sound of bells from the city. "They'll be celebrating for weeks," my brother murmured, smiling.

I sighed. The palace would be overflowing with visitors and well-wishers.

"Let me know when affairs settle down," I told him. "I'll collect him then."

My brother grinned then glided into a spear of sunlight aimed for the main hall of the palace. I chuckled as I raised the jug to my lips. He did enjoy a party.

It took almost a month for life to settle back to whatever was normal for a royal court. The apple blossoms were long gone by then. The scent of roses that replaced them drifted through sheer curtains as I stepped into the nursery. Bent over the cradle, singing softly to her child, she didn't notice me at first. She wore silk and lace now. The russet and cream colors suited her. Deep yellow gold glittered around her throat, dangled from her ears and encircled every finger. What a vision she was. She looked up, more composed than I expected. A shiver, no more than a pebble falling to the ground, went down my spine. I had been prepared for tears and pleading, not this cool and measuring look.

My brother, still posing as her servant, hovered in the shadows behind her. He glanced at her and smiled as she gently lifted her son and held him close. My brother glided up to her left side, a short length of peeled willow branch in his hand. He held it close to his side, out of her sight, but not mine. His smile deepened and his eyes took on a hungry, feral shine.

"You thought I wouldn't find out," she said. Her words distracted me from my brother.

Find out what? I stepped back, wary, and reached for the stone. Earth magic, unlike fire, is slow to cast. Better to flee, if I needed to.

"I know your name," she said softly.

My brother lifted his wand. I cursed and flowed down into the stone, or tried to. Just as I started sinking, she stepped forward and shouted my name, then two words of mortal magic. With the wand, my brother swiftly traced binding wards that wrapped around my soul like an ivy vine around an oak. He flicked the wand out of sight as she turned to him, triumphant and anxious.

"Did I say them correctly?" she asked.

My brother bowed deeply. "Perfectly, your highness."

Pain, sharp as a hunter's arrow, shot through my limbs. Half sunk and trapped in the stone by my brother's wards, I screamed as the spell she had spoken dissolved my flesh into dust and shards. The baby stirred and cried, frightened. The last thing I saw was her, silhouetted in the window, comforting her child.

"Shh, my sweetling. You're safe. No harm will come to you now, my sweet Tristin."

I surged up to the limit of my stone tether. At last! I had the name I needed! I remembered! Over and over, I said it, my soul humming with the sound of it. Even unspoken, I felt it beginning to weaken the bonds my brother had set on me. As the child had been mine before he was even conceived, so was his name. But before I could free myself, I needed to speak it in the mortal world.

In the far corner, near where the water trickled down, I had let the moss grow in random patches. I focused my will and felt the growth patterns shift. Three times, the walls would be my voice. Three times and I would be free. When I claimed my payment, my power would return in full. Then, hidden in that flesh, I would let it grow at a mortal's pace before I claimed retribution.

I settled back and watched the mother mouse nurse her newborn pups. I must remember to leave a way out for them.

With the return of the name, I remembered everything. I remembered how my brother had told me of how he had deceived the queen by pretending to be me. Pretending to be moved by tears and pleading to offer her a way out of a fair bargain. How he had strutted and preened when he had told me of how the "faithful queen's servant" had stumbled across the little man prancing around a fire, drunk, and singing his name. As if any fae would be so foolish as to shout his name where a mortal might hear it.

And I remembered why he had betrayed me. His face loomed in my mind, dark and full of hate.

"You cost me flesh, dear brother. Flesh to walk the world a hundred centuries. Lost! Because of your dithering the last time you renewed.

"Her death was not my fault."

"Liar!" Fire and lightning had flashed from his fingers to scorch the wall I was trapped in before he'd streaked back to the surface world.

I roused from the memory and sighed. After I had claimed the child that time, she shouldn't have run after me in the darkening wood when shadows trick the eye. She'd stumbled on a gnarled root and struck her head on a rock. I'd doubled back when I'd heard her cry out as she fell. But by the time I reached her, she and the child she carried within her were already dead. The child who would have been my brother's renewal. I understood his anger, even his hatred. But he had betrayed me when I could have helped him find another. That demanded justice.

I smiled then as I remembered his name, Tristin. A short name. An easy name to speak. There is power in names.

NO GOOD DEED

Jody Lynn Nye

Jody Lynn Nye lists her main career activity as "spoiling cats." She lives northwest of Chicago with two of the above and her husband, author and packager Bill Fawcett. She has published more than thirty-five books, including six contemporary fantasies, four SF novels, four novels in collaboration with Anne McCaffrey, including *The Ship Who Won*; edited a humorous anthology about mothers, *Don't Forget Your Spacesuit, Dear!*; and has written more than a hundred short stories. Her latest books are *An Unexpected Apprentice*, and *Myth-Chief*, co-written with Robert Asprin.

A thickset man in a jumpsuit with a hand control box guided a train of loaded antigrav skids marked for transit off-planet and let them drift a little too close to the bench where Androye Clesborn sat huddled. Androye looked up, wary eyed, and braced himself. An opportunity like this was not going to come again, not in time. The other prisoners sent the skinny healer rueful glances that offered fearful wishes of good luck. He would need it.

He edged closer and closer to the side of the bench, away from his guard's line of sight. If the blue-uniformed woman would just look away for one second . . . there! The fat man ran one of his skids into the legs of a well-dressed man looking the other way. The ensuing altercation attracted the attention of spaceport security, several onlookers, and the uniformed guard. Androye sprang from the bench and dashed away into the gathering crowd.

The alarm didn't go off when he slipped through the portal and out onto the concrete apron where atmosphere transports let off their passengers who arrived to travel off-world from Danton. The temporary RFID tattoo on his arm permitting him to pass through the doors had not yet been purged from the spaceport security system. It was his second piece of luck. Perhaps Fate meant to let him get away this time. He took a deep breath of the surrounding damp, hot air before he remembered not to.

How horrible this planet smelled! Androye choked on the stink of chemicals and decay held close to the surface by the heavy, damp inversion layer of the geosphere. He just managed to suppress the wrench of his internal organs trying to force their way upwards. He couldn't afford to draw attention by vomiting up his meager breakfast on the edge of the pavement. His worn, beige shipsuit was nothing out of the ordinary among the travelers. No one dressed up to go anywhere since the Dominion had conquered half of known space. If one wore ostentatious clothes or jewelry, one was apt to find oneself being stripped of it publicly. The same went for knowledge or talent. The individual character of every planet was being compressed into a characterless, bland average.

If that were true, every planet would smell alike, too, and his allergies wouldn't be bothered by every single change in atmosphere he had undergone. If only he had had three more minutes at the end of the battle of Triusk. He would be home on sweet-scented Orskia, back in his little flat, back in his inoffensive medical practice. Back with his wife.

He could hardly picture Meriglen's face as a face. He thought of individual features, each precious and beautiful, but should anyone have asked him to put them together, he would have been embarrassed at his lack of observation. With every breath in his body, with every bone, with every blood cell, he wanted to get back to her. They had been separated for three months, the longest they had been apart in their eight years of marriage.

Making his saunter look as casual as he could, Androye strolled toward the edge of the apron, past an airbus dropping off a gaggle of giggling girls in white jumpsuits—cleaning staff, all under twenty standard years of age—and surveyed the burgeoning, green and purple plant life as though he were thinking of buying it. As soon as the last girl hefted her carryall to her back and turned away, he plunged into the undergrowth. Thorns whipped at him, tearing his face and hands, the only parts of his skin showing out of his shipsuit. Underfoot, roots and creepers grabbed for his booted feet. He thought of running barefoot and immediately dismissed it. Danton was useful as spaceport only because large portions of its terrain were flat, once the jungle full of poisonous lizards, snakes and plants was cleared away. Androye didn't dare expose himself to the local biology any more than he could help.

Within two meters the spaceport was invisible over his shoulder. He leaped over roots and tripped on creepers. He had to find a place to conceal himself long enough for the transport to take off without him. He wasn't the most valuable of the prisoners of war from Orskia, and they had other doctors. They would do without him.

In the back of his mind, he knew that wasn't true. He was the most experienced healer they had captured, and the Dominion never let a living prisoner escape. But the guards had been in a hurry to lift ship. Perhaps he would be lucky. Plenty of independent traders, too slippery a commodity to be subsumed by the Dominion's rules, landed here. He would wait until he saw one land, then thresh his way to the landing strip under cover of night and beg to be taken on board. His profession, coupled with the obligatory mental block that prevented him doing harm to others, was a passport anywhere. Maybe even back to Orskia.

The irony was he had been due to be demobilized after this battle. Free at last of travel in military transports, of sleeping eighty to a room with other people, all of them restless and unhappy, away at last from the war which he hated but understood needed to be fought to maintain the independent worlds' freedom against the Dominion. He had been pinned down in a field with a host of wounded waiting for evacuation. An unlucky movement of the flanking forces left him and his patients exposed. The evil empire's monotanks moved in, surrounding them. The small, nearly indestructible vehicles held two men—or, rather, beings. The Dominion soldiers shot all the wounded, but seeing the medical insignia on his uniform and the plaswraps in his hands, figured out that he was worth something to them. They hauled up his sleeve to find the tattoo with the implanted capsule that guaranteed he was a certified healer, a permanent noncombatant. At gunpoint he was bundled into the rear seat of a monotank and taken away.

Ever since, he had been shuttled around the Dominion

and its newly captured systems, treating illness and injury in species they didn't understand. He had learned to treat many new species. He was a good doctor, and the long-forgotten Earth had given him the Hippocratic Oath that he had sworn to upheld, no matter what the circumstances. All the time he kept asking when he could go home. The Dominion guards ignored his questions, which meant that he had to take matters into his own hands. This was his fifth attempt at escape. Maybe this time he would get away unnoticed.

Too late! Angry voices in the distance meant that the guard had discovered his absence and was raising the alarm. Androye put his arms up to protect his eyes, and hurtled blindly into the undergrowth.

It would take them time to work out where he had gone. He had followed no path, squeezing past prickly tree trunks and slimy lianas, wherever he could fit. He shied away from the slightest movement, fearing attack wasps and snakes. Thorns ripped his jumpsuit and left long, aching scratches in his scalp. He dared not look at his beautiful, long surgeon's hands. They twitched and quivered with sharp agony, as if they had been dipped in acid.

The hot sunlight was cut by more than half. He squinted through the shadows, trying to make sense of what he could see. He heard a warning beep pulsing ahead of him. That was probably the automated air traffic control tower. Maybe he could hide there. Those towers were usually surrounded by a repulser field plus several fences and other protective measures to keep out intruders and local wildlife. From experience, Androye knew the fields weren't as impenetrable as the designers wished. He had overseen the removal of the sad remains of small children in his neighborhood who found the meshwork tower irresistible and perished in their attempts to climb it. Ani-

mals, too, would find their way into the dog-proof
sanctuary and often died there. He'd saved some.
They stiffened when he picked them up, afraid to accept help, but they couldn't help whimpering with
the pain.

He thought he heard whimpering then, in the stifling
wilderness. Androye cudgeled his imagination for playing tricks on him. Then he realized he wasn't imagining it.

Something was sobbing, off to the right, only meters
from him. He pushed forward, determined to ignore
it. Freedom was near.

But he *couldn't* ignore it. All his instincts forbade
him from going on without investigating the sound of
a fellow creature crying not in sorrow but in pain. It
could be a child.

He dithered for a moment. The animals on this
planet competed hard for available prey. Who knew
whether one of them had figured out that making distress noises might attract a curious scavenger? Why
expend the calories to hunt if your quarry came to
you? He kept running toward the safety of the control tower.

The sobbing changed to a low moan. Androye's feet
made the decision for him, turning toward the noise.
He couldn't help himself.

He pushed underneath a low-hanging vine as thick
as his wrist. The sunlight was even more spare here.
The only illumination seemed to be coming from a
pair of glowing eyes. A strong, sour, musky smell hit
him straight in the nostrils.

Androye pulled up short. The eyes flashed. The
keening stopped abruptly, and a low warning growl
came from the depths of the shadows. He held up
both hands to show they were empty.

"It's all right," he said in Orskian, then reframed it
in Dominion Basic. "I am a healer. I will not harm

you. Do you see?" He held out his right hand and peeled back the wrist of his jumpsuit with the left. The skin on the back of both was flayed. He cringed at his own touch, but the pattern of red bars and crescents on his skin was intact. The eyes narrowed at him. "You are in pain. I can feel it. Let me help you."

"I will kill you." The voice was weak. Androye knew that if the voice's owner could have killed him it would have happened the moment he appeared.

"Don't. I have medicine. What happened to you?"

A hand thrust itself forward into a thin shaft of light. It was strongly made, long, with knobbly knuckles and covered in thin, golden hairs. Rich, purple blood dripped from the wrist. Androye winced when he saw the cluster of thorns that pierced right through the joint. In spite of the possessor's efforts, the limb trembled.

"That must hurt," Androye said. His eyes were becoming accustomed to the dimness. He could see the face now. The glowing green eyes sat to either side of a blunt, bewhiskered muzzle. Round, golden ears sat on the flat-skulled head. "You're a Corex, aren't you?"

"I am the Corex," the lion-man said. "I am Lraou."

"I'm Androye. I come from Orskia. What are you doing here?" The Corex didn't answer. The healer sat on a heap of rotting leaves and secured the limb between his knees. He felt in the pouches of his shipsuit and brought out what he needed. A general purpose styptic that worked on more than 80% of the species in the Dominion and the surrounding systems halted the bleeding and numbed the area. With an extractor that resembled an electronic technician's pliers, Androye pushed each of the thorns out through the exit wound. They had barbs that prevented them being drawn the way they had gone in, as the tearing and irritation of the skin attested. The Corex had tried to remove them himself, but they had hurt him too much.

Battlefield medicine had trained Androye to operate swiftly. In no time he had cleaned and disinfected the wound and added a skinpatch of antiseptic/anesthetic to cover it against infection. He put the tip of one of the thorns into the ancient analyzer he carried in his breast pocket. The indicator turned orange.

"It's toxic," he said, pointing at the light. "Alkali-based. That's why you feel sick. Give me a minute. I have some antidotes." He thumbed through his pouches for the correct envelope. He tore off the guard strip and applied the adhesive to the male's palm, one of the few patches of bare skin he had. "That'll work within a couple of days." *If not, you're dead,* he thought but did not say. Both of them understood.

"I thank you, Androye," the lion-man said. "You have the gratitude of the Corex." His head went up suddenly.

Androye felt as though all the bones in his body had disintegrated. Boots threshed down the vegetation outside the copse, and the sound of a hoverbot tore the air overhead. They had been discovered.

"Hold your hands out where we can see them, or we will level this area," a man's harsh voice boomed, amplified by a uniform speaker. Androye realized that his vow to heal all creatures had just put him back into the hands of the enemy, and his new patient, too. All hope gone, Androye put his arms outside the enclosure. Voices exclaimed in surprise, and muttered among themselves. Androye wondered whether it was he they were not expecting to find out there. A whole troop of guards in spaceport uniform burst into the clearing with guns and blankers.

The female guard from the transport pushed through

the others. She grabbed him by the hair and tossed him to the ground.

"Tell me why I shouldn't kill you!" she demanded. Androye lay still. Once she had controlled her temper, she hauled him to his feet. "We have lost our launch window. Now we must wait until tomorrow, and it is your fault! You will have no rations today." Androye nodded miserably.

The lion-man didn't want to be captured. He leaped at the guards, claws out, and succeeded in taking the face off one man and the throat out of another before a dozen moved in to club him to the ground and blast him unconscious with blankers. The charge wouldn't keep him out long, but it was long enough to fasten a yoke around his neck and bind his wrists behind him. The Corex hissed in pain. Androye leaped forward to help him and was clubbed back.

"This critter's been gone a couple of weeks," the lead guard told Androye's escort. "I don't know why he came back this way. He coulda been clean gone, if it wasn't for your guy's tracer implant."

He needed medical help, Androye thought miserably. *And I supplied it. Unluckily for both of us.*

The uniformed Dominion troops dragged the lion-man upright. One of his eyes was swollen half shut. He winked the other one at Androye.

"I don't blame you," he said. "And I won't forget it." Before any of the uniformed guards could stop him, he leaned over and shoved his cheek hard against Androye's. "There."

"Come on!" Androye's guard said, taking him by the back of the neck.

"Good luck," he told the lion-man before he was pushed back out into the blinding sunlight.

"It's a good deed you're doing," whispered Tomping, huddled next to him on a bench in the anteroom.

He was a field laborer who had once been an artist on Melaysi. "We all appreciate it."

"You know what they say about good deeds," Androye said, with a calm smile for the guards.

"We care that you try," Tomping murmured.

"Clesborn! On your feet. The governor will see you."

Androye stood and carefully smoothed down his patched shipsuit. With an air of unhurried professionalism, he followed the secretary. The sergeant-at-arms stayed close to his side, a blanker held in Androye's ribs.

The next day's ship out of Danton had taken Androye and his fellows to the plague- and injury-ridden host of prisoners and low-level workers they expected him to cure with promises and a pocketful of bandages. The guards kept a closer watch on him than before. Instead of just an implant, they lock-sealed a heavy ID shackle around one ankle. Now there was no mistaking his status as a prisoner no matter where they took him. No longer could he pass unnoticed in a crowd, even if he could get away. The first new planet's atmosphere stank of simmering metal from the smelting plants. It gave him and his fellow prisoners a rash. The next was a morass of swamp gas thoroughly mixed with the exhaust from outdated engines that hauled precious timber in from the waterlogged forests. This third system, Imsan, was a center for agriculture and industrial assembly. Androye thought he would soon die if he couldn't get away from the reek and pollution and the endless work that sent him exhausted to an unpadded cot at night. He repaired flesh wounds and reattached limbs as best he could. So many of his patients died for want of better care. Androye worried about them, but he worried about his wife back on Orskia. As soon as he could, he would make another break for freedom, but in the meanwhile he tried to negotiate for better equipment and better conditions for himself and his patients. Even an air filtration system would go a long way.

He was neither by training nor nature much of a negotiator, though he did his best to express the desperate need exacerbated by the primitive conditions. In the healing halls on Orskia, he had access to all the most modern advances in medicine. With increasing frustration, he took his complaint from his guards to their supervisor. It was a risk. As the supervisor was unable to answer his demands, she passed him up the chain of command, to the next tier, where an officer heard him out. He couldn't make decisions of that level and sent Androye upward, and so on until he had reached the limits of the echelon. He felt heartened, knowing he was making progress toward getting what he wanted.

He had rehearsed what he would say to the governor. Providing better conditions would restore the Dominion's conscript workforce to full strength, enabling them to carry out tasks as ordered. He would offer himself as a consultant. If he could work his way up to a position of trust and authority, perhaps he might be able to secure communications with his family on Orskia, even leave time.

The governor, a stout, beetle-browed man barely glanced up from the glowing array of screens beneath the transparent surface of his desk.

"Well?"

"I am Androye Clesborn, Lord Governor."

The piggy eyes beneath the brows glared up at him. "I know who you are! What do you want?"

Androye smiled. Here was the opportunity he had been hoping for. "Lord Governor, I don't know how well acquainted you are with the medical facilities to hand for your, er, foreign workforce." He began to outline conditions in the fields and the mines, the injuries and illnesses that were being sustained by the workers, and the bare measures he felt were needed to ameliorate them. He outlined point after point of the deficiencies in the infirmary and in the field units at each work station. "Now, I have made a study of the nutritional requirements of the various races that you have in your . . . employment. . . ."

He looked at the governor for a response, and his voice ran down to a stop. The fleshy face wore an expression of exasperated boredom. The beady eyes had gone stony. Androye peered at him hopefully.

"Sir, may I have your feedback on my suggestions?"

The teeth bared like an animal's. "Certainly not. Such things are not in my interest."

Androye felt his face grow hot. "Then why did you listen to me?"

"I heard you out only to see how long you would go on. You make demands as if you have some measure of importance on this outpost. You are nothing. Less than nothing. Slaves die. We replace them when they do. They will work as long as they can. You're here to use until I have no use for you and discard you once I do. I don't care about the conditions. My workforce, as you call it, is lucky to get what it has."

"Then why let me go on and tell you all the plans I . . . that I offer?"

He did not understand until that moment the stories of how dangerous the governor was, nor that he had earned the fear in which his underlings held him. The beady eyes burned like coals. "To see if you would ever become amusing. You did not." He moved a finger toward the sergeant at arms. "Take this fool to the arena! At least he'll have entertainment value for a moment or two. Inform me when he is on the schedule. I'd like to see him die." He gestured through the door at the workers huddled on the benches near the entry door. "And take that scum with you! All of them! I may as well enjoy my afternoon."

"Yes, Lord Governor," the sergeant said, tugging Androye out of the room. The healer tried to pull away.

"But Lord Governor!"

The sergeant poked him in the chest with the blanker. "Don't speak again, or I'll kill you here."

"I tried," he told Tomping, as they were hustled into the gray corridor toward the steel lifts.

"I know. We're going to die here."

Tomping's prediction came true within an hour. They hauled his body, dead, from the sands to the cheering of the live audience, a thousand or so locals, Dominion citizens only, who crowded the stands. Androye clung to the grate of a cage full of remote cameras, one of a cluster containing the day's victims to be.

A young man with an earpiece poked a skinny sword through the wires. Androye took it, knowing he would never be able to use it. "Here you go, friend. Now, remember, the crowd gets bored if the bouts last more than ten minutes. Try and cringe a little as we lower you. The governor likes to see cringing."

"Will it spare my life?" Androye asked desperately.

The attendant gave him a sympathetic look. "No. But it might keep us out of trouble. Be good. We've got families."

"So have I!" Androye shouted as the crane hauled his cage out into the air over the gleaming sands.

The lights on the field were blinding. Androye winced at the hot beams that lanced through his cage. An armored figure waited below. By the thick legs and wide, webbed feet, he could tell it was a Nourin.

It was unsteady on its feet, giddy from the heat. An intelligent amphibian, it should have been back on its waterlogged world among the gigantic black roots of varol trees.

His cage thumped down, and the door creaked open. The Nourin leaped for him. Androye backpedaled. His heel hit the threshold of the cage and he sat down hard. The crowd laughed. He threw up the sword, just deflecting a blow. His arm went numb from elbow to fingers. He couldn't kill. All he could do was die.

But the Nourin had done all he was able. Through the eyeholes of the helmet, Androye watched the big, round eyes roll up toward the ceiling. The Nourin collapsed in a heap. The crowd booed. Androye ran to its side to see if he could help it. The creature was too far gone. When he pinched up its skin to test for dehydration, the pinch stayed high. It was dying. Men in black leather masks kicked Androye away. They took one big floppy foot each and hauled the Nourin away.

"Fight!" one of them growled over his shoulder. "Make it look good, curse you!"

Androye's next opponent was already in the ring, a tall figure in a half-mask standing on the toes of huge, gold-furred feet. He knew the scent immediately, not to mention the shape. It was a Corex. He scrambled to his feet. It would tear him apart in seconds. He held out the electronic sword, trying to look threatening.

"I am a prince of my people," the Corex declared. "I will not yield to you, no matter how skilled you may be."

"I don't want to hurt you," Androye said.

"Lie! Die like the Orskian slug you are."

They circled one another for an eternity. He knew about swordplay in theory, though his medical training prevented him from making any attacks. The lion-man feinted and drove in. Androye dropped to the ground. The sword passed over his head.

Androye had a perfect view of the furry hand and arm as it extended through where he had been standing. A small cluster of round scars still showed purple on the wrist. He knew this male!

"Lraou!" he exclaimed. The lion-man jumped back surprised, ruining the recovery from his lunge. He stared down at the prone man.

"I know no Orskians," the Corex snarled. He drew back his hand and spread his claws to strike.

"It's me," Androye said desperately, eyes flicking to the glinting crescent-moons. "I'm the healer who patched you up on Danton."

The eyes in the half-mask widened. Lraou leaned down and smelled Androye's cheek.

"Ah," he said. He pulled Androye to his feet and slapped him on the back. Androye staggered at the lion-man's casual strength. "Yes, I remember you! You're mine! I won't kill you."

"You'd better make it look like you will if you want to live," Androye warned him, backing away. He looked over his shoulder. The hovering cameras were invisible behind the brilliant white lights. "We don't have long. They told me ten minutes."

"My people know where I am. I await rescue. This is the day. If I had not been in the arena they would have freed me from my cell." Lraou's brilliant eyes widened. "I owe you life, healer. You shall come with me."

Such a hope seemed unlikely, but it was enough to lift Androye's heart a little.

"They want blood within ten minutes, or they will send in the professional fighters," he said.

"Then we will give them a little blood. We must prolong this encounter as much as possible. Let us give them a fine show until my ship arrives!" Lraou beckoned him with one claw and brandished the sword. "Engage!"

Androye swallowed hard. "I can't fight you, Lraou. My oath as a healer prevents me harming you or anyone else. Only one of us can live. It must be you."

The furry lip curled under the edge of the half mask. "Intolerable. I cannot poke holes in a being who won't fight. Very well, you shall be as a cub who is learning the skill. Will you pretend? Can you?"

The crowd was already growing restless. Androye heard boos and jeers coming from the stands. He had no choice. He held up the sword as if preparing to fight. Lraou went on guard. Androye imitated his movement.

"That is very good. They circled one another, making passes. It half-killed Androye to be making threatening gestures with the thin sword, going deeply against his training, but if they could live . . .

The unseen crowd jeered them.

"The round is forfeit," a voice came over the public address system. "Warriors, to the center of the arena! Kill or die!"

That's it, Androye thought hopelessly. Out of the glare trotted a double file of bare-chested men in black leather trousers and black masks. They brandished an array of ancient weapons that looked like primitive surgical equipment. The blades were stained with many colors of blood, the residue from today's kills. The healer's oath demanded that he save life whenever possible. There was only one way.

He dropped his sword and spread out his arms. "I can't hurt you, Lraou. Kill me. Save yourself."

"I owe you my life," Lraou roared. "I will protect you. Get behind me."

The professionals had seen attempts at a last minute alliance before. The leaders even grinned at Lraou and Androye as they spread out in a ring around the pair. It would be over in moments. Androye braced himself to die.

That was when the screaming began.

A narrow craft like a lightning bolt streaked across the arena. It disgorged a barrage of round lumps. Each lump took flight in a different direction. Three of them dropped directly toward Androye. He threw himself on Lraou to shield him. A BOOM! deafened him and sand flew up in a choking cloud. More stunners pelted the stands, the grounds, the lighting fixtures, until the entire complex was in a welter of confusion.

The sleek craft whisked around against the now blackened ceiling and skidded in for a landing. Androye dashed sand out of his eyes in time to see nine huge Corexes bound toward Lraou and dig him free.

"We are pursued, your grace," the leader said. "We must hurry."

"We take this Orskian," Lraou announced, seizing Androye by his arm. "He is my new physician. He has saved my life twice. I claim him."

"As you please, your grace! Hurry!"

Lraou threw Androye over his shoulder and sprang after his rescuers into the ship.

It did not take long before pursuit began. Security was tight around the government's main buildings. The sleek ship was more nimble than the gunships, and it had speed. Androye did not feel a single blast shake the hull before they cleared atmosphere.

"Good riddance," he said. "Lraou—your grace—I can't thank you enough for saving me."

"A life for a life," the Corex said. He peeled off the half-mask and threw it aside. "I still owe you one."

"I will trade that gladly if you will take me home to Orskia," Androye said, thinking of Meriglen happily. "Or get me to a neutral port where I can take ship home."

"Orskia?" Lraou asked, cocking his head. "No, my friend, you're coming home with me! We have many patients who could use your skills. Our healers were scattered and killed by the coming of the Dominion. Now they have provided us with a most worthy substitute. You will live well. You shall be my personal physician. I will pay you well. You shall have a title, a manor, anything you require."

"But, my wife . . . ! I haven't seen her in months. I want to go home to her."

"My personal guard will retrieve her and bring her to Corex. She will enjoy it there. It is very beautiful. You will see." Lraou looked at Androye in outrage. "You are not thinking of declining? It is a tremendous honor! You will be with me until I die. You belong to me. I marked you when you saved my life the first time. You cannot decline."

Androye took a deep breath to argue, and started coughing. The air inside the ship was laden with the heavy smells of musk and urine. Lraou waited, his eyes glowing. Androye realized that it would not be politic to disagree, not yet. He shook his head. Lraou smiled and sat back.

"Relax, my friend. This will be the beginning of a new life for you, a good life."

A stinking one, Androye thought miserably. He leaned forward and put his head in his hands. He had just traded one form of servitude for another.

I could have let him die, he thought. And just as quickly, an inner voice retorted, *No, you couldn't.*

No, he couldn't. He knew it. His oath forbade him, his training prevented it, and his personal morals were upset even to entertain the notion. He had lost his chance of freedom yet again. He was a prisoner again, but a prisoner of his own ethics.

Full of gloom, he sat back in the heavily cushioned couch. Maybe one day he'd get used to the smell.

THE RED PATH

Jim C. Hines

Jim C. Hines has been writing since 1995, which makes him feel old, so he tries not to think about it. His latest book is *The Stepsister Scheme*, a quirky mash-up of fairy tale princesses and Charlie's Angels. (Roudette will probably return for the third book in the series.) He has also written a trilogy about a nearsighted goblin runt named Jig, as well as close to forty short stories for markets such as *Realms of Fantasy*, *Sword & Sorceress XXI*, and *Turn the Other Chick*. You can find him online at www.jimchines.com. As always, he would like to thank his wife and children for putting up with him. Living with a writer ain't easy.

Roudette had sinned twice by the time she closed the door. Her first sin was theft. Father had been baking for the past three days in preparation for the Midsummer Festival, when he and the other elders would ask God to renew his blessing upon the town for another year. Even though Roudette believed the church would have smiled upon her goal, she had still taken the muffins and cakes without permission.

Her second sin was disobedience. Though her parents hadn't explicitly forbidden her from visiting Grandmother this morning, Roudette knew what they would say if she asked. Respect for one's elders was a central tenant of the Savior's Path. She would be punished, and rightfully so, upon her return.

"Roudette?"

Perhaps punishment would come even sooner. She turned to see Mother standing in the doorway. Roudette's little brother, Jaun, peeked from behind brown-painted shutters and stuck out his tongue.

Roudette's fingers tightened around the handle of her basket as she planned a third sin. The instant her mother turned away, Jaun was getting a muffin right between the eyes.

"Inside. Now." Mother kept her voice low, to avoid drawing the neighbors' attention. Her gaze slipped past Roudette to the whitewashed homes on the opposite side of the road. Roudette's father was a Patriarch of the church, the highest office in which a human could serve. Even in a small town, it was a position of great respect. It wouldn't do for his daughter to be seen quarreling with his wife.

Roudette spoke softly, out of respect. "Grandmother has been back only a few days. Why can't I visit—"

"Your grandmother turned her back on us," Mother interrupted. "She left the Path. I won't allow you to follow her into temptation."

"But isn't devotion to family an important part of the Path?"

"So is obedience."

Roudette used one hand to pull her cloak tight. Her fingers brushed the gold symbols embroidered into the blood-red wool. Each symbol was said to represent one step of the Savior's Path. Descended from Heaven with the rest of fairykind during the uprising, the Savior had sacrificed himself on the cross to protect humanity from God's wrath.

Her mother wore a similar cloak, though hers was blue. Roudette would receive her blue cloak when she turned thirteen at the end of the summer. Mother had embroidered hundreds of such cloaks over the years; her skill with the silver needle was unmatched by mortal hands.

"What if Grandmother hasn't truly strayed?" Roudette asked, trying a different tactic. "What if she's simply lost? Perhaps all she lacks is a guide to lead her back?"

Mother's hesitation was brief, barely noticeable to anyone who didn't know her. "Your grandmother has never shown any interest in guidance."

"Are you sure?" Roudette asked, pressing her advantage. "Do you know what's in her heart?"

It was an unfair question. Only magic could reveal one's thoughts, and human magic was forbidden by church law.

"I remember when she left us," Mother said. "My father tried to stop her. He told us later that she had done terrible things."

"Then isn't it even more important to guide her back?" Roudette asked. "So that she might find forgiveness and be reborn? Midsummer is a time for forgiveness, is it not? The Savior forgave even the human who drove the iron nails through his flesh."

Roudette bowed her head and waited. She knew scripture almost as well as her father. They both knew who would win this argument.

"You'll return by noon," Mother said at last. "And for trying to sneak away, you'll rise early tomorrow and scour the ovens."

"Yes, Mother," Roudette said.

"The lies of the fallen are seductive," Mother said. "Don't let her lead you astray."

"Thank you, Mother." Roudette pulled up her hood

and walked away, stopping only when she heard the door close behind her. After making sure nobody else was watching, she opened her basket.

The muffin struck the left shutter, slamming it against the frame and making Jaun yelp. The Savior would frown on her actions, but he hadn't grown up with a little brother.

Roudette pulled a fairy cake from the basket and ate as she walked. Her father used a special brass brand to burn the sign of the cross onto the top of each cake. The jam inside was supposed to represent the blood of the sacrifice.

Until she was five years old, Roudette had believed the Savior tasted like strawberries.

She was finishing off the second cake when the cottage came into view. It stood alone in a small clearing atop a hill. Roudette stepped carefully onto a fallen tree that spanned the stream winding past the hill. She crossed the makeshift bridge quickly, as she had done many times through the years. There, looking up at her grandmother's cottage, she hesitated.

Curiosity had always been Roudette's weakness, whether it was exploring the woods or reading the "adult" books her father kept locked away in the church. As far as she could tell, they were the same as the books she had studied when she was younger, only her father's versions had more begatting.

It was curiosity that had brought her back to Grandmother's abandoned cottage each year, trying to imagine where Grandmother had gone. Her last visit had been shortly after Jaun's birth.

Then, three days ago, Roudette had discovered smoke rising from the chimney. When she peeked through a window, she had been stunned to find Grandmother butchering a pair of squirrels in the kitchen.

The sight had wiped all semblance of manners from Roudette's mind. She burst through the door, squealing like the child she had been when last she saw Grandmother.

To be fair, Grandmother had smiled to see Roudette's joy. They embraced, and then Grandmother had studied Roudette for a long time, until the girl began to feel uncomfortable. Finally, Grandmother had shooed Roudette away, saying, "Your parents would spit hellfire if they saw you here with me. Please go, and leave me in peace."

What peace could Grandmother have, alone and lost? Curiosity had led Roudette here before, but it was duty that made her return today. Duty to family, to try to save a loved one who had strayed. Brushing crumbs from the front of her cloak, Roudette made her way to the door.

The air was still today, and the woods were silent, save for the faint trickling of the stream. The green door was open, though the windows were shuttered tight. Roudette stopped in the doorway. She blotted her forehead on the sleeve of her cloak.

"Grandmother?" There was no answer. Roudette rapped her knuckles on the doorframe as she stepped inside.

The kitchen was a mess. Flies swarmed over the remains of a rabbit on the floor. Roudette wrinkled her nose.

A low growl made her jump. The sound had come from the bedroom. Perhaps another animal had snuck into the cottage. A fox or a wolf, or even a wildcat. That must be what had killed the rabbit.

Roudette grabbed a knife from the counter, clutching the bone handle in sweat-slick fingers. A part of her longed to flee back to the safety of town. But what if the animal had attacked Grandmother? She couldn't leave.

"God protect me." She imagined she could feel her cloak grow warmer in response to her whispered prayer.

Smears of blood darkened the hard dirt floor leading into the bedroom. Holding the knife in front of her, Roudette peered through the doorway.

Stretched out on the cot was an enormous silver wolf. Blood matted its side, soaking into the blankets.

Roudette's hand shook. She nearly dropped the knife. But there was no sign of Grandmother. Holding her breath, she started to back away.

Though she made no sound, one of the wolf's big ears twitched. It turned toward Roudette, its huge eyes spearing her in place.

The wolf bared its teeth and growled again. Such enormous teeth, no doubt all the better for eating foolish girls who didn't listen to their mothers' advice.

Should she flee, or would that just encourage the wolf to chase her down? Wasn't that what such beasts did?

She looked the wolf in its eyes. Was that another mistake? She knew dogs would take a direct stare as a challenge or threat.

Such big eyes it had. Round and gentle, belying the terror of those teeth. They were pale gray, tinged with blue. A fleck of black marred the ring of the left eye.

Roudette swallowed, remembering her previous visit and the way Grandmother had stared at her. Grandmother's left eye had been flecked in exactly the same way as the wolf's.

"Grandmother?" Roudette whispered. Thoughts of demons and devils raced through her mind. Those who strayed from the Path were said to be vulnerable to such things. But the wolf had relaxed, and made no move to attack as Roudette took a slow step into the room.

"What's happened to you?" She moved closer, her

attention drawn to the wound on the wolf's side. Blood continued to drip from the dark gash between the ribs.

The wolf sniffed the air and its—*her* lips drew back in a snarl.

"What is it?" Roudette asked.

The wolf sprang from the cot, moving too quickly for Roudette to react. The knife spun away as huge paws clubbed her chest. She slammed to the floor. Teeth snapped at her throat, locking around her cloak. The wolf dragged her farther into the bedroom.

Roudette tried to break free, but a sharp shake of the wolf's head left her stunned. The wolf yanked again, and the cloak tore free. The wolf backed away, taking the cloak with her. The gold embroidery was lit up like tiny flames. The material had caught in the wolf's teeth, and appeared to be causing her pain. The wolf stumbled toward the doorway, pawing at the cloak.

There were no windows, and the wolf blocked the only escape. Roudette fled into the closet and yanked the door shut behind her. Peeking through the crack, she saw the wolf tearing the cloak apart. The fur around her jaws was blackened, as were her paws where she had touched the cloak. The light from the symbols flickered like candlelight, slowly dying as the wolf destroyed the cloak.

Roudette held her breath. Her basket lay spilled on the floor, crushed muffins and cakes scattered in the dirt. Blood dripped over torn scraps of red as the wolf limped to the cot, pausing only to growl at the closet.

Roudette's hands shook. The door was flimsy. No doubt the wolf could smash right through. But whatever magic had blossomed from Roudette's cloak had clearly weakened the wolf. Even as the wolf climbed back into the cot, her rear legs collapsed, and she had to try twice more to pull herself onto the sagging mattress.

"What have you done?" The voice was male, the enunciation clear and perfect. Again the wolf snarled.

Roudette watched through the crack as a tall man stepped into view. He wore hunter's garb, a vest of dark green leather over a loose black shirt. Green bracers circled his wrists, and a quiver of arrows was slung over his right shoulder. A golden crucifix hung from a chain round his neck.

Roudette silently made the sign of the cross. That symbol marked the hunter as a bishop of the church. Roudette had never seen one of the fey so close. Surely he could counter whatever curse had taken her grandmother. She started to open the door.

The wolf lurched to her feet, yipping loudly. In response, the hunter drew a silver-bladed knife. "Don't play the vicious beast with me. I know what you are." He nudged the scraps of Roudette's cloak with his boot and then stooped to pick up one of the bloody pieces. "Feasting on your own kind? You're lucky the cloak didn't destroy you."

The hunter lunged forward, driving the knife into the wolf's chest. The wolf's yip muffled Roudette's gasp.

"Or perhaps not so lucky." He yanked the blade down, and then ripped the skin back with his free hand. His body concealed the gruesome details, but when he finished, he dropped a bloody wolf skin on the floor. Roudette's grandmother lay curled on the cot, naked save for a leather necklace. Her chest and side were bloody, though the hunter's blow hadn't been a deep one.

He kicked the skin away and then wiped his hands on his trousers. "Filthy, primitive magic."

Grandmother coughed. "Grand Bishop Bernas didn't think so."

Roudette started. Grand Bishop Bernas had been one of the founders of the church, more than a hundred years ago. He had died a martyr, fighting a demon to protect his followers.

The hunter raised his knife and then caught himself. "If you confess, I am authorized to be lenient. Who are you working with, human?"

Grandmother smiled. Her lips were burned and blistered, her teeth stained with blood. "I work with God. Who do you serve, you fairy serpent?"

Roudette closed her eyes. Mother was right. Grandmother would never return to the Path. To speak to one of God's chosen in such a way . . .

"Are there other skins?"

"Why, Bishop Tomas, is that fear in your voice?"

Tomas' snarl was as frightening as the wolf's had been. "Very well. Then you shall feel the fires of damnation." Without another word, he spun and left.

As soon as the cottage door slammed behind him, Grandmother rolled onto her side. She groaned and clutched her side. "Roudette?"

Roudette pushed open the closet door. "Grandmother? I don't understand. What—"

"Hush, girl," Grandmother said. "Tomas will be outside, preparing his 'cleansing fire,' and I haven't much time." She lay back in the cot. "The fey poison their blades."

Roudette picked up one of the crushed fairy cakes that had spilled from her basket. The cross on top was mostly intact. "There's still time. If you repent before the poison takes you—"

Grandmother took the roll from Roudette's hand and crushed it. Jam ran between her thin fingers. Her smile was both warm and gruesome. "The church garbs you in curses," she said, glancing toward the scraps of Roudette's cloak. "Those symbols your mother copies so carefully? Enchantments that would burn you alive for attempting the simplest magic."

Roudette stared at the remains of her cloak. "Mother never said anything—"

"She doesn't know. It's one more way to keep us controlled."

"No," Roudette said. "It's because man is weak. Because magic tempts us from the Path, leading us to . . . to *this*." She pointed to the wolf skin. "Only God's chosen have the wisdom to use magic properly."

Grandmother coughed again, spitting blood. Roudette used a corner of the blanket to wipe her mouth.

"Thank you." Grandmother lay back. "I have been to lands where the Church of the Fey is looked upon with scorn and derision. I have seen magic wielded by men and women to heal the sick. I have met those who believe humans, not fairies, are God's true children."

Roudette shook her head. "Please stop," she said.

"I never should have returned. But the opportunity was too great."

Curiosity forced Roudette to ask, "What opportunity?"

"The Midsummer Festival. They say the Grand Bishop himself plans to attend this year."

Despite her fear, Roudette's heart leaped at the thought. The Grand Bishop visited only one human town each year. That he would bestow such an honor on her father's town—

"I thought I could use the skin, as my great-grandfather used it to kill Bernas." Grandmother looked away, almost as though she were ashamed. "I was too eager. I allowed them to discover who I was. I never even noticed Tomas tracking me."

She touched the deep cut on her ribs. "His spear pierced my side before I realized he was there."

"But why would you want to hurt the Grand Bishop?" Roudette asked.

Burned fingers stroked Roudette's hair. "Because I couldn't bear to see my grandchildren live as slaves." Her voice grew raspier. "You must go, child. The wolf has taken too many of his kind over the years. Now that he's found me, he'll seek out your family. He'll kill them all to protect his people."

Roudette backed away. "My family has never strayed from the Path. He wouldn't punish them for—"

"That's what I thought too." Her voice was distant. "The gift of magic is carried in the blood. Your mother. Your brother. Even if the flames took this skin, you have the power to create another. Tomas won't risk your survival."

Outside the cottage, Roudette could hear flames crackling to life. "Grandmother, let me help you." She reached out, but Grandmother pushed her away.

"I'm beyond saving," Grandmother said. "But your family needs you. Take the skin. Save them from Tomas."

"I can't—"

"Please, Roudette." Grandmother coughed again, spitting blood into her hand. "Isn't it the child's duty to honor the wishes of her elders and to comfort those who are dying?"

"Of course," Roudette said automatically. "But—"

"Well, I'm both. Take the skin."

Slowly, Roudette nodded.

"Thank you." Grandmother slumped. One hand closed around her necklace. The pendant was a simple cross made of three iron nails. Roudette had never seen the forbidden metal, but its blackened appearance matched the descriptions her father had read to her.

Grandmother began to mumble. She was *praying,* though the prayers were unfamiliar to Roudette. Her face was twisted from the pain, but her voice was serene. At peace. The kind of peace the church said was impossible for those who left the Path.

Smoke darkened the air. Roudette dropped to her knees, where it was easier to breathe. She touched the wolf skin, half-expecting it to burn her the way her cloak had burned Grandmother. She thought of her parents and of Jaun.

"Goodbye, Grandmother." Roudette picked up the skin and fled.

The wolf skin was heavier than Roudette had expected. The head and front paws dragged through the dirt as she fled the burning cottage.

Though the flames soon engulfed the thatched roof, the trees appeared untouched. Bishop Tomas was already gone. On his way to Roudette's home, if Grandmother was right.

As Roudette moved farther from the fire, the breeze chilled the sweat on her skin, raising goosebumps along her arms.

Wood cracked, and a section of roof thundered down with an explosion of sparks. She had never imagined a fire could be so loud.

"Grandmother . . ." Smoke and tears stung her eyes. She turned toward the sky, amazed to see the sun still hours from its peak. How had her life changed so much in so little time?

The wolf skin was stiff, like badly tanned leather. Sweat and blood stained the inside. Roudette could see a gash on the side, presumably from Bishop Tomas' spear. Roudette looked more closely, finding older cuts, all carefully repaired with silver thread.

The skin smelled like Grandmother, full of autumn leaves, fresh-baked apple bread, and stale ginger beer. Grandmother, who had died a sinner, whose soul was damned for all time. How many of God's chosen had she killed?

Mother couldn't have known. She never would have allowed Roudette to visit if she had suspected Grandmother of such evil. To murder the Grand Bishop during the festival . . . "Evil is seductive," she whispered, quoting one of her father's favorite verses.

This was what Mother had warned her against. Not a villain luring her from the Path with promises of forbidden pleasure and lurid decadence, but a loved one begging for help.

"God help me." Bundling the skin under her arm, she hurried toward home.

Even from the road, Roudette could hear Bishop Tomas preaching to her family. Both Jaun and Mother were crying. Their voices came from the kitchen, at the back of the house.

Her fingers dug into the fur of the skin. Her grandmother's blood had begun to dry, stiffening the fur into bristled spikes that scratched her arms.

She circled through the alley between her house and the next. She nearly dropped the skin as she scaled the fence into their garden. The smell of crushed tomatoes wafted through the air as she hurried toward the storeroom window and climbed inside.

The voices came from the kitchen. Roudette crossed through the room, pressing her body against the stacked firewood as she peeked in at Tomas and her family.

Heat from the stone oven rippled the air. Her parents stood in front of the oven with Jaun between them. Jaun's face was buried in Father's apron.

Bishop Tomas rested one hand on the hilt of his knife. In his other hand, he held a piece of Roudette's cloak.

"That's hers," Mother said, her voice faint. She reached toward the scrap, and then drew back. "I made that cloak myself."

"I'm sorry," said the Bishop. "The old woman gave herself over to evil. To devour her own kin . . ."

Jaun's cries grew louder. Father put a hand on his shoulder.

"I should have been stronger," said Mother. "I should have ordered her to stay away."

"Yes, you should have." Bishop Tomas stared at her for a long time, then asked, "How long have you known of your mother's sins?"

Mother bowed her head. "She strayed years ago, when I was very young. But I promise, I never knew what she had become. If I had—"

"You couldn't have stopped her," he said, not unkindly.

If not for Grandmother's words, Roudette probably wouldn't have noticed the way Tomas' hand never left his knife, or the way he studied her family . . . like a farmer trying to decide which animal to butcher.

"It's written that the sins of the parent live on in the child," Bishop Tomas continued.

Both of Roudette's parents stiffened. Father swallowed and wiped his hands on his apron. "My wife has never strayed."

"But she will," the Bishop said softly, drawing his knife. "Her blood is tainted by her mother's sins."

Or by her mother's magic? Grandmother had said magic was carried in the blood.

No! Grandmother had planned to murder a Grand Bishop. She had admitted so herself. To murder God's own tool in this world . . . Roudette set the skin atop the firewood and backed away. Her father was a Patriarch. She couldn't turn her back on him. She refused to follow Grandmother to damnation. But did that mean giving herself up to Tomas and his knife? Allowing him to kill Roudette and her family?

"What do I do?" she whispered. If this was truly

God's will, who was she to fight it? Would God condemn her family for her Grandmother's sins?

She had lost her way. The revelation felled her. On her knees, she begged, "Please guide me, Lord. Lead me back."

"Please!" Father was almost shouting. "Her faith is as strong as any I've known."

"Then she will be rewarded."

The Bishop's thrust was quick and sure. Mother grunted and stumbled back. She made no further sound as she collapsed at the base of the oven.

Tomas used the bloody knife to make the sign of the cross. "Go with God, and be reborn into grace."

"Mommy!" Jaun broke away and ran to Mother. He touched her shoulder, gently at first. When she didn't respond, he began to shake her, yelling louder and louder as tears dripped from his cheeks.

Roudette didn't realize she was crying until one of her tears landed on her arm. She jerked back, unable to look away from Mother . . . from Mother's body.

There had been no sign. No divine guidance to tell her which was the right choice. She had waited, and now her mother was dead. Because of her.

"I'm sorry," said Tomas, stepping toward Jaun. Father started to move between them, then turned away, his shoulders shaking.

Roudette rose and grabbed the wolfskin. "Leave him alone." Her voice was still hoarse from the smoke at Grandmother's cottage.

Father spun. "Roudette!" For a moment, joy filled his face. Then he looked at Tomas, and his expression turned to despair.

Jaun ran toward her, wrapping his arms around her waist. Roudette ran one hand through his hair, holding him close. With her other, she pulled the skin over one shoulder.

"No!" Tomas shouted. "Don that skin, and you join your grandmother in hell."

Roudette gently pried Jaun away, pushing him behind her. She drew the skin tight around her body.

"Roudette, please," said Father. "You mustn't turn away from the Path, not now. Not when—"

Tomas leaped at her. Roudette grabbed a log from the firewood and hurled it at his chest. Perhaps grief gave her strength, or maybe the skin's magic had already begun to take her. The log felt light as a twig, smashing Tomas backward.

She could feel the wolf's skin embracing her. Pain crushed her fingers and feet, pulling them into the wolf's paws. Her vision darkened momentarily as the head pressed down on her own. She blinked, her ears twitching to follow Tomas' footsteps as he came at her again.

Roudette bounded past him. She shook her head. Already her eyesight had returned, keener than before. She could see the sweat beading Tomas's forehead. She could smell his terror.

"The beast has taken your daughter," he said, brandishing his knife. "She will kill us all."

Father started toward her. Roudette growled, and he jumped back.

In that moment of distraction, Tomas attacked. But Roudette heard his footsteps and leaped easily away from his knife. Her claws gouged the bloody floor.

"Help me, damn you!" Tomas shouted.

Father didn't move. And Jaun was too afraid to act. Baring her teeth, Roudette pounced.

Removing the skin was painfully difficult. Roudette's fangs pierced her own skin several times as she struggled to rip the seam back from her stomach. She pulled harder, cramping her neck and shoulder until she finally freed one arm from the wolf's skin. Once she had the use of her hand, she was able to peel the rest of the skin from her body.

Her clothes were little more than tattered rags. She lay on the floor, trying to adjust to the blurred vision, the abrupt loss of scent.

"Roudette?" Jaun stood in the doorway, looking from her to Father.

"What have you done?" whispered Father.

The bishop lay crumpled on the floor, his throat a bloody mess. Roudette brushed her mouth with the back of her hand. Her lips were blistered, and her mouth felt as though she had bitten hot coals, seared by Tomas' magic. The taste of blood in her throat made her stomach convulse, and she fought to keep from vomiting.

"I've saved my brother," she said. If this had been the right choice, shouldn't her doubt be gone?

Father shook his head. "At the cost of your soul. Bishop Tomas was right. Your blood is cursed."

"No, Father." But there had been truth in Tomas' words. At the moment her teeth closed around his throat, Roudette had experienced a thrill like nothing she had ever known. An animal pleasure. Even now, a part of her longed to feel such freedom again. "Maybe," she admitted, bowing her head. "But he—"

"Don't." He knelt beside Mother. Without looking up, he whispered, "Get out."

Roudette's throat tightened. "What?"

"Your mother died to serve God. You turned your back on him. I'll not have you in my home."

"Mother died because . . ." Because Roudette had hesitated, waiting for God to decide for her.

"She died because of your grandmother's evil. The same evil you now embrace."

Hearing the grief in his voice, Roudette realized it didn't matter what she said. Father was a Patriarch of the church. To turn away from the Path meant abandoning everything he believed. More importantly, it would mean Mother had died for nothing, and that he had stood by and watched as Tomas murdered his wife.

"I'm sorry," Roudette said. "I hope someday you can forgive me."

He didn't answer. Roudette rose, carrying the skin in one hand. With her other, she reached for Jaun.

"What are you doing?" Father asked. He started to rise.

Something in Roudette's eyes stopped him. "Taking Jaun somewhere he'll be safe." She hesitated. "You could come with us. Tomas died in your home. You'll be punished if—"

"Would you trade your mortal span for an eternity of suffering? If you lead Jaun from the Path, you damn him as well."

Roudette thought about the necklace Grandmother had worn, the reverence with which she had cradled the iron cross. She squeezed her brother's hand. He pressed close to her in response. "Perhaps God will help us find a different Path."

LOST CHILD

Stephen D. Sullivan

Once upon a time, Stephen D. Sullivan wrote comic books. He spun tales of mutant turtles, and speeding race drivers, and dark-winged ducks, and star-bound boy robots, and the occasional faerie story. Sometimes, his narratives went unpublished—often for lack of a suitable artist. Then, one day, Steve said to himself, "If I wrote prose, I wouldn't need artists to help bring my tales to life." He's been writing books and short stories ever since, with only the occasional foray back to his graphics-bound roots. "Lost Child" has followed the author through the publishing wilderness for many years, waiting for the right venue in which to reveal itself (or for Charles Vess to become available to illustrate it). Steve is pleased that this twisted faerie tale's time has finally come. Some of Steve's recent work, including *Zombies, Werewolves, & Unicorns*, is available from Walkabout Publishing, www.walkaboutpublishing.com. In his guise as Manwolf, Steve is the co-host of Uncanny Radio—*www.uncannyworld.com*. More information about the author and his upcoming projects can be found at *www.stephendsulli-van.com* or on his blog, *http://stephendsulli-van.blogspot.com/*.

Amber Thomas hated England. She hated the weather, she hated the countryside, and she especially hated the big manor house her parents had rented. Mostly, though, she hated the shouting. It seemed as if ever since they came to England, the shouting never stopped.

Her parents had been fighting from the moment they stepped off the plane. They didn't think she noticed, but she was six years old now, and she understood a lot more than she had last year. She wasn't deaf, either. Even in her grand bedroom, even with the door shut, she heard them arguing every night. She knew what they were yelling about, too: England. It *had* to be England.

Either it was England, or it was *her*.

Had they been fighting like this before summer vacation? Their house in America was just as big as their rented manor, but the rooms were more spread out. Noises didn't travel as far back home, maybe because there weren't open grates in the floors to let the heat move around.

Not all the nighttime sounds that drifted to Amber's room were fighting. Every night, the huge old building groaned and sighed. Sometimes, Amber heard whispers outside her window. Other times, the brilliant blue fireflies that danced in the summer evening sang to her. And some nights—maybe four or five times since she moved in—Amber glimpsed the face of a boy pressed up against the room's wide, tall windows. The boy always smiled at her.

That was impossible, though. How could a boy be at her window? Her room was on the second floor, and there was no balcony outside.

Despite the strange, dreamlike quality of these visitations, Amber liked the boy. His face seemed friendly—though he never said anything. Unfortunately, whenever she looked at him directly, he was never really there after all.

Each time he appeared, Amber called to him. "Hello!" she whispered into the night, "Hello!"

She listened very intently for the boy's reply, but none ever came. Sadness welled up. She needed an English friend so desperately—someone to play with, someone to take her mind off the . . . trouble.

Even now, her parents were downstairs fighting. During their first week in England, Amber had covered her head with her pillow and tried not to hear. For the second week, she'd put her fingers in her ears and sang songs from Sunday school. That didn't work any better than the pillow had.

It seemed no matter what the family did during the day, no matter how many lovely castles they saw or how many wonderful zoos and parks they visited, no matter how many presents they bought in expensive stores or how many carriage rides they took, the night always returned, and with it came the fighting.

After two nearly sleepless weeks, Amber knew she had to do something. She didn't know *what* to do, but anything would be better than listening to the endless shouts. Even having them yell at her, rather than at each other, would be better.

Amber crawled out of her warm bed with the pink pillows and the fluffy comforter. She walked through the gilded bedroom doors and into the cool, dark corridor beyond. Winston went with her. Amber knew he would keep her brave enough to do what had to be done—whatever that might be. Winston stared at her with his big button eyes and a friendly smile on his fuzzy brown face. Even if Amber didn't have any *real* friends in this strange, noisy country, at least she had her bear.

The shouts grew louder as the two of them crept down the hallway toward the long, winding stairway that led to the first floor. The carpet felt cold under her bare feet, and the patterns—so colorful and intricate during the daylight—looked like crawling snakes and insects. Light from the full moon streamed through the high windows at the corridor's end, painting the staircase in zebra-striped shadows. The pattern reminded Amber of the bars of a cage.

Her windows back home had bars on them. She didn't like that; it was the only part of home that she didn't like. Her parents said the bars were to keep bad people out, but Amber didn't believe that. They were to keep her in—like a precious bird in a large and lovely cage.

Her parents had lied to her about England, too. They'd said this would be a fun family time. "Don't worry, sweetie," her mom had told her. "You'll love it," her dad agreed. They'd been wrong, though. England was just a bigger, noisier cage.

Amber crept down the stairs and through the darkened hallway to the door of the study. Brilliant light blazed from within the room. The crystal chandeliers glittered, and a small fire—to ward off the chill of the summer evening—crackled in the fireplace. Amber paused at the doorway, caught between fear and the desire to end it. The big double doors were cracked open—none of the manor doors shut correctly—and inside, her parents were shouting.

"For Christ's sake, Gwen . . . !" her father's voice boomed. "What more do you want from me? We have the biggest house in Travis County. We have a swimming pool. We have a Lexus, a Jaguar, and a BMW convertible. We pay more in taxes than most of our friends make in a year, and your wardrobe allowance could feed a small country. Plus, I've spent a fortune on this vacation. How on God's green earth is that not enough?''

Amber peeked through the crack in the doors. Inside the big room, her father paced angrily, furiously puffing on his cigarette. Her mother stood stock still in the center of the room, her fists clenched at her sides, her face pale, her eyes dewy.

"A little compassion might be nice," her mother hissed. "Or maybe some actual *understanding*. I'm not one of your possessions, Shawn. I have a good job, too, and I make a good salary. Maybe I don't earn as much as you do, but I contribute plenty to my so-called 'wardrobe allowance.' I've paid for a few of your midlife-crisismobiles, too.''

Her father glared. For a moment, Amber feared he might hit her mother, but then he turned his back to her.

"Don't turn away, dammit!" her mother snarled. "Listen to me!" She stepped forward, reached toward his shoulder. Then she changed her mind, stopped, and backed away.

"I am listening, Gwendolyn!" He kept his back to her, kept smoking. "I've been doing nothing but listening ever since we came to this absurdly expensive place.''

"The hell you have! You're still off in your own world, worried about finances and promotions and God knows what else. I don't know why I thought this vacation would make any difference, because, clearly, it hasn't!''

"You got that right," he snapped. "We travel five thousand miles, and still it's the same old thing: nag nag nag, bitch bitch bitch.''

"Are you calling me a bitch?''

Amber didn't know what that word meant, but her mother's face turned red with fury.

Her father almost smiled. "If the shoe fits."

"Bastard!" Her mother hurled the word like a rock.

Her father turned, slowly, and flicked the smoldering remains of his cigarette at her mother. The butt struck the neckline of her mom's blouse, just above the breast, and tumbled to the floor, trailing sparks.

Her mother's mouth formed a silent, shocked O, and she stared at her husband for a moment. Then tears welled in her eyes, and she cried, "I wish to God we'd never come to England!"

Her father blew a long trail of smoke and lit another cigarette. "We can stop in Haiti and get a divorce on the way home."

Amber felt as if someone had hit her hard in the chest. *Divorce!*

Her mother remained frozen, fists clenched at her sides. "If only it were that easy," she muttered.

Her father chuckled nastily. "Easy?" he hissed back. "You think it's been easy putting up with your whining for the last few years? Getting divorced *has* to be easier than that. Besides, what's the big deal? We've already got his and hers property: my work, your work; my car, your car; my wardrobe, *your* wardrobe. You have your life, I have mine. How hard can divorce be? Everybody does it."

Tears streamed down her mother's face. Her voice was barely a whisper. "What about Amber?"

"Grow up, Gwen. Parents get divorced all the time."

"Not *us*."

"Yes, us. Of course, us. Who the hell else are we talking about?"

"Keep your voice down." Her mother smeared the tears from her cheeks with the back of her hand. "You'll wake her."

Her father laughed, a short hurtful burst. "She's slept through louder fights than this."

Amber pressed herself back against the wall, out of the light.

Divorce.

She understood what that meant. She had friends back home whose parents were divorced. Divorce meant that you moved from one house to another— shared like a doll at a daycare center.

Amber knew what divorce felt like, too. She'd seen the sadness in the eyes of her friends. Some pretended to be happy. They told her about all the toys they got—a new present every time they switched homes, it seemed like.

Every time.

Switched homes.

Her friends weren't fooling her. The presents didn't matter. They weren't happy; they were never happy.

And she wouldn't be happy either. No happier than she was now. Their family was broken.

Amber wanted to rush inside the study. She wanted to tell her parents to stop yelling. She wanted to tell them not to get divorced. But despite Winston's warm furry paw clutched tightly in her hand, she couldn't find the courage.

Her parents didn't want to be a family any more. They didn't want each other, and they didn't want her, either. She would never be able to stop their shouting. Even the divorce probably wouldn't stop that. She'd watched divorced parents at the daycare center— watched them carefully, as though they were strange animals at the zoo. They never came to pick up their kids together, and if they met accidentally, they usually looked angry. Sometimes they shouted.

Clutching Winston close to her breast, Amber backed away from the study doorway. At the far end of the corridor, moonlight shone through the glass-paned front door. In the glade beyond, blue fireflies danced in the summer night. It looked so lovely outside.

Her father continued his rant. "Besides," he said, "what does it matter if I wake her? What if she *does* hear, Gwen?"

The fury in his voice stabbed at Amber. The anger seemed directed at *her*. She remembered the sadness in her friends' eyes at the daycare center. Suddenly, she understood something new—her friends were part of the problem. Parents got divorced because of their *children*.

"Amber isn't stupid, Shawn," her mother hissed. "I'm sure she knows we're *this far* away from divorce."

Far away.

That's where Amber wanted to be. Maybe if she were far away, her parents would stop fighting.

The moonlit doorway beckoned. Outside, merry shadows whirled across the lawn.

Amber dashed across the hall and out the door. The echoes of her parents' angry voices chased her out into the night.

The cool air raised goose bumps on her pale skin. The dew-soaked lawn felt chilly beneath her bare feet.

"Be brave, Winston," Amber whispered, hugging the bear tight. Behind her, the many-paned windows of the manor house glowed merrily in the darkness— almost begging her to return.

It was a trap, though. She knew that. The house was a pretty cage in the larger cage of England. Every house would be a cage as long as her parents continued fighting. That was why she had to go. If she went away, maybe they would stop.

A great forest lay beyond the manor's carefully manicured lawn. The woods silently patrolled the edge of the grass, as if awaiting permission to move closer to the house. By day, the forest was a bright green place, filled with tall trees, soft moss, and gentle ferns. The moonlight made the woodland dark and foreboding, though fireflies still flitted among the shadowed bows. To Amber, the lightning bugs looked like friendly lanterns beckoning her onward.

The forest was the only part of England that Amber liked. Playing in the woods got her out of the house, and she knew the landscape well. Surely the forest had to be the same at night.

"Nothing to be scared of," she told Winston as they ducked into the trees. "We'll just find a quiet place to rest a while."

The forest floor wasn't as soft under her feet as the grass had been, and the leaves and twigs seemed even wetter and colder. Amber wished that she had brought her shoes, or even her slippers, but it was too late now. She didn't want to go back. This was the first night in weeks that she couldn't hear the yelling; she had to keep going.

Despite her brave words to Winston, the nighttime forest seemed strange and menacing. Frightening shadows flitted beneath the dark boughs. As she stumbled further into the woods, it became harder to see—especially when, one by one, the fireflies flickered out. Soon only a single bug remained, its blue light dancing into the distance.

Amber wanted to call to the insect, wanted to ask it to wait, but she knew it was useless. Fireflies couldn't understand human talk.

Amber's lips trembled at the idea of being alone in the darkness. She clutched Winston tight and kept going. Fingerlike branches clawed at her nightgown as the last firefly vanished into the foliage. As the bug disappeared, darkness closed in around her.

"Don't worry. I know where we are," Amber told the bear, but that was only for his benefit. She *didn't* know where they were. The forest looked very different in the night, and she felt completely lost.

She stumbled, skinned her knee, got up and looked around, trying to regain her bearings. Returning home was starting to seem like a good idea, despite the shouting. Unfortunately, she was no longer sure in which direction the manor house lay.

"Help!" she gasped, though she knew there was no one to hear. Even if she yelled as loudly as she could, her parents' own shouting would drown out her cries.

"I will keep walking," she told Winston as they went. "I will keep walking until I recognize something and figure out where we are." She didn't want to scare Winston by crying, but tears streamed down her face nonetheless. Perhaps running away hadn't been such a good idea after all.

A branch snagged Amber's nightgown, jerking her to a sudden halt. With a great heave, she pulled the fabric free, but the action sent her tumbling. She rolled downhill over twigs and bracken before finally thudding to a halt beside a small pool. She looked around, disoriented. Winston lay sprawled on the damp ground next to her. Amber picked him up, hugged him, and began to cry in earnest. The moonlight streaming through an opening in the canopy set her teardrops sparkling.

Amber smeared the tears from her face with the back of her hand—a motion she'd seen her mother repeat many times. The six-year-old looked at the pool; it was clear and beautiful in the silvery light. She leaned down, cupped her hands, and splashed the chilly water on her face. Her reflection gazed sadly back at her. Then something moved in the tree branches overhead.

"H-hello!" Amber gasped, frightened.

"Hullo," replied an unfamiliar voice.

Amber looked up and saw the face of a boy not

much older than she was. He was sitting in the bough of a tree, smiling. A leafy tunic covered his pale body and a tiny blue firefly circled around his head. He looked just like the imaginary boy Amber had seen at her window.

"My name's Pan," the boy said jovially, "but you can call me Perry—all my friends do. What's your name?"

"A-Amber."

Perry hopped off his tree branch, drifting lazily to the ground. The firefly continued circling him, as though it were some kind of trained pet.

Amber clutched Winston to her chest, hoping he might protect her. She kept her eyes fixed on the boy. Perry seemed friendly, but there was something strange about him—and not just the fact that he was wearing leaves for clothing.

"Amber . . ." Perry said, grinning, "a precious gem if ever there was. Did your parents name you that?"

"I guess."

"Then they must treasure you very much."

The words hurt. "I . . . They're always fighting."

Perry cocked his head, like a bird examining a bug. "I'm stunned to hear that," he said. "Stunned . . . and sorry." To Amber he didn't look either stunned *or* sorry; he looked full of mischief.

"Where's your home, Amber?"

For an instant, her eyes sought the manor home. Then she remembered herself and said, " 'Merica."

The strange boy nodded. "A long way off, then," he said. "A far, strange country there, and a far strange country here. Are you lost, Amber my jewel? I have a shadow that gets lost sometimes. Right now, for instance." He looked down at his feet, and Amber noticed for the first time that Perry had no shadow.

She checked her own feet; the moonlight made her shadow stand out plainly atop the cold moss. Could this be some kind of trick? She looked back at Perry and, sure enough, his feet rested on the ground with not a trace of darkness beneath them. It was almost as if he wasn't really there at all.

"Belle and me were just looking for my shadow, in fact, when we ran into you," Perry said. "You haven't seen it, have you, Amber Amber bright as gems?" The blue firefly circled Perry's head twice and then zipped into the woods nearby.

"How can you lose a shadow?" Amber asked, curious. The boy seemed less frightening now, despite his lack of shadow. Amber had lost a few things during her life—she'd lost her mother's keys once—but she'd never heard of anyone losing a shadow.

"I'm not sure," Perry said, "but it seems to get away from me most every full moon."

In the woods nearby, the firefly glowed more brightly. In the glow, Amber thought she saw a struggling figure—a shadow! A shadow moving on its own!

She pointed. "P-Perry!"

As Perry turned, a tall, slender woman stepped from the woods. She was very pale and nearly naked. Scraps of translucent cloth, not quite rags but not clothing in the traditional sense, covered her body. Her flowing silver hair cascaded down over her smooth shoulders, and a crown of white flowers adorned her forehead. A soft blue glow surrounded the woman's entire body. In her slender hands, she held a struggling figure.

The figure looked almost like a boy. But it wasn't a boy; it was flat—or nearly flat anyway—like a long scrap of black cloth that you could almost see through.

"Who's that?" Amber asked, gaping at the woman. She'd never seen anyone quite so beautiful in her life. Yet, there was something frightening about the woman, too. The dark, thrashing figure was scary as well.

Perry leaned close to Amber, as though he feared

someone might overhear him. "Who? Her? That's just my friend Belle," he said. "You saw her before."

"Did not!"

"Sure you did, unless you're blind! Belle goes everywhere with me. She was circlin' 'round my head when we first met."

"That was a firefly," Amber said, worried. Perry seemed very strange once again. Could he be crazy? "Can't you tell the difference between a woman and a firefly?" she asked.

"Can't you tell the difference between a firefly and a faerie?" Perry replied. "That was Belle. And, look! She's found my shadow!"

The glowing woman held out the struggling transparent figure, and Perry took it by the shoulders. He held it in front of him, like someone trying on new clothes. The shadow struggled.

"I s'pose we could sew it back on," Perry mused. "Got any thread, Amber?"

Amber shook her head; the whole idea of a shadow that could run away scared her. And it definitely didn't like being caught. She wondered if Perry and Belle ever shouted at the shadow. Was that why it had run away?

"Ah, well," Perry said cheerfully. "If you've got no thread, I'll just have to stuff it in my pocket, then."

Amber didn't see how the shadow, which was even taller and more grown-up looking than Perry, could fit in his pocket, but Perry didn't seem to notice this problem. The shadow wiggled and flailed—clearly not wanting to go—as the strange boy balled it up. In just a few moments, Perry had the entire thing tucked away within a pouch in his leafy coat.

Belle, the faerie, watched impassively, as though the struggle between boy and man-sized shadow were the most natural thing in the world.

Amber couldn't help but gawk. "What will you do with it?" she asked.

"Sew it on when I get home, I suppose," Perry replied.

"You have a home?"

"Of course I do, Amber bright and sparkling!" he cried merrily. "Doesn't everyone?"

Amber said nothing. The ache in her chest returned, and she clutched Winston closer. Her legs gave out, and she sat down on a nearby log. Belle came and stood over her, smiling, shining as brightly as the moon. Looking at the lovely, glowing woman, Amber felt dizzy.

"How can a lady be a firefly?"

Perry grinned. "She's my faerie may, found me when I run away. Sometimes she's big, sometimes she's small, sometimes you can't see her at all. But she's always with me. Always always and a day, ever since I run away."

The dizzy sensation was making Amber feel very tired. Had the world always been this confusing? She rubbed her eyes. "I ran away, too," she said wearily. "My parents were being bad."

"I know how that goes," Perry said, dancing lightly around the glade. "Parents are a mean lot, always scolding, always telling you what you can and *can't* do. Are they frightful mean to you, Amber?"

"I don't think they mean to be," she said, stifling a yawn. "But they do yell an awful lot."

"I wouldn't put up with parents yelling at me," Perry said. "Never have, never will."

"Oh, no," Amber replied. "They don't yell at me. Not lately, anyway. Mostly they just shout at each other." She sighed and lay down on the log, putting Winston under her head as a pillow. "It's my fault, though."

Perry took her hand. His fingers felt warm and soft.

"I thought maybe they'd stop when I ran away," Amber said, yawning in earnest.

Belle came and stood behind Perry. She gazed down on the boy and the lost child like a loving mother. For a moment, the faerie's face appeared almost human. Perry looked at Amber, too, and he smiled. "Don't worry," he said. "You're not lost any more, Amber my gem. I've found you now."

Amber smiled back.

Perry's voice dropped to a whisper. "I know a place," he said, "where there are no grown-ups, and you can do whatever you like, for however long you like. There's good food and good faerie friends and— the best part of all—no one to yell at you."

"No yelling?"

"Nope."

"Not ever?"

Perry grinned. "Not ever, except in fun. It's fun forever, and you never, ever get old. Want to go with me, precious Amber?"

"If I go, will my parents be happy? Will they stop yelling?"

"I promise," Perry said, "you'll never hear them yell ever again."

Amber nodded. " 'Kay. I'll go."

Gently, the strange boy pulled her to her feet.

Belle extended her hand to Perry. In her palm, she held a fine powder that glittered like stardust.

"Faerie dust to help you fly," Perry explained.

He took the dust and sprinkled it over Amber. As he did, Belle shrank down smaller and smaller until she was only the size of a firefly again. She flitted into the sky, circling Perry and Amber, dancing in the cool night air.

Gentle laughter echoed in Amber's ears. Then she was light as a cloud and happier than she'd been in ages. She no longer felt cold, or worried, or lonely. Her dress wasn't damp, and her limbs didn't feel tired and sore. She couldn't feel the warmth of Winston's fur in her hand, either—but that hardly mattered any more.

The stars shone brightly in the sky overhead; Perry's eyes twinkled in the moonlight.

As soft as a summer wind, Amber's glowing form lifted into the air. Perry held her hand lightly, guiding her, urging her on. Far below them, the manor house glowed bright and warm, but Amber heard no shouting.

She smiled.

Belle flew circles around the young girl and the strange boy as they flew off together, setting course for the nearest star.

Gwendolyn and Shawn didn't notice that Amber was missing until breakfast the next morning, and by then the happy child was long, long gone. Her parents searched the house frantically until the authorities arrived.

Shortly after moonrise, the police located Amber's body. They found her lying on a tree trunk in a small glade next to a clear pool, her head resting serenely on a stuffed teddy bear.

In the space on the police report marked "cause of death," the coroner wrote "exposure." It was the best he could come up with. He found no good explanation for the demise of a healthy young girl on a fine summer's night in the English countryside. In his experience, under such conditions, it usually took lost children much longer to perish.

Nor could he explain the strange, contented smile on Amber's face—a smile that not even the best mortician in the county could wipe away.

RAPUNZEL STRIKES BACK

Brendan DuBois

Brendan DuBois is the award-winning author of eleven novels and nearly 100 short stories. His short fiction has appeared in *Playboy*, *Ellery Queen's Mystery Magazine*, *Alfred Hitchcock's Mystery Magazine*, and numerous other magazines and anthologies, including *The Best American Mystery Stories of the Century*, published in 2000. He lives in New Hampshire with his wife Mona, a hell-raising cat named Roscoe, and a ball-chasing English Springer Spaniel named Tucker. Visit his website at *www.BrendanDuBois.com*.

So there I was, cooped up in my tiny third-floor bedroom, trying to get through my advanced algebra homework, when my brother knocked on the door and opened it. Creep. He never bothers to wait, never bothers to call out to see if I'm decent or not. No, my older worm brother gave the one-knock signal—as if he's doing me a favor or something—and then strode in, like the perv wanted to catch a glimpse or something.

Like dozens of times before, Alan had a Shaw's

grocery paper bag in his hands, folded twice at the top. He put it on my dresser, which is by my bedroom's sole window. Alan turned and gave me a smirk.

"It's ten o'clock, Patti," he said. "Lights out."

"Not done with my homework," I said.

"Too bad." He walked over and flicked off the light, leaving me in the dark, save for the light coming in from the hallway. "You know the house rules. Lights out by ten."

"My homework is due—"

"Then get up earlier and do it," he said. "And remember. Tomorrow night. It's going to be very important."

My voice rose some. "How can I forget? That's all you been talking about, all week."

"So remember some more. It's on for tomorrow night."

Then he closed the door, leaving me in darkness.

Okay, so not total darkness. Outside light from streetlights and other buildings came through the window, which gave me a bit of illumination, but not much. So I sat there and waited and waited, as I'm supposed to do, and stared at my desk and open books. My advanced algebra homework.

My brother was preventing me from finishing it, a young man who probably couldn't spell algebra if you spotted him an "a" and a "g."

Other young ladies in my position would have gone to Mother and Father to complain, which would have been nice, except in my case, Father is dead and Mother is on "vacation" in Florida with a long-distance trucker she met two years ago.

And other young ladies would have gotten undressed in the dark, and would have gone to bed.

But I'm not like other young ladies.

I waited.

I saw a tiny red dot of light appear on my ceiling, near the window.

Sighed.

Time to get to work.

I got up from my chair, went over to the window, and slid it open with a bit of work. It's an old apartment house built around the turn of the century—not this century, the last one—and the window was heavy and made a creaking noise as I lifted it. I leaned out into the cool spring air and looked down, my long red hair cascading about my shoulders.

The view from my window looked over a narrow alley in this part of the west side of Manchester, the biggest city in New Hampshire—and this particular neighborhood was the meanest. Not mean like some streets in L.A. or Chicago or New York City, but for me and the others who lived here, it was rough enough.

I looked down the three stories to the two young men down there looking at up me, one of them holding one of those hand-held laser pointers in his grubby hand.

One whispered, "Hey, hon, is the store open?"

The other said, louder, "Sure, baby, show us your wares. C'mon."

I kept my mouth shut and went back into my room. From underneath my window I pulled out a length of thin rope attached to a straw basket. I lowered the basket down to the level of the two young men, felt tugging on the rope as they played with it for a moment, and then I hauled the basket back up.

In the basket was a square piece of white cardboard. I held it, and with the help of a nearby streetlight, I saw the numeral "4" written there in my older brother's handwriting. I went back to the grocery bag, opened it up, and after a bit of trial and error, picked out a plastic-wrapped package, about the size of a cigarette pack and with the same number written on its side. I put the package in the basket, lowered it back to the waiting customers—or low-life druggies, depending on your point of view—and made the transaction.

The first of several that night, one after another, me being prompted by the laser red dot of light on the ceiling, some of the guys down there giggling and chortling at me, one calling out, "Hey, babe, your hair gets long enough, I'd love to climb up on it and give you some lovin'."

A long night supplying illegal substances to my alleged neighbors. Somehow, I didn't think Mister Burke, my advanced algebra teacher, would buy that for an excuse for not getting my homework done.

When midnight came and went, I leaned out the window for one last look at my neighborhood. The buildings around me were tenements built more than a hundred years ago for the French-Canadian immigrants who came in to work at the famed mills on the Amoskeag River. When the mills collapsed and the work went to the South and then to Africa, the brick buildings of the mills were rebuilt into upper-priced condos and art galleries.

But the immigrant housing didn't have such luck. It was bought up cheap by out-of-town landlords who did the very minimum upkeep, charged as much rent as they could, and pretty much ignored their tenants. From where I looked out, the alleyway was narrow, with clotheslines spanning the gulf. There were lights on and loud music and the smell of wet trash, and a block or two away, the warbling of a police siren. I glanced up into the night sky, but I only saw the orange glow of streetlights.

I held onto the edge of the window sill. In a way,

my brother Alan and were immigrants here. Just a few years earlier, the four of us lived in a small farm in a forgotten town up by the Canadian border, where the stars were so very bright at night, and the silence in the darkness was so loud it could keep you awake. Father loved his little farm, loved hunting and fishing and trapping in the mountainous woods nearby. Mother had no interest in spending time with Father and neither did Alan, but there were plenty of times when I went along with Father as he stalked deer or turkey, or cast a line into one of the streams, or set his traplines for muskrat and mink.

I had loved this life, as only a young girl could, until one wintry day when Father was working a trapline and got caught on an underwater snag and drowned during the long night.

My Father, my hero, my king, dead . . . and here I was, marooned and imprisoned in this third-floor walkup, dependent on my stupid brother for the rent and everything else, with no prince in view to save me.

I closed the window and went to bed.

So I got up early and did my homework and went to school. No big deal. Just an average-looking gal in an overcrowded and underfunded high school. As the day progressed, I got nabbed in the hallway by one of our guidance counselors, Mrs. Hanratty. She was in her late fifties, dressed for her age, and didn't pretend to be our best bud. She took hold of my elbow and pulled me to the entrance to her office and got right to the point.

"There's a half dozen college applications waiting for you, Patti," she said. "When are you going to come by and go over them with me?"

I clenched my textbooks tighter against my hip. "Soon, Mrs. Hanratty, real soon."

She shook her head. "The deadlines won't wait, you know that. What's the matter, Patti?"

I shifted the textbooks from one hip to the other. She said, "If it's money . . . Patti, with your grades and background, you'll be a cinch to pull in some hefty scholarships. That won't be a problem. So—"

I kept quiet.

"Patti . . . so what's the problem?"

I pulled away from the office door. "Sorry, Mrs. Hanratty, I'm going to be late for biology. Later, okay?"

Once Father had been buried, Mother started drinking more and more heavily. On the nights without Father bustling around, talking about the farm, about the gossip in town, about his latest scheme to make some money to fix the roof or shore up the far barn, she would sit and just stare into space. So when an uncle offered her a job working as a waitress in a diner outside of Manchester, we three left the farm and moved south. Uncle Jack got us this crappy apartment, and for a while it seemed to work. Alan got a job at a local dealership, washing cars and doing light mechanic work, while Mother did okay at that waitressing job, and I tried to fit in at a high school where the freshman class—of which I was a terrified member—had three times as many students as the entire population of my little regional high school back home.

We adjusted, hung in there, until Uncle Jack's job sent him to Washington, and then Mother started drinking again, and Alan decided a life of crime was more interesting and lucrative than washing muddy minivans.

Mother didn't know a thing, but I picked up on it after a couple of weeks, when I noticed that Alan no longer had oil stains on his hands or dirty fingernails and that he had a new gold chain around his neck. So after dinner and dishes one night, I asked him in the hallway outside of our bedrooms, "What are you up to?"

"What's that, Patti?"

I said, "Nice gold chain, no more visible dirt, what are you up to now?"

He smirked—one of his favorite expressions, as if he were putting something over you—and said, "Amateur pharmaceuticals. How does that sound?"

"You better not get caught, and you better be sure Mom doesn't find out."

Alan said, "Mom's working on her own amateur drug status, or haven't you been seeing the empty Smirnoff Ices in the trash?"

"Leave Mom out of it. And Dad—"

"Dad," Alan snorted. "Just a dumb hick who—"

I grabbed his wrist and said, "Don't you dare—"

And he slapped me, hard, and I fell to the floor. "Sister, you keep your mouth shut. All right? Just keep your mouth shut."

And that was the first time he had slugged me in a long while, and it wasn't going to be the last.

From the bus stop to our tenement building was a three-block walk, and I kept my head down and did just that. There were pawnshops and tiny grocery stores and bodegas, and New Hampshire may have this image of a white-snow state with white church steeples and white people, but there were minorities here, and they tended to cluster in cities like Manchester. In that three block walk, I heard Spanish and Portugese and Cambodian. The streets were a mess, and the sidewalks were cracked and buckling, and as I reached the steps of our tenement building—a type of three-story building known down in Boston as Irish battleships—a couple of guys sitting around the stoop whistled and said, "See ya tonight, babe, see you tonight. You get that long hair ready for us, okay? Mmmmm."

I felt the flush of anger and embarrassment, and ran upstairs to the apartment.

One night, Mother didn't come home from work, and I didn't worry that much, knowing with a queasy sense of shame that Mother still had needs and desires. But then one night went into two, and then three, and on the fourth day when I came home, Alan was going through the refrigerator and said, "She's gone."

"I know that." I dumped my books on the kitchen table, a round table that I hated because none of the legs were even, meaning it always tipped when you sat at it.

Head still in the refrigerator, Alan said, "No, dummy, I mean she's really gone. I went to the diner today and she left a note for us. Seems she met up with a trucker named Gus or George or something like that—you know how her handwriting sucks—and she's on her way to Florida. For a vacation."

Something cold clutched at my heart. "For how long?"

"How the hell should I know? What am I, her friggin' travel agent?" He stepped away from the refrigerator. "Hey, I'm getting hungry. Get supper going."

"Get it yourself," I snapped, and then he came over to me, and I found myself on the floor, ears ringing. He looked down, breathing hard, and said, "With her gone, bitch, I'm in charge. And if you don't like it, get the hell out. But I'm going to be paying the rent and utilities and the groceries for this crappy slice of heaven, and you're going to do your part, understand?"

I slowly nodded my head and put a few fingers to my sore lips. Sure, I understood.

In the apartment I was glad that Alan wasn't home, for it gave me a little time for myself. I made myself some toast and a glass of orange juice and watched TV for a while; I had that dull ache of jealousy that practically every one of my classmates had not only their own home computer but also a cellphone, and I had neither. And when friendships and alliances in school were made by e-mail and by texting your classmates, and you didn't have the tools to participate, you were left behind.

Yeah, left behind. I thought about what Mrs. Hanratty had said earlier, and I knew I had to do something to get out of here. The tantalizing hint of going far away to college, where the bills would be paid . . . it sometimes made me crazy with desire.

Yeah. Crazy. My brother Alan had clearly and forcefully told me with his words and fists that college wasn't in my plans, that I was now in partnership with him, and there was nothing else I was going to do except work for him.

I thought about what Mrs. Hanratty would say to that, that I was a prisoner in my home—and someone's home being a castle, so I guess I was a prisoner in a castle, hah-hah-hah—and that my psycho older brother said he would break my bones if I ever tried to leave him, and that I had no choice to believe him, because I had seen what he could do.

I got up, turned the television off, and then went to do my homework, though a cheerful little voice inside of me asked, what's the point? What's the point of good grades, when Alan wouldn't let you free?

Good question, and I told the little voice to shut the bleep up.

*   *   *

A year after Mother had departed, Alan brought me out to the hallway connecting the other two third floor apartments and said, "Lookee here."

"Here" being a small door at the end of one of the hallways, which was now open. I followed Alan up a very steep set of stairs and then into a cold and damp attic with exposed beams and uneven floorboards. At the end of the attic was a wide bench, and on the bench were a couple of hotplates, some glassware, and bags and other stuff.

"What do you think?" he asked.

"Not sure what to think," I said. "What the hell is it?"

"My own little production facility, that's what. You take some drug store meds, some other chemicals, and follow the right instructions . . . pure crystal cash, Patti, pure crystal cash."

I stared in disbelief at what he had done. "A drug lab . . . here? Are you out of your mind?"

"Not at all. This is a wide-open market in this part of town, and with the right product, I'll do just fine, thank you very much."

"How did you get up here in the attic?"

"Broke the door open, put in a new lock."

"And you don't think the landlord will notice?"

He laughed. "Oh, that's nice, Patti. What the hell, you think we're living on Park Avenue or something? When did you tell the landlord about the leaky toilet, and how long has it taken him to fix it?"

"Hasn't been fixed yet, you know that," I said.

"My point, Patti. They don't care, they've never cared, and I found a place to set up a little production line."

I turned to him. "I don't like it."

He leaned into me, close enough that I could smell his breath. "Tough. You don't like it? Then move out. Or quit school and get a job and pay your share of the rent and the groceries. I'm supporting the two of us, Patti, and a little goddamn appreciation would be nice."

I held out my hand. "You want me to appreciate this? A drug lab over our heads?"

He pushed by me, heading down the steep stairs. "Fine. Be all pure and holy. But I know you, sister. You're gonna stay and live off what I can do, and that's just fine. If not, well, go up to the diner where mom used to work. I bet they're still looking for a waitress."

In the small kitchen I spotted the two faded post-cards from Florida that we had gotten from Mother, both more than a year old. In each she just said she was having fun with a man whose name began with G—Gus or George, neither Alan nor I could figure out the scrawl—and looking at those faded postcards just made me choke up some.

And to take the mood further, I guess, I went into Mother's bedroom, which we'd both left pretty much alone. Alan uses it as a place to dump junk and old shoes and torn clothes. I opened the closet and bur-rowed my way past some of Mother's belongings until I reached a big green torn trash bag shoved into a corner.

I sat and opened up the bag, and inside was the last of Father's stuff. Some old shirts and trousers and his dull khaki leather coat. I pulled the coat up and brought it to my face and smelled the old scent, and then the tears really started to flow. The old musky smell just brought back all the memories of being out with Father in the woods, in both daylight and in the dark, and I remembered all the times I'd be asleep in my bed and there'd be a gentle little tug on my foot, and Father would lean over and whisper, "Wake up, princess. Your king wants to take you on an adventure," and that would always make me laugh, and I'd roll over and pretend to be asleep until I gave in and got up and went out with him.

Oh, some of my friends back then couldn't believe that I would get out of a nice warm bed and go out in the cold air with Father, but they didn't understand that it was our time alone, just the two of us, and he took such pride in teaching me how to shoot, how to set traps, and how to read the sky and the stars.

Once, out in the woods in late November, a snow squall came up suddenly, making us stand nearly still in white-out conditions. I was scared, but Father quietly and quickly got to work, made us a lean-to shelter out of boughs and branches, and built a fire. He made a bough bed as well, and we cuddled in the shelter, out of the wind, watching the snow fall and feeding the fire.

And Father had said, "Remember this, Patti. We're better than those flatlanders down south. They lose power, they panic after half a day 'cause they can't see their television or play with their computers. They lose power for a week, and they'll be fighting in the streets over a loaf of bread. Up here, we lose power that long, it'd be rough, but we'd make it."

He tossed a length of dead pine onto the fire, as the white flakes battled their way down to the ground. "That's because we take care of ourselves. Don't rely on anybody else. You remember that, honey, and you'll go far."

I held the coat closer again to my face, willing the tears to stop. Then I put the coat back into the bag, felt around, found Father's shaving kit, some medals and patches from when he was in the Army, some of his smaller traps and traplines, his favorite pipe, and a couple of other odds and ends. Missing, of course, were his good rifles and shotguns. Father's idiot son had pawned them years ago to buy God knows what.

I closed the bag, thought some, and then left the room.

One evening, soon after he got his drug lab up and running, Alan came to me and said, "You know what the biggest problem is for guys like me?"

I was looking through the day's *New York Times* to prepare for a current events quiz in my sociology class tomorrow. "Good grooming skills?"

"Hah, Patti, very funny." He sat at the kitchen table and put his elbows on it, which caused it to shift and make me drag my red pen across the page. If he noticed that he was ticking me off, he was keeping it to himself.

"The problem is marketing, Patti. Getting customers to buy what you want without getting nailed by the cops or the State Police drug task force or anyone else. You start getting a rep, you start getting known, and then you get watched. You get followed. And if you're seen passing over little packages in exchange for cash, you'll get your ass busted for possession. And possession with intent to distribute is another pretty way of saying getting some additional serious jail time."

I folded the newspaper. "So my smart drug dealer older brother has come up with a plan."

That famous smirk made its reappearance. "That's right. Look at this."

From his coat pocket he took out some square pieces of cardboard. On each square was written a numeral, from one to ten.

I looked at him and said, "What? You have problems getting your shoes off to figure out how to write above ten?"

His face colored. "Lucky for you I'm in a good mood, Patti, or your ears would be ringing. Now listen up. This is important."

He stabbed a finger at the white card marked with

the numeral three. "Let's say I'm hanging out at the mall one day, okay? And some guy I know comes by and sits with me on a bench, and we talk about the Red Sox and shit, and he says, well, you selling today? And I say, yeah, and he says, how much? And I say, fifty bucks. And if that's agreeable, we talk some more, and he leaves and goes to a store in the mall— like one of those clothing stores—and I follow him a bit, and he drops off an envelope with the cash in it, okay? Maybe in the dressing room or something. So I pick up the money. No big deal. Some cop rousts me, I just make all innocent like and say, so what? I found this cash. No name. No ID. Finders keepers, right? You following me?"

"Sure," I said. "It's fascinating."

"Good, glad to hear it." And my brother went on, his sarcasm detector obviously off the for the day. "Then it's my customer's turn. He follows me, and maybe by a trash can or something, I toss in some trash from a breakfast burrito or something, and at the edge of the trash can, I leave this number one. That's his claim ticket. Got it?"

I stifled a yawn. "Oh, yeah, I got it."

"Good," he said, "because this is where you come in, where it gets all neat and tidy."

I stopped yawning. "What do you mean, where I come in?"

He was really grinning now. "Got it all figured out. My stuff is in your bedroom, and at the right time, the guys use a flashlight or a laser pointer or something like that, and they get your attention. You open your window, you lower a basket or something, and they put the ticket in. You bring up the ticket, find the matching baggie, and lower it down. Boom. Transaction complete, and I'm blocks away, and if any cop is watching me, they see nothing. It's all done quietly in the rear alley, no fuss, no muss."

I stared at him, finding it hard to believe that this creature was my brother, was actually my own flesh and blood.

"No," I said.

"What?"

"No, I'm not going to do it. Don't even think about it."

His face colored some more, and he abruptly left the kitchen table, went out to the living room, and my heart thudded some, me thinking, well, at least I got away from that.

Then the television set came on, and Alan boosted and boosted the volume, and I realized what he was doing and tried to make it to the door leading outside, but he grabbed me before I got there.

And about a half hour later I agreed to do anything he wanted, and I stayed home from school the next two days, humiliated at how my face looked.

Dinner was by myself—which was fine, some carrot sticks and corn beef hash out of the can—and then Alan let himself in and grinned and said, "The night of nights, Patti. This is gonna be great."

I was drying the dishes by the sink. "I still don't see the big deal."

"Deal? Deal?" Alan went to the refrigerator, opened it, and took out a can of Budweiser, which he popped open. "Here's the deal, you moron. There's this guy, Duff Horton, who's connected with some activity up on the northern blocks. He's heard of my little deal and little production facility, and he wants to do some investing. So tonight, he's gonna sample my wares."

"Lucky him," I said, putting the chipped plate back in the cupboard.

Alan took a long swallow of his beer. "No, honey, lucky me. He likes what he sees, how he scores, and this could mean something big. More business. More distribution. More of everything."

"And more police attention," I said. "Alan, look, you've been lucky so far. Why not do something different? Why not step away? Why keep on gambling like this?"

Another long swallow. "It's worked, so why should it change?"

I wiped my hands on the towel and threw it on the counter. "Because you never asked me, Alan, not ever . . . and I want out. I want to stop."

His eyes glinted at me. "Don't talk like that, Patti."

"I'm tired of being cooped up in here, tired of being your prisoner, tired of everything. How much longer, Alan? Huh? How much longer am I going to have to do this?"

Moving quick like a snake, he had his hand around my throat. "As long as I want, princess. And you want to know the truth? You're gonna do it tonight, and you're gonna do it right, with no fuss and muss. Remember, sweetie, you're part of this deal, and if the cops ever do arrest me, why, I think you might have put them up to it, and I'll give you up."

My breathing was getting raspy. Alan went on. "And if that doesn't get your attention, remember this. This guy, Duff Horton, doesn't take no for an answer. Got it? One time, I heard somebody made a move on Duff Horton's girl, and they found the guy's hands in a trashcan a month later. Nothin' else. Just the hands. So he's not a guy to dick around with."

I tried to move away from his grasp, but I couldn't. "So tonight, Patti, I'm gonna be right by Duff's side as he signals you and you lower the basket. Do it right, and we'll all make out. And don't screw it up, sister."

In the darkness I sat, waiting. On the bed was Father's old jacket. I had gone into Mother's bedroom for ideas and moral support. A few minutes ago, I had taken the jacket and had drawn in the scent again, remembering Father's firm but gentle ways. I'm sure he would be some pissed at Mother and at what Alan had done, but I also think he would have been disappointed at what I was doing. Or not doing.

Father would have expected more from his princess.

Something caught my eye. I looked up at the ceiling and there it was, the bright red dot of the laser pointer. It was a cold night, so I put on Father's old jacket as I went over to the window. I lifted up the window and heard voices down there, and I made out the shape of my brother and a large, hulking man that must have been Duff Horton, and a couple of others.

"Princess, princess, let down your wares," someone called out, and everyone laughed.

I ducked back in, got the heavy basket, gingerly lowered it down, looking closely, seeing it approach, even noticing the eager way Alan was holding himself, the basket going down, now at eye level, Duff Horton talking and reaching in and—

snap

Maybe it was my imagination, maybe not, but the next sound I heard was certainly loud enough, as Duff Horton screamed and took his hand out of the basket, one of Father's old leg-hold traps snapped tight around his hand. Duff Horton screamed and screamed, and then the other men were on top of my brother, and I dropped the thin rope.

And as I ran out of the apartment house, my few belongings safe in a knapsack, I thought of Father, and the tears came, but in the tears, too, was joy and pride.

His princess was free, and she had done it all by herself.

REVENGE OF THE LITTLE MATCH GIRL

Paul Genesse

At the ripe age of four, Paul Genesse decided he wanted to be a writer. It took him a few years before he started selling professionally, though. He loved his English classes in college, but he pursued his other passion by earning a bachelor's degree in nursing science in 1996. He is a registered nurse on a cardiac unit where he works the night shift, keeping the forces of darkness away from his patients. Paul lives with his incredibly supportive wife, Tammy, and their collection of frogs. He spends endless hours in his basement writing and is the author of several short stories featured in *Pirates of the Blue Kingdoms, Blue Kingdoms, Shades and Specters, Fellowship Fantastic, Furry Fantastic, The Dimension Next Door, Catopolis,* and *Imaginary Friends.* His first novel, *The Golden Cord, Book One of the Iron Dragon Series* was published in April of 2008. Visit Paul online at *www.paulgenesse.com.*

The girl shuddered as a gust of freezing wind blasted through the thin apron in which she carried her bundles of matches. Tall men in thick coats jostled past her in their rush to get home.

"Only a penny a bundle." She held up the matches as the men hurried along to see their families on this last evening of the year—New Year's Eve. Carriages raced home in the muddy streets. No one even gave her a second glance as her fair hair became white with snowflakes. She brushed the snow from her brow with fingers that had started to go numb, wishing dearly she owned a scarf or a bonnet.

After wandering in the cold for several more minutes, she took shelter beneath the awning of a shop; it would give her some small protection. Darkness would come soon, and she asked a man who came out of the doorway if he wanted to buy some matches.

"Get away from my shop, you filthy wretch." The merchant raised his fat fist to strike her, and she bolted into the muddy street. Her heavy clogs slowed her, as they had been her mother's and were twice the size of her tiny feet.

A carriage thundered toward her, the driver's uncaring eyes locked onto hers. He barreled ahead, and the little girl clumsily ran for the other side of the road. Another carriage came at her from the opposite direction. Horses' hooves pounded and sloshed through the mud as the wheels cut ominous furrows.

One of her clogs became stuck in the mud. The carriages continued toward her. She slipped out of the shoe and staggered through the frigid mud as fast as she could. The other clog fell off, and one of her bundles of matches slipped out of her apron and into the street as she dove onto the sidewalk.

One of the carriages ran over the matches and one of her shoes, pressing her lost items deep into the muddy street. She started to reach for the lone clog still above the surface when a boy with cruel eyes and a mocking grin snatched it up.

"Steal shoes that fit next time, you stupid little girl!" He scraped the mud off and flung it at her face. She could barely feel the sting on her numb cheeks. She wanted to tell him the shoe had belonged to her mother, but he wouldn't care. No one listened to her anyway.

The boy laughed and ran off down an alley, holding her clog high.

She sat on the sidewalk and scraped the cold mud from her feet and face. Her belly ached with hunger. Her toes had turned blue and throbbed with pain when she touched them.

She thought about going home, but she didn't dare. She had not sold any matches, and her father would beat her—as he did every time she came home without any pennies. Besides, their home was little warmer than the street. Wind whipped through the roof of the tiny attic where they lived, though rags and straw had been stuffed into the cracks. Living there had gotten worse, especially since grandmother had died. The frail old woman had been the only one who had ever shown the girl kindness.

The streets were starting to ice up now, stealing the last bit of warmth from the little girl as she picked her way forward. Light shone from every window, and she could hear voices raised in celebration of the new year. She lingered near one house, inhaling the scent of apple pie, until a man going inside shooed her away.

Darkness came quickly, and the little girl huddled between two houses farther down the street. She crouched and pulled her legs to her chest, trying to get her naked feet off the cold stone. Her hands were numb, and she thought a match would be such a comfort. It was good she had not lost all the bundles. She took a match and struck it against the wall—*scraaatch*! It crackled and blazed with light. The beautiful flame warmed her as if she were in front of a big iron stove. She loved watching the orange halo of light as it snapped and burned along the wood. The smell of faint smoke entered her nostrils and invigorated her fading senses.

But the small flame died quickly. She lit another, and the friendly light warmed her feet, but she knew it wouldn't last long. She needed to light a real fire if she was going to get truly warm. Her favorite thing was watching a fire in a hearth. That was the only time when she forgot about how truly alone she really was. The little girl looked for something to burn, but the alley was barren. It would be so easy for her to sit and light the rest of her matches, then let the cold take her.

Or she could get up and keep going. Endure the pain in her feet and find something to burn. She tiptoed through the layer of fresh snow, her feet feeling as if they were being poked with a hundred sharp nails with every step. The few people on the dark street pretended not to see her.

A shrill laugh caught her attention, and she saw the boy who had stolen her shoe duck into a rundown shack attached to an old stable. She crept toward it and peered through a hole in the wall. Five boys sat in a circle on a floor covered with moldy straw. Gold watches, wallets, embroidered handkerchiefs, and coins spilled across a dirty rug. They ogled the loot and congratulated each other, then the oldest boy handed each of the others a round pastry. They all tore hungrily into their meals as the oldest pickpocket counted the stolen loot. The boy with the cruel grin tossed her mother's clog on the fire. It began smoldering in the hearth as the boys ate and prodded the pile of items on the floor, recounting the details of their robberies.

The little girl watched her dead mother's shoe go up in smoke. Tears came to her eyes, and she felt as if the thieves were taking her mother away from her forever. It didn't matter that her mother had died when she was born. She felt as though she had known her mother through those shoes. Her mother was solid, strong, and through those shoes went with the little girl wherever she went.

Now the connection was gone.

The pain in her heart hurt worse than the pain in her blue feet. She was tired of being walked upon by everyone around her, and the thieving boy had destroyed what little comfort she had left. She had walked all over the city in those shoes.

The boy had taken her most valuable possession.

Oblivious to her spying, the boys sat warming themselves beside the fire and stuffed their faces with sweet bread. The little girl's stomach ached. She couldn't remember the last time she had eaten. It wasn't fair. Why should the mean boys be warm and fed when she was not?

Something burned within her and told her to take action.

She was done letting every person in the city walk all over her. Just because she was a poor little girl didn't make her any less important. Her grandmother had always told her that, but until this moment she didn't believe it. This would be her chance to prove her grandmother right. She would finally make sure people knew how special she really was.

She got out a match and crept toward the entrance to the shack. She struck it against the wall; for a moment she watched the flame, and then she slid it under the door. The straw on the floor caught fire, and she barely felt the pain in her feet as she ran to the other side of the shack and peered into a knothole.

The piles of straw caught fire at once. She stood warming herself and watching as the orange flames grew into a bonfire and climbed up the wooden walls.

The boys came running out the other side, cursing and coughing as the smoke rose into the sky. The fire spread, and she basked in the heat.

She stayed and watched the pain on their faces as their hideout and stolen plunder went up in flames. Now they would be on the street in the cold, just like her.

When a small crowd appeared, the little girl finally backed away from the flames and fled down an alley toward the main street. The girl found herself across from the shop where the merchant had raised his fist at her. In the darkness, she couldn't see any sign of her lost shoe still buried in the road. No carriages trundled down the empty street, so she crossed it, trying to stay on the frozen parts of the ground. But her bare feet were soon covered in icy mud. She made her way to the back of the shop, which had the façade of a house. She could see through the glass of a tall window where a great table had been laid out with a magnificent feast.

The smell of a roast goose and fresh baked bread wafted out, and she saw the fat merchant stuffing meat into his mouth. He licked his greasy fingers as the woman and three children around the table kept their heads down and their mouths shut. She reasoned that he used his fat fists against them as well. They all seemed miserable, even as they ate from fine porcelain plates on a clean tablecloth. One of the children pushed away his plate and crinkled his face. Did any of them even know how much they had when so many had nothing?

Her gaze lingered on the goose that had to be stuffed with plums and apples. She imagined it rising up from the table and dancing toward her. The little girl shook her head and noticed the pile of broken crates beside the house. They had been shielded by the roof and very little snow covered them. She lit a match and used a piece of her tattered dress for the tinder. The cold wood refused to burn, but she struck match after match until the crates started to smolder. She warmed her feet as the flames spread and the merchant's house caught fire at last.

The flames went up the wall, and in the glow of the light she imagined the tallest and most beautiful Christmas tree she had ever seen. Thousands of candles and ornaments adorned the branches. She sat staring at the beautiful tree and bathed herself in the heat. The candles on the tree rose high into the air and became stars. The brightest candle on the top of the tree turned into a shooting star that streaked across the heavens.

"Someone will die tonight," she whispered to herself, remembering when her grandmother told her that a shooting star was a soul going up to God.

Screams inside the house made her flinch. The stars and the tree disappeared. The fire had spread under the roof and smoke belched out of the eaves and the windows on the second floor. The fat merchant stumbled out of the doorway and his family followed. The little girl hid in the shadows and watched them as they stared in horror as the fire consumed the roof. Flames spread to the white tablecloth on their feast table and the merchant cursed God for his misfortune. If the man and his family only knew what misfortune really was.

The little girl wondered if they would appreciate what they once had now that it was gone. She scurried away on bare stone, as the snow around the house had melted from the heat. The warmth in her feet soon faded, and she wished for the comfort of her mother's overlarge shoes.

The deserted streets gave her no comfort, and the raw soles of her feet ached as she walked on the ice and snow. There was still one bunch of matches tucked in her apron. One more fire might see her through the night.

A cold wind blew from the cemetery where her mother was buried. The girl hurried past it. The stone bridge over the canal was covered with ice, and she used the railing for support to avoid slipping to the ground. The snow was deeper in the decrepit neighborhood where her father had his tiny house. As she trudged onward, the air burned as she sucked it into her lungs. The cloud of steam coming from her mouth became bigger, and she forgot what it felt like to be warm and safe.

The back door to her father's house was open, and she slipped inside. His two hauling carts piled with canvas sheets occupied the lower level. All the shovels and picks that had once hung on the wall were gone, sold off to pay for her father's time at the taverns.

The stairs up to the attic where they lived creaked, though she heard no sound of movement above her. The door opened with a loud squeal, but her father didn't stir from the bed where he was passed out. A large mug lay on its side beneath the bed, and the smell of a strong drink lingered in the air. He wouldn't give her a beating on the last night of the year. She was finished getting beaten by him.

The wind whistled through the roof as the little girl glanced at the empty hearth. There was nothing to burn. She remembered when her grandmother died that her father stripped the body of its woolen garments as fuel for their fire. If he hadn't spent all of their money at the alehouses, they could have bought wood or coal. Grandmother might still be alive.

The little girl went back down the stairs, consumed

with a loathing for her father. She climbed into the cart with a canvas sheet that her father used to cover the loads that he hauled. She could barely feel the last bundle of matches in her apron because her hands were so numb. She failed to bring the first three matches to life, ruining them as she kept scraping the heads against the cart until they broke. Her fourth try succeeded, and the yellow-orange glow lit up the dark room.

She found the edge of the fabric and teased it with the flame. The canvas smoked, and then caught fire. A black ring appeared, and then spread quickly. She climbed out of the cart and pulled the burning canvas under the stairs. She pulled the sheet from the other cart and added it to the burning pile.

One match remained, and she held it tight as noxious smoke filled the room as the flames came to life. She backed into a corner where she could still feel the heat. The fire leaped onto the staircase and headed toward the door to the attic where her father slept.

The room filled with smoke and heat. She heard her father coughing, and the fire became so hot that the little girl's body began to thaw at last. It was a glorious feeling, even though her feet ached as they warmed. The glow reddened her cheeks and dazzled her eyes. The cart house had been ugly and gray, but now it was alive with scintillating light. The flames danced, forming little fairies in the air. The girl knew in her heart that fire was the most beautiful thing in the whole world.

The smoke made her eyes fill with tears, but she blinked them away to witness the glorious display. She coughed, and the heat filled her lungs, melting what had to be icicles inside her chest. Sparks swam across her vision, and she realized she couldn't breathe. If she got up now, she could go outside, escape the smoke and flames. But the fire was so captivating. It became a roaring blaze in a giant hearth that she could not look away from.

Out of the brightest light came the ghostly form of her grandmother. The old woman's eyes glowed like embers as she reached out with long fingers made of black smoke.

"Grandma! You came back for me," the little girl said as she noticed the slightly crooked grin on the old woman's face. "Please take me with you! I'm ready."

The little girl's hunger turned to a gnawing pain as her grandmother took her into her arms. She felt hot and smelled the sulfurous odor of burning matches. The warm embrace became hard and constricting. Her grandmother's face changed to an ugly scowl and the little girl felt the fear that came on the darkest nights. Something was terribly wrong as they went down through the base of the fire to a place where it would never be cold and everyone understood the need for revenge.

CLOCKWORK HEART

Ramsey "Tome Wyrm" Lundock

Ramsey "Tome Wyrm" Lundock uses the nickname instead of his "meat body" name in e-mail. His first article, "Marybelle for Arrivers," appeared in *Polyhedron Magazine* in 1999, published by the gone but not forgotten TSR. In college he was involved in the Role Playing Gamer's Association, eventually becoming the Campaign Director for Living Verge. He graduated from the University of Florida in 2002, with degrees in Physics and Japanese, and went to work on his parents' longhorn cattle and thoroughbred horse farm. On June 7th, 2003, he had the incomparable thrill of watching their horse Supervisor run in the Belmont Stakes. He worked on the farm and wrote freelance until restlessness drove him back to academia in 2005. He spent one year at the University of Florida and is currently a graduate student in the Astronomy Department at Tohoku University in Japan. His hobby is visiting Japan's castles and ruins.

With all of her clockwork heart, Pinocchia wanted to be a real girl. If she were a real girl, she wouldn't have to spend all day doing the cooking, cleaning, laundry, and any other task Master Geppeto dreamed up for her. And Master Geppeto wouldn't beat a real girl for the slightest mistakes.

As if on cue, Pinocchia felt the familiar boot smash down on her back, forcing her to the floor.

"I told you to scrub the floor, not just move the dirt around, you worthless puppet!"

It was true, Pinocchia was only a puppet. But she was not an ordinary puppet. Like all of Master Geppeto's inventions, there was more than simple clockwork under her skin. When gears and springs alone would not meet his needs, Master Geppeto resorted to components like fairy dust and unicorn blood.

The kick had landed just as she was reaching to wring out her scrubbing rag, so she had been up able to catch her fall. Her outstretched hands had knocked over the water bucket, and now Master Geppeto's foot held her to the ground as the cold, dirty water soaked into her tattered work dress.

"I ought to rip you apart and start over! Can't even scrub the floor right. A machine without a useful purpose has no reason to exist!"

He lifted his foot. Pinocchia raised herself to her hands and knees and waited for the next blow. Instead, Master Geppeto turned and walked away. He muttered, "Clean up that mess."

Geppeto was at the washbasin, strapping a leather and wire contraption over his shoulders. It encompassed his head like deranged scaffolding. He buckled a leather strap around his forehead to hold the demonic halo in position. Finally, he wound the key on the chest harness and pressed the release lever. Three brushes jabbed viciously in and out of his mouth, contorting his lips into lunatic expressions. The rhythmic ticking of the mechanical assault continued as a mint-scented foam ran out of his open mouth, reminiscent of a rabid dog. The contraption yanked his head backward. A metallic "sprong" sounded, followed by another as two springs uncoiled, shoving rubber stoppers up his nostrils. Water from a small copper tube filled his gapping mouth to the brim. He stood there, making the gurgling sounds of a drowning man, with water trickling down his face and neck.

The gurgling noise stopped. Master Geppeto's eyes went wide with fear. He clutched frantically at the framework surrounding his head. Without warning, his head snapped forward and the water in his mouth gushed onto the floor. He panted as he unstrapped the leather and metal contraption.

Master Geppeto found his small, thick wire-rim glasses and examined himself in the mirror. He was showing his age. His white hair was thinning on top. He let the rest grow long and wild to make up the difference. He had three days' growth of stubble, except for the ugly acid scar on his right cheek where no hair would grow. He stretched his lips with his fingers and nodded in satisfaction. "No fresh cuts on the gums or cheeks. I think this mouth cleaner is coming along. Maybe add some guide rails to make sure the spit ends up in the basin, and figure out why the gargle timer keeps sticking."

He glanced down at the water and white foam on the floor. "Pinocchia, clean this up."

Pinocchia left her current task. Master Geppeto loomed over her as she wiped the floor around the wash basin. He didn't speak again until she had finished. "Bedtime. Time to put the tools away."

"No! Maser Geppeto, please don't lock me in the closet."

"You can go in the closet, or I can throw you in the closet. Your choice."

Pinocchia knew there was nothing figurative about his threat to throw her in the closet. He was remarkably strong for his advanced years. She whimpered and shuffled past Master Geppeto. She opened the door to the workshop's small storage area and stepped inside. She heard the door slam behind her and the tumblers turn inside the lock.

She could hear Master Geppeto moving around the main room, probably undressing for bed. She heard the bed springs sag under his weight. With a soft "huff" the weak candlelight creeping under the door disappeared.

The darkness was absolute. Pinocchia wasn't afraid of the dark. She had been locked in this closest too many times to be afraid. And come morning, without fail, Master Geppeto would beat her for "hiding" in the closet instead of getting up early to make breakfast. She sat down ever so slowly and softly, scared to make any noise, lest she wake the master from his sleep and incur his wrath.

In years past, she would have only had to wait a little while until her gears ran down; then next thing she would know it would be morning. But Master Geppeto had gotten tired of her running down at inopportune moments and had installed a self-winding coil made from fairy gold and Egyptian iron. All she could do was wait until morning and wonder how Master Geppeto would beat her. Today, he had used only his feet and his bare hands, so he was overdue to strike her with his belt or with a twitching rod. The one bright side, he probably wouldn't use one of his heavy or sharp tools, which would make major repairs necessary.

The worst part was that Pinocchia couldn't cry. She wanted to cry, to let all of her fears and pain drain out though her tears and lighten the load on her clockwork heart. She had asked Master Geppeto once to give her the ability to shed tears. The only thing Pinocchia wanted more than to be able to cry was to be a real human girl.

The first faint rays of dawn came early, hours too early. This light was blue instead of the customary red of first light. As the light strengthened, Pinocchia could see that the illumination was coming from within the closet, not under the door. At the heart of the cool glow was a beautiful fair-skinned woman who was only three inch tall. Her long blonde hair cascaded down between the iridescent butterfly wings flapping slowly on her back. She was wearing a lightweight blue toga, with her bare feet dangling in the air beneath her. She carried a golden wand crowned with a pentangle star.

"Who are you?" Pinocchia whispered.

"I'm the Blue Fairy, Pinocchia." Her voice was like the high-pitched tinkling of a bell. "And I'm here to grant your heart's desire."

Pinocchia lunged forward, almost ramming the Blue Fairy with her nose. She stared cross-eyed at the delicate figure in front of her. "You can make me a real human girl?"

"Yes, dear. If you are sure that is what you really want."

"Yes, it's what I want!" Pinocchia shouted, and then she clasped her hand down over her own mouth. She listened, scared that she might hear Master Gepetto lumbering toward the closet, but instead heard only his continued snoring.

"Well, then, close your eyes, and I'll grant you this one wish."

Pinocchia did as she was told. There was a soft tap on the bridge of her nose and a tingling, like a spark of electricity. That was it. She didn't feel any different.

"Open your eyes. You're a real human girl."

Pinocchia opened her eyes. It was true! Where before there had been gaps between the wooden segments of her fingers, now in the pale blue light, she could see skin covering her joints! She jumped up and looked at her feet. She had real toes, not those blocky, cloglike puppet feet. She wiggled her toes in delight.

"Thank you, Blue Fairy! Thank you." Then a groan arose from Pinocchia's stomach. A sharp pain in her belly caused her to double over. She looked at the glowing blue figure through cloudy eyes.

"When was the last time you ate something?"

"I don't eat." Pinocchia replied.

"You mean puppets don't eat. Honestly, now that you're human, you must learn to take better care of yourself." Then, laughing, the Blue Fairy faded from view, taking her light with her and leaving Pinocchia in the darkness.

Pinocchia's stomach growled like a tormenting demon. She remembered there was food on a counter by the stove. She could almost taste the bread and the cheese, but it only intensified her hunger. She reached up and tried the door knob, knowing full well that it would not turn.

At least now she could cry. Tears streamed down her face. Wasn't crying supposed to make you feel better?

It wasn't working. But that didn't matter, Pinocchia just had to get through the rest of the night. In the morning, when Master Gepetto saw that she was a real girl, they could eat their fill in celebration together. Now that she was a real girl, she wouldn't have to do the drudgery all day long. She could help Master Gepetto with his inventions. He wouldn't beat her any more, and they could live happily ever after. Her stomach groaned again. If she could just get through this night.

She awoke to the sounds of the lock on the door clanking open. Her eyes stung. She rubbed them in the darkness. Her hands were warm and soft, not cold and wooden.

The door burst open. "So this is where you're hiding!"

Pinocchia stepped out. "Look, Gepetto!" It wouldn't feel right to call him "Master" since she wasn't a clockwork doll anymore. "I'm a real human girl."

Gepetto's jaw worked up and down, but no sound came out. His face flushed bright red. "You ungrateful piece of scrap! After-market modifications by an unlicensed third-party vendor? Are you insane?"

He unbuckled his belt and pulled it off in one smooth, well practiced motion, "I'll teach you not to sneak around behind my back!"

Gepetto brought the leather strap slashing down on her. Pinocchia raised her arms instinctively. The belt bit into them. Even as a puppet she had felt the pain, but it wasn't half of what burned in her forearms now. Gepetto took the opportunity while her hands were raised to whip the belt back and forth across her stomach.

A new human sensation welled up in Pinocchia: panic. She bolted past Gepetto and out the open door. She ran as hard as she could. Tears blinded her, but it didn't matter. Once she was past the garden wall, she didn't know where she was going or what to look for.

"Come back here and take what's coming to you!" Gepetto screamed from the doorway.

Pinocchia ran until the cobblestones under her feet turned into a packed dirt road and until the dirt road turned into a foot trail. Then the trail turned into soft, fallen leaves. She collapsed, panting and rolled onto her back. Strands of her long, black hair draped across her face. She had never seen so many trees. Is this where Gepetto had gotten the wood to make her? She tried to sit up, but everything went black.

She was guided back to consciousness by an unfamiliar voice. It was deep and strong, like the arms cradling her. "I found her in the woods. I think she's sick."

A bony thumb pressed against Pinocchia's upper eyelid and forced the eye open. A wrinkled old crone with a gold earring and a red bandana stared her in the face. The same knobby hands pulled open Pinocchia's lips, squeezed her arms, and then finally poked her in the stomach. The last caused Pinocchia to whimper.

"Food is the medicine this child needs." The old woman said. "Come and set her by the fire, Big Rob. Young Bert, go and fetch a blanket to keep the chill off her."

Big Rob gently lowered her onto a log. Pinocchia looked around groggily. Master Gepetto had had visitors sometimes, but she didn't recognize any of these people. They were dressed in bright clothing and wore lots of jewelry.

"Here, eat up." The woman thrust a steaming bowl of gray, gritty gruel into Pinocchia's hands. At first Pinocchia thought that she was too weak to eat. Her trembling hand raised half a spoonful up to her mouth, and of its own accord her mouth wrapped around the spoon. She shoveled the gruel into her mouth as fast as her hand would move. She swallowed without chewing, but she relished the taste of each new mouthful. After she had scrapped the bottom of the bowl with the spoon, she licked both of them clean.

Pinocchia looked up just in time to get her head out of the way of the old woman's ladle as she filled the bowl back up to the brim with more piping hot gruel. "Eat lots. You've had a tough day."

A young boy with black hair came up. He wore a silver ring on a string around his neck. "Here's that blanket, Granny."

"Why don't you put it around her?"

The boy stepped behind Pinocchia and draped the blanket over her shoulders. "My name's Robert. Everyone calls me Bert."

"We call him Young Bert," Big Rob said.

"I won't always be the young one," Bert shot back. "What's your name?"

"I'm Pinocchia."

When she had finished her fifth serving, Pinocchia held out the wooden bowl to Granny.

"I'm sorry, that's all there is." She showed Pinocchia the empty cooking pot to prove the point.

Pinocchia looked up pensively. "I'm sorry. I didn't mean to eat it all."

"Oh, don't worry. Missing one meal isn't going to hurt a couple of strong young men like those two," Granny laughed.

Bert opened his mouth, but Granny cut him off with a glare. "Young Bert, go string up a hammock for Pinocchia in my wagon."

Pinocchia was feeling groggy. She hadn't realized just how much humans eat and sleep. As she drifted off, she heard voices outside the wagon.

"What are we going to do with her, Granny? The townspeople say that we gypsies steal children. We should oblige them by taking one now and then."

Pinocchia didn't think being stolen by these people would be such a bad thing, and so she stayed with them for days and months and a handful of years.

On day, when she saw Bert twisting his silver ring around his finger, she asked: "Bert, why don't you get that resized?"

"I could still grow into to it," Bert insisted, as he threaded the ring back onto its string and tied it around his neck. He changed the subject. "You're a whirling dervish with that tambourine. My fiddle could barely keep up with you, Pinocchia."

"The more frenzied the dance, the more the crowds like it, I guess."

"What the crowds like is that the faster you twirl, the higher your skirt rises."

Pinocchia blushed. It was their normal banter, but tonight her heart wasn't in it. Something was nagging at her, but she couldn't figure out what.

They had reached their campfire in the wagon train. Big Rob thrust a bowl at each of them as they sat down. "I had a rabbit in my snares today. We have meat in the pot tonight!"

Meat usually made the stew taste better. But tonight it seemed bland to Pinocchia. She held the bowl and let her elbows rest on her bare thighs sticking out through the slits in her dancing skirt.

"Not a bad catch, that rabbit." Big Rob beamed. "Meat for dinner, a soft white pelt that will make a nice purse, and a good pocket watch to boot. I forgot to tell you the rabbit had a watch and kept looking at it, claiming he was late for something."

Big Rob passed Bert an ornate watch about an inch and a half in diameter.

"At least he wasn't late for dinner," Bert chuckled.

Pinocchia wasn't in the mood for cheer. "I don't think the rabbit would think that was very funny."

"That's okay. A rabbit's point in life is to get eaten," Big Rob replied.

That's what was bothering her, "And what is our point in life?"

"Tonight, it is to eat rabbit."

"I'm being serious. We perform and beg and poach and steal all day, for what?" Pinocchia muttered. "To eat and sleep so we can get up tomorrow and do it all over again?"

"It's better than not eating."

"I know." Pinocchia grimaced at the memory. She looked downcast, her sweaty black locks spilling over her shoulders. "But we work to survive and we survive to work. It's like we don't have any purpose beyond that."

The words echoed in her head "A machine without a useful purpose has no reason to exist."

"We only have to go on living like this until we hit the big score," Bert said as he passed the watch to Pinocchia. She took it without looking. Bert reached down into his knee-high leather boots. "Speaking of such, I lifted a fat bag of gold off a foreign woman at the market today."

He pulled out a cloth bag the size of two fists. Even in her distracted state Pinocchia noticed that it didn't jiggle like a coin purse. He raised and lowered his hand, weighing the purse, and then tentatively opened the draw stings. A sickening odor was released: dung.

Bert threw his prize to the ground, and Big Rob burst into hearty laughter.

"I swear that was heavy with gold when I stole it."

"Just admit it, Young Bert, that woman must have gotten one step ahead of you." Big Rob roced side to side with amusement.

"Why would a woman carry a bag of animal manure just to teach pickpockets a lesson?" Pinocchia asked.

Big Rob stopped laughing. "That's fox droppings. Boy, you crossed a fox spirit. We'll be lucky if you don't get us all cursed." He rose and pulled Bert up by the collar. "You are going to go tell Granny right now what you've done and find out how to apologize to the fox."

Burt groaned, "Last time Granny cured a curse, I had to dance around with antlers on my head for two hours."

Pinocchia was last in line as they marched to Granny's wagon. No one noticed that she fell farther and farther behind, then turned to exit the camp. No one noticed either that she was still carrying the pocket watch. There was a lake near the camp that seemed as good a place as any to be alone with her thoughts.

When Pinocchia arrived at the lake, she wasn't alone. Sitting on a boulder was a woman with a long braid of black hair. She had a tan completion, like the people from east of the mountains, and she wore a simple white robe with blue trim, belted at the waist. When she stood, Pinocchia could see that the robe only reached mid calf level, and below the hem a mass of bushy white tails flicked and twitched. The light of the full moon turned the robe and tail silver.

"There are nine of them," the woman said of her tails.

Pinocchia made eye contact.

"You were staring." The woman smiled.

Pinocchia looked back to the tails and started to back away. "You're a fox. I've been told not to trust foxes."

"Who told you that? Humans?" The fox lady laughed. "Are you any better off with them?"

She sat back down and patted the rock beside her. "Why don't you sit with me for a while?"

When Pinocchia was seated, the fox continued, "Actually, I was rather looking forward to the antler dance of the gypsies, but I thought that you might need someone to talk to. My name is Inari. What is yours?"

"Pinocchia."

"That is a nice watch you have, Pinocchia."

"It's not mine. It's stolen. But I didn't steal it. I was just marveling at it. Second after second, minute after minute, it ticks off the time without ever getting tired or asking to be thanked. Just quietly fulfilling its function," Pinocchia said. "Like a clockwork."

"If only humans were as diligent about their purpose as that watch," Inari mused.

"That's just it. What is their purpose?"

Inari raised an eyebrow in surprise. "Why do you say 'their' purpose?"

"I used to be . . ." Pinocchia swallowed hard, "a mechanical puppet."

Inari looked back and forth between Pinocchia and the watch and then nodded. "Purpose? That is something that every human has to find for herself."

"So once they find their purpose, humans, everything is all right?"

Inari sighed. "If that were true, there would be no disenchantment, no crises of faith, no abandoned hope. Saying that humans have to find a purpose for themselves is really the same as saying that they don't have one, I guess."

"How do you deal with the . . ." Pinocchia searched for a word. "Pointlessness?"

The fox picked up the end of one of her tails and cradled it in her left arm. She stroked it lovingly with her other hand. "When I was granted my eight extra tails, I was given the sacred duty to protect Good and oppose Evil in all of its forms. That never-ending quest gives my existence meaning. I have a purpose. But, then, I'm not exactly human."

"Can you give me a meaning?" Pinocchia asked.

"Even I can't give humans a purpose," Inari admitted. "They're not like machines, which have an innate purpose."

It took several heartbeats for the significance of Inari's words to sink in. The former puppet looked up to see the fox woman's mischievous grin. "Yes, I can do that. If it is what you really want."

Pinocchia thought hard before she opened her mouth again. "I wish you could turn me back into a clockwork puppet. But I want to have toes, not those ugly blocky feet like before. And if it's not too much trouble, could you make it so I can still cry?"

The fox lady leaned close, until their noses almost touched. "I can do that."

Pinocchia sat paralyzed by the intense gaze. Inari breathed out a soft puff of air that tickled Pinocchia's upper lip. Pinocchia tumbled off the rock, and Inari rocked back, laughing.

Pinocchia grabbed her head in an attempt to regain her bearings. Her hand was cold and hard against her temple. She still had toes, but they were wood and metal. She tried to hold her breath, to see if she could hear her clockwork turning. Not only could she hear the gears, she discovered she wasn't breathing at all.

Pinocchia jumped to her feet. "Thank you. Is there anything I can do to repay you?"

"Would you please give the pocket watch to me?"

Pinocchia handed it over.

"I think one of the White Rabbit's sons should have it," Inari said. "Deep down, every rabbit knows that it is his final destiny to be eaten. That's why they have so many children—so that there is always a replacement ready."

Pinocchia nodded. When a rabbit had fulfilled its purpose, it was replaced. When a machine could no longer fulfill its function, it was discarded. But without a clear purpose, humans stumbled through life. She pitied them for that.

Master Geppeto's wake-up clock screamed like a banshee. The bell wasn't actually ringing, but the gears and springs, which were failing to ring the bell, shrieked and moaned as if they worked in opposition.

"Breakfast is ready, Master."

Master Gepetto looked up at her with sleep-filled eyes. Then he leaped to his feet and clasped her shoulders.

"It's really you!" He beamed. "You've come back to me!" Then his mood turned darker. "Do you think that you can just waltz back in here like nothing has happened? I'm going to turn you inside-out for running away."

"Let me set your breakfast down so I don't spill it."

Master Gepetto grabbed his belt from the bedside stand and glared at her suspiciously as she put the tray down. "Do you actually want me to beat you?"

"I'm a puppet. I don't want anything," Pinocchia lied. Fortunately, her nose didn't grow enough for him to notice. She did want some things. She wanted to clean the years' worth of dirt which had accumulated in this house since she left. She wanted to make sure Master Gepetto had good food to eat, unlike the leftover slop she had found in the kitchen. But right now, what her clockwork heart wanted more than anything was a sound thrashing. Now she understood, Master Gepetto didn't beat her for failing in her functions. Taking his blows was one of her functions.

Fifteen days later tears streamed from Pinocchia's painted brown eyes. The tears weren't caused by the smoke filling the room. Nor were the tears from pain, as the flames licked up her wooden legs.

Master Gepetto was dead.

He had passed away quietly in his sleep.

She had set fire to the cottage, to consume the old master and all of his machines.

She cradled his head in her lap and stroked his wild white hair. She was sad that the old man had died. He had given her life, but more importantly, he had given her a purpose.

The half-burned ceiling beams creaked ominously.

Without Master Gepetto, she had no function, and a machine with no useful purpose had no reason to exist.

THE HUNDRED-YEAR NAP

Skip and Penny Williams

Skip and Penny Williams profess a love of old things, such as classic Hollywood movies, musty old books, the century-old farmhouse they share, and each other, though not necessarily in that order. Penny has degrees in chemistry and Russian. Skip has numerous role-playing game credits, and has dabbled in many other things. When not dreaming up new twists on old tales, Penny enjoys many different crafts and teaches chemistry and broadfield science. Skip putters in his vegetable garden and orchard (which keep many deer and rabbits fed) and works to reclaim the fields around the farmhouse from the obstinate weeds that blanket them. He also paints toy soldiers. The Williams house is the site of an annual Christmas cookie bake that draws friends from both sides of the Atlantic; it's also the permanent home to a growing pride of unruly housecats.

The chamberlain shuffled through the pile of scrolls heaped on the council table and sighed heavily. "How far down the peerage must we go, Your Highness?"

The stately woman across the table rested one slender, pale hand on the cluttered table, the other on her swelling belly. "All the way down the list, Gerald," she replied with a beatific smile. "We're inviting all the peers; they can decide which knights and retainers to bring along."

The chamberlain's expression turned dour.

"Now Gerald, it's not every day that the royal heir is christened," added the queen. "We have waited long for this day, and everyone expects a celebration like no other."

Indeed, Queen Meldarerna and her husband, King Galameade, had waited long for a child—so long that they had begun to believe their kingdom would have no heir and their hearts no joy. But at last their prayers were answered, and Meldarerna became pregnant. Never was there a happier mother-to-be nor a prouder prospective father. Indeed, the whole kingdom rejoiced that the royal family would soon be complete. Planning a mammoth celebration for the christening before the child was even born was perhaps a bit premature, but Meldarerna believed in being prepared.

"We'll rely on the guilds and privy council members to assist with the rest of the guest list," continued the queen, "except for the fairies. Brynmor will handle the preparations for them."

The chamberlain rolled his eyes. "That old coot of a court wizard? Just put him to work entertaining the kids."

"Oh, no, Gerald," answered the queen. "Brynmor is our expert on everything magical, and I'm counting on him to make sure the most important fairies in the kingdom will be present at the celebration. It will be vital for the child to have the blessings of the fae."

The chamberlain only snorted by way of reply.

"Don't be so familiar, Gerald," said Meldarerna, wagging a finger. "And don't let either my husband or Brynmor hear you carrying on like that. Brynmor worked some impressive battlefield magic in his day, if even half the king's tales are true. If he's limited himself to parlor tricks recently, it's only because he hasn't been challenged. Perhaps you've forgotten the little matter of the dragon last fall."

"I heard it was about the size of a newt," muttered the chamberlain. He fell silent as two men entered the hall. One was the king—a handsome, strapping man, going gray at the temples but still lean from a lifetime of hard campaigning. His companion was older-looking, wearing a robe decorated with constellations of magical symbols and spattered with candle wax. He wore a pair of spectacles on his nose and carried an oak staff in one clawlike hand.

The king stooped to plant a kiss on his wife's cheek. "You look positively luminous, my dear. How goes the planning?"

"We were just discussing the matter of the fairy guests," replied Meldarerna with an affectionate smile.

At this, King Galameade turned to his robed companion. "What have you to say about that, Brynmor?"

The wizard produced a slim scroll from his sleeve and unrolled it, looking the chamberlain in the eye as he did so. "Here is the list, my liege," he replied. "We have thirteen fairies living in or near the kingdom who merit invitations by virtue of their magical prowess, their standing in the fairy community, their service to the kingdom, or . . ." The wizard paused to adjust his spectacles and shot a glance at the queen. "Or their generosity toward mortals." With that, the wizard passed the scroll to the chamberlain. "And all will have to be served from golden plates."

King, queen, and chamberlain responded in unison. "Golden plates?"

The wizard planted his staff and drew himself to his full height—a head taller than the king. The chamberlain put a hand to his forehead. "Here comes another one," he murmured. The royal couple, however, gave the wizard their full attention.

"To make the best possible impression on the fairies, we should provide a golden plate for each fairy guest," the wizard began. "Nothing shows mortal respect more than a gift of gold, even if it's only lent for a short while. Unfortunately, the royal treasury includes only twelve gold plates. The more junior fairies might be served from silver, which is also a magical metal, but doing so would be a minor affront."

The king shook his head: "No, the fairies are our most special guests. We should not slight any of them."

"Surely there's enough gold in the treasury to make another golden plate or two?" suggested the queen.

"Perhaps not," cautioned the chamberlain, digging though the pile of scrolls. Locating a ponderous ledger, he flipped it open, ran one slender finger down a page, and said, "With the loss of tax income due to the new holiday, renovations to the nursery, the costs of the party, and the rebuilding expenses from the dragon attacks—I guess it was bigger than a newt—we're very nearly broke. We'd be better off melting down the plates we have and making them anew."

"Wouldn't that leave us with thirteen rather flimsy plates?" wondered the king.

"Fourteen, Your Majesty," piped up a rather nasal voice from the doorway.

"Oh, now the circus is complete," muttered the chamberlain, rolling his eyes heavenward.

"Ah, Armand! I wondered where you'd gone off to," exclaimed the queen. "We can hardly plan a party without our Chief Protocol Expert."

The newcomer bowed to the king and queen, his stylish green trousers, aquamarine shirt, and peony sash making the rest of the group seem drab. "Your

Majesty looks particularly radiant this morning," he said to the queen with a fawning smile.

The king stepped forward. "Here now, Armand. How did we get to fourteen plates?"

"Oh really now," said Armand with a pitying glance at the king, "you never seat thirteen at a dinner table. It simply isn't done."

"Oh. So where are we going to get another fairy?" the king wondered aloud.

Brynmor waved a hand. "A matter of little import, sire," he said. "We can find some other guest from the mystical realm to make the fae party even. It might be a good idea to invite a gnome, a dwarf, or even a giant."

"A giant? Oh, no!" exclaimed the queen. "Perhaps we should trim the guest list instead. Who was that disagreeable fairy you mentioned, Brynmor?"

The wizard's bushy eyebrows shot up. "Xyhille? Oh, no, Your Highness, it would be a grave error to risk offending her. If we don't want to invite Xyhille, we should invite no fairies at all."

"And we couldn't possibly hold an event of this magnitude without the fairies," said Armand. "Think of what people would say!"

"So," Gerald interjected, "to keep our fairy guests—and our queen—happy without either breaking the treasury or stretching the gold in our current supply of plates too thinly, we need to borrow two golden plates for a day." The chamberlain paused to consult his ledger. "We can borrow the gold. We can sell the plates afterward to cover the cost. Or perhaps our esteemed court wizard could just conjure us two golden plates?"

The wizard stroked his chin. "It can be done," he said after a moment. "It's against my better judgment, but it can be done. No spell can make lasting gold, but I could fake it for a time. A silver plate or two could be transformed—or I could simply create a couple of temporary gold plates, which we could give to the most junior fairies. Of course, if the ruse is discovered, we could have a nasty scene on our hands. It's not a great idea, but it's less dangerous than snubbing Xyhille."

"Very well," declared the king. "Conjure up an extra pair of golden plates."

"And, Your Majesties, I wanted to talk about the colors for the decorations," said Armand, taking the king's arm. "We simply cannot wait until the birth to choose them—besides, pink and blue are SO common. I suggest forest green with touches of rose gold, in honor of our fairy guests . . ."

In time, Queen Meldarerna bore a daughter, whom the joyful couple named Rosalind Aliena (after two of the queen's childhood friends). The christening celebration was announced that very day.

In the weeks before the event, Brynmor, Gerald, and Armand were three of the busiest men in a bustling kingdom. The wizard filled his days perfecting his transformation spell, making arrangements for the fairy guests, and casting auspices for the blessed event. This latter task vexed him greatly because the auspices for the christening were mixed. The wizard foresaw great trouble but also great hope. He shared his disquiet with no one.

Meanwhile, Armand sketched fantastic designs for the Great Hall decorations and endlessly altered the seating arrangements according to which noble was angry with whom. As for the chamberlain, he dashed furiously about, seeing to most of the practical preparations for the celebration. Some days, it seemed his tasks would never end, and he wondered—with increasing rancor—just what the wizard was up to, locked away in his tower day and night.

The day before the celebration, Brynmor approached the chamberlain. "I'm ready to create the extra golden plates," he said. "I'll cast the spell just before the celebration and place them on the table myself. Please instruct the staff to set the junior fairies' places without plates."

The chamberlain's eyes narrowed as he bit back a scathing reply. "You have a place in the procession, Brynmor, as do I. It would be best if you can have the plates ready in the morning. If not, then as soon as possible. We'll label them, and the staff can set them where they belong."

The wizard shook his head. "This is a bad idea, Gerald," he declared. "I suppose there's no help for it?"

"None at all," the chamberlain said, a gleam of triumph in his eyes.

The morning of the christening celebration, the wizard brought a stack of fourteen golden plates—including the two he had conjured—to the scullery in the royal castle. He found the chief scullion and carefully explained the plan. Taken aback by the presence of the royal wizard, the scullion promised that all would be done as required.

Less than an hour later, a harried potboy hustled into the scullery burdened with a tray stacked high with cups and saucers. No one had told him about the golden plates—but, then, no one ever told him anything other than "hurry up." He was hurrying now, and tray collided with stack, sending plates, cups, and saucers tumbling to the floor in a cacophony of crashes, pings, and clangs. The noise brought the chief scullion running. "Ooops," said the pot boy, cringing.

The chief scullion briefly stood aghast and then boxed the potboy's ears. "Clean this mess!" he shouted. "And mind how you restack those golden plates—they're labeled." The pot boy scrambled to obey. But most of the labels had fallen off the plates. *"Which label belonged to which plate?"* wondered the hapless potboy. The messages on the labels looked sort of like names—single words starting with big letters—but since he hadn't learned to read, he couldn't be sure. Anyway, what possible difference could it make which label was on which plate? All the plates looked the same. As long as each had a label on it, he couldn't possibly get in any trouble. Besides, the chief scullion couldn't read either.

Later in the day, the serving staff carefully laid the golden plates at the fairies' table, placing each beside the appropriate name placard, according to its label. Draped in silver mesh and set with golden plates and fine crystal glasses, the table shone like the sun on fresh snow. A touch of color in the form of calendula flowers completed the table of honor.

And not a moment too soon. The trumpets sounded through the great hall, and the chamberlain himself, dressed in a blue satin suit with silver trim, began to announce the guests as they arrived. Liveried servants escorted the guests to their tables, amid exclamations of awe over the sumptuous green and gold décor artfully sculpted into a faux forest. And at last the fairies arrived, flying in on their gossamer wings like jeweled butterflies clad in shades of pink, aqua, seafoam, daisy, rose, and lavender. Twelve fairies flew gracefully into the hall, alighting one by one before the chamberlain, who checked the crib notes on his cuff and announced their names to the awed crowd. Most had never seen a fairy before, and even those who had been so blessed had never seen so many in one place!

As they were escorted to their table, one more arrived—an older fairy of considerable girth, with bright red-orange hair and flowing robes of white and gold. "And Grand Dame Xyhille!" announced the chamberlain, as the fairy lighted before him.

"Xyhille? By the fiery forge, they'll let anyone into these places," said a gruff voice from the doorway. All eyes focused on the newcomer, a rotund dwarf clad in brown and gold, wearing an outlandish broadbrimmed hat with several colorful feathers.

"Well, look what the dragon dragged in," said Xyhille, whirling to face the newcomer. "Hanar Throngand Dwin, what are you doing here? I thought I got rid of you when I dropped you into that quicksand bog six hundred years ago."

"Six hundred forty-seven years ago, to be precise, my dear. And that experience did give me the distinct impression that our marriage was over," said the dwarf, advancing on Xyhille and the chamberlain. "But fortunately for me, a lovely bog sprite was there to aid me. A bit on the smelly side, perhaps, but she had her own sort of charm—especially to someone drowning in quicksand. Those months were special in their own way."

"Aha! I always said you'd chase anything in a skirt, and I was right!" shouted Xyhille, drawing back her hand as if to cast a spell. Crashing sounds ensued as several peers of the realm dived under their tables.

"Please, Dame Xyhille, allow me to lead you to your seat," said the chamberlain with an edge of desperation in his voice.

"Never mind, Lord Chamberlain," said the dwarf, holding up a hand in protest. "I shall escort my dear wife to her chair." He approached the seething fairy with crooked arm extended, and after glaring at him a moment, she took it. "Now, my dear, this is a party, so let's try to be civil, shall we?" he said.

"Oh, this is terrible! Just terrible!" fretted Armand, standing with Brynmor at the edge of the crowd.

"How could Gerald have invited her estranged husband of all people?"

"You heard him say it was more than six hundred years ago," said Brynmor. "Fairies hold grudges for a long, long time."

"I'd better warn the king and queen—oh! It's too late! Here they come now!"

"All we can do now is take our places and hope for the best," said Brynmor.

At the first flourish of trumpets, Armand, Gerald, Brynmor, and several other key members of the court formed a processional at the end of the hall. Slowly they walked to the throne and parted, revealing King Galameade and Queen Meldarerna, with the baby girl in her arms. Once the queen was settled, the king stood up and addressed the crowd. "All of us have waited long for this happy day, and we are glad that you have come to share our joy. I would like to announce Princess Rosalind's betrothal to Prince Edgar the Charming, heir to the neighboring kingdom—a match that will strengthen both our realms and one day unite them. We also wish to extend special welcome to our fairy guests, who have graced us with their presence this day." He extended an arm to the fairy table, and all except Xyhille inclined their heads and smiled.

"Humph. They just want magical gifts for the kid," she said loudly enough for all to hear. "Oh, well, at least they set a nice table."

"I see that long separation from your husband has not sweetened your tongue," said Hanar dryly, as the king continued his speech. The other guests resumed their seats, though those near the fairy table still watched its occupants with wary eyes.

"Perhaps you're right," said Xyhille. "So what have you been doing with yourself all these centuries?"

"Making and selling spinning wheels," replied Hanar. "Mundane and magical—I have all sorts. In fact, I was thinking of gifting the young princess with one that spins straw into gold. But I think not. Those have been known to cause all sorts of jealousies. And besides, gold makes mortals act strangely."

Xyhille snorted. "You couldn't make a spinning wheel like that if your life depended on it," she said, as a servant picked up her plate and piled it high with berries and greens from a large bowl, then set it down in front of her. "Dwarves are so unmagical."

"All right, so I got Zelhandra to enchant them for me," said Hanar, extending his cup toward another servant for a refill. "I have to admit that my own gold-spinning ability is a tad unreliable."

"Zelhandra! So you've been fooling around with this worthless sack of river silt, have you?" Xyhille shouted at a fairy two seats down from her.

"Mother, please!" said Imavia, one of the younger fairies from the far end of the table. "This is a formal, affair. Try to be nice."

Xyhille glared at her daughter, and the other fairies shrank back. "Oh, very well," she said, taking a bite of salad. "Hmmm, interesting dressing. Tastes faintly magical."

The meal continued fairly peacefully through the next two courses, and the royals and their courtiers began to relax a bit—all except for the three advisors. "We'd best be on our guard," said Brynmor. "This whole situation could go south at any moment."

"Of all the dwarves in the kingdom, Gerald, what made you choose that one?" whined Armand. "Inviting squabbling spouses makes for very difficult dinner parties! And then you sat them together!"

"I thought someone to talk to might keep her occupied," snapped the chamberlain. "How was I supposed to know?"

As the meal progressed, the fairies came forward one by one to give their gifts to the baby. One gave her beauty unsurpassed, another grace, a third merriment, a fourth wisdom, a fifth intelligence, and so forth, until all except Xyhille, Hanar, and Imavia had bestowed a magical gift.

"Why did you two get married anyway if you hate one another so much?" asked Hillaria, as the main course was being served.

"She bewitched me," moaned Hanar. "There I was, seeking my fortune in the mountains, gathering gold nuggets with nothing but a pickaxe and the sweat of my brow . . ."

"And some fast fingers," finished Xyhille. "Nuggets indeed. You could hardly stagger away under the weight of the gold coins and jewelry you stole from those travelers while they slept."

"So maybe the gold was a bit more refined than I recall," snapped Hanar. "But it still took skill and daring. Doubtless what attracted you to me." He puffed his chest with pride.

"Well, you were a rather handsome brute in those days. I'll give you that much," said Xyhille, handing her empty plate to the serving lad to be filled with duck a l'orange, red cabbage, and petite peas. "But I did not bewitch you. You saw a pretty face and sparkly earrings and wanted them both."

"Well, I can't hear what they're saying," declared the chamberlain. "But they seem to have settled into a decent conversation."

"Yes," the chief of protocol observed. "Perhaps it's well that the formidable Xyhille is seated next to someone of her, uhm, intellectual caliber. And familiar faces do encourage casual conversation."

"The calm before the storm," observed the wizard, fishing in his sleeve for some unseen magical implement. "Look out for squalls."

"Ah, you were quite lovely then," said Hanar, with a fond smile at his wife. "Pity it was only fairy magic hiding that ugly puss of yours."

"Oh, no," said Hillaria, ducking.

Xyhille's face darkened. "Why you miserable, ugly, no-talent . . ." she shouted, drawing back her arm, the iridescent light of unformed magic dancing about her fingertips. "I'll teach you a lesson I should have taught you six hundred years ago!"

"You forget—I don't have to take spells from you! Exhabispex!" yelled Hanar, thrusting a hand toward Xyhille just as the servant finished filling her plate and started to set it down on the table. The magical light vanished—but so did her plate, dropping the entire serving of dinner into her lap.

"Uh-oh," said Hanar.

Xyhille regarded the colorful mess all over the front of her white gown with an expression of unmitigated rage and then turned her wrathful gaze on the king and queen. "So! You offer us conjured plates, eh? We aren't good enough for real gold!"

The enraged fairy sprang to her feet like a flame catching in tinder. "Greedy for fairy gifts, are you?" she sneered. "Well, here's a real keeper!" Xyhille's eyes settled on the child.

Chamberlain and protocol expert turned to the wizard as one. "Do something!" they urged, each grabbing an arm.

"I'm trying!" the wizard gasped. "Let go of me!" Shaking himself free, he produced a wand and waved it about. In a heartbeat, a pale glow had settled over the royal family. "There's no stopping a fairy curse, though," he muttered.

Xyhille's reddened face flashed a deep shade of purple, and she continued. "Before her eighteenth birthday, she'll prick a finger on a . . . a . . ." Xyhille glanced at Hanar, whose fingers had begun to twitch. "Spinning wheel!" she finished triumphantly. "And die, die, die!" Xyhille's face split into a malicious grin. "Indeed, there's a gift for you—she'll never grow old!" With that fearful utterance, Xyhille vanished in a thunderclap and a puff of acrid smoke.

"Gee, thanks," muttered Hanar. "That'll improve sales."

"This is all your fault!" chorused the three counselors, pointing at one another.

After a moment of stunned silence, pandemonium erupted in the Great Hall. The king shouted, the queen fainted, and the baby cried. Loud voices decried fairy curses, and people began to race for the exit. Eventually, King Galameade's authoritative voice restored calm.

"This curse is a calamity indeed," he said. "But we must and shall find some way to mitigate it." His gaze turned to the fairy table. "My esteemed guests, I apologize deeply for this incident. Please know that we hold you in the highest esteem, and the matter of the plate was a grave misunderstanding."

The fairies conferred among themselves for a few moments, while Hanar looked on with an amused expression. Finally, Imavia stood and walked over to stand before the royals. "The fault for this debacle lies with you," she said sternly. "Serving my mother from a conjured plate was a grave offense. However, we realize that mortals cannot see beyond their own immediate interests much of the time. And the child is not at fault for this insult. I haven't the power to lift my mother's curse entirely. Her magic and mine stem from the same line, and she is my elder."

Moving to stand before the child, Imavia reached a hand toward her and said, "You shall not die from the prick of the spindle. You shall only sleep—a deep sleep lasting for at least one hundred years—and you will awaken when a prince of the blood bestows a loving kiss upon your lips."

"No!" cried the king and queen in unison, ignoring the frantic waving of the court wizard. "Not a hundred years! She will be as good as dead to us!"

"A century is but an eyeblink in fairy terms," said Imavia sternly. "Be happy that your punishment for this affront is so light." With that, she flounced back to the fae table, where the rest of the fairies were busy trying to determine whether their own plates were real.

The meal finished in subdued silence, and at last the guests took their leave. The last from the hall, Hanar looked around and then up. "You shan't get away with this, my dear," he said to no one in particular. Then he glanced at the king and queen, and finally fixed his gaze on the child. Making a rolling motion with his hands, he said:

> "May that which you sow
> Also be what you reap.
> You'll share one fate
> From spindle prick
> To century's sleep."

With those cryptic words, he left the hall.

"What did he mean by that?" whispered the chamberlain.

"I'm not sure," said Brynmor, stroking his chin.

"Here now, Brynmor," said the king, crossing to stand before the three courtiers. "You must find a way to break this terrible curse."

"I'll do what I can to find a way around it. In the meantime, keep her away from spinning wheels."

The very next day, the king sent forth a proclamation banning spinning wheels in his kingdom. All spinning wheels were seized and burned in a huge bonfire in the palace courtyard. The country's economy, fueled for so long by the textile trade, slid into decline, but eventually rallied when the populace learned to create fine cloth from imported thread and mastered the art of leatherworking.

During the months following the curse, Brynmor worked feverishly on counterspells, but he could tell that none succeeded. He did, however, manage to make Rosalind immune to minor scratches and abrasions of all sorts.

Now known as Briar Rose for her ability to waltz through the thorniest areas, the princess grew into a young woman of dazzling beauty, thanks to her many fairy blessings. She enjoyed spending time in the woods around the castle, cataloging the animals, birds, and plants, and she also became quite adept with the needle—in fact, her embroidery was ranked among the finest in the kingdom.

The king, the queen, and Brynmor marked off her birthdays, hoping against hope that she would reach the magical age of eighteen without the curse coming to pass. The neighboring king and queen, having heard about the curse, stalled the children's nuptials. "I suppose it's only natural," said the chamberlain to the distraught monarchs, "that they'd be unwilling to marry off their son only to have him deprived of a wife within a few years."

As Briar Rose's eighteenth birthday approached, king, queen, and nearly everyone in the kingdom kept a strict watch over the princess' every move. The king led squadrons of soldiers through every town and hamlet searching for spinning wheels that might have escaped the christening day edict. The queen made the royal castle her special hunting ground. Brynmor was frequently seen with his nose in a dusty old tome—that is, at those times when he wasn't walking about with the smell of brimstone (or something even more acrid) hovering about him. Everyone—even the king—thought it best not to inquire just what the wizard was doing.

For her part, Briar Rose became vaguely aware that everyone around her had gone slightly mad, but in a caring way, and she did her best to endure their devotion. She found that everyone seemed to breathe easier if she confined herself to the castle, so she devoted herself to her embroidery. On the eve of her eighteenth birthday, she sat at her chamber window with her needle and hoop. As she worked on a particularly elegant rose petal (one of her favorite subjects for needlework) she suddenly realized that the castle had fallen unusually quiet.

Rose glanced out the window. Her room overlooked the castle garden, which was planted with dozens of rose bushes in her honor. But instead of the garden and the courtyard beyond, she found herself staring at a thread of iridescent gossamer, at once delicate and handsome in its perfection, floating just outside her window.

"Is that a spiderweb?" she wondered. She leaned out the window, looking for the spider, but there was no arachnid in sight. Rose's keen eye traced the thread up to a high turret of the castle, where it emerged from a broken shutter. *"I know that chamber,"* she thought. *"It's an abandoned guardroom, home only to a collection of pigeons and bats."* Her curiosity aroused, Rose put aside her needlework and set off for the tower.

After a long climb up the tower stairs, Rose pushed open the door of the chamber. A toothless old woman with a leathery face and long, nimble fingers sat near the rotted shutter working a contraption Rose had never seen—a wheel that whirled around as the crone worked a treadle. The woman was spinning a mound of downy wool to produce the entrancing gossamer thread that had floated past the shutter to dangle before Rose's window.

"Never seen the wheel and distaff before, my dear?" asked the crone in a gentle and sibilant tone. If Rose's curiosity hadn't been running so high, the voice would have sent a shiver down her spine.

"No, Grandmother," said Rose.

"Well, then, come over here, my dear," the old woman cooed. "Try your hand. I have a feeling you'll surprise yourself." She beckoned to the girl.

Feeling all volition drain from her mind and body, Rose walked toward the wheel as if in a trance. She touched the wheel and promptly knocked her hand into the spindle. But thanks to Brynmor's spell, the touch didn't hurt her.

"Awww, prick your finger, dear? Feeling sleepy?" cackled the crone, leaping to her feet. Her fairy disguise melted away as she spoke, revealing Xyhille, her face etched in malicious glee.

"Uhm, no and no, whoever you really are," Rose replied. "I never worry about cuts, scrapes, and pricks. I don't even use a thimble when I sew."

"What?" snapped Xyhille, her face reddening with rage.

The room darkened as Brynmor literally flew through the open shutter, oaken staff in hand. "Avaunt, Xyhille!" the wizard commanded. "You've kept an entire kingdom in fear for nearly two decades. Be content and begone!"

"Not on your life, mortal!" shouted Xyhille. "You have no power over me. Leave us or spend the rest of your days as a slug!"

"You're on my turf here, Xyhille," Brynmor retorted.

Rose wasn't sure exactly what was going on, but she prudently edged toward the door and looked about for anything she might use as a weapon.

"Not so fast, girlie!" ordered Xyhille. With a wave of her hand, rose briars slithered through the shutter and snaked through the room, seizing girl and wizard.

Brynmor thumped his staff on the floor, sending a shockwave through the room. The vines withered, and Xyhille went tumbling, along with the spinning wheel, distaff, and wool. The whole collection landed in a heap, with the enraged fairy on top. As Xyhille struggled to her feet, tossing aside bits of the smashed spinning wheel, her scrabbling hand brushed the spindle, and she felt a sharp prick. "Ouch!" she screamed, more out of frustration than pain.

As she tried to shake the sting from her hand, Xyhille felt suddenly sleepy. Her expression of surprise rapidly changed to one of ire. "Hanar Throngand Dwin, this is your doing! I'll get you for this, make no mistake!" With that, she abruptly slumped to the floor. Brynmor stared at the sleeping fairy for a split second and then turned to Rose. "Are you well, Princess?" he inquired.

But Briar Rose made no reply. Eyes closed, she tottered for a moment and then collapsed into the wizard's arms. As he eased the girl to the floor, the wizard recalled certain lines of doggerel he'd heard years before:

> "You'll share one fate
> From spindle prick
> To century's sleep."

Brynmor slapped himself on the forehead. "*It's always the detail you overlook,*" he thought. The wizard gazed out the tower window and saw the tangle of briars from Xyhille's final spell. "*How will I explain this to the king and queen?"* he wondered, starting to pace the floor. Shortly, an idea dawned on him.

Brynmor chanted a spell of his own. The king and queen, in their chamber, fell asleep together. In the scullery, where the potboy was getting his ears boxed again for some new indiscretion, the servants set aside their work and settled into sleep. And so it went, down to the flies on the walls. A terrible silence fell over the castle, unbroken by even a snore.

Brynmor carried Rose down to her chamber and laid her in her bed, leaving Xyhille snoozing amid the wreckage of the spinning wheel and the dead briars. The wizard glanced out the window at the thorn bushes entangling the Princess's tower and decided to give them a little boost before finding his own bed.

The sun rose that day over a sleeping castle wrapped in a formidable hedge of thorn bushes. As the years passed, it grew higher and thicker, until it became a veritable forest of vines, leaves, and wicked thorns that flourished even in winter. Only the very tops of the castle's towers remained visible. Without the king's guiding hand, the kingdom languished, and one by one, the citizens packed up and moved on—most of them to the neighboring kingdom, where King Edgar the Charming now ruled.

As the seasons passed, tales of the castle wrapped in briars and the princess sleeping within spread through the adjoining lands. Gallant young men resolved to hack at the briars and win through to the sleeping beauty, but the thorns defeated them all. Their skeletal remains and rusting armor, left hanging in the bushes, provided a stern reminder of the perils of the hedge.

But not everyone found death in the briars—some found opportunity. A hundred years after the hedge had appeared, Hanar stood at its outskirts, gazing inside and dreaming of the good old days. "Damn you,

Xyhille! Spinning wheels were a good, solid business. Lots of growth potential." He turned away from the hedge with a sigh. "But one has to make one's own opportunities, I always say. Ah, here comes a fresh client now," he said, glancing down the road at a young man approaching astride a swaybacked, knock-kneed horse.

"Ah, come in search of a princess to wed, young fellow?" said the dwarf, stepping into the road before the horse.

"Yeah . . . I mean, yea, verily," said the young man, trying desperately to keep his horse from trampling the dwarf. "Is this the place where the beautiful princess sleeps?"

"You've found the very spot!" said Hanar, nimbly dodging the horse's hooves. "I can provide you with a map to her outdoor bower for the low price of . . . twenty-five shillings," he said, sweeping an appraising glance over the young man.

"But . . . she's in the castle, right?" asked the young man, his brow furrowed in confusion.

"No, no!" said Hanar. "That story was put forward to discourage suitors. In actuality, she lies within the hedge, in a natural bower."

"Oh, I can find her then," he said, urging his horse toward the hedge.

"Well, if you want to try," said Hanar, surreptitiously pulling on a wire. Suddenly, a branch moved aside to reveal the lifeless corpses of an armored knight and his horse, snared in the briars and impaled in dozens of places by the foot-long thorns.

The young man stopped short. "On second thought, I believe I'd like to buy that map of yours," he said.

The exchange completed, Hanar pocketed the money and waved goodbye to the young man. Withdrawing a small notebook and quill from his pocket, he made a note. "Twenty-five shillings for map, report successful match to Iphigenia's parents, and collect final payment." He pocketed the book just in time to greet the young man as he emerged, this time with a pretty young woman perched ahead of him on the saddle. The two waved, and the young lady winked.

"Got to get a priest on board, so we can collect for weddings on the spot," Hanar mused. "That'll save money in beauty draughts too, since I won't have to keep them pretty for so long." He flipped a few pages in the notebook and ran a stubby finger along a hand-written column. "Ermina the miller's daughter is next," he mused, snapping the book shut. "Who'd have thought so many peasants could produce ugly daughters?"

"Hanar, you stop this right now!" said a feminine voice from somewhere above.

The dwarf looked up and squinted. "Ah, it's you, Imavia. How is my favorite fairy stepdaughter today?"

"None of that," she scowled, wagging a finger at the dwarf. "This business of yours is shameful! Using the princess' misfortune to lure young men into matrimony with unmarriageable girls—all for your own profit!"

"Why, nothing of the sort!" replied Hanar, spreading his hands wide. "I run a legitimate matrimonial brokerage. Parents pay me to take their ugly daughters off their hands. I simply pretty them up a bit, hide them in the briars, and let the suitors pay me for maps and advice. Everyone ends up married and happy. Besides, I had to do something to make a living after your mother stripped me of my spinning wheel business."

"But what about the young men that you defraud into marrying peasant girls?" Imavia asked.

"They would've married peasant girls anyway," said the dwarf with a laugh. "If they knew how to read the tale, they'd know that only a prince of the blood can awaken the real princess. Why shouldn't I make a bit of profit from an event that's inevitable anyway? And besides, if I didn't redirect them, they'd all die in the briars. This way, they're alive, married, and whelping more stupid, ugly peasant brats to sustain the local economy."

Imavia snorted. "Mother was right about you. But the century is up today. That means Briar Rose is due for her kiss, and I'm going to see that she gets it." With that, the fairy vanished in a shower of rose petals.

"Humph," mumbled Hanar to himself. "Sometimes there's just no reasoning with a fairy."

As the dwarf tidied up the bower where the last "princess" had lain, he heard the sound of horses' hooves. "A profitable day indeed," he said, rubbing his hands together as he emerged from the bower. "Perhaps Constance in bower 6G will also end this day wed."

"Ho there, dwarf!" shouted a young man from the back of a caparisoned charger. "Is this the castle wherein Princess Rosalind sleeps?"

"This is the place, your lordship," said Hanar, bowing low. "But she lies in a rose-scented bower here inside the hedge, not in the castle itself."

"Poppycock!" said an ancient man, nudging his beribboned mule out from behind the young man's steed. "She's in the castle all right, Junior. Ignore this pompous tub of lard and go on."

"But, Grandpa," protested the young man. "What if he's right? We could get killed for nothing."

"We won't get killed," said the old man with a snort. "You're a prince of the blood, and the century's up. Why, lookee there!" he cried, pointing a gnarled finger at a path that had suddenly opened in the hedge before them. "See? Now get that overbred bucket of oats moving so we can get this land annexed officially, like your daddy wants."

"Damn you, Imavia!" stormed Hanar. "All this work I've done, and you just let in the first prince of the blood who happens by. Not to mention the oldest human in the . . . wait!" Hanar peered at the old man and then did a double take. "King Edgar the Charming, as I live and breathe!" he said under his breath. "Not exactly well preserved."

Hanar sighed and slipped through the briars to another bower. "Up you get, Constance!" he barked. "We're closing up shop." Leading the bawling girl to the edge of the briars, he snapped his fingers to summon his pony, hoisted her aboard, and set off for her home. "Just kills me to have to return money," he muttered.

Meanwhile, the ancient king and his great-grandson had tied their horses outside the silent palace. "Where do you suppose she is, Grandpa?" asked the young man.

His great-grandsire heaved an exasperated sigh through his toothless gums. "Don't you ever listen to your tutors, Junior? Beautiful princesses in distress are always stuffed in some high tower. Like that one," he said, pointing up.

"Let's go then," said Junior, pulling open the castle's main doors and entering the silent, cobwebbed hall.

"She was a pretty one, I'll give you that," said the old man, smacking his leathery lips. "But these royal princesses are all alike. Soon as they've borne the requisite heir, they suddenly get the vapors every night and don't want anything to do with you anymore. Just like your great-grandma—the princess I married after Rosalind went down for her nap. That's why I never took another wife after she died. Give me a buxom scullery maid any day," he cackled, as he followed the young prince up the tower stairs.

"I've been meaning to ask you, Grandpa," said the young man. "Why did you give up the throne all those years ago?"

"Easy there, boy," wheezed Edgar. "Not as spry as I used to be. But to answer your question, I fell into a bog while hunting when I was about your daddy's age. A pretty little bog sprite saved my life and kept me as her play toy for years. Didn't care much for her perfume, but she was a fun girl. Naturally, my son—your granddaddy—had to take the throne when I didn't come back right away, and when I did show up, I didn't ask for it back. I was happier being a prince again and having my days free to chase women and hunt foxes. They figured I'd die soon enough, but that bog sprite gave me long life as a parting gift—so the family has had to feed and support me in royal style."

"Pity she didn't give you eternal youth to go with it," said Junior, pulling the tower door open. "Here I am, Rosalind!" he cried. "Your prince has . . . Grandpa!"

"What's the trouble, Junior?" asked Edgar, holding onto the doorframe and gasping for breath.

"This can't be Rosalind! She's . . . she's UGLY!" said Junior, pointing at the sleeping Xyhille.

"Ugly?" said the old man, coming forward to look. "I wouldn't say that. Maybe not a spring chicken, but not bad. Got some nice love handles there too—I like a woman I can hold onto. Yessir, this here's my kind of woman!" And with that, Edgar seized Xyhille and planted a long, loud kiss on her lips.

The fairy's eyelids fluttered open, and she began to struggle, pushing against Edgar's chest until he dropped her back into the pile of dusty wood. "Who in the nine hells are you?" she demanded, wiping her mouth and gasping for breath.

"Prince Edgar the Charming, at your service!" cried the old man triumphantly, seizing her hand and pulling her to her feet.

"Charming, eh?" said the stout fairy, looking her rescuer up and down. "Not much charm left in you now. But you've got more energy than most mortals half your age."

"There may be snow on the roof, but there's still fire in the furnace, girlie," chided Edgar, pulling Xyhille closer.

"Well, now," said Xyhille with a half-smile. "You must have been quite a catch in your day. Maybe with a little fairy magic, you'd be almost passable." The twinkle of magic formed around her fingers as Edgar pulled her closer.

"I don't think I wanna watch this," said Junior, edging over to the door. His great-grandsire and the fairy ignored him, and he made good his escape, sprinting down the tower stairs two at a time. Once he reached the castle's second floor, he opened the first door he came to, slipped inside, and slammed it shut.

"Who are you?" asked a sleepy voice from within. "And what are you doing in my bedroom?"

The young prince whirled at the sound and then stood transfixed for a moment at the sight of the loveliest maiden he had ever seen, yawning and stretching in a canopied bed. "I . . . I'm Prince Harold," he said, haltingly. "And you're Princess Rosalind, aren't you?"

She nodded and yawned again. "Call me Briar Rose," she said. "But that still doesn't tell me what you're doing here. Daddy will be most angry if I have a boy in my room."

"Well," said the prince, his mind working feverishly.

"I just kissed you, see, and woke you up from a century of sleep."

"You must not be much of a kisser, if I can't even remember it," she replied.

"Well, you were asleep. Let's try it again," said Junior. Crossing to her bed, he took her in his arms. Just then, he noticed a movement in the hallway.

"Who are you?" he asked the three men standing outside the door.

"Oh, that's Gerald the Chamberlain, Armand the Protocol Expert, and Brynmor the Court Wizard," said Rose, waving to the three.

"Well, go ahead boy, kiss her!" said the chamberlain impatiently. "We don't have all day."

"But she's already awake," protested Armand. "He must have kissed her before we got here."

"Nothing says he can't kiss her again," said Brynmor with a yawn.

"What's that noise?" asked the chamberlain, frowning in the direction of the tower.

"Do you MIND?" asked Harold, glaring at the three until they withdrew. "Now where were we?" he asked, smiling down at Briar Rose and then kissing her gently.

"Hmmm, not bad," thought the princess. *"But not that great either."*

"Now the spell is broken and we can get married," said Junior, rising and offering Rose his hand.

"Whoa, there," she said, rising from the bed under her own power. "I'm engaged to Prince Edgar the Charming."

"Well, I don't think you'll want him now," said Junior. "He's my great-grandfather. Wouldn't you rather have me?"

"I don't think so," said the princess, crossing to her mirror. "Eww, how did I get all these cobwebs in my hair?" She seized a brush and began to brush out her long tresses. *"He does have the family chin,"* she thought with a pitying glance at the prince. *"A shame. But he could always grow a beard."*

"I'm not sure I want to get married," she said aloud. "And even if I did, one kiss doesn't make an engagement. Or even two."

"Oh, this is terrible!" whined Armand, peering into the room. "Everyone knows the beautiful princess has to marry the handsome prince in a situation like this. What will people say?"

"Yes, you have to do something," said the chamberlain, glaring at the wizard. "He's of Edgar's line, and the king always intended to join their realms with that marriage."

"Looks like it's time for a love potion," muttered Brynmor. "Now where did I put that eye of newt?" The three walked off down the hallway, bickering all the way.

Around the two young people, the rest of the castle began to awaken. Down in the scullery, the cook yawned and boxed the potboy's ears to awaken him. The king and queen stirred in their chamber, and then looked about with a start. They stared in wonder at the briar thicket outside their window, gasping with astonishment as the vines budded and exquisite roses bloomed. They closed their eyes dreamily, breathing air perfumed with thousands of fragrant blossoms. Then a shared recollection struck them.

"Rose!" they shouted together. With that, they dashed to their daughter's room. On the threshold stood the court wizard, carrying a small, empty bottle. "Brynmor, what has happened?" blurted the queen.

The wizard bowed. "It will take some explaining," replied the wizard. "Suffice it to say, we have circumvented the curse. And now all of us have considerable work to do."

Inside the chamber, Prince Harold stood bewitched

as Rose reached out her window to pluck a namesake blossom. "I don't recognize the species, but these climbing roses are fabulous—fairy work, I'll bet. She offered the blossom to the prince, who bowed and accepted it. *"He's really rather cute after all,"* she thought, wiping the traces of the chocolate drink that Brynmor had brought from her lips. Rose threw a leg over the sill and extended a hand to the prince. "Come and see the castle. But mind the thorns!"

As the lovely princess scrambled down a vine, the prince tucked away the blossom. One glance at the thorny tangle outside the window convinced him it would be best to keep his armor on. Suddenly, he heard a shout from above.

"Whee!" yelled his great-grandsire, as he flew past the window in Xyhille's arms. "So long, Junior! Tell your folks I won't be home for dinner for a few decades!"

"Hanar Throngand Dwin!" shouted Xyhille, banking around to accost the dwarf on his pony. "Release me from my promise. I'm going to marry a prince."

"A little old even for you, isn't he?" asked the dwarf, looking up at Edgar.

"He's a hundred and twenty-two, toothless, and wrinkled," said Xyhille. "But he's got one thing going for him—he's not you."

The dwarf shrugged. "Fine. You're free, Xyhille. Enjoy your prince."

The fairy waved and flew off, the prince becoming younger and handsomer as they went. "Wonder what that bog sprite is doing this century?" muttered Hanar, clucking to his pony.

Junior shook his head. "I don't believe it," he said. "Grandpa gets a girl, and I've no guarantee of it."

"Well, are you coming or not?" demanded Rose. Feeling doubly giddy from the height and Rose's nearness, the prince stepped onto the sill. "So, you've made a study of plants, have you?" he asked as the two clambered onto a sturdy vine.

King, queen, and wizard watched the youngsters vanish beneath the windowsill, their hearts full.

Later, in the castle's great hall, the wizard explained the events of a century ago to the royal couple. The king nodded gravely. The queen looked thoughtful for a moment. "I think," she said, "we ought to begin with a birthday party."

The chamberlain heaved a sigh. "Here we go again."

FIVE GOATS AND A TROLL

Elizabeth A. Vaughan

Elizabeth A. Vaughan is the author of *The Chronicles of the Warlands* and *Dagger-Star*. She still believes that the only good movies are the ones with gratuitous swords or lasers. Not to mention dragons. At the present, she is owned by two incredibly spoiled cats and lives in the Northwest Territory, on the outskirts of the Black Swamp, along Mad Anthony's Trail on the banks of the Maumee River.

Snowdrop was the prettiest.

White from the tops of her floppy ears to the tip of her tail, with dark hooves and dark eyes, she was the prettiest, the smartest, and absolutely the cutest of the goat herd.

And magic, as well, but, then, they were all magic.

She pranced down the path, well ahead of the others, enjoying the sun as it scattered through the leaves, warming her back. Ting-tang, ting-tang chimed the bell around her neck as she moved.

The rest of the herd stayed with their humans, behind her on the trail. The humans were slow, because they would stop to press their faces together once in a while. This wasn't something that impressed the herd, but the humans seemed to enjoy it.

They certainly did it often enough.

But the waiting bored Snowdrop, so she'd prance ahead in the warm sunshine. Happy and content, because everything was as it should be for a goat.

The herd and its humans were going back to where they'd come from. It was a place of lush, sweet grass and clear, cool water. The humans called it Athelbryght, but what is a name to a goat?

It mattered not to the herd what it was named, so long as they were going back there. Names were a human obsession and mostly ignored.

Of course, Snowdrop knew her name, for it could mean treats and scritches under the chin. Of course, it could also mean she was in trouble, but Snowdrop was rarely in trouble. She was the prettiest, after all.

So she kicked her heels and danced along the path as it twisted and turned. The forest ended, and the trail led right to a bridge, made of sturdy rope and wooden planks. Snowdrop never paused, just danced out onto the bridge over the rushing river.

Trip-trap, trip-trap went her little hooves as she started over the wooden planks.

Ting-tang, ting-tang chimed the bell around her neck.

Pleased at the sounds, at the rush of water, of the sun on her back, Snowdrop turned around danced back to the end of the bridge, making as much noise as she could. She did a leap back on to solid ground, then turned and started back again, happy, pleased, and excited about—

A troll stood there in the center of the bridge.

A big, mean, evil-smelling troll with fur and claws and nasty eyes.

She bleated in surprise and danced back, her hooves clattering and her bell ringing.

An answering bleat came from the trail behind, and Snowdrop knew that her herd was close, which was a relief, because while she was the prettiest, she was also the smallest.

The troll growled and took a step toward her.

Kavage came around the corner, she of the brown coat, who was as small but not quite as pretty. Kavage bleated as she saw the monster, and she raced for the bridge to stand at Snowdrop's side.

Trip-trap, trip-trap, their hooves rang on the wooden planks.

The troll advanced, swinging its long arms, growling, snarling . . . talking like a human.

Snowdrop took another sniff, and she wasn't so afraid when she understood that this was a human dressed in skins and smeared with mud and dung. Still dangerous, still ugly, but not so much a troll.

Another bleat from the trail, and Dapple and Brownie rounded the corner at a run. They were both a bit bigger and, being male, had horns. They charged the bridge, their added weight causing the rope and wooden plank structure to sway back and forth. Their hooves made a clip-clop sound, ringing hollowly on the wood.

The troll lost its balance and grabbed for the railings. Snowdrop and Kavage darted under its arms and ran past him, headed for the other side. They stopped where the ropes tied off to the edge, and bleated their defiance fiercely.

From a safe distance, mind.

The troll regained his balance, glaring back at them. But it turned and advanced on Dapple and Brownie, who retreated at the same pace. But as the troll advanced, they heard the sounds of Fog coming down the trail at a fast clip, calling as he ran.

Fog was gray, and big, and male, with horns to

prove it. Unlike his name, he came on hard and fast, on sharp hooves, bleating and calling to the others.

Snowdrop and Kavage stood at the far end of the bridge and bleated back, pausing to investigate the ropes wound around the pillars planted deep in the earth. The pillars were strong and sturdy, and the ropes smelled good.

Dapple and Brownie charged the troll, first one then the other, setting the bridge to swaying back and forth. Once again, the troll grabbed for the rope railings in order to steady himself. Dapple charged through, darting under one arm, while Brownie charged a few steps behind, brushing against the troll and forcing his way past.

Fog didn't bother to stop. His hooves hit the wood of the bridge, sounding tromp-tramp, tromp-tramp as he rammed right into the troll.

The troll yelled then, a high screech as he lost his balance. He fell, his long clawed hands reaching for the ropes and the planks. He caught himself, dangling in midair, making loud noises and glaring at the goats.

Fog snorted, and stomped to the end of the bridge, to gather with his herd.

The troll swung back and forth, trying to get a leg up.

Snowdrop and Kavage started chewing the ropes, one at the base, and the other at the railing.

The troll made angry noises and tried harder to climb up.

Dapple and Brownie started chewing as well, crowding at the edge to get their teeth in the tasty ropes.

The troll cried out, and the noises changed, sounding more like bleating.

Fog struck the rope at the base with his hard sharp hooves. The rope strands parted, even as the railing broke away from the stump on one side.

Snowdrop delicately nipped through the rope on the other side.

With a snap, the ropes broke, and the bridge fell, collapsing against the cliff on the other side.

The troll fell into the rushing waters, screaming.

The goats clustered at the edge, watching the man fall. Then all five lifted their heads to see their humans emerge from the forest on the other side.

"What are you fool goats doing over there?" Asked their woman, dressed in armor and wearing red gloves.

"More to the point, what happened to the bridge?" Their man said, looking down over the edge. "Didn't the innkeeper say there was some kind of monster guarding it?"

"If there was, it isn't now."

The goats milled about, bleating and cavorting, quite pleased with themselves.

Their woman crossed her arms over her chest. "This is all mucked up, what with them over there and us over here."

"Red," their man straightened. "Don't forget, they are—"

Snowdrop and the others gathered on the edge of the chasm, above the rushing waters below, and leaped, disappearing—

—and appeared next to their humans.

"Magic goats," their man finished with a smile. Snowdrop butted his leg, and he reached down and scratched her ears.

"Magic," their woman shook her head. "I'll never get used to that."

Kavage pushed her head under the man's fingers and demanded attention. Snowdrop butted their woman's leg, and she reached down and scratched Snowdrop's ears with gloved fingers. Fog, Dapple, and Brownie all begged for their fair share of attention.

"Magic goats." Their woman sighed. "At least they don't talk."

"Good thing you love me," Their man said with a smile, reaching out his arms to pull their woman close to him. The goats watched at their humans pressed their faces together.

Fog grumbled and went to bed down in the grasses along the trail. The others followed, including Snowdrop, the whitest, the smallest and the prettiest.

SOMETHING ABOUT MATTRESSES

Janet Deaver-Pack

Janet Deaver-Pack has also written fiction and nonfiction as Janet Pack. She begins her days before dawn at her computer with a large mug of tea and her cats trying to snuggle in the office chair with her. Janet has written fifty fantasy, science fiction, mystery, and horror short stories. She has written three nonfiction books for children, and her articles appear in magazines and newspapers in southern Wisconsin. She has edited four anthologies based on mythology and cats for DAW, coedited by Martin H. Greenberg. Janet works part-time as an assistant librarian, and does professional editing for Walkabout Press as well as for individuals and businesses. She also knits custom designs under the name Cobweb Creations. In her spare time she leads writing seminars for teens and adults. Janet is an inventive cook. She also reads, walks, enjoys wildlife, and plays with her cats, Tabirika Onyx, Syrannis Moonstone, and Baron Figaro de Shannivere.

She's currently working on a fantasy novel with coauthor Bruce A. Heard.

Dave Spenser led his customers through the Cloud City Mattress shop, halting at the most expensive display. "This is a revolutionary design in beds," he announced, gesturing with a long hand. He hoped his smile was sincere and didn't droop. He was wiped out.

"Space-age foam, no springs at all," he continued. "This mattress self-adjusts to your every curve. No more back pain. It's warm, comfortable, and makes no pressure points. You won't ever bother your partner if you get up during the night because it doesn't transfer motion—"

A tug from something he didn't understand made Dave's attention shift suddenly up and to the right. A suggestion of exotic spicy-flowery fragrance tickled his nose. He looked into the back corner of the display room. What he saw there between the ceiling and the walls made his jaw drop.

"She's here!"

The customers twisted their heads, looked at the corner, and saw nothing other than paint and the gleam of recessed lighting. They traded sidelong glances as Dave continued staring.

"Excuse me," the man said in a loud voice. "You were saying—"

Co-owner Sharron Tucker bounded from the office. Stepping in front of Dave's tall form, she took over the spiel. "That's right, this mattress doesn't transfer motion at all. And it comes with a thirty-day free in-home trial. You'll love—"

A sharp motion from Sharron's hip pushed Dave away from the trio. Eyes still transfixed by his vision, he stumbled to another bed across the aisle and sat on the edge.

"Beautiful," he mumbled. "Just beautiful. She's closer than before. I can see her burgundy eyes!"

The woman he gazed at stood in a chamber of golden wood and polished stone that looked like marble. She wore floor-length layered robes of deep fuschia trimmed with pink and metallic silver. Her wavy black hair hung past her shoulders and curled a bit at the ends. She carried herself with the natural poise born of long experience dealing with people. Dave pondered her concerned expression for the dozenth time.

"Wonder how tall she is?" he muttered. "Wonder where she's from?" He sighed, shaking his tawny head. "I'd like to meet her—"

The door to the shop slammed shut. Sharron's heavy, quick footsteps thundered against the rug. She planted herself in front of Dave, hands on hips, her pale face blotched with anger.

Dave's vision disappeared. "Wait," he moaned to the corner, leaping to his feet. "Don't go."

"What the hell do you think you're doing?" Sharron spat. "Those customers will probably go straight to Bennet's Beds and buy what we could have sold them right here, if you'd just been paying attention! You used to be our best salesman. Do you realize our sales are down twenty percent? That's twenty whole percent! I don't know how we're going to continue to support this store with that big a drop in income." She shook a finger beneath his nose. "And I think you're the cause of it. No, I'm sure of it. Have you looked at yourself today?" Her disgust was clear.

Dave blinked at her. "I combed my hair and brushed my teeth. I know I did."

"That's not the trouble." Sharron grabbed his arm and dragged him into the women's bathroom, which had a large mirror. She snapped on the light. "Now, would you buy a mattress from someone who looks like that?" She pointed to his reflection. "Would you buy anything in the world from him, even if you needed it?"

Dave squinted, almost not recognizing himself. His long angular face was puffy. There were reddened circles beyond the bruise-colored ones surrounding his hazel eyes, and the bloodshot orbs themselves darted to a new focus every few seconds. His hands trembled, and he slapped at unseen things in the air. He'd lost about ten pounds in the past few weeks: his shirt, sports jacket, and slacks drooped like flags in disinterested wind on his six-foot-seven frame. And he hunched, as if his broad shoulders had befriended his ear lobes.

"Good," he muttered. "I *did* remember to shave."

"How long has it been since you slept?" Sharron snapped. "I mean really deep normal sleep?"

"Uh, about three months," Dave mumbled.

"Uh-huh." She cocked her head, making her cedar-colored hair swing the same direction. "So, this is serious. Chronic. Been to a doctor?"

He nodded. "Several."

"And?"

Dave shrugged. His eyes felt gritty and fatigued, as though he'd been standing in a sandstorm of bright light for several hours. "None of them offered much of a reason. They can't find the little pellet in my lower back that keeps me awake and hurting, so they're no better at explaining it than I am. Except for one thing."

"What's that?" Sharron asked.

"Every doctor I've been to said my condition sounds exactly the same as the one in the kid's story called 'The Princess and the Pea'." He pushed past Sharron into the store, rounded the partition to the office, and flomped down at his desk.

"One doctor thinks it's displaced pain," Dave continued as she followed him, "possibly because of my height. But I've never had problems before, except with growing pains. Another doctor asked me if I've been in the military, or was injured in some bar brawl. She seemed disappointed when I said no to both. I've already tried everything she recommended, such as flipping the mattress, vacuuming it daily, and buying a new pillow top pad for it. Twice. Or more, I can't remember. Oh yeah, and I've had a CAT scan, too. They couldn't find anything, except that I don't have sinus problems. The doctors seemed to think that was remarkable." He looked into the display room. "Do you think I could find a mattress I can sleep on out there?"

"Are you nuts?" she spluttered. "This is our display room—it's for customers!"

"I was just considering the possibility," Dave tried to mollify her. "After all, no one looks at the mattresses after we close. I could test each one, add my comments to the advertising spins, put up a Hot List of recommendations. People might like that. It would let them know we're personally involved in choosing our products."

He scrubbed a hand through his hair, over his face.

Sharron's impossibly turquoise eyes, made so by contact lenses, didn't waver from his face. "Tell me what this—this thing is that you were looking at in the back corner. Why is it so important that it took your attention away from customers?"

Dave couldn't help himself: he almost smiled, remembering the gorgeous face that had been regarding him only minutes ago. "I'm getting . . . I have . . . well, I call them visions."

"Visions! Visions of the Second Coming?" He'd triggered Sharron's sarcastic mode. "Predictions of Nostradamus? Sight of Armageddon?"

"No." Dave didn't want to tell his co-owner about the beautiful lady, but his mind was too foggy at the moment to come up with another explanation. "A . . . it's a woman."

Sharron's eyes widened, and she sat. "You're a twenty-nine-year-old man fixating on a woman in a vision. Oh, I get it. What dating service is she from?"

"No, no," Dave protested. "You've got it all wrong. I haven't joined a dating service. She just . . . she just appears. We can see each other. I think. She reacts to me, but she doesn't talk, and . . . and—"

"How long?"

"Have I had the visions? Ah, about two weeks, maybe three."

Sharron's eyes slid away from his to stare into the beach scene on the screen saver.

Right, he thought. *Now I've really blown it. What would I think if I heard this story? Sharron is a conservative church-going Midwestern entrepreneur with a husband, a dog, and two kids. I can just imagine how she's mixing the details of my situation into something bigger. Something uglier. I shouldn't have told her. I should have made something up.*

The round gold clock on Sharron's desk discarded seconds with each *tick*. To Dave's ears, every one sounded louder than the last. They seemed to be collecting somewhere behind his eyes. His head ached, and his shoulders tightened with tension. He wanted to beat that clock into tiny shards.

"So," Sharron's voice startled him. Her tone wasn't sarcastic any more, it was concerned. "You're not sleeping, you look like you've been a month in hell, and you're seeing visions. The next two things I'd consider are acupuncture and some intensive psychotherapy. How long has it been since you ate? Not nibbles—I mean a solid meal?"

"I don't know. I think I had a breakfast sandwich yesterday." Dave frowned and swiped at something in his peripheral vision. He missed. "Or was that the day before? I'm not hungry. Lack of sleep is doing a number on my appetite."

"If you can't remember when you last ate, it's been too long." Sharron pulled out the bottom drawer on her painted metal desk and rummaged in her three-gallon handbag. "Here," she poked a twenty at him. "Buy something to eat. Take a few days off. Play some racquetball. Exhaust yourself so you CAN sleep. Drink warm milk. Get some serious calories into that bony frame. Check yourself into that sleep clinic on Highway 83 for a few days. Clean yourself up. Then come back."

"Do you really think any of that will help?" Dave asked.

"Maybe mattresses have been your life for too long," his co-owner stated, refusing to look at him. "There are other things to make money at. You might be happier. Maybe you need a change to get all this weirdness out of your system." She finally swung her face toward him. "Bottom line, Dave. I'd hate to lose you as a partner: You're good. But we need both of us consistently at top form to make money in this place. So you get yourself right or let me buy you out." She slammed her desk drawer closed. The sound was the period to her speech even though there was a great deal she'd obviously left unsaid.

Dave sucked in a lungfull of air. "Well, is it all right with you if I try sleeping here?"

He heard the irritation in her voice, but Sharron managed to control most of it. "If you have to. I can't really stop you." One of her eyebrows rose. "You're not going to sleep nude, are you?"

As if that would make any difference to the mattresses! Dave thought. *But it might startle the cleaning crew.* "No," he replied. "I've been carrying pajama bottoms and a toothbrush in my car for a while."

"Good. Now get out of here. Get something to eat."

Her sigh was a gust. "Let me try and repair some of this crap you've caused." She picked up the phone, beginning the follow-up calls that Dave had ignored because of fatigue.

He rose, stretched, loosened his tie, and headed for the door. "See you," he called just to end the conversation. Sharron didn't reply.

Sighing, Dave slouched across the small parking lot Cloud City shared with a kitchen design shop and a thriving sushi bar.

Maybe Sharron was right: I've been staring at mattresses too long. The warm air of early summer stirring through his hair felt good. Traffic and hurrying pedestrians filled the area around the lot and the larger mall beyond with color and noise. He allowed his mind to wander toward the gorgeous woman he'd seen twice recently in his—

Visions, Dave admitted. *They couldn't have been dreams. I can't sleep. Unless it was a waking dream.* He turned toward the sidewalk dividing the mall from the eight-lane highway.

I wonder if she's tall enough for me? he asked himself. *But that really doesn't matter—if I could get a woman like her interested, I'd marry her in a split second.* Dave found her enticing and quite disturbing. He smiled at the combination. Smiling instead of yawning felt good.

Like I have a real chance of meeting her. She's just a vision. He sighed. *But she seems so real! And the edges around her are more substantial than at first, almost like a picture frame.*

"Come on, Dave," he mumbled to himself. "Get over it! You're hallucinating big time!"

Enticing smells wafted from somewhere nearby; his stomach reacted with a roar. Checking the money in his pocket, Dave grinned.

"I can get a really good meal at a Thai restaurant

for less than twenty," he said. He found the restaurant, went in, ordered Mongolian Beef, and ate until he was stuffed.

Feeling more normal than he had in weeks, Dave left the restaurant and continued walking. He decided to cross the highway at Westmere Avenue. The intersection had the only pedestrian lights for blocks. Dave hit the silver button to activate the walk light and waited, for the first time he could remember enjoying the cacophony of passing traffic. Other people gathered around him, waiting to cross.

He strode into the intersection as the human outline on the pedestrian light glowed. Then he tripped over nothing, flailed the air, recovered his balance, and looked up.

"Holy sweet Moses, she's here!" Dave stopped, and stared.

The man behind him bumped into his back, splashing coffee on his sports jacket. "Watch it, ass!"

"You're an idiot to stop in the middle of this street," snapped a woman.

"C'mon, buddy, this is a short light!"

Their comments were lost on Dave. Enraptured, he gazed at the lovely woman featured in the midst of a dark cloud hanging at the same height as the stoplights. This time she was sitting at a desk, her hands holding a peculiar book. A silvery light glowed from a nearby lamp. Dave swore its head angled automatically as she shifted position. Her clothes were more subtle in color than the fuschias and pinks she'd worn in his first visions, and she had pulled her hair back from her face. It was tied with a metallic ribbon at the nape of her neck. There was a steaming cup of something within reach of her long fingers. The cup looked like fine porcelain, painted with a delicate scrollwork design bordering animal figures that played with one another.

"She's working." Dave gaped at her profile. "I wonder what she's drinking? I wonder what she does? Maybe she's a diplomat, or some sort of business negotiator. Wish she'd talk to me. Wish I could meet her."

He stared, drinking in the vision. Then a thought occurred to him.

"This all seems so real. Wonder if I can just jump to where she is? That's only about six feet away."

He gathered himself for a great leap. "If I can catch that lower edge, maybe I can swing my foot up and pull myself through—"

Something yanked on his jacket, twisting Dave to the right. "Hey, stop!" he cried, losing sight of the lady. Something else caught him roughly by the collar and sleeve, dragged him to the concrete divider between north-and southbound traffic, and dropped him. He clenched his eyes shut as the skin on his left cheek hit the abrasive surface and tore.

"Ow! What the—"

A huge rush of air and noise passed inches from his shoes. Dave realized a truck horn was blaring. It had been blaring for long seconds. At him.

"Shouldn't look at birds when the light's against you."

Dave opened his eyes and turned his head to regard the chin of the burly bald man who'd saved him. "Th-thank you," he whispered, full of disappointment. His hands trembled.

The man pulled him to his feet. "That Freightliner would'a made you a hood ornament in another second."

"Yeah," Dave replied. Every bone in his body ached, and he also now owned a raging headache. His fatigue, chased away by the meal he'd eaten a short while ago, returned with double force. He stood on the divider, slumping and feeling stupid.

"C'mon, buddy, light's green." The same burly man

partnered him across the second part of the highway. "You okay?" he asked when they reached the curb.

Dave forced himself to nod. "Sure. Sorry. Uh," his mind groped for a plausible explanation. "I'm on a new prescription. It wipes me out sometimes."

"Bummer. My wife went through that with her heart condition." His rescuer lifted a hand in farewell. "Watch yourself."

"Right," Dave acknowledged, watching the man disappear among the people on the sidewalk. He wondered if he could function well enough on his own to reach his apartment. He had no choice.

The few friends I have are all at work. I can't disturb them for a ride in the middle of the day.

Bennett's Beds was just a few doors away on his right. If he could reach that, he'd be safe until he felt well enough to make the trip back to Cloud City.

Maybe I'll follow Sharron's advice. I can call a cab to take me home. I'll pick up my car in the parking lot at work some other time. He shook his head, noticing again how sore his muscles felt. *I'm in no shape to drive. Or do much else right now.*

Enticing aromas from the coffee shop he was passing made him turn inside. At the counter he ordered a double hot chocolate and asked for two aspirin. The understanding manager dug two tablets from her own stash and presented them with Dave's cup. After paying and thanking her, he took his chocolate to the bistro tables in the tiny trellised garden between buildings.

Peaceful. No one else here, Dave thought, popping the aspirin into his mouth and chasing them with a mouthful of rich chocolate. *Nothing at all to worry about. Except my future. What the blazes is happening to me?*

But he couldn't keep his thoughts on himself. The

lovely lady from his visions intruded. He remembered how intent she'd appeared seated behind her desk, working. Dave lost himself again while visualizing her.

She looks so real. His tired eyes widened. *Wait, that's more than . . . she IS real!*

This vision, which opened along the upper back wall of the garden, showed Dave a worrisome view of the lady seated in a carved armchair. An angry man, much larger than she, confronted her. It seemed that the longer she kept her composure, the more disturbed her visitor became.

Wish he wouldn't throw his fists around like that, Dave thought. *He's going to hurt her.* Despite his aches, his muscles were already tensed to help. *But how can I get to her?* Frustration bloomed in his mind.

The substantial appearance of the vision intrigued him again. *Maybe I CAN climb into it,* Dave thought. Abandoning his chocolate, he chose the table closest to his vision. Stepping first on the chair, he set his other foot on the uneven wrought iron. The table wobbled as Dave reached up.

"What the hell do you think you're doing?" The manager's voice ripped Dave's attention away from his goal. "I'm calling the cops!"

His vision winked out. Sighing, Dave returned to his feet to the patterned brick beneath the tables of the coffee garden.

"No need. I'm going, I'm going." Feeling as if something very precious had been torn from his grasp, he again joined the other pedestrians on the sidewalk.

Pushing through the door into the air-conditioned atmosphere of Bennet's Beds a few minutes later offered Dave a sense of something familiar he welcomed. The brands of the ideal posture bed, the one called "perfect sleeper," and the new space-age springless foam mattress felt like old friends.

Dave stopped, startled. *If these are my friends, maybe Sharron was right—perhaps I DO need analysis and a new job.*

He glanced around the trendy place, hoping he looked the part of a customer who'd entered the store for the first time. Like Cloud City, the store was built on the outlot property of a group of medium-sized stores forming a small mall. Bennet's had the room to stock a few lamps, duvets, quilts, and comforters in addition to mattresses. The walls were all hard dark surfaces in purples, greens, and granites, which contrasted against the pale mattresses. Woven sisal covered the floor. The lighting was modern and upscale, with a background of wordless rock music.

"Help you?" A chunky young woman with a gold bolt through one thick black eyebrow and a ring with a black bead in her lower lip approached him. Part of the dark blue and green jewelry around her neck was tattooed there. She wore a scooped neckline to show it off.

"No, thanks," Dave replied. "Just looking."

"You're the fifth one 'just lookin' today. Well, if you need anything, my name's Brandie." She'd already begun to sway back to the office area, her thick black boots thumping on the carpet. "It's from some old song. My parents are the ultimate hippies."

"Thanks," Dave said, turning toward the main display. Suddenly his fingers itched to grab a mattress and drag it into a corner. The far corner.

What is it about that corner? Dave thought, studying it. He clenched his hands and shoved them into his jacket pockets, hoping to keep them still. They wanted to slap the invisible gnats he could barely see in his peripheral vision.

Spotlit, the area contained the store's primary display of a reproduction antique sleigh bed covered by a beautiful cream and gold quilt with matching shams and a dust ruffle.

Easy, Dave cautioned himself. *I'm here to comparison shop. Brandie doesn't have to know I'm from the competition down the street.*

He felt suddenly odd, odder than he had all day. *No,* Dave corrected himself. *This is more odd than I've felt in a month or more.* His hand tremors turned into uncontrollable tics. His feet wanted to run, but his knees felt like water. Muscles throughout his body cramped.

Can't have been dinner, Dave reasoned as that and wilder possibilities chased one another through his mind. *Too soon for food poisoning to kick in. Can it be something in Bennet's air conditioner? Maybe I've got an allergy.*

Then he saw her. His mouth opened in amazement. The willowy form, the dark hair, and the wine-colored eyes—no mistake, it was the poised beauty again. This vision hung in the upper back corner of the shop, above the expensive sleigh bed.

This is the fourth time I've seen her today. And this time she's looking straight at me!

Dave gasped as a man in blue robes with long pulled-back hair stepped into view beside her. *That's got to be a weapon,* he shuddered, looking at the thing clamped to the man's left forearm. It looked like a cross between a Star Trek phaser and an overlarge pea shooter. When the man raised that arm, Dave reacted.

"Attack!" Dave screamed, suddenly diving behind the nearest mattress, willing his mind to think fast. "We're being attacked! She's being attacked! Got to save her—she's in danger!"

"What?" Brandie trotted into the display area, bending in half to peer at Dave behind the bed. "You're yelling."

"Get down, they're firing at us! Mattresses—the mattresses will help protect us. Grab one. We've got to pile them all in that corner. It's the best place, the safest place. I'll be able to get to her from there." Dave looked at Brandie, eyes blazing. The knowledge of what he needed to do consumed him. He no longer felt worn out or peculiar. "We have to get to that corner without them seeing us."

Brandie didn't move. She stood still, gaping, pale blue eyes expressionless with shock.

"Why don't you understand?" Dave hissed. "We're in danger here. Help me!"

"Uh, yeah," Brandie replied, looking at him like he was a refugee from a loony academy. "Sure." Reaching into her skirt pocket, she flipped her cell phone open and began punching buttons with both thumbs.

"Don't do that! They can triangulate on those things and find us instantly!" Dave surged forward, backhanding Brandie's cell phone into the air. It landed, skittering across the carpet beneath a bed on the far side of the display. Dave grabbed Brandie's wrist and dragged her behind his shelter.

"Hey, that hurts! Now I'm in trouble," the girl whimpered. "I'm gonna end up as a statistic on 'Cold Case Files'."

"Get down!" Dave pulled on her arm, making Brandie crouch beside him, and whispered, "Hey, look. I'll bet these things flying by my head are what her enemies use to watch her. That means they've been watching me!"

"Oh, you believe in all those conspiracy theories." Brandie's voice wavered as she tugged against his hand. "I really think you ought to calm down. There's nobody here but you and me."

"No, see? She's right there." He pointed over the top of the mattress, and then took a quick look around the shop before hunkering down again. "We've got to save her!"

"Save who?"

"The woman with wine-colored eyes in the corner!"

"I'm the only woman here, Mister."

There wasn't time to explain. Launching himself from a kneeling position was hard, but somehow Dave rolled across the display bed and landed with both feet squarely beneath him. He still gripped Brandie's wrist. She bounced along behind.

"Mister, I don't—ooowwww!" She hit the floor on one hip, her boots adding thunder to her landing.

"We've got to get over there," panted Dave, nodding to the far side of the room. "But how do we get there without them seeing us? Without them firing at us?"

"I thought this was gonna be a no-brainer cush job," whimpered Brandie. "I quit! Yeowwwwww!"

Dave scrambled up, ducked his head, and tumbled across the next bed. This time, his rotations broke his hold on Brandie's arm. She managed a lopsided somersault that angled away from him and scuttled crablike across the aisle between and under the displays, aiming for her cell phone.

"Yeuch," Brandie's voice sounded muffled from beneath a thick mattress and box spring set. "Dust bunnies!"

Something within Dave's mind allowed no hesitation during his assault. "Come on, come on, we've got to make it to the portal and save her!" he cried, diving over another bed. "Help me—give me a diversion, anything."

"You're the worst nightmare ever!" Brandie screamed. Dave heard her scuffling as she worked her way beneath the next bed. "Go away. My karma's low on beauty, and I—I must be asleep. This is definitely my worst nightmare ever!"

"That did it!" Dave was only two beds from his goal. He could see the beautiful lady more clearly now. She was bracketed by two men as tall as she.

They were wearing dark blue robes. The second carried what looked like a small notebook, and wrote on it with a metal stylus. All three watched Dave with an intensity he found uncomfortable. Only the lady's eyes showed sympathy.

Sympathy? Why should she be sympathetic? It's her I'm trying to save!

Dave abandoned caution. Roaring defiance at his lady's captors, he rose to his full height, grabbed a mattress in both hands, and threw it into the corner atop the store's expensive sleigh bed. The bed creaked and bounced, but it held together. Dave followed the first mattress with another, and another, and another.

Brandie howled her delight as she reached her cell phone and activated it. "Yeah, 911," she yelled. "This is Brandie Carter. I'm at Bennet's Beds at the corner of Westmere and Highway 87. I work here. Send someone fast—there's a crazy man in here throwing things."

Brandie's call did not divert Dave's concentration. "No one else will help you, but I'm going to," panted Dave to the woman in his vision, tossing another mattress onto the pile. They formed an unstable jumble reaching halfway up the wall. He didn't feel the sweat running down his face and body. He also didn't notice his arm muscles straining, didn't notice when his jacket seams split, didn't notice when his favorite shirt caught a sleeve against something and tore its whole length. The rags followed every movement he made, tattered flags accompanying his crusade.

"Right, right," Brandie's voice floated to his ears, but Dave paid no attention to what she was doing. "I'll hang on as long as I can. I don't want to be alone with this nut. He's tearing up the whole display, tossing mattresses right and left, know what I mean? No, I'm all right for now, I'm under a bed. He's not yanking me down on the floor any more. Sexual attack? No, he hollered something about seeing a woman, and that *she* was being attacked. So he's trying to save her, I guess. No, I'm the only person in the store, other than him."

Dave flung the last two mattresses. The final one teetered on the top of the pile, the other slipped halfway down and stopped. "Doesn't matter," he panted. "I can reach her now. To the mattresses!"

He began toiling up the slope. It was more slippery than he'd imagined. Frustrated at having to waste a few more seconds, he sat and tore off his shoes and socks.

"I can do this." He attacked the pile of mattresses like a rock climber. "I can do this, I can save her!"

"Stop right there."

Dave hadn't heard police car sirens, nor seen their lights. Surprised, he glanced over one shoulder toward the door and saw an officer in black leveling a gun at him.

"Thanks." Brandie emerged from beneath a bed, streaked with dust and an occasional ball of pale fluff. She snapped her cell phone closed, and ran as fast as her stocky frame and thick boots would allow to the protection of three additional uniformed people squeezing through the door.

"I'm Officer Peterson." The gun pointed at Dave didn't waver. "Come down nice and peaceful."

Dave's pile of mattresses shuddered. His mind handed him an uncomfortable thought. *If I go down, I get arrested. There's no other direction to go.* He looked over his shoulder again. *Unless my visions are real.*

The policeman's cold eyes confronted his. "Come on, buddy," Officer Peterson said. "Back down real quiet, and you won't get hurt. Nobody needs to get hurt here."

For a moment, the ludicrous situation overwhelmed Dave.

Another nasty thought washed a wave of despair through him. *Everything I've ever worked for is in ruins: my job, my good standing as a citizen, and the respect of my friends. To think it's all been brought about by a few weeks without much sleep and visions of a beautiful woman.*

He almost wanted to die right then and there. But there was a little steel still left in his psyche.

"Dave."

The breath of a voice with a foreign lilt tickled his ears. He looked up. The man with pulled-back white hair had put away his strange weapon, and was now gesturing for him. The lady beside him nodded encouragement.

"Da-ve."

She spoke for the first time. It sounded like "Da-vih." Her voice was pure velvet.

The first word I hear out of her mouth is my name! Elation overcame Dave's fear and despair. He forgot the police and gaped at the lady's lovely face.

The officer's voice held little patience now. "I've tried to make this easy for you, buddy. If you don't come down from there now, I'm gonna have to use tear gas. Pass me my mask, Finnegan."

The tall man still beckoned, and now even the lady held out her hand, urging him closer.

"Da-ve."

He moved before he knew he'd made a decision, surging up with the last strength in his trembling legs.

In that instant the lady's hand vanished. She vanished, and so did both men in blue robes. As he passed the edge of his vision, icy cold and blackness beyond any he'd experienced in his life enveloped him. Dave felt an odd, sickening rotation, twirling headfirst down a bottomless well where an occasional star winked.

It was too much. Freezing, disoriented, he blacked out.

* * *

Dave's first conscious thought was that he wanted the beautiful lady to come back and say his name again.

But she won't be here, he reasoned, slitting one eye, and then closing it in despair. *This place is cold, dark, and musty, and I'm lying on a hard surface. I've got to be in jail. I've failed.*

Disappointment clouded his mind and made his heart stutter. A tear leaked across the bridge of his nose, leaving a trail that cooled rapidly. It was hard to think; wads of cotton seemed to absorb each thought. His throat was as dry as the Sahara, and his muscles bunched as he pulled himself into a fetal position.

He tried to reach out, then groaned and pulled his arms tighter against his chest. Even the tiniest muscle in his body hurt, from the roots of his hair to his toenails.

A calm voice beat against his pulsing eardrums. An insistent hand urged him to rise. Dave forced his eyes open and found himself in a small wood-paneled room.

A man knelt by Dave and fumbled something into his right ear.

". . . edniash trum fimbiar wos—" suddenly turned into ". . . hope you can walk."

Dave squinted in the dim light, recognizing the man with the notebook who'd been standing with the beautiful woman in his last vision.

My eyes are playing tricks on me, Dave reasoned slowly. *That's the only explanation.*

"Where?" he croaked aloud.

"You will soon find out." The man again urged him to rise. "This way. This way."

Dave staggered to his feet. *Cold, so very cold.* He looked down, realizing for the first time that his sports jacket and shirt were in shreds. His slacks were creased and dirty. He couldn't stop shaking as he walked with the man along an interminable corridor on bare feet. The stupor from his mind invaded the rest of his body, and he allowed himself to be led along, his eyes downcast.

"Here." Dave's guide finally opened a door.

Following him, Dave noticed a glowing light in the dim chamber, looked up, and stared in amazement.

The three-dimensional display of several solar systems swam in a hanging ball of golden light half his height. Three solar systems were closely grouped to one side. On the other side, at some distance, hung a planet that looked familiar. Dave squinted. The little blue, green, brown, and white ball was Earth.

And from the back of the room came a scent that made his nose lift in appreciation: good strong tea.

"T-tea," Dave whispered. "Hot. Please."

"Yes, Trithelmarn, please serve our guest some tea." Dave's guide disappeared as the older man with the white ponytail from his visions stepped from the shadows. He wore a sapphire-colored robe, and he was smiling. Within moments, his guide pushed a steaming mug into Dave's hand.

Dave sucked down several scalding mouthfuls. It tasted wonderfully normal. The heat gathered in his belly and in his hands and then spread throughout his body. His shaking lessened.

"Welcome to Lhangficsaria, Mr. Spenser," the man with the ponytail continued. "And congratulations. I have the singular honor of presenting to you the good wishes of Queen Quilfrineczia and the entire Central Galactic Council."

"Who?" Dave cocked his head at the strange names, trying to understand. His mug tilted. Tea splashed on his naked chest. He glanced at the cooling liquid, embarrassed. Dressed in rags, barefoot, he looked like a bum.

Maybe I am a bum. And I must be dreaming.

"You've had a difficult trip after a difficult time, Mr. Spencer," continued the ponytailed man in a gentle voice. "My name is Alterfarr Quentarion. I am Advisor to Princess Shrondranaris and to Queen Quilfrineczia. Trithelmarn, bring that green robe for Mr. Spencer. And a chair. He looks none too steady."

Nodding thanks, Dave shed what was left of his shirt and sport jacket, sopped up the spilled tea with them, and put on the robe. His fingers trembled as he tried to work the unfamiliar fasteners. He sank into the armless chair before he finished. Clean clothing made him feel better, although the texture and the cut were strange.

"That's better," approved Alterfarr. "Now, we owe you an explanation. Mr. Spenser, you were brought here because of one reason: Of all the humanoid races we tested, you achieved the best results." He hesitated.

"I must also apologize. We are the reason you haven't been sleeping. We are the reason for your visions."

Dave shook his head, not understanding.

"Lhangficsarians are hundreds of years older than the humans of Terra. We stopped needing more than two or three hours of sleep per night long ago. Skedasthinaz, one of our brilliant scientists, proposed that by changing a bit of our DNA, we could give up sleep entirely. Our ruler at that time, Ladiskivesyk the Inquisitive, convinced the Lhangficsarians that changing our DNA was a thoughtful and wondrous thing."

Trithelmarn settled a new mug of tea in Dave's hand. This one was three times larger than the first and looked like porcelain with patterns of active color twining across it. Dave sipped the steaming brew and listened hard, staring at Earth's solar system in the display as Alterfarr continued.

"There was one drawback to the change, and it turned out to be an inconvenient one. Our urge to mate disappeared. That was fine, because we all live such long lives now. There is little need for reproduction. But every once in awhile, we require replacements, or a new generation for the throne. That time is now."

Dave almost laughed, thinking, *I'm not a bum, I'm going to be a lab rat!* He croaked, "So what do you need from me?"

"Allow me to explain further. Bear with me: this is difficult. Our best scientists can't tell us why ancient urges of some Lhangficsarian females are triggered by males who do require sleep. Obviously, we must seek such males from worlds beyond ours. You, Mr. Spenser, passed the test. You proved you can survive and function fairly well on little sleep. And your drive to assist a woman you did not know was both generous and impressive."

Dave's control neared the breaking point. He wasn't certain what he'd heard, and how it applied to him. "So what do you want?" he growled.

Alterfarr nodded. "Your fatigue is ruling you. That's understandable. So I'll truncate explanations." He straightened, made a quarter turn, and bowed low. "Mr. Spenser, it is my very great honor to present you to the Queen's Primary Negotiator, the Royal Representative to the Central Galactic Council, and heir to the ancient Throne of Penderancys, Her Most Royal Highness Princess Shondranaris Cymbardas of Lhanficsaria."

Where are the trumpets? Dave almost laughed again. *I really must be dreaming!* He clutched his mug tighter.

A shadow stirred in the darkness across the room.

A self-assured tread sounded, accompanied by the rustling of silklike cloth.

"Hallo, Da-vih." The voice was pure velvet. "I hope I have your name right." She stepped into the light from the three-dimensional display.

Dave stared at her lovely face, her dark wavy hair, and her luminous eyes, which he knew were burgundy. He felt encased in boneless idiocy.

"I wished to surprise you. I hope you do not mind."

Her words were not coming through the translator. *She's speaking English!*

Dave forced himself to stand. Forgotten, his mug fell from nerveless fingers and bounced on the hardwood floor.

Tall—she's taller than me!

"I do hope we can learn to work well togezzer."

"M-me, too," he managed. "Uh, what is it exactly you want me to do for you? Some sort of security?" *I could stand a job like that,* Dave thought. *As long as I get to be around her.*

"Forgive me, Mr. Spenser, my explanation was not clear," stated Alterfarr.

"Let me, Alterfarr," said the princess. "Da-vih, you are not here to be security for me." She touched his arm. Shock waves erupted from the contact, streaking down his body. He couldn't breathe.

"You gave up your job, your friends, and your world to become my consort." Her eyes clouded suddenly with concern. "I hope."

"You . . . your . . . consort?" Dave gasped. "As in married? Us?" He truly had the shakes now.

"Of course," the princess said, "but we have much time to discuss zat. I wish not to rush you. Alterfarr, please tell the queen that Mr. Spenser has arrived. We will be in the gardens by the pool and will dine zere." She smiled at Dave, a somewhat shy expression meant for him alone. "We can get more acquainted."

"Yes, Princess," responded Alterfarr with a bow.

"Now, Da-vih." She tucked her hand above his elbow, drawing him along. He paced her, still numb, as she led them out the door and into the hallway. "I think you are hungry. And you must call me Naris. That is my short name, used by family and good friends only. I will answer your questions. But forgive me, sometimes I must speak Lhangficsarian because my English is not yet good."

Dave halted. "How do you say 'perfect' in your language?" he asked, looking at her profile instead of at the beautiful vista beyond the window.

Princess Naris faced him, pronouncing the word with care so he could hear each syllable. "Prondolfcir."

Dave looked into her wonderful eyes and took a deep breath. "Prondolfcir."

She understood. Her smile eclipsed the double sun shining beyond the window.

THREE WISHES

Kelly Swails

Kelly Swails is a clinical microbiologist by day and a writer by night. When she's not dealing with enteric pathogens or unruly characters, she spends time with her husband, Ken, and their three cats, Kahlua, Morgan, and Moonshine. In her spare time she likes to read, bake cookies, exercise, and play Guitar Hero. A rumor has surfaced that she sleeps, too, but that has yet to be proven. Please visit her online at *www.kellyswails.com*.

June in Illinois made Alice happy to be alive. The air was warm but not yet humid, the spring allergens had settled, the skies were sunny more often than not, and birds swooped over the waist-high corn fields. All this was even more glorious if one had no obligations. It just so happened that on that Friday afternoon Alice didn't—not work or rehearsal or voice lessons or anything. She walked along the downtown streets, nibbled at an ice cream cone, and window shopped.

She was so busy feeling content that she nearly missed the teddy bear in the window of an antique store. She breezed past the shop before backtracking a few paces and taking a closer look. It was a brown bear in a miniature rocking chair in the corner of the display, small by adult standards but big to a three-year-old. Age had dulled the fur, and a previous owner had ripped one of the ears.

Alice's heart skittered in her chest. It wasn't just any bear, she was sure of it. She had fallen asleep clutching that bear for too many years to not know her childhood toy when she saw it. She walked into the shop without thinking.

An ancient bell jangled as she entered the cramped space. This was one of those places that called itself an antique store when really it was just a junk room. It smelled like a combination of mold and rotten cabbage. Dim lights shone on shelves packed with mismatched dishes and tableware. Rickety furniture crowded the center.

There wasn't anything cheerful about the store, but Alice felt light-hearted nonetheless as she squeezed past the dusty assortment and retrieved the bear from its perch. Any doubts she had about this being her bear were erased the moment she touched it. The fur was rough and comforting, just as she remembered, and the back sported a shiny patch where she had held it too close to a candle flame. It should have smelled musty, but when Alice sniffed it she could smell the Tide detergent her mother used.

"Find something you like?" A deep voice said behind her.

Alice gasped and turned. She hadn't heard anyone approach. "This bear, I think it was mine when I was a kid," she said around a lump in her throat.

If the old shopkeeper found anything unusual about her statement, he didn't show it. "Let's see." He examined the bear with one hand as he pushed his glasses down his nose with the other. After a moment, he cocked a brow. "You used to live in England?"

"No," Alice said, "But my dad was stationed there when I was born."

"This is a Steif bear, made in the seventies. Sound about right?"

"Yes," Alice said. "The date, anyway. I didn't know teddy bears had brands back then."

"They most certainly did," the man said. "Steif is a fairly well known one." He handed her the bear and slid his glasses up his nose. "It's in good shape, too. You took good care of him."

"I didn't see a price marked." She suspected that he'd raise the price simply because he could see how badly she wanted it.

"Six dollars."

Alice tried not to look surprised. "Sold." She followed him to the back of the room where a register sat on a glass-topped jewelry case. She peered through the glass while he wrote up the purchase. "You have lots of nice things in there," she said, just to make conversation.

He scowled and waved his hand. "Don't be so nice. It's mostly costume crap for old women."

Alice giggled at his candor. What age must a woman be before this man considered her old? He looked like he was pushing eighty.

He looked up from his pad and said, "Do you want to see the good stuff?"

She looked out the shop window. The shadows were lengthening, and she'd wanted to eat a late lunch in the park after shopping. Her head told her she should just leave, that she had bought what she needed, that she didn't need to spend any more money. However, her heart whispered that the man had just sold her the bear for next to nothing and humoring him was the least she could do. She smiled and said, "Sure, why not?"

"Indeed." He fished a key from his pocket, opened a display case, and pushed a lever. The green-felt bottom sprung up and hinged open at the front so that the jeweler could root around inside without the customer seeing anything. The owner chose an item and shut the compartment before Alice could begin to fathom what could possibly be valuable enough to keep hidden.

When the man showed Alice what he had selected, though, Alice knew he had been right to hide it. A flower-shaped pendant with amethyst petals and rope-and-beaded accents hung from a simple gold chain. The shop wasn't in a bad part of town, but this neck-lace's beauty could have made a nun steal.

"It's beautiful," she whispered.

"Try it on," the man pushed it toward her.

"No, I couldn't. It's much too expensive."

"Please? Make an old man happy."

Alice relented and carefully plucked the piece from the man's outstretched hand. The pendant was nearly as big as her palm, but she found it to be surprisingly light. She fumbled with the clasp as the man pulled a mirror from behind the counter. She looked at her reflection and smiled. The color brought out the warmth in her skin. It was the sort of piece her grand-mother would have called a lavaliere.

"It fits you."

"Yes."

The man watched her enjoy her reflection for a moment before saying, "If you could be granted any three wishes, what would they be?"

She tore her eyes away from her reflection and looked outside at the lengthening shadows. "I'd be able to stop time so I could enjoy days like today for as long as I wanted."

The man smiled and cocked his head. "That's your heart's truest desire?"

Alice kept her gaze averted. "I wouldn't mind being a successful actress. Famous. Respected. I know it's silly." She picked an imaginary fuzzball from her shirt. Alice thought she felt the pendant warm against her skin, but it had to have been her imagination. Or maybe baring her soul to a stranger had made her flush a bit. She moved to take the necklace from her neck.

"Perhaps it's not as expensive as you thought."

"What?"

"It's included with the bear."

Alice couldn't speak as the information sunk in. He couldn't be serious, could he? She didn't have a trained eye, but she suspected the necklace was an estate piece that could fetch thousands of dollars. After a few moments she found her voice and said, "Oh, I couldn't. It's too—"

"Expense is a relative term. Please."

"Really, I—"

"Consider it a favor for an old man." He placed his hands together as though begging her.

"Favors don't pay the rent," she blurted.

"You can pay me when you become famous."

Alice laughed. Oddly, that made her feel better. At the very least, she could sell it on eBay and give him the money. Most of it. A girl had to eat. "You've got yourself a deal."

She moved to take the necklace from her neck but the old man stopped her. "Oh, keep it on. It looks so nice."

"Okay." She looked in the mirror again and had to agree. She paid the six dollars and allowed the owner to walk her to the door. As she left, he said, "Bear."

"What?"

"That's the word you'll need to use. And don't forget you still have one wish left."

She looked at him, the sun warming her back, the pendant light against her chest. "I don't understand."

"You will." He winked and closed the door, the bell jangling softly behind him. As she watched, he placed a tarnished silver platter where her teddy bear had been.

Later, she would wonder whose platter it was.

Alice had just arrived at her studio apartment when her cell phone rang. She dropped her purse and the bear onto the floor as she fumbled the phone from her pocket. "Hello?"

"Oh, Alice. Thank God I didn't get your voice mail," said the speaker on the other end. It was Gene, the manager of her theater troupe, and Alice had never heard him so panicked. "We need you to come in tonight."

"Why? What's going on?" She checked her watch and started shedding her clothes.

"Tonya fell from the trellis during a run-through."

"God! Is she okay?" Her stomach jumped as she said the words. Tonya played one of the two leads.

"Fine, but they think her ankle might be broken. She's at the hospital getting X-rays now. The thing is, though, we've got a reviewer from the Chicago Tribune in the audience tonight. We can't cancel, and—"

"Give me fifteen minutes." She closed her phone, threw on a pair of sweatpants and tee-shirt, grabbed her keys, and bolted from the apartment. This could be the break she needed. If she did well tonight, she'd have a shot at the lead for the next play. She might even get a raise.

Alice arrived at the theater twenty minutes before curtain. Gene met her at the back door with her costume in one hand and a bottle of water in the other.

"Do you need time to warm up? I don't want to start late, but—"

"No," Alice lied as she grabbed the dress for the first act and headed for the closet the cast called a dressing room. As she changed, her nerves jumped and her stomach tightened. She was glad she hadn't eaten. A castmate helped her with her hair just as Gene called for everyone to take their places.

Alice scrambled to the wings and took a few deep breaths. From the murmurs of the crowd, the auditorium sounded half-full, which would be the most people Alice had performed for at once. She had to nail this performance. She gave her arms and legs a quick stretch. As she straightened her skirt, she saw the necklace resting on her bodice. She'd forgotten she still had it on. "Shit." She looked on stage and saw that everyone was ready. Her cue came up within thirty seconds of the curtain rising; there'd be no time to dash to the dressing room. As she moved to tuck the necklace into the high-necked dress, she remembered what the shopkeeper had told her. She whispered "bear" before she could tell herself she was being silly.

Instantly, the noise of the audience stopped and her castmates froze. Alice dropped the pendant as if she'd been burned. "Sally? Toby?" When they didn't acknowledge her, she said their names louder. Finally she walked on stage and touched them with shaking hands. They didn't move.

"Oh no, oh no. This isn't real." She peeked through the curtain at the audience and found them similarly frozen. Some looked at the curtain, most read the program, a few picked their nose, and one couple looked to be serious about examining each other's tonsils with their tongues.

Alice snapped the curtain closed and began to pace. "This can't be happening. It isn't real." She flicked

Toby on the ear. He didn't flinch. She touched the necklace and mentally replayed the afternoon's transaction in her mind. As she remembered her wishes, her eyes snapped to the industrial wall clock hanging backstage. The second hand didn't move. Tonya's accident, the reporter . . . she shivered. Her wishes had been granted.

Alice bit her lip and returned to her place in the wings. Clutching the pendant, she whispered "bear" and gasped when the audience noise started again as though it had never stopped. On stage, Toby and Sally found their marks and waited.

Alice dropped the necklace and said "bear." Nothing. She touched the pendant and said it again. Everything stopped. Again. Movement. Again. Stillness.

Alice smiled. She'd have plenty of time to warm up for her performance.

First thing the next morning, Alice rushed to the nearest newspaper stand and looked for the reporter's review. She seemed neutral about the play and the rest of the cast, but she spent a whole paragraph rhapsodizing about her performance. Alice read it twice more before buying every copy the stand had.

After another sold-out performance a week later, Alice received a call from the ICM Agency in LA. One of their junior agents had read about her, and was she interested in screen acting? Alice was. She packed her bags, sublet her apartment, and sent a check for two thousand dollars to the shopkeeper on her way to the airport.

A year to the day after she had purchased the necklace, Alice had lost twenty pounds, filmed three commercials, played a waitress in two different independent films, and landed a spot as a regular castmember on a half-hour sitcom. While not rich by industry standards, she was making more money in a week than she ever thought she'd see in a year. Her ability to memorize lines after seeing the script once became legendary, as did the unusual necklace she took off only when the cameras rolled.

During the winter hiatus, Alice lounged on a private beach in Mexico and sipped a margarita. She thought about stopping time so she could enjoy the solitude for as long as she wanted, but the last time she'd done that, she'd fallen asleep and got sunburned as hell. The makeup ladies would have killed her had she shown up for taping that way, and so she'd had to keep time frozen long enough to heal. At first it'd been cool seeing an entire city stopped as though they were playing Statue. After a few days, though, she felt like a creepy, lonely voyeur. She didn't want quiet bad enough to go through that again.

Her iPhone rang, and she groaned. Just because she didn't use the necklace didn't mean she wanted to talk to anyone. She checked the display. Her agent. She sighed and said, "Hello?"

"Alice, Brent," he said. He sounded as though he was on a speaker phone. "You need to get home right away. There's—" his words became lost in a jumble of blowing horns and curses.

"Brent? What's going on?"

"People need to learn how to drive on the 405, I swear," he said.

"Why'd you call?" She knew she shouldn't have answered the phone.

"Judd Apatow wants a meeting with you. He's casting for a new comedy, this one about two brothers and the woman they fight over. I need your ass in LA, pronto."

"I'll take the next flight." Alice found a pen and

paper in her beach bag and scribbled the information Brent gave her.

"Be careful," Brent said. "Call me when you get here."

"Of course," she said. Brent probably cared more about his meal ticket than her well-being, but she appreciated the sentiment.

Before two hours had passed, Alice sat in the back of a little commuter plane that would take her to the first of two layovers. The only others on board were the pilot and a slim woman with dark hair and sunglasses. Once the plane left the ground, the woman opened a magazine and pretended to read it as she snuck glances at Alice. Alice looked out the window. Sometimes she wished she could turn fame on and off as easily as she could time.

Alice looked out the window at the clouds as she absently rubbed the pendant around her neck. Over the past year she had come close to using her last wish, but something held her back. Using it to secure a role seemed like cheating somehow, as did wishing for all the other actresses she auditioned against to fail. A role in a major motion picture, though . . .

Alice's thoughts were interrupted by a loud thunk somewhere underneath the plane. She grabbed her armrests and said, "Did you hear that?"

"Yeah," the woman said, closing her magazine. "What do you think—" Another thunk.

"Murrda," the pilot said. "Pajaros."

"What'd he say?" Alice said to the woman next to her.

"I don't know. 'Birds,' I think."

"Right." Alice didn't need to pull out her Spanish-to-English dictionary to know the man sounded scared. Her stomach dropped as the engine quit. Silence had never sounded so horribly wrong. Alice's bowels loosened as the woman next to her screamed. The plane's nose tipped forward and her body strained against the seatbelt. As they plummeted to the ground, the pilot crossed himself and prayed the Hail Mary.

Alice looked out the tiny window. The wings wrenched through the air, twisting this way and that. She had no idea how long they'd stay on the plane. Her ears popped as the ground rose to meet them. Her death would be a quick and messy one, and she felt unreasonably calm. At least the waiting was over. Briefly she wondered if she were famous enough to rate an obit in *The New York Times*.

"Do something, oh, God, save us, do something," the woman screeched.

Alice moved to slap her—hysterics wouldn't do anyone any good—when she remembered the necklace hanging from her neck. Of course. She clutched it and yelled the word that had saved her neck more times than she could count.

Instantly the plane stopped moving. The woman sat frozen in midscream while the pilot had covered his eyes with his hands. Alice could see the man had wet himself and felt a moment of pity for him.

Alice took deep breaths until she stopped shaking. She had one wish left and all the time in the world to think about how to word it. She turned it over in her mind a dozen different ways before she clutched the necklace, closed her eyes, and said, "I wish this plane hadn't taken off yet."

Nothing happened. Alice opened her eyes and found herself surrounded by the same frozen chaos as before. She chuckled and tried without success to get her hands to stop shaking. "Bear."

The woman's screams and the scent of urine filled the cabin as the plane hurtled toward the ground. Alice clutched the necklace in both hands and yelled her wish again.

Before her eyes everything changed. One moment

she hung suspended from an airplane seat by a seatbelt and the next she sat in the waiting room of the
little airport in Mexico. It had worked. She'd saved
them all. The sudden transition left her shaking and
dizzy.

A woman sat a few chairs down from her. "Are you
all right?"

Alice looked up to find the woman from the plane,
her relaxed and tan face smiling. "I'm fine," she said.
"Just got a little light-headed for a minute."

"I bet you're dehydrated. If you're like me, you
won't drink the water down here." She pulled a bottle
of water out of her bag and offered it to Alice.
"Want some?"

"Thanks," Alice accepted the bottle and drank half
of it down at once. Her face felt flushed and sweaty,
and she knew she must look horrible.

"You're on that show, aren't you? The one about
the neighbors in New York?"

That described about half the shows on the air.
"Yeah."

"I don't really watch it myself," the woman said,
"but my boyfriend loves it. Could I get your autograph? He'll never believe I met you otherwise."

"Sure. Just don't sell it on eBay," Alice made the
familiar joke before she could stop herself. "Cool
paper," she said as the woman pulled a notepad from
her bag.

She smiled and blushed. "Thanks. It was a birthday
gift from my mom." She ripped of the top sheet and
handed Alice the pad.

Alice scribbled her name on the paper as a man
approached them. It was the pilot. She couldn't help
glancing at his dry pants.

"We're ready for taking off," he said in accented
English.

"What plane are we taking?" Alice said.

The man pointed to the small tarmac. It was the same plane that she had boarded before.

"Has it been inspected? Are you sure it's safe?"

"Si, it's only a short flight, you be fine."

"I'm not getting on that plane," Alice said. "Find another one."

"There is no other," the man said, his impatience apparent.

"We need to find another. That plane isn't safe. It's got some mechanical malfunction."

"It's probably fine," the woman said. "I've flown these little commuters before. They look scary, but I've never crashed." She giggled at her wit.

"There's a first time for everything."

"Aren't you a bright ray of sunshine." The woman didn't look as starstruck now.

"I'm not boarding that plane, and neither should any of you. I'm serious. It's going to fall out of the sky."

The woman gave her a wary look as she took the autographed pad of paper from Alice's hand and backed away. "Suit yourself."

"You wait for next one if you like," the pilot said.

"Please, don't go." Alice clutched the man's arm. When she'd made her wish she hadn't counted on this.

The pilot extricated himself and led the woman from the waiting room. Once they were a few feet away Alice heard the woman say something about celebrities and their need for attention. The pilot laughed as they walked toward the plane on the tarmac.

Alice ran to the ticket counter where a man sat reading a newspaper. "You've got to do something."

"Just a moment, Señorita," the man said.

Alice reached over the counter and yanked the newspaper from his hand. "There's a plane that's getting ready to take off. You have to get on the radio and tell them they can't leave."

"This the plane you have ticket for?"

"Yes."

He shrugged. "You miss plane, you wait for next one."

"No, you don't understand. The plane's going to crash. You have to call them back."

The man didn't move. "You know this how?"

Alice nearly screamed. "I can't tell you how I know. I just do. Please."

"You plant a bomb?"

"No, but—"

"Then is fine." The man pulled the paper from Alice's hand and refolded it. "You transfer your ticket to the next one."

"You're really not going to do anything?"

"Your ticket, Señorita."

Alice gritted her teeth and pulled the ticket from her bag. For the first time in her life she felt guilty to be alive.

When she arrived at LA, she walked into the first bar she found, paid the bartender to put CNN on the television, and watched. She drank Kahlua on the rocks and waved off offers of food as she watched the scrawl on the bottom of the screen. There was no mention of a plane crash, Mexican or otherwise. She finished her drink and left the airport.

The next day Alice drove to Brent's to prepare for her meeting with the director. She walked into his office and plopped into a squishy chair.

"You look like hell," Brent said.

"Thanks," Alice said.

"I mean—"

"I know. I didn't sleep well." She'd stayed up all night surfing the web for any news.

"Wanna see something funny?"

"Sure."

Brent turned his laptop around. "Bid's up to twenty bucks."

Brent had an eBay page pulled up on his browser. Alice leaned over and enlarged the picture. A piece of flowered notepaper with her writing on it filled the screen. Gooseflesh prickled her arms. It was the autograph she'd given the woman in Mexico.

"Oh, thank God," she said as tears blurred her vision.

Brent pulled the laptop back around. "I thought you'd get a kick out of it."

"Yeah. You could say that." She plucked a tissue from the box on Brent's desk and blotted her eyes.

"I just took a call yesterday from a girl who said she was the next Alice Griffith. Plenty of actors in this town wish they were in your place right now, you know that?"

"Sometimes wishes come true." Alice fingered the pendant around her neck. She wondered how many of those actors had a way of making it happen.

THE ADVENTURE OF THE RED RIDING HOODS

Michael A. Stackpole

Michael A. Stackpole is an award-winning author, editor, game designer, computer game designer, graphic novelist, and screenwriter. He's best known for his *New York Times* best-selling *Star Wars* novels *Rogue Squadron* and *I, Jedi*. Last year he celebrated two milestones: his thirtieth anniversary as a published game designer, and his twentieth anniversary as a published novelist. When not writing or attending conventions, he enjoys playing indoor soccer and dancing (both of which can be tough on the toes).

Gray skies and a persistent mist brought a chill to late October. I had not seen my good friend for a fortnight. An outbreak of the swine influenza had laid low many a nightsoil mucker and bonepicker. By nature of my calling, I was obliged to care for my cloven-hoofed brethren. This I accomplished while refusing all payment, as I have little use for fertilizer or bone meal, and they need every farthing they earn.

So it was a great relief to receive a message from my friend in the morning post. He requested, were I free, that I visit him that evening. He directed me to bring a traveling satchel and, as he put it, "that fine machine by Webley *et fils*." The promise of adventure made it difficult for me to concentrate for the rest of the day. Still, as he had known, the influenza had broken and by day's end, the torrent of patients had become a drought.

I paid the hansom cab driver a crown and mounted the steps to 427 Butcher Street. A light was on in his window, but I detected no silhouette. He had learned well the lesson of that curious affair of the giant bat of Borneo.

His landlady, Mrs. Hanihan, met me at the door and took my overnight bag. She left me my medical kit. Alarm flashed through her bovine eyes. "Thank goodness, it's you, Doctor."

"There is nothing wrong with him, is there?" I glanced up the stairs anxiously. "Tell me, quickly."

"No more than the usual, I suppose. His appetite is up, and he asked for pork, despite the flu. And then the piano-forte . . ."

"I hear nothing."

"Exactly, Doctor." Glass earrings flashed as she flicked an ear forward. "He is up to something."

I bleated a quick laugh. "He's back to himself, my good cow, fret no more."

I mounted the steps, knocked once at his door, and then entered unbidden. Discourteous it might seem, but I had been invited previously, and such was my friend's nature that, lost in thought, he would not notice my knocking or absence until well into the morrow.

It was half as I expected. He reclined on his davenport, stretching his long legs toward the fire. He had slouched down enough that his back rested where his buttocks should have. Slender, as were most of his kind, and of a grayish fur with only the first hints of white around his muzzle, he stared at the soft glow of embers. His fingers touched tip to tip above his chest, but he looked past them. His ears remained flattened back against his skull.

Then his nostrils flared. For the briefest of moments his lips curled back, flashing fangs. Then he smiled, displaying those fearsome teeth in a much more friendly manner. He did not move, save for the smile and his ears flicking forward, and then in one smooth motion he rose to his slippered feet.

"Ah, my good Woolrich, so kind of you to come." His dark eyes narrowed and he sniffed. "By way of the fish market. And there, you saw two females—one Human, one a Sea Weasel—engaged in a struggle over a basket of fish heads."

Despite my having known V. August Lupyne these many years, and having witnessed great feats of ratiocination, I could not conceal my shock. "I understand, Lupyne, catching the scent of fish and knowing the market, late in the day, can be a fast route from my practice here. How ever did you deduce I witnessed such a fight?"

"Your nature betrays you, Doctor." Lupyne shrugged off his red velvet smoking jacket and replaced it with a brown tweed that matched his trousers. "Though you are courageous beyond the norm for your people, you instinctively shy from conflict and seek the company of others. Just a hint of fear on you, Doctor, which does you no discredit. Many a foolish man has been filleted by a fishwife's knife."

"But, Lupyne, anything could have caused me a fright on the way here. Before I came, perhaps."

"Doubtful. No trace lingers on you of the mucker-folk, whereas lavender and wet wool do. Overlay fear and fish, well, the conclusion is inescapable." Lupyne sketched a brief bow, then kicked off his slippers and began the search for his shoes. "No matter, however. I direct you to the cable on the mantle there. Pray, remove your cloak and read by the fire so your pelt may dry."

I did doff my cloak but kept jacket, shirt, and waistcoat fastened. I had dried myself after bathing, hence my coat was a bit more fluffy than I am comfortable displaying. Not out of any fear of a wolf like Lupyne, but because being unkempt really did not do in polite society.

The cable in question had arrived early that morning from Aldershot-on-Wick, an ancient village on the Eiran Sea. Earl Northcutt, Andrew Benbrook, had sent it and included instructions that an immediate reply was requested. The cable read:

> Lupyne
> A matter demands your urgent attention STOP One of your kind is accused of murder STOP He denies it STOP I need the truth STOP
> Andrew Benbrook
> Earl Northcutt

I read it twice, wishing my eyes were as sharp as those of my companion. "What do you know of this murder?"

Lupyne, seated again, slipped his feet into shoes and began buttoning them. "There was a mention in *The Times* two days ago of a Wolf being apprehended in the matter. There was no doubt to his guilt."

"What did he do?"

"In transit, Woolrich, we have no time to lose. We are catching the night coach to the coast." He pulled a cloak about himself and donned a deerstalking cap. Damping the fire, he grabbed his own luggage and into the night we flew.

On the train, in a B carriage, we accommodated ourselves well. Two young Sea Weasels in their Royal Navy uniforms sat across from us and slept. A family of Badgers gathered at the far end, and the only Man to disturb us was the conductor. He seemed pleasant enough, and if he recognized Lupyne from his transit permits, he gave no sign at all. He did address me as "Doctor" after examining mine, and I detected no hints of sarcasm in his voice.

Lupyne explained that T. Bruce Carrington worked for Northcutt on his estate as a gamekeeper. He was accused of murdering an old woman who lived in the woods. Her granddaughter and a woodcutter discovered the body, with Carrington standing above it, covered in blood. Because he had murdered a Man, the case would be resolved in the Higher Courts. With a jury chosen from Men, the verdict and sentence was hardly in doubt.

We each got a little sleep, and then we were met at the station by Earl Northcutt's coach. The driver and groom, Stoats both, proved adroit at handling the matched pair of chestnut geldings. Prior I'd only seen them handle pony carts, as befitting their size. They were pleasantly disposed, as their kind often is, and I sensed in their manner a pleasure at working for Earl Northcutt.

Lupyne addressed the driver directly. "Would it be possible for you to take us through the woods and past the old woman's home?"

"The witch cave?" The groom made a sign to ward off evil.

The driver cuffed him. "Hush, idiot. Begging my lord's pardon, the earl asked for you to be presented to him straight away. Now, I would be willing to do as you ask, but that cave is set near no track. It would be a mile through mire and more, my lord."

"Very well. To Northcutt Manor, then."

We passed into the village and on toward the hill atop which lay Northcutt Manor. The people of Aldershot doffed caps and bowed heads as the carriage clattered down the cobblestone street. Lupyne watched for a bit and then let the shade close.

"You would be quite welcome here, Woolrich, wouldn't you? See some Ewe who catches your eye, settle down, raise a lamb or two?"

I turned from the window. "There are a number of Sheep here, herding, no doubt. Aldershot wool is prized, if I recall correctly."

"So you do, Doctor." My companion gave me one of his inscrutable smiles. "Some day I shall retire to the country. Not here, I think, but to the north, where places are yet wild."

I had, through the years, of course, heard many plans advanced for his retirement. I doubted I would live to see them come to fruition, for I was older than he, and Lupyne could never resist a challenge. And challenges constantly sought him out.

The carriage quit the village outskirts and started up the hill. The original Northcutt holding had come down during the Civil War, but it had been rebuilt tall, strong, and square. The grounds were impeccably maintained, especially the vast beds of roses. Northcutt retained Swine to care for them, and both Boars clearly knew their work and delighted in it.

Though the earl's household staff appeared to be drawn from Men alone, at no point did I gain the impression that the butler or his aides thought Lupyne and I should have been received in the courtyard. We were welcomed openly in the foyer, with our cloaks and hats being taken away without hesitation. I even imagined mine would be brushed, not to collect Ram's wool but just as would be done with *any* guest's coat.

We found the earl in his library, with tall shelves filled to bursting. Leather-bound volumes everywhere, chased in gold. I recognized a few volumes.

The bindings were custom and I luxuriated in their scent despite my full knowledge that many were bound in lambskin.

This is a misapprehension common concerning Walkers such as myself. Though Men resist the comparison, as they are to the lesser apes, so we are to our more common brethren. While I eschew mutton, it is less because it comes from an animal quite close to me than that I digest meat very poorly. The presence of lambskin gave me little concern. Were it the flesh of a Walker, then I should have serious misgivings, but the skin of a lesser ovine discomfited me not.

The man's florid face brightened as he turned from the fire. "Best Lupyne, I am so glad you have come."

They clasped hands and shook. Lupyne smiled easily. "Doctor Jameson Woolrich, Earl Northcutt."

"A pleasure, Doctor." The man took my hand without hesitation, nor did he wipe after. "May I offer you something to drink? I'm having whiskey. To settle the nerves."

"Why is it you are nervous, sir?"

The earl bade us sit while his butler poured us each a slant-glass of cool water. "Carrington has been with me for years. He is somewhat disreputable and inclined toward sloth, save for two things. He is, without a doubt, the most diligent gamekeeper this estate has ever seen. He's made my woods into his territory. I should sooner expect him to kill himself than do anything to dishonor the land or my name."

His lordship savored some whiskey before continuing. "Second, when I was very young, I was involved in an indiscretion that does not bear examination now. Carrington saved me from a great deal of embarrassment. I do not fear his speaking out now, but out of gratitude for his silence, and in the hopes of saving my grandson some embarrassment, I should like to help Carrington."

Lupyne's ears flattened. "The woman who was slain?"

"Mrs. Smeed, though folks around here called her Grandmother, the crone, the witch, or worse. She's been ancient since I was a boy. Back a generation or two it was common and even favored for every estate to have a hermit—a holy man, usually. In that spirit I allowed her to live there, affording her some protection against the villagers. Superstitious lot, they believed she was a witch. They came to her for cures and help, or other things."

"I should like to interview Carrington and then see the murder site. I would also like to interview the girl and the woodsman who found Carrington."

Northcutt nodded eagerly. "I shall arrange all that, gladly. Thank you, Best Lupyne, for your help."

The arrangements were made for us to interview the Wolf first, then to visit the murder site. The weather was expected to turn nasty later on, but the earl had hopes the girl and woodsman could be interviewed at the manor that evening. The coach bore us back into town, and Lupyne brought a letter of introduction to the sheriff.

It was hardly necessary. The slender, nervous Man smiled broadly, albeit briefly. "Why Best Lupyne, word of your exploits in dealing with the West End Ripper have reached us even out here. It's an honor." He gathered the keys to the gaol cells and bid us to follow, bearing a lamp to guide us into the dark, dank recesses of the building's cellar.

We did not find Carrington in very good condition. Even though he had been confined in a cell with stout bars, he'd been fitted with an oak collar as wide around as his shoulders. Not only did it prevent him from being able to slip between the bars, but it made lying down comfortably impossible. While law permitted such treatment of Walkers, it did not demand it, and use of such barbaric methods often marked prejudice.

Though, as Carrington snarled and charged the bars when we approached, the sheriff's caution might not have seemed imprudent.

Lupyne held up a hand. "If you will, Sheriff, give me the keys and then quit this place. You have my word of honor that Best Carrington will not escape."

The Man handed my companion the keys and left us the lamp. Lupyne beckoned the other Wolf to the edge of the bars and unfastened the lock on the yoke. "Rest yourself and be sensible, Best Carrington. You'll soon be free."

"They'll kill me. They want to kill me." He tossed the yoke aside with a crash and then pointed toward the street. "Men. Sheep, they hate me."

"Not all of them, you fool. The earl sent for me."

"And who are you?"

"V. August Lupyne, and this is my friend, Doctor Woolrich." Lupyne flashed fang. "Tell me what you know."

"They hate me."

"You've established that. You may go to the gallows with that on your lips and dance, or tell me all you know of the murder, and I will save you."

"I don't know much." The older Wolf, gray in muzzle and ears, arched his back and snarled. "Had a feeling something was wrong with the old woman. I went to her cave and found her dead, her head smashed, her body slashed like someone was fixing to skin her. Then I remember feeling strangled, then nothing else until I woke up to the girl screaming. She hid her face in the folds of her dark cloak and the woodcutter clopped me with an axe handle aside the head."

Lupyne waved me forward. "If you will, Doctor, examine his head."

"I am a physician, Lupyne, not a phrenologist."

"I seek signs of trauma, my friend, not an analysis of character."

Carrington submitted to my examination through the bars. I found easy evidence of swelling where he'd been hit with the axe handle. "Good Heavens, Lupyne, there is another bump here and some crusted blood. A blunt item, yes, but more like a rock."

Lupyne's eyes narrowed. "One blow or two, Carrington?"

"One."

"Are you certain?"

"He stunned me, but I retained my wits."

"Good, very good." My friend scratched at his throat fur. "What was your relationship with the old woman?"

"We traded some. I'd bring her meat, she'd give me wine. The earl didn't approve of me drinking, but it was just a wee touch now and again."

"Were you drunk the day you found her?"

Carrington gave Lupyne a glance that had not bars and civil convention separated them, would have precipitated a quick battle. "I might have had a drop or three that morning."

"You're huntsfolk. How long dead was she when you found her?"

"Fresh. Blood was still warm."

"Good, excellent." Lupyne gave his brother Wolf a nod. "One last thing. How much do the Sheep herders hate you for poaching from their flocks?"

You'd have thought Lupyne had produced my revolver and shot Carrington right between the eyes. "But I never, Best."

"Come now. They graze on the Northcutt estate.

You warn them off. They fail to listen, you punish them. It happens all the time. They must hate you.''

"A lamb goes missing, they blame me. Most keep their flocks away. The Oliver Rams, though, they don't listen."

"Thank you." Lupyne picked up the lamp. "Remain quiet, and we shall get you out of here."

We retreated up the stairs, and the sheriff welcomed us back as if we'd been to the Dark Continent and had found the source of the Nile. We apprised him of our intention to visit the cave, and he came with us. The coach brought us as close as it could get, then we trooped through the woods. Once within sight of the cave, Lupyne held a hand up and went forward alone, watching the ground and sniffing as he went. He produced a magnifying glass from his pocket and quickly studied overturned leaves and other things that baffled me, then would wave us forward and signal for us to stop.

The cave itself was not terribly remarkable. The front had been left as nature had designed, narrowing to a crack, which had once been sealed to form a brick chimney. Much of it still remained, and the witch had used the base for a firepit, but the back wall had long since crumbled. Beyond it stretched a darker part of the cave, and Lupyne straightened up having returned from his examination of it.

"Storage beyond there. A number of unsavory things." He looked at the sheriff. "There was more that you removed, yes?"

The sheriff nodded. "A few things shouldn't be seen by Man nor Beast, if you'll take my meaning, Best Lupyne. The whole district knew Granny Smeed was a witch. Weren't need to have proof of it paraded around the village."

Lupyne crouched beside a wooden cot covered in bloody rags beside the fireplace. "You saw the body?"

The Man crossed himself. "Every time I close my eyes. She was tore up something powerful bad. Cut fit for skinning. Carrington's knife was there beside the body, covered in blood."

"But that wasn't the only odd thing, was it?" He rose, bearing a lock of long, gray hair. "Her head had been shaved."

"Like she was a nun."

"No, Sheriff, not like a nun." Lupyne held the lock up and studied it with his glass. "She was shorn for a most unholy purpose."

I frowned. "What do you mean, Lupyne?"

"That should not concern you, Doctor." Lupyne lowered his glass. "Instead you might want to consider how it is that the murderer had three arms."

We returned from the cave by way of the village, dropping the sheriff off at its outskirts. We arrived by early evening and were informed that there would be guests for dinner. Lupyne and I retired to our rooms to bathe and dress. I did the former with alacrity and the latter more slowly, not wishing to inflict the scent of wet wool upon my companion.

I thus had much leisure time to ponder what my companion had said. I confess I made little of it. Carrington's story did not deny him the opportunity of having committed the crime. He might have slain her when she refused him wine. Of course, then the question would have been about what he had done with her hair and why he had taken it, but this matter did not seem to concern Lupyne in the least.

Of course, Carrington did not possess a third arm, but that fact provided me no insight into the murder. I would have thought a triple-armed murderer would have been easy to spot, but the sheriff had made no more of the question than I. Nor did he seem to have a list of suspects that had three arms. As often happened with Lupyne, what seemed transparent to him was opaque to me no matter how I tried to pierce that veil surrounding it.

I had made no headway into the mystery when we were called to dinner. The earl sat at the head of the table, with Lupyne to his right. His grandson, a handsome, strapping lad up for the weekend from Oxford, sat opposite the host, and I sat at his right hand. The other two visitors faced Lupyne and me respectively. Burton Hill, the woodcutter, and Blanchette, the girl who had discovered the body, had joined us. While neither of them wore the finery our hosts did, the girl had a delightfully crocheted lace shawl around her shoulders, and the grandson, Desmond, clearly found it fascinating. Hill, while more humbly dressed, was clean and sharp witted, while Desmond proved, unfortunately for the earl, to be as dull as his clothes were fashionable.

Conversation remained slightly stilted. The earl asked Desmond about his studies, and Desmond responded with many stories—few of which actually involved academia. We all laughed politely—Blanchette the most, Hill the least—perhaps because Desmond addressed himself primarily to her. Hill hesitated to offer opinions, wisely thinking better than to show up his superiors.

At last dinner was over. In deference to me, the salad course had been generous, and no mutton had reached the table. I contented myself with bread and greens and then indulged gluttonously in the bread pudding offered for dessert. The others enjoyed some beef dish tasty enough that Lupyne savored rather than bolted.

Finally we retired to the library, with everyone aware of the agenda. Desmond stepped up to offer a protest. Standing behind the wing-back chair in which Blanchette had settled, he gave Lupyne a stern stare.

"I am aware, Best Lupyne, that you wish to ask Blanchette about the murder. I want you to know she is innocent of any involvement. You have my word on that, the word of a Gentleman."

"I appreciate that, Mister Benbrook, but were you to give me your word that, at this very moment, the sun was at its zenith, I should doubt you. That said, I wish only to ask her and Mr. Hill a couple of questions, merely to test the veracity of what Carrington told me."

Blanchette reached up and patted Desmond's hand. "I don't mind answering."

Lupyne nodded carefully and then packed his pipe with the dark tobacco the butler offered. "Carrington said you were wearing a dark cloak. Did you bring it with you this evening?"

"No, Best Lupyne."

Desmond glowered. "What sort of question is that? This is the nature of the woman you question, Lupyne: She and I were out walking two days ago, and she insisted I wear her red riding cloak because I looked cold. I have yet to return it to her, but I had planned to do so this evening."

"Nonsense, Desmond, you should wear it back to Oxford, to keep you warm." She smiled prettily at him, and he returned the smile.

"You are most kind, Miss Blanchette." Lupyne swung his head about and smiled toothily at Hill. "And you, sir, must be as well."

"Best?" The man eyed Lupyne carefully. "I don't follow."

"You discover a Wolf, covered in blood, over the body of an old woman. Instead of slaying him with your axe, you stun him and capture him."

Hill lifted his chin. "I, Best, do not suffer the prejudices of other Men. There could have been a reasonable explanation. I hope and trust you will find it."

The earl raised a glass in Hill's direction. "You are exactly the sort of Man this district needs. Welcome to you."

"Thank you, your lordship."

My companion continued to pack his pipe, but his eyes had grown distant. The Men looked expectantly at him, and I did nothing to break the silence. I had seen this before, as he turned inward. He prided himself on being a ratiocinator of the first order, and it was in times of silence such as this that he did his best thinking.

Finally he returned to his wits and waved away the offer of a match for his pipe. He rose and tucked his pipe away in his pocket. "Your lordship, Carrington is innocent, and I know who did it. Do any of you know where I can find the Oliver Rams?"

The earl frowned. "I don't know for certain, but many of the Sheep herds congregate at the Black Sheep."

"Then we are off. All of us." Lupyne's fangs gleamed. "It is time to put this affair at an end."

It was my impression that the advent of a Wolf into a public house full of Sheep caused less of an uproar than that of the four Men accompanying him. My friend, who is never at a loss for theatrics when it serves his purpose, strode into the middle of the room. My brethren, though we fight it, shrank from him, save for three robust Rams nearest the fireplace. The largest of them had a pretty Ewe under each arm and was last to take notice of Lupyne.

"I have come here to solve not one murder, but two." He pointed to the largest Ram. "Your name, Best, if you please."

The Ram stood slowly, pulling his braided vest closed around his middle. "If it's any business of yours, I am Roderick Oliver."

"Why is it you wear boots when your brothers do not?"

I had taken notice of Roderick's boots, but up to that point had attached no significance to them. Walkers often wear boots or shoes, especially in the cities or polite company. While a herder might have them for a time of snow or for a visit to city, with its cobblestone streets, his occupation hardly demanded he wear them.

Roderick shrugged convincingly. "I was thinking perhaps of walking to Rumford this evening, but these Ewes may have convinced me otherwise.

The Ewes tittered.

My companion sniffed. "Remove your boots."

"Here now, what is it you're accusing me of? The murder of the old woman? The Wolf did it, we know."

Lupyne smiled. "If you believe that, then you have no reason not to remove your boots. Or to explain," he continued in a growl, ". . . where that fancy braid on your vest came from."

Roderick blinked for a moment, and then he made to run. Desmond, deep in the throes of affection for Blanchette, hurled himself upon the Ram and wrestled him to the ground. Roderick struggled, but fruitlessly. Apparently, the tales Desmond told of wrestling matches at Oxford had not been exaggerated.

My companion nodded to me. "Remove his boots, Doctor. Tell me what you find. Here, use my glass."

I took the magnifier from him and did as bidden. The left leg was unremarkable. The right had been shorn short over the hoof and up the cannon, just shy of the hock—a fact the boot had hidden. I brought the glass up.

"Good gracious, Lupyne, there are singed hairs here."

"Which were singed when you darted back through the chimney in Granny Smeed's cave. You'd slain the woman in a rage and set about to butcher her. You heard Carrington approaching and hid, darting over the fire. You were singed. Then when he came in and had his back to you, you slipped your crook around his neck and pulled him hard against the chimney with enough force to knock him out.

I stood. "The shepherd's crook, of course, that was the third arm you mentioned. That's why Carrington felt strangled."

Roderick struggled, but Desmond held him tight. "She had it coming. The Wolf, too. I would have killed him, but . . ."

"But you were too intent on your revenge. Framing him, yes, would allay suspicion from you. And you hated him for taking some of your lambs. But she had taken something far greater from you, hadn't she?"

"Yes."

Lupyne shook his head. "No, Roderick, no. Her denials were true."

The earl frowned mightily. "What do you mean, Lupyne?"

"I said I came here to solve two murders. A brother, Roderick?"

The Ram shook his head with resignation. "A cousin, new to the district."

"Of course. Innocent, easily duped." Lupyne turned and pointed at Blanchette. "Easily led to the slaughter, Blanchette?"

"I don't know what you're talking about."

"Of course you do." Lupyne opened his arms. "Blood wool."

As accustomed as I am to my friend's ways, even I cringed. Among the superstitious and those unschooled in science, there is a belief that blood has power. That power is best exploited in magicks most foul, and blood wool plays a part in many of the legends. Just as the rope woven from a virgin's hair shorn after death—and after her post-mortem deflowering—will never part, so wool shorn from a Sheep and soaked in his blood can do many things—especially those related to the opposite sex.

My mouth gaped. "Her cloak."

"Precisely, Woolrich." Lupyne's lips peeled back in a feral grin. "Blanchette set her cap for Desmond, to marry him and inherit the Northcutt fortune and title. She plotted in concert with Mister Hill."

Hill raised his hands. "I had nothing to do with this."

"But your hands bear witness to your lies. Soft hands, sir, and hands that are so little acquainted with an axe that you cannot split a wolf's head, but instead stun him when you overshoot your target. But he was not your target, was he? You knew of Desmond from college. Oxford. Cambridge? You ached to correct him at dinner, sir, do not deny it, not a word of it."

"But I did not kill a Sheep. She did it!"

Blanchette slapped Hill, spinning him to the floor, and made to run, but the low growl coming from Lupyne's throat froze her in place. The earl grabbed her, and she fainted.

Desmond released Roderick and started toward his grandfather, but Roderick's two brothers tackled him.

"Burn the cloak, my lord, and Desmond's wits will return to him. Likewise, get rid of that vest and the braid—the braid woven from the witch's hair. You took it for the wrong reason, Roderick. You should have reported the murder and let justice take its course."

Roderick remained on the floor, slowly gathering his boots to himself. "Justice? You joke. There is no justice."

"You will find, Roderick Oliver, there is quite

enough justice to suit you." Lupyne shook his head. "You doomed yourself, and you will now pay a terribly price for it."

Lupyne's prediction proved true. Roderick Oliver was found guilty of Granny Smeed's murder and sentenced to hang until dead. Blanchette Putnam was found guilty of Odo Oliver's murder. She was transported to Van Dieman's Land, there to labor in the penal colonies for no less than seven years. Burton Hill, for his involvement, took enlistment in the Royal Navy, never to be heard from again.

We had come down to Aldershot for the trial. Lupyne's testimony was accepted by the jury, but the earl had taken great pains in its choosing. After Blanchette's conviction, the earl invited us to his home for a meal. He informed us that Desmond had returned to Oxford and was doing well at his studies.

The earl swirled brandy in a snifter. "I am quite pleased with how this all resolved itself."

Lupyne lit his pipe. "But you needn't blame yourself, my lord, nor suspect your secret will come out."

The earl's glass stopped halfway to his mouth, then came down again. "I should have known you would have puzzled it out."

I looked from one to another. "Puzzle what?"

"It was a different time, Doctor, and I was a different man, very young, before I went to the Sudan." The earl looked into the amber depths of his drink. "I loved a girl who did not love me, and a flux spread through the village. It killed only Sheep, and I helped clean up. We found one Sheep, Carrington and me, a young Ewe, barely alive, sure to die, suffering. I tell myself she was suffering, you see. Carrington said she would not live the night. So I killed her and sheared her wool, and Granny Smeed wove it into a scarf that I gave my beloved. She fell under its spell. She promised to marry me, and she did when I returned from the Sudan. By then I was changed, and everything I have done here to promote understanding, it was because of all that."

I said nothing.

"My wife never knew. I buried her without that scarf, freeing her from its magick. I tossed it on the fire with that damned cloak." The earl looked at each of us in turn. "You now know why I let Granny Smeed live here. A bargain struck and kept."

"Yours being one of many secrets that died with her."

The earl nodded. "I hope so. Am I a monster?"

Lupyne blew a perfect smoke wreath, which floated toward the ceiling. "A monster would have let Carrington die, your lordship. As my friend, a creature of science, will tell you, there is nothing to the idea of blood wool. Superstitious nonsense. You were lucky enough that your wife saw your true nature and fell in love. Would she love a monster?"

"Never my sweet Caroline."

"Then take it that you are not a monster." Lupyne gave him a courteous nod. "It has been my experience that those who ask the question never are monsters, and those who hide from the answer most assuredly are."

ABOUT THE EDITOR

Jean Rabe is the author of two dozen books and more than four dozen short stories. She primarily writes fantasy, but she dabbles in the science fiction, military, and horror genres when given the opportunity. A former newspaper reporter and news bureau chief, she's also edited anthologies, gaming magazines, and newsletters. When not writing, Jean works on her growing to-be-read stack of books, plays roleplaying and board games, visits museums, and fiercely tugs on old socks with her three dogs. Visit her web site at *www.jeanrabe.com*.

Once upon a time...

Cinderella—real name Danielle Whiteshore—did marry Prince Armand. And their wedding was a dream come true.

But not long after the "happily ever after," Danielle is attacked by her stepsister Charlotte, who suddenly has all sorts of magic to call upon. And though Talia the martial arts master— otherwise known as Sleeping Beauty—comes to the rescue, Charlotte gets away.

That's when Danielle discovers a number of disturbing facts: Armand has been kidnapped; Daniellie is pregnant; and the Queen has her own Secret Service that consists of Talia and Snow (White, of course). Snow is an expert at mirror magic and heavy-duty flirting. Can the princesses track down Armand and rescue him from the clutches of some of Fantasyland's most nefarious villains?

The Stepsister Scheme
by Jim C. Hines

"Do we *look* like we need to be rescued?"

There is an old story...

...you might have heard it—about a
young mermaid, the daughter of a king, who
saved the life of a human prince
and fell in love.

So innocent was her love, so pure her
devotion, that she would pay any price for the
chance to be with her prince. She gave up her
voice, her family, and the sea, and became
human. But the prince had fallen in love with
another woman.

The tales say the little mermaid sacrificed her
own life so that her beloved prince could find
happiness with his bride.

The tales lie.

Danielle, Talia, and Snow return in

The Mermaid's Madness
by Jim C. Hines

Coming in October 2009

"Do we *look* like we need to be rescued?"

John Zakour

The Novels of
Zachary Nixon Johnson
The Last Freelance P. I.

"If you like your humor slapstick and inventive,
you need look no further for a good fix."
—*Chronicle*

Dangerous Dames* 978-07564-0496-3
(The Plutonium Blonde & The Doomsday Brunette)
Ballistic Babes 978-0-7564-0545-8
(The Radioactive Redhead* & The Frost-Haired Vixen)
The Blue-Haired Bombshell 978-07564-0455-0
The Flaxen Femme Fatale 978-07564-0519-9
*co-written with Lawrence Ganem

"No one who gets two paragraphs into this
dark, droll, downright irresistable hard-boiled-
dick novel could ever bear to put it down until
the last heart-pounding moment..." —*SFSite*

To Order Call: 1-800-788-6262
www.dawbooks.com

Tanya Huff

The Finest in Fantasy

To Order Call: 1-800-788-6262
www.dawbooks.com

Tanya Huff
The Blood Books
Now in Omnibus Editons!

"Huff is one of the best writers we have at contemporary fantasy, particularly with a supernatural twist, and her characters are almost always the kind we remember later, even when the plot details have faded away." — *Chronicle*

Volume One:
BLOOD PRICE   BLOOD TRAIL
0-7564-0387-1 $7.99

Volume Two:
BLOOD LINES   BLOOD PACT
0-7564-0388-X $7.99

Volume Three:
BLOOD DEBT   BLOOD BANK
0-7564-0392-8 $7.99

To Order Call: 1-800-788-6262
www.dawboks.com

DAW 20